Anne and Louis Forever Bound
Book Four of the Anne of Brittany Series

"A vibrant and dynamic retelling of Louis XII and Anne of Brittany's life, this novel moves at a quick pace that pulls readers into the story. Gaston's prose is lovely and compulsively readable, driven by and in service of the dynamic plot. Anne's voice shines through the page. As a protagonist she captivates and balances well with Louis, whose story feels fresh and new."

—*Publishers Weekly BookLife Prize*

"In this fourth installment of a series revolving around Anne of Brittany, Gaston once again displays an extraordinary knowledge of the period, an erudite mastery evident on every page. She achieves an impressive historical authenticity, translating an intricate story into a captivating drama. Anne is a mesmerizingly complex character—decent yet calculating, fierce yet vulnerable. Gaston's writing avoids melodrama—but not at the expense of flair and emotional poignancy. An engrossing and rigorously researched work of historical fiction."

—*Kirkus Reviews*

Praise for
Anne and Louis: Rulers and Lovers
Book Three of the Anne of Brittany Series

"Fresh and original ... Fast-paced and filled with marital drama and court intrigue, this book will please any lover of historical fiction."

—*Publishers Weekly BookLife Prize*

"In this engrossing volume of the Anne of Brittany Series, the author deftly recreates the complex political landscape of Europe … This is a delightful blend of historical rigor and dramatic entertainment, delivered in easily companionable prose."

—*Kirkus Reviews*

"A powerful historical read that requires no prior knowledge of the era or French culture to prove satisfyingly engrossing to newcomers—even those who rarely read historical fiction."

—*Midwest Book Review*

"In addition to bringing to life the political machinations of the time, the author does a fine job of taking the reader beyond the throne room into the privy chambers and personal lives of Anne and Louis. A well-researched, entertaining tale."

—*Historical Novel Society*

"… a must-read for anyone interested in the French court at the turn of the sixteenth century and the life of a uniquely powerful woman of that era."

—Frederic J. Baumgartner, author of *Louis XII*
Professor Emeritus of History, Virginia Polytechnic
Institute and State University

"Gaston's evocative portrayal of Louis XII and Anne of Brittany as the ultimate royal Renaissance power couple is enjoyable and highly satisfying. Details on Anne de Beaujeu, Louise de Savoy, and Germaine de Foix provide a historically accurate glimpse of women who held political power in the first decade of 16th century France."

—Susan Abernethy, *The Freelance History Writer*

"Realistic and vivid, *Anne and Louis: Rulers and Lovers* offers an intriguing insight into the life and times of Anne of Brittany and Louis XI of France."

—Judith Arnopp, author of *The Beaufort Chronicle*

"A fascinating portrait of two complementary rulers with conflicting aims who steered France into the modern age. An engaging read from the very start."

—Claire Ridgway, author of *The Anne Boleyn Files,*
Founder, *UK Tudor Society*

Praise for
Anne and Louis
Book Two of the Anne of Brittany Series

"Sharp and engaging...a memorable adventure to the French Renaissance."

—*Publishers Weekly 2018 BookLife Prize*
Winner, General Fiction

"A dramatically engrossing and historically searching tale about a powerful duchess."

—*Kirkus Reviews*

"*Anne and Louis* is a masterpiece that paints an extraordinary vision of its times, capturing the facets of a social and political milieu with historical accuracy and vibrant emotional resonance ... satisfying, educational, and hard to put down."

—*Midwest Book Review*

"It's a treat to see a historical woman brought so richly to life."
—*Historical Novel Society*

"A lively, engaging story, rich with historical detail that brings the story of a forgotten queen to life. Reminiscent of Philippa Gregory and Jean Plaidy, *Anne and Louis* gives voice to Anne of Brittany, allowing her to step from the historical shadows and illuminating her as a determined and influential political figure, as well as a bright and devoted woman in her own right."
—Eleanor Brown, *New York Times* bestselling author, *The Light of Paris*

"A lively narrative filled with strong women."
—Susan Abernethy, *The Freelance History Writer*

Praise for
Anne and Charles
Book One of the Anne of Brittany Series

"Gaston's blend of royalty, young love, and the French Renaissance is enchanting."
—*Publishers Weekly*

"A historically sharp and dramatically stirring love story."
—*Kirkus Reviews*

"A delightful read with sparkling dialogue, Gaston puts a human face on these captivating historical personalities from the French Renaissance."
—Susan Abernethy, *The Freelance History Writer*

"A romance for the ages, Ms. Gaston masterfully conveys the passion, heartbreak, and determination of this royal couple."

—*InD'tale Magazine*

"... a brilliant historical compendium and a moving love story. Reading *Anne and Charles* is like making an effortless journey into a past that does not seem so distant anymore."

—*Readers' Favorite*

"Francophiles, feminists and fans of history and romance alike will delight in *Anne and Charles.*"

—Dominique Padurano, Ph.D., Crimson Coaching LLC

Also by Rozsa Gaston

The Anne of Brittany Series
Sense of Touch: Prequel
Anne and Charles: Book One
Anne and Louis: Book Two
Anne and Louis: Rulers and Lovers: Book Three

The Ava Series
Paris Adieu: Book One
Black is Not a Color: Book Two

Other Novels
Budapest Romance
Running from Love
Dog Sitters

Novella
The Least Foolish Woman in France

ANNE *and* LOUIS FOREVER BOUND

THE FINAL YEARS OF ANNE OF BRITTANY'S MARRIAGE TO LOUIS XII OF FRANCE

Book Four of the Anne of Brittany Series

ROZSA GASTON

Renaissance Editions

New York

Cover image of Anne of Brittany by unknown artist, Chateau de Chaumont, France
Photo by C.S. Carley, courtesy of Castles and Coffeehouses.com
Cover image of Louis XII by unknown artist, courtesy of Wikimedia.com
Cover image of Blois by Pikist, courtesy of Wikimedia.com

Back cover image of Louis XII by unknown artist, 19th century engraving
Back cover image of Anne of Brittany statue by Jean Fréour, Nantes, France
Back cover image of Anne de Beaujeu from a triptych by Jean Hey, c. 1498
Back cover image thought to be of Louise de Savoy by Robinet Testard, c. 1496-98

Cover design by Cathy Helms/Avalon Graphics

Spine image of Anne of Brittany by Jean Bourdichon, c.1503, from
The Grandes Heures of Anne of Brittany
Courtesy of Bibliothèque Nationale de France, Paris

Interior images of coat of arms of Anne of Brittany
Courtesy of Wikipedia.org

Published by

Renaissance Editions
New York

www.renaissanceeditions.com

Printed in the United States of America

ISBN-13: 978-1-7325899-7-1 (pbk)
ISBN-13: 978-1-7325899-6-4 (ebook)

"It is difficult to quench a great fire
when once it has seized the soul."

—Pierre Brantôme on Louis, Duke of Orléans' love for
Anne of Brittany before he became king of France

Portrait of Louis XII of France
Artist unknown, French origin
Courtesy of Wikimedia Commons, public domain

Detail from Portrait of Anne of Brittany
Artist unknown
Chateau de Chaumont, Loire Valley, France
Photo by C.S. Carley, courtesy of Castles and Coffeehouses.com

Author's Note

Anne of Brittany is the only woman in history to have been twice crowned queen of France. While queen-consort to Louis XII of France she ruled neighboring Brittany, conducting a separate domestic and foreign policy agenda for her own realm from that of her husband. Despite their differing political aims at times, Anne and Louis were devoted to each other.

Anne of Brittany was born in Nantes, Brittany, on January 25, 1477. At age ten she was named hereditary successor to the ducal throne of Brittany. She ruled Brittany alone from ages eleven to fourteen, then co-ruled her duchy with her first husband, Charles VIII of France.

After Charles' death at age twenty-seven in April 1498, she married his successor, Louis XII of France, in January 1499. Her marriage contract with Louis stated that she was to retain sole sovereign rule over Brittany, which Louis respected.

Anne and Louis lived together at their royal residence in Blois, France, until Anne's death on January 9, 1514. Louis joined her less than a year later on January 1, 1515.

Brittany became part of France in 1532, eighteen years after Anne of Brittany's death.

Coat of Arms of Anne of Brittany
Arms of the king of France (fleur-de-lis) to the left
Arms of the dukes of Brittany (ermine tails) to the right
Courtesy of Wikimedia Commons

Map of Brittany and France

late 15th century

By Alexey Tereschenko, courtesy of Quora.com

Contents

Cast of Characters

Anne of Brittany, Duchess of Brittany and Queen of France

Louis XII, King of France, formerly Louis, Duke of Orléans

Claude of France, elder daughter of Anne and Louis

Renée of France, younger daughter of Anne and Louis

Louise de Savoy, Countess of Angoulême, widow of Charles d'Angoulême, cousin to Louis XII

Francis de Valois-Angoulême, also known as Francis d'Angoulême, the future Francis I, King of France

Marguerite de Valois-Angoulême, also known as Marguerite d'Angoulême, the future Marguerite of Navarre

Valentina Visconti, Duchess of Orléans, paternal grandmother of Louis XII, and successor to the ducal throne of Milan through her father Gian Galeazzo Visconti, first Duke of Milan

Georges d'Amboise, Louis XII's senior minister and Cardinal of the Church in Rome

Anne de Beaujeu, Duchess of Bourbon, also known as Anne of France, former regent of France as older sister to Anne of Brittany's first husband, Charles VIII, during his minority, and daughter of Louis XI, the spider king.

Gaston de Foix, nephew of Louis XII, King of France

Margaret of Austria, also known as Margaret of Habsburg, Governor of the Habsburg Netherlands, daughter of Maximilian I of Austria

Maximilian I of Austria, Holy Roman Emperor

Charles of Habsburg, also known as Charles of Luxembourg, the future Charles V, Holy Roman Emperor and King of Spain, grandson of Maximilian of Austria and Ferdinand of Spain

Ferdinand of Aragon, King of Spain

Germaine of Foix, Queen-consort of Spain, niece of Louis XII

Henry VII, formerly Henry Tudor, King of England

Henry VIII, King of England

Catherine of Aragon, Queen of England, youngest child of Isabella and Ferdinand of Spain

Pope Julius II, formerly Guiliano della Rovere

Pope Leo X, formerly Giovanni de Medici

Alfonso d'Este, Duke of Ferrara, future father-in-law of Renée of France

To the memory of Louis XII, King of France,
who recognized quality when he found it
and fanned its flame forever after.

Chapter One

August 1508

A Queen's Cross to Bear

"The king had placed in her all his pleasure and all his delight
So much so that there was never a woman better
treated and more loved by her husband."
—*Claude de Seyssel, secretary to
Louis XII, King of France*

She had been gone only a week, but already she missed him. A quick side trip to Tours then she would be back in Blois, berating him over the bad care he had taken of himself in her absence. The moment they were alone he would slip his hand around the back of her neck, working his way up into her scalp. It would be heavenly.

Stretching in her carriage, Anne's thoughts fell on her rival. Louise de Savoy would have heard of her son's mishap by now. She could imagine the woman dropping to her knees the moment the news was delivered, begging God not to take him before his time.

Francis d'Angoulême, heir apparent to the throne of France, had arrived at the Royal Abbey of Fontevraud on the third of August 1508 without his mother in tow, mirabile dictu. The strapping young dauphin had been ordered by the king to leave his home in Amboise to join the royal court at France's most prestigious monastic address, nestled deep in the Loire Valley countryside.

Louis had said it was time for the fourteen-year-old to begin training for the crown he might one day wear as closest male to the throne of France's ruling House of Valois.

The dauphin had arrived at Fontevraud with only his tutor, unescorted by Louise as per the king's explicit orders. To Anne's merriment Louis' exact words had been that Louise was not to tag along like some sort of attachment to her son's body. Her overprotection of the boy she referred to as her 'precious Caesar' was a topic of rich amusement at court.

All had gone well for the first few days. With his usual bravado Francis had cavorted with his male companions, teasing the demoiselles and showing himself fearless at sword practice.

Anne had found herself half-charmed and half-annoyed. Francis d'Angoulême showed none of the humility her husband did, although it was at the king's pleasure that the youth had been designated his successor. The boy who might one day be king had not yet been checked by a single lash of life's blows.

But all that had changed two days earlier as members of the court had strolled outside the abbey's grounds in the golden long rays of a summer sunset. Francis had been up ahead, disporting with a group of youths when gay laughter had turned to cries.

A loose tile from a low-hanging roof had hit the dauphin on the forehead, knocking him to the ground. Anne had rushed to his side, calling for help as her thoughts flashed back to ten years earlier.

"Get the carriage. We'll bring him to the nuns," she commanded. Barking orders for water, a cool compress, and a blanket, she guessed the abbess and her capable nuns would nurse him better than any doctor, although not as well as her Breton cook would back in Blois.

While they awaited the carriage, Anne remembered how Charles had first seemed fine after hitting his head on a door lintel, laughing and talking as they took in a tennis match. Then, suddenly, his head had snapped back and he had fallen to the floor unconscious.

France's former king had been dead before midnight. From sad experience, she knew the twelve hours after a blow to the head were critical. Francis would either wake up feeling better the next morning or not wake up at all.

That evening she prayed for the boy's recovery. But as she prayed, her mind drifted to prayers for a son of her own to take his place as France's dauphin. It was the one prayer that blotted out all others.

As queen it was her foremost responsibility, above all else, to produce an heir. God knew she had always sought to do her duty. But in this sole regard, she had not been able to accomplish what her insufferable rival had done—bear a son who lived.

The next morning Francis had awakened with a smile and a jest, sporting a nasty graze above one eye.

"Don't tell my mother, Your Grace," he had begged. "She will find out soon enough, and I would not worry her with such a thing as I am now fine."

"She will hear of it, but I will send the messenger on a slow horse so that she will not rush here against the king's orders," Anne promised, glad to have an excuse to prevent Louise from arriving at Fontevraud while she was still there. Due in Tours the day after next, she would watch over Francis carefully before she left, but, already, his bright expression told her the injury was not life-threatening.

"Bless you, Your Grace. It is nothing but a scratch and I will be as good as new in a few days."

Anne smiled wistfully at the youth's boundless confidence. She had felt similar confidence at age fourteen. But such assurance had ebbed in her over the years, sucked out by countless unexpected deaths of those she had most loved. Well could she appreciate the pain Louise de Savoy would feel on hearing of her son's brush with death. A thumbnail or two closer to the youth's temple might have ended every one of his overreaching mother's hopes.

Two days later Anne set out for Tours. She had told her entourage she would visit the tomb of two of her princes, then the workshop of the sculptor who had created it to discuss his latest commission.

Guilt pricked her at thought of her lie. Would God forgive her for what she intended to do?

Leaning over, she drew back the carriage curtain with the edge of her fan. Phantoms of her dead children visited frequently; whether to comfort or haunt her, she knew not which. If only she had living sons, thoughts of her dead ones would have no further power over her. Could God blame her for doing whatever she could to make that come to pass?

"Your Grace, allow me." Madame de Dampierre reached out to help her with the curtain.

"Nonsense, I've got it."

"Are you comfortable, Your Grace?"

"I am thinking of my sons," Anne said. "Go back to your nap and leave me to my sorrows."

Madame de Dampierre gave her the sort of deeply sympathetic look that Anne hated.

She frowned until her lady-in-waiting closed her eyes and fell back to sleep. How fed up she was of her courtiers peeking at her with their great cow eyes after the death of yet another son, whispering amongst themselves over her failure to produce an heir for France.

Anne placed a hand on her belly. She always knew when life was inside. But her belly was no warmer than the rest of her body on that hot August day. Since her latest prince had arrived stillborn in January, her womb had not ripened. Was her time up, or was she still in the game?

Snapping shut her fan, she tapped it on the carriage seat as she went over her plan. She would slip out the back door of Colombe's workshop while her attendants waited for her in the sculptor's anteroom.

The wise woman's home was a stone's throw from his studio. It would take only minutes to visit her then return to the studio without her ladies knowing she had been gone. The moment her mission was accomplished, she would fly home to Louis in Blois.

Thinking of his sure fingers moving up her neck she closed her eyes.

A horse's loud squeal jolted her awake. Immediately, another joined it in horrible neighing shrieks. With a sickening judder, the front left side of the carriage careened down, causing Anne's stomach to drop.

Madame de Dampierre fell violently into her lap as men shouted and horses screamed around them.

"Madame, hold steady!" her lady-in-waiting cried.

"God save us," Anne gasped, clutching at the wooden handle inside the door.

"Cut the straps, quick!" one of her Breton guardsmen shouted.

"Cut the harnesses," another yelled.

Anne and Madame de Dampierre clung to each other as the front of the carriage lurched down toward the river below the wooden bridge they were on.

"Hold tight, Mesdames! Hold on!" voices shouted from outside.

"Put your hand here and hold fast," Anne ordered her companion, bracing herself against the back of the carriage which was now higher than the front. Were they about to be hurled into the river? She prayed her time was not yet up.

The door of the carriage flung open and two of her guardsmen appeared.

"Your Grace, come quickly!" the senior one called out, his face pale beneath streaks of sweat and dirt.

Grasping his extended hand, Anne climbed from the carriage and onto what remained of the bridge.

Her throat closed as she gasped. The bridge had collapsed only a few arms lengths ahead and the front left side of the carriage dangled off the end of what remained. Neither of her horses were in sight, but their screams fell on her ears like the cries of souls in Dante's ninth circle of hell.

Looking down to the river below, Anne took in the ghastly sight. The two beautiful beasts thrashed and whinnied piteously, helpless and doomed in the swirling waters.

"Come, Your Grace," her guardsman urged, grasping her arm and hurrying her off the bridge, her lady-in-waiting close behind. Focusing on walking well instead of giving in to her limp, Anne tried to blot out the terrible shrieks of the horses behind her. Quickly, they reached the side they had come from.

"Are you hurt, Your Grace?" Her guardsman's face was a mask of worry.

"I am fine," Anne replied, running her hands down her gown to restore herself. Order and duty were foremost for her in all situations, save moments alone with Louis. Such self-possession had served her in the past; it would serve her now.

Despite herself, a shudder seized her from head to toe. She

had been an arms length from losing her life. Had the accident been a warning that she was on the wrong track?

"Madame, bless God you are safe!" the man cried, relief flooding his features.

"And may God take those poor creatures home to Him." Anne pointed to where she had last seen the horses, now swept farther downriver.

"Your Grace, it is a loss, but what matters is that you are unhurt!" The guardsman bowed deeply as he wiped the sweat from his brow.

A trunk was taken from the baggage carts and set next to a tree. There, Anne and her lady-in-waiting sat and settled their nerves while the carriage was eased off the bridge and fresh horses were found.

"Your Grace, thank God your time is not yet up," Madame de Dampierre exclaimed.

Anne started, surprised to hear her lady-in-waiting use the same words she had thought to herself only moments earlier. Her time was not yet up. She was still in the game. But was there a message from above in what had almost befallen her?

Her conscience twinged as she thought of the amulet in Tours she was on her way to pick up. The wise woman had said it would guarantee the future birth of a healthy son.

Yet she knew the Church frowned upon its people turning to soothsayers and amulets. Her confessor had been firm on the point, reminding her of the first commandment: "Thou shalt have no other gods before me." Her instincts told her the accident had been a sign that God did not want her to carry out her errand. Had He not called her closer with what had almost happened?

Rising, she shook out her gown then turned to her head guardsman.

"We will change course and go directly to Blois," she ordered. The message was clear. Her only chance of bearing more healthy children was to remain within His will for her. She would get back to Louis as soon as possible so they could achieve that aim without help from dark sources.

Wait for me here. I wish to pray alone," Louis told his attendant. The King of France entered the chapel of his ancestral home, genuflected, then went to the altar of the Virgin in the far corner near the main altar. Behind the statue of the Holy Mother, a door hidden by a crimson velvet curtain opened into a corridor that led to a lesser-known section of Blois Castle.

It wasn't the Virgin Mary he would pray to that day. Instead, he planned to spend a few moments before his grandmother's portrait in an unoccupied wing of the castle. It was there that Valentina Visconti had lived out her days until her death in 1408, widowed and exiled from the royal court in Paris.

With a backward glance to ensure his attendant had not followed, Louis slipped through the hidden door and set off down the corridor. As he moved deeper into the unused wing, he felt like a boy again, escaping his nurse and scampering to the untouched rooms where the portrait of his mysterious Italian grandmother hung.

Some said the rooms were haunted. Louis thought of them as inhabited by the spirit of one who could not embrace her final rest until her wishes were carried out.

Soon, he reached the bedchamber where the portrait hung. There the daughter of Milan's first duke, Gian Galeazzo Visconti, had died one hundred years earlier. She had been widowed after the assassination of her husband, Louis' grandfather, for whom he was named. The powerful Duke d'Orléans had been hacked to death in the streets of Paris in 1407 by murderers hired by his cousin.

Jean of Burgundy had disputed Louis, Duke d'Orléans' powers as regent of France during the reign of his older brother, Charles VI, who had become insane. The duke's murder had been a horrendous act, setting off the Armagnac-Burgundian civil war for the next thirty years.

"Madame, bless me and guide me in what I set my hand to," Louis murmured as he bent his knee to the portrait of his father's mother, her image as beautiful as it was sad. His blood ran cold at thought of what she had gone through after learning her husband had been toppled from his horse, his hand chopped off at the wrist, then his skull bashed in until his brains decorated the cobblestones of a dark narrow Parisian street.

The stern noblewoman stared down at him, withholding her favors. Gazing at her, he sensed she was waiting.

"Madame, you know I have vowed that as King of France I will not seek to avenge wrongs done to the Duke d'Orléans," he said. After three years in prison at the hands of France's regent, the powerful Anne de Beaujeu, he had vowed not to allow thoughts of revenge to imprison his mind, once his body had been set free. He had never forgotten the lesson, and upon ascending the throne of France, he had publicly promised his subjects to leave behind redress of personal wrongs to pursue the greater good of his people.

The eyes of Valentina Visconti's image remained unmoved as if he had missed her message.

"Madame, do you ask me to claim our lands in Italy for France?" he asked.

At his words, the great lady's gaze seemed to soften.

Straightening his back, Louis squared his shoulders. As King of France he had the wherewithal to answer her call. He would strive to claim his ancestral rights, not only for his family but for France.

Thinking of his predecessor's failed efforts in Italy, his determination grew. Charles VIII had tried and failed to claim Naples, based on the flimsiest of distant ancestral claims. But he, Louis, had a direct claim to Milan and Asti, one that his grandfather would have pursued if he had lived, or his father, if he hadn't been held hostage in England for most of his adult life.

"You are the only one," a silver bell of a voice tinkled.

Of course, he was. And with no son to whom he could pass on his claim, he was the only male member of his family who could pursue it.

"Only you, Louis. Only you," Valentina's voice murmured as if whispering to her murdered husband.

Louis' insides tightened. He must succeed in Italy where Charles VIII had failed. Then all of Europe would know that he was no accidental king, but one who belonged on France's throne.

"'Tis the Queen! The Queen is back!" the broad Breton accents of the head cook at Blois rang out as a hubbub of voices floated up from the courtyard.

Louis' jaw dropped. His wife was not due back from Fontevraud until the day after next. She was no fan of Italy, especially not Italian women. Her first husband had dallied with too many of them while on campaign there.

With his wife's feelings hardened against Italy, Louis kept secret his visits to Valentina Visconti's rooms. His *Brette* would never understand the depths of his desire to claim his hereditary holdings there.

As he rose, his knees creaked with age; he did not have forever to accomplish his dreams. Moving to the portrait hung high on the wall, he brushed his grandmother's feet with his lips.

Turning, he strode to the main section of the castle, a renewed energy propelling his long legs at thought of seeing his spirited consort. Wondering what her early return was all about, he tucked away his secret thoughts. The call from Valentina Visconti to claim his legacy for France was for him alone. Nothing and no one would ever pry it from his heart.

"My lady, you are back early. Is all well?" Louis asked as he helped Anne from the carriage.

"A change of plans, my lord. My head guardsman will fill you in."

"My lady, did something happen?"

"It did, my lord. Or almost happened and I'm going straight to my oratory to thank God for what didn't happen."

"Speak to me, Wife."

"My men will tell you. Meet me in my rooms so I may greet you properly once I'm done."

At the door to her rooms, Anne's two Italian greyhounds welcomed her with joy that matched her own at still being alive. Giving them each a pat, she quieted them and dismissed her attendants before entering her private oratory. She didn't trust herself to tell Louis about both accidents before she had unburdened her heart.

"Forgive me, Father," she prayed. "My thoughts and plans have fallen short of Your glory. Forgive me for my impure heart and for being unable to surrender my will to Yours."

Even as she prayed, she felt her will override her prayers. "Father in Heaven, how am I to relinquish my desire to bear a son who will be king when it is my duty to do so?" she asked, wondering why God would have made her a queen twice over if He didn't intend for her to bear an heir to either of her husbands' thrones.

No answer came, but Anne knew Louis soon would.

"Forgive me for thinking to seek help in dark ways to see my prayers answered," she confessed, feeling her heart lighten as she thanked God that He had prevented her from carrying out her plans in Tours.

Hearing a rustle in the outer room, she stopped.

"Thy will be done," she concluded, although all she could think was that she wanted her will done. She and Louis needed a son and heir. Why did God not listen to her when everyone else did?

Dissatisfied, she rose. Once again she had sent up the wrong sort of prayers. No wonder they weren't being heard.

"*M'amie*, what is this about a bridge collapsing under your carriage?" Louis burst out as she opened the door of her oratory.

"I just thanked God for saving my life." *And asked Him to forgive me in matters I will not share with you.*

"Good God, Wife, I would not have been able to live without you."

"You would have managed, but poorly." Her smile was wry.

Louis returned it. "I would rather not, my lady. Life is trouble enough without you to soothe me."

Anne moved into his arms. "Usually you complain that I rile you," she challenged, looking at him from under her lashes.

"You are expert at both."

"Well-spoken, Husband."

"Did you tell the attendants to stay away?'

"I did, my lord. You know I think of everything."

"That you do, *m'amie*. And how fared you with Francis in Fontevraud?"

Her eyes flickered as she thought of her mixed feelings toward the boy. "He, too, had an accident."

Louis' face blanched. "What happened?"

"A loose tile fell from a roof and hit him square on the forehead."

"Good God, so much like Charles' accident," Louis exclaimed.

"Fortunately not." Anne felt her conscience tug at the thought that she would not have been so sad if the tale had turned grimmer.

"How is he?"

"Fully recovered. The nuns assured me and I saw it for myself before I left."

"Did someone tell Louise?"

Anne laughed. "I promised Francis I would send the messenger on a slow horse."

Louis raised a brow, his eyes brimming with amusement. "He didn't want her there?"

"Your dauphin seemed happy to be out from under her skirts."

"'Tis a good sign, but the stripling needs supervision."

"His tutor is with him and there are plenty of attendants to keep an eye on him."

"Then let us worry no more and thank God you are alive and well."

"There is another matter, my lord."

"What is it?"

"You have not yet kissed me."

With a groan Louis embraced her as Anne of Brittany's hounds retreated to a far corner.

Chapter Two

August 1508

Louise de Savoy

Louise de Savoy was fed up. Her life was devoted to looking after her two children, but neither of them obeyed her anymore. First, her son had been nearly killed within days of being taken from her per the king's orders. Now her daughter had rejected the king of England's suit, saying she would never leave France and, besides, Henry VII of England, at age fifty-one, was too old.

There was nothing she could do about Francis, with the king ordering their separation, but what was she to do with her stubborn daughter?

Tucking a stray strand of red hair under her headdress, she rued raising Marguerite in the heady fumes of Europe's new humanist learning. Never had she thought that her own daughter would take it into her head that she would be allowed to have a say in who she was to marry. It was enough to infuriate any mother trying to do the right thing by her child.

"*Maman*, you rejected him yourself! Why would you want me to marry an old man and leave you and Francis behind for a country with bad weather and bad food?" Marguerite railed.

"My daughter, you must think of your position, not of yourself. The higher your position the less you are able to choose.

Those closest to the king are most valuable to him in the alliances he seeks to make." She left out the queen. Why mention that backcountry midget who carried herself as if she were Empress of Europe? It was the king her children were kin to, not his insufferable wife.

"Lady Mother, if I am not to choose who I will marry then at least let me choose who I will not." Marguerite stood abruptly, sending her lapdog yelping into the corner.

Louise eyed her firstborn. At sixteen, Marguerite was too tall and too independently-minded: her husband's fault on the first score, hers on the second. She had always promoted the highest education possible for both her children. But she expected them to accede to her wishes in the matter of who they were to marry.

"What is wrong with the king of England? He is older, but he is much grieved of his wife's death. A man who mourns one's wife so dearly has the capacity to love again," Louise argued.

"*Maman,* what exactly do you know about marriage, seeing as you have avoided it all your life?" Marguerite shot back.

"I know enough about marriage to know that marrying well is never a mistake," Louise retorted. Marrying into France's ruling House of Valois had been an inarguable step upward, arranged by her guardian, France's regent at the time. Even at age eleven, she had grasped her good fortune in securing a husband from the royal house that had produced France's kings since 1328.

"Then why don't you marry him yourself?" Marguerite asked.

Louise's face flamed. "What did you hear of that?"

"Only that he asked for you before he asked for me."

"Where did you hear such a thing?" Indeed, it had been the case, but she would never relinquish her dream of getting her son onto France's throne. When she was carrying him, the holy man Francis de Paule had told her she would bear a future king. Her life's goal was to ensure his prophecy came true.

"*Maman*, do you think that word did not get out of the English ambassador's original offer when he came to court last spring? Why didn't you take it?" Her daughter's violet eyes mocked her. "Already, you think yourself a queen. Why not become a real one?"

"It was out of the question." She would never marry such a stiff, humorless man, even if he was a king. Before becoming Henry VII of England, Henry Tudor had spent the formative years of his youth in that backwater Brittany, from where the queen hailed.

She had heard there had been talk long ago of Anne of Brittany's father marrying her to him. It would have never worked, as the Breton snob was as supremely self-confident as only those born to wealth and rank could be. Henry Tudor had been insecure and fatherless, a royal outlaw running from Edward IV then Richard III in England with only the thinnest of claims to the English throne.

Louise, too, had grown up insecure and motherless, raised by the previous king's older sister. Anne de Beaujeu had been France's most powerful woman from 1483-1491 when she had ruled in Charles VII's minority. Louise intended to be France's most powerful woman in her footsteps once her son was on the throne.

"Why so, *Maman*? Why for you, but not for me?" Marguerite pressed, hitting her target as only close family members can do.

"Until your brother ascends the throne, I must guide and protect him. But you have your life ahead of you. Why would you not think to bring further glory to our family by accepting the offer of a king?" Her life's work was here, molding her precious Caesar into France's next king.

"For the same reason you wouldn't. I would never leave you, Francis, or France."

"Daughter, it is the duty of highborn princesses to travel to foreign lands to make alliances with kings and princes. It has ever been so and ever will be."

"I'm not going, *Maman*. You must think of another for me."

"It will be the king who decides on another for you. And it will not be a king since I cannot think of any besides the English one who is looking for a bride at this time."

"Fine. I do not require a king. I require a man closer to my own age who shares my interests." Marguerite crossed her arms and gazed over her mother's head.

"You can be sure that whoever the king decides on for you will be the husband you require," Louise retorted.

"*Maman,* why is it that a woman has no say in who she is to marry?"

"Do you think your brother had a say in the choice the king made for him? It is not a question of sex, but of rank," Louise said. "Those in the highest positions are of most value to their rulers. And those are the ones who have less say in the matter."

"None at all, it would seem."

"It would seem you have just had a say in this affair by saying no to what would have been a splendid match," Louise flung back.

"Lady Mother, don't be ridiculous. We are 'our trinity' and ever shall be," Marguerite said.

Louise's heart tugged. There was no more powerful phrase for her, except the four words she most lived for: *my son, the king.* "Our trinity" the epithet she had given to her close-knit family of three, came a close second.

Trying not to show her daughter that she had won her point, she held back the tears that threatened to well up. Talk of their trinity was sacred. The rock on which she stood wasn't the one from above, but the trinity of love she shared with her two children.

"You will still need to marry one day soon," Louise said, scolding herself for having lost the argument. How vexing to have educated her daughter to the point where the girl presumed to overstep her mother's authority.

"To a Frenchman, *Maman.* So we may continue 'our trinity.'"

Marguerite smiled the sweetest of smiles. "Nothing must break it up," she whispered.

Shot in the heart by her daughter's deft arrow, Louise folded the headstrong girl into her arms. She must not let her see the tears spilling from her eyes.

But as her tears dropped, her mind moved to her next plan. She would bid her contact at court to encourage the king to return to Italy. The more time he spent there, the less chance his wife had of producing an heir who would knock her own son from the line of succession.

Releasing Marguerite, Louise hurried from the room. She must find her steward to get a message to Blois.

Anne of Brittany and Louis XII
By Adrien Thibault
Courtesy of Wikimedia Commons, public domain

Chapter Three

Fall 1508

Joyous Entry to Rouen

Most were intimidated by the queen,
but for those who knew her… "There was no
one as soft, as humane, and as approachable."
—Jean de St.-Gelais, *Histoire de Louys de France*

She'd had enough. On their official entry to Rouen, she had been forced to bury her face in her handkerchief to escape the odor that assailed them the moment she and Louis passed through the town gates.

"Madame, this is nothing compared to the stench of the army camps," Louis chided as he waved to the crowds on either side of the road leading to the large and wealthy town's main cathedral.

"Yet another reason to avoid war. Especially when you are not defending your own kingdom," Anne said. She smiled at a young girl standing spellbound near her right stirrup.

For the girl's enjoyment, Anne shifted on her mount, making the ruby and aquamarine stones of her jeweled necklace glitter in the bright September sun. The child's eyes lit up at the sight.

"The Duchy of Milan is mine by inherited right. It is my duty to defend and preserve it for France," Louis pushed back, giving a short wave to someone behind her.

"The sooner you realize France does not belong in Italy, the happier you will be." Anne reached over and swept a stray clump of hair back from Louis' face.

The crowd roared its approval.

Smiling widely, she enjoyed the moment. She couldn't abide Louis' carelessness with his lank locks. On their first official visit to Normandy's seat as King and Queen of France, it was important to offer the crowds the royal splendor they expected from their monarchs.

"Lady, shall this be a political swordfight or a joyous entry?" Louis jested. Grabbing her wrist he kissed it, stoking the cheers of the crowd even further.

"I shall try to express my joy, but it's hard with the stench in my nose of sloppy men disregarding civility's most basic rules." Flaring her nostrils, she brought her handkerchief to her face.

"Head up, hand in the air, my lady. You know the people count on you to dazzle them with your airs," Louis encouraged.

"I can hardly breathe in this particular air," she hissed back.

"Largesse, largesse, my queen!" a beggar with a crutch called out near the head of the white palfrey Anne rode, his hand extended.

Anne brightened. Long ago memories danced through her head of her and her sister tossing coins to the crowd in Brittany in processions behind her father. Duke Francis had counseled her to err on the side of generosity when deciding how much to give. "Your subjects will speak of the day their royals noticed them for the rest of their lives. Best to give them a memory that reflects well on you," he had advised.

Giving the mendicant a gracious smile, she turned to an attendant. "Hand him double the usual. And don't throw it at him, he will fall."

The attendant bowed and carefully placed the sous in the old man's hand, batting away more able-bodied types trying to move in and snatch them.

Louis raised a brow. "Madame, the stench was even stronger coming from your side of the street. Yet, suddenly, it no longer offends you?"

"Husband, what a cripple cannot help is not his fault. But what able-bodied men do in public, to the disgust of all, is a disgrace. I will see it stopped if you do not." She glared at him then waved to the throngs with a smile that welled from her heart. The moment they returned to Blois, she would ensure that Louis signed into law an ordinance forbidding public urination. The common people of France's towns deserved higher standards. She would see to it that they were raised.

If she touched his hair again, he would tie her to the bedpost that night then tickle her with the same unfavored locks she was now frowning upon. Whose hair was it, anyway, and what did it matter if it was in front of his collar or behind it? Was he not King of France? No one bothered him about his hair when he was in Italy.

But his wife had a point about evil odors. The smell in every army camp in Italy he'd stayed in had been atrocious. No one washed anything for months, and everyone pissed anywhere convenient. Certainly, it was not a civilized thing to do, but what could one do when nature called and there was no other convenient spot to relieve oneself?

Someone ought to do something about it, he thought. Then it came to him that his wife had just told him that he would.

"*Vive le roi, vive la reine*!" rang out on both sides. Louis basked in his subjects' good will as they approached the cathedral. His senior minister had been archbishop of Rouen since 1493. Georges d'Amboise wore many hats, including a red cardinal's cap since 1499, presented to him by Cesare Borgia with compliments from his supposed uncle in Rome, Rodrigo Borgia, Pope Alexander VI.

The cardinal's hat had been part of the annulment package Louis had received from the pope in exchange for granting his nephew, whom all knew to be his son, a title. In addition, Borgia had required French landholdings, an annuity for life, and a noblewoman for a bride from amongst Anne's ladies' court. It had been a large ask on both sides.

Looking over at his queen, Louis chuckled. Anything concerning his wife was a large ask.

Brittany's ruler and France's queen lived largely, gave generously, and demanded much in return. It was the least the men of France could do for their queen to relieve themselves somewhere more privately than the public streets of its towns and cities. He would see to it right away. Better yet, he would do nothing and let his wife and Georges handle it. God knew that they would.

"Did you see the way she flicked the hair off the king's face?" a woman in the crowd asked.

"I'd have done the same if my man rode about in public with his hair hanging in his eyes like some sort of sad mop," the woman next to her said.

"How can a mop be sad, woman?" a man behind the second woman scoffed.

"I don't know, but that one on the king's face just now certainly was."

"Nonsense, Thy name is woman," the man chided her.

"Fortunately, he's got a wife to see that he stays tidy," his wife harrumphed, ignoring the barb.

"A court full of attendants too."

"Yet his wife looks after him, despite all their helpers."

The man gave his Fleurette a sly look. "You know what that means."

"Looks like those two still canoodle when they get the chance," Fleurette said matter-of-factly.

"Who wouldn't canoodle with a woman as fine as she?"

"Shut your ravings or you won't be canoodling with anyone," his wife huffed.

"Says who?"

"Do you think any would care to, with your looks?"

"Lady, 'tis not a matter of looks but rather of—"

"I'm the one who knows what it's a matter of, and I can tell you that whatever looks there are need to be in order or a woman will quit looking."

"Ah, so you enjoy mine, then." Her husband straightened, smoothing down the front of his jerkin. For the first time, he noted some grease spots on it.

"What little there is to work with I try to keep up to standards." Fleurette's face was grim.

"What standards, my lady?"

"Ones higher than yours, Husband."

"As high as all that, then? Lucky for you, mine are lower."

"Then you won't mind sleeping in the pig stall tonight."

"Not as low as all that."

"I'll set you up with a nice blanket. You'll be snug as a bug." Fleurette crossed her arms over her chest, her face a study in connubial satisfaction.

"I'll set you up with a gift that'll make you forget all about looks, my high and mighty one—"

"You'll need to take a bath before you offer any gifts."

"Did I not take a bath at Eastertime?"

"It's harvest time now."

"Good God, woman, what do you want from me?"

"Higher standards."

"I don't know what you're talking about."

"I do, and I'll make sure you do, too."

"Lady, you try me."

"If you want me to, you'll be taking a bath tonight."

"All this just because the queen didn't like the king's hair in his face," the husband grumbled.

"All this because you'll be sleeping in the pig stall, otherwise."

The man's scowl was fierce. "I'm not taking a bath."

"I'll have it ready just before supper."

"I don't need a bath."

"No bath, no supper."

"Papa!" a high-pitched voice sounded as a small girl ran toward them.

Smiling, the man reached down and scooped her up into his arms.

The little girl squealed with laughter as he tickled her, then buried her nose in his chest.

In an instant her face reappeared. "Pee-yew, Papa, you stink. Let me down so I can breathe." The girl giggled as she held her nose.

Heaving a great sigh, the man set her down while his wife stood by, a catlike smile on her face.

"Go wait at the church door with your mother for the queen," he told his daughter. "When she comes out, cheer for her so she sends coins your way."

"Ooh, good idea!" the girl squealed, grabbing her mother's hand and rushing off.

The man drifted along behind. Sniffing at his armpits, he cursed the fairer sex.

A pox on them all and their high standards, he thought as he raised his head. Just as he did, the queen turned her face in his direction and smiled at him.

He froze as if struck by lightning. Never in his life had he seen such a radiant sight. Queen Anne was as regal and proud as any queen fair France had ever had. With such a sweet face and noble stature, one could even forgive her for being foreign. What glory she added to his country as its queen.

His pride swelling to be a Frenchman, suddenly he remembered the grease stains on his jerkin. Peeking at the queen again, he felt her eyes flicker as they swept over him. He knew what that flicker meant. It wasn't good.

Perhaps he could get Fleurette to wash his jerkin that evening. She could use the water from his bath after he took it.

Georges d'Amboise, Archbishop of Rouen, cardinal of the Church in Rome, and senior minister of France, moved out into the sunlight through the great double doors of the cathedral. Two years older than the king, he was as round and dumpy as Louis was tall and lean. They made a perfect complement and had done so since he had entered Louis' service at age fourteen.

The cardinal beamed as the king and queen rode toward him. A shift in the crowd took place just steps from where he stood as all the beggars rushed to the queen's side. Everyone knew where the alms were most likely to be tossed. Their king was as good at saving money as the queen was at giving it away. Together, they offered all that their common subjects looked for in their rulers.

Georges bowed deeply as the King and Queen of France entered the cathedral, greeted by a wave of bended knees as they proceeded up the center aisle. The royal monarchs would be his guests for the next few days at his country estate southwest of Rouen. He had spent the past six years building it and had done his utmost to ready it for their visit.

The Chateau de Gaillon was his haven of respite and calm. It was to Italy that he owed its inspiration, more splendid than any other estate in Normandy, his retreat in fair weather months when the king wasn't enlisting him for yet another venture across the Alps.

He had wearied of the Italian campaigns but his eye was on the papacy itself, once Julius II was gone. The King of France needed a good friend on Saint Peter's throne—one whose aims were in lock-step with his own. Who better but himself for the job?

Either the will of God or a powerful prince or two would nudge the present warlike pope off his throne; when that moment came, Georges intended to get himself elected with Louis' help.

Chuckling to himself, he watched his monarchs leave the cathedral, then slipped out the back door behind the altar and straight into his carriage. He would speed to Gaillon to oversee final arrangements before the royal couple arrived later that day.

The queen's tastes were as discriminating as his own, so he would pull out all stops to ensure she was pleased. Both understood the ineffable calculus of how to increase France's prestige in the world. It was something the king wished for but did not fully grasp how to achieve. No matter. Between the queen and himself, they would see to it, with Louis reaping the reward.

After visiting the cathedral, Anne nudged Louis as they came out into the sunlight onto the square.

"It is time to pay our respects to the Maid, my lord."

He nodded, then whispered a word to his head equerry. The

royal procession set off for the Rouen marketplace, the crowd moving with them like a wave every step of the way.

Dismounting, the monarchs knelt in the unprepossessing market square, paying homage to the woman who had saved France and been burned at the stake by the English in that exact spot in 1431.

As Anne prayed, Louis thought with disgust of the rebel branch of the House of Valois who had sold out the Maid of Orléans to the English. His distant cousins, the Valois-Burgundians, had handed her over. She had saved France by marching the Armagnac king from Louis' own House of Valois-Orléans to Rheims to be crowned. But after she was captured, the weak Charles VII of France had done nothing in return to save her.

Louis bowed his head in shame for his ancestors' actions. "Let me honor you, great lady, by holding together the kingdom you fought for and allowing no civil wars under my rule." Never would he allow Burgundy to regain the power it had held and abused less than a century earlier. If it hadn't been for Jeanne d'Arc, France might now be ruled by a Burgundian-English alliance. But the incomparable Maid had spooked the English from France after her death, her legend igniting a fire far greater than the one that had burned her alive.

Raising his head, Louis took Anne's hand and helped her up as the crowds cheered. He watched in wonder as his wife raised a dainty hand, quietening the throngs.

"She may have lost her life but she won her cause ..." the Queen of France proclaimed.

As cheers began, her voice carried to every corner of the square. "... for the glory of God and the glory of France."

The crowd went wild as Louis' heart filled with admiration for his regal queen. His subjects might not love her, but they loved what she gave them: a sense of France's importance and their place in its story.

Bending to her ear the scent of her skin filled his senses, at once calming and igniting him. "My queen, may we both win our cause, in this life and after it," he told her.

As they regained their mounts it struck Louis that, likely, neither one of them would win their respective causes because of their claim on each other.

For the sake of France, his duty was to ensure Brittany would be folded into France one day to prevent a Habsburg-Breton hedge around his kingdom. As for his own deepest desire, he knew well that Anne would do whatever she could to dash his Italian aspirations, thinking his time better spent at home. Both were invested in defeating each other's dearest dream. Yet he couldn't imagine life without her.

Chuckling, he marveled at the perfect absurdity of it all.

"My lord?" Anne glanced at him sideways as she waved to the crowd.

"'Tis a rich secret, my lady."

"One you can share?" she gaily asked.

"Not this one, *m'amie*."

Looking as if she were about to grill him further, the excited squeals of a group of young women saved him, making further conversation impossible. Some secrets were too rich to share. This one was one of them.

"What say you to these naughty lads, my lady? Should they be directed to do their business elsewhere?" Louis eyed the statues of two sturdy young boys voiding into the lower basin of the fountain he stood before. At seven arm's lengths high, the two-tiered Carrara marble fountain formed the centerpiece of the inner courtyard of his senior minister's chateau.

"They are playful, not like grown men who spout malodorous streams in public that offend all civilized souls," Anne shot back. She would make no apologies for her fastidious nature. As a girl, her tutor had taught her that the ancient Hebrews had valued cleanliness next to godliness and she agreed. She was as devoted to frequent baths as she was to the Church. If the people of France found her too fine for their tastes, she would make it her duty as their queen to see to it that their tastes became more finely honed.

Their host, Georges d'Amboise, chuckled behind her. "Your Grace, do you know what the king says when someone complains about your strict standards?"

Anne tilted her chin. "I can't imagine, but I'm sure it's far less severe than what I would say if someone grumbled to me."

At this, the king let out a guffaw, nodding to d'Amboise to tell her.

"Madame, he always says that much must be accorded a woman of such high virtue," the senior minister related.

"Am I to understand that such grumblings occur often?" Anne gave Louis a sly look. How she loved him for his genteel nature, so much like her father's. And how she feared for him in Italy where such gentility would be taken advantage of. It was her job as his wife to keep him home in France where he was appreciated.

"Ah, Madame, that is a question for the king and not for me," d'Amboise deflected.

"And as for these bounteous ladies?" Louis asked, admiring the next row of statues forming the central column of the two-tiered fountain. Lactating nymphs in classical Roman style spouted water from abundant breasts.

"Superb. Tell me, Georges, what artist designed this?" Anne asked.

"Your Grace, it is the work of the Sires Bertrand de Meynal and Girolamo Pacchiarotti," d'Amboise said.

"It was Pacchiarotti who assisted on Sire de Colomb's tomb

of my two princes in Tours." Anne's conscience pricked at thought of her recent aborted trip to Tours.

"So you know his work." D'Amboise looked exultant to see her interest.

"It is genius. The faces so lifelike ... so laughing and playful." *Just as my two princes should have been with each other*, she thought. Would she ever again hear the sound of her own son's laughter?

"Your Grace, you have captured it. A melding of the ancient with the modern that brings alive its subjects."

"You have outdone yourself, Georges," Anne remarked as she drank in the rich details surrounding her. She would work on Louis' minister to convince the king to confine himself to bringing Italian art to France rather than the French army to Italy.

"Tell me, Georges, how did you pay for all this?" Louis asked over dinner. "That fountain alone must have cost a fortune."

D'Amboise looked nervous. Anne could guess why. Any question from her frugal husband about money was a sensitive one. "Sire, the fountain was a gift from the Republic of Venice," their host replied.

"How generous." The king bit into a venison pasty made with a red wine sauce. "Mmm," he murmured, relaxing.

"It was in thanks, Your Grace, for ridding Milan of Il Moro," d'Amboise added.

Anne had heard Il Moro had died in prison just a few months earlier. Ludovico Sforza, the former strongman who had ruled Milan, had been captured at the Battle of Novara in 1500 and brought back to France in chains. He had spent the rest of his days locked up in a dungeon.

"Dead and gone, a relief to all." Louis flicked his fingers as if flicking away a recently solved problem.

"We did the Venetians a favor to lock him away," d'Amboise agreed.

Louis looked pleased. "A well-deserved gift, Georges. Your efforts merited it."

Anne chuckled to herself, guessing that her husband was happy not to have had to pay for such an expensive gift from France's coffers. A stickler for fiscal conservatism, Louis' subjects loved him for keeping taxes low.

"And are you still on such good terms with the Venetians now?" she asked Georges. She had heard that the upcoming conference in Cambrai was being held to form a league against the lagoon republic.

Louis and his minister exchanged guarded looks as Anne sipped her wine. Savoring its verbena and honeysuckle taste, she awaited the cardinal's reply.

"The Venetians have begun to irritate many of Europe's princes, Your Grace." D'Amboise's tone was tentative.

"And has this European prince tasked you with forming a league to push them back to their lagoon?" Anne asked with a nod toward her husband.

Their host choked as he put down his wineglass. Dabbing at his mouth with a cloth, his eyes sought Louis', giving Anne her answer.

"It is simply a matter of putting them in their place," Louis answered for his minister.

"To carve out a bigger place for the rest of you who don't belong there?" she asked.

Her husband's eyes flared, and she saw she had struck a nerve. Best not to pluck it.

"Madame, it is very much a good question as to who belongs in northern Italy," d'Amboise hedged.

"As for who does not belong in northern Italy, you can be

sure that the pope takes the position that Europe's princes best stay home and out of his game," Anne told them.

"Madame, as usual, you are well informed," d'Amboise equivocated, giving the king a sideways glance.

Anne said nothing but took another sip as she thought of how she would frame her next letter to Julius II. Seeing the steel in Louis' eyes, no further inroads would be made on her husband's plans in Italy tonight. She would support d'Amboise in pursuing the king's agenda at Cambrai, then encourage the pope to join whatever alliance was formed there. Best to keep Julius II in the fold against Venice to delay the moment when he would seek to clear all foreigners from Italian soil.

Of that objective, she had no doubt. The pope didn't want foreigners ruling parts of his homeland any more than she or her father could stomach the French ruling over Brittany. It was a viewpoint that Louis didn't choose to see but as clear as a summer sky to her.

"Let us drink to our host, who does well all he sets his mind to," she rerouted as Louis joined her in raising a glass to his minister.

D'Amboise colored, looking relieved. She could see the cardinal was happy to get off sensitive topics. Best to stick with thanking him for a hospitality which pleased them both—she, because his good taste matched her own, and Louis, because someone else had paid for it.

As for Italy, Louis wanted Milan and his minister wanted the papacy. For the moment, there was no swaying either of them, so she would let the matter rest and enjoy the evening.

Chapter Four

Fall 1508

A Secret Errand

Watching the back of her contact disappear down the hill, Louise de Savoy heaved a satisfied sigh. The news from court boded well, with the king determined to return to Italy the following spring. If the queen wasn't with child by the time he left, so much the better for Francis' chances of ascending the throne.

And even if the queen was with child, if the child failed to live, as so many of Anne of Brittany's already had, then Louise's son's position was secure.

As she scanned the countryside to the east where Italy lay, a devilish notion came to her. If the king were to be felled across the Alps either in battle or by illness, her moment to rule France as Francis's regent would arrive sooner.

Smiling, she savored the thought. The king's will of 1505 stipulated Queen Anne would share regency with Louise during Francis's minority. But knowing the queen, she would fly back to the realm she ruled the moment the king died, just as she had prepared to do in 1505 when he had appeared to be mortally ill. Who could blame her for her devotion to her provincial backwater? Louise would encourage her to go, all the better for her to rule France alone without interference from anyone else.

Laughing out loud, she attracted the attention of her steward in the next room.

"My lady, something amusing to share?"

"No, Jean. Just a thought I should not put into words."

Her steward gazed at her with dry affection. It was comforting to have him in her confidence. But that exact thought she would confide to no one.

Louise didn't particularly believe in God, but she believed in maintaining the king's goodwill. Knowing how desirous he was of expanding his holdings in Italy, she would focus on fanning his flame so that he set off soon—come what may once he was over there.

"Perhaps you will tell me later," Jean de St.-Gelais suggested, his eyes soft.

"Perhaps not," Louise checked him. How perfect it was not to have a husband ruling over her. When she became regent she would ensure that Jean was promoted to Francis' *valet de chambre* to ensure access to her rooms through the young king's. In fact, she would see to it that he had direct access too so as not to disturb Francis and Claude, who she hoped would have better luck breeding than her high and mighty mother had had.

"Will I see Madame at the midday meal today?" Jean asked.

"I think not. I have errands in town and won't be back till suppertime."

"Anything I can pick up for you to save you the trip?"

"Not this time, Jean."

"Then I look forward to reporting to you later," the steward said, a subtle shade to his tone.

"Umm," Louise hedged, although she looked forward to seeing him at the end of the day too. It was their custom and a comfort to her in the lonely evenings now that her son had been called up to court.

But her errand that afternoon was one she needed to take care of alone. No one must know of it, and no one must know what she planned to do with the items she picked up.

Setting off for town, she bid her coachman to drop her at the corner of one of its main streets then meet her there again in an hour. After draping the hood of her mantle over her head, she disappeared into a shop, then exited by the back entrance into an alleyway. At its end, she came out on a side street where she made her way to a lesser-known part of town. There she would obtain what she needed from the wise woman who sold herbs and amulets from her home.

Leading Louise to the privacy of her storeroom, the woman shut the door behind them. "My lady, what is it you wish accomplished by this charm?" she asked.

"My good woman, it is a sad tale," Louise began, "but I wish to affect the outcome of a pregnancy in a case where there is no father to claim the child." She gave the woman an earnest look.

"My lady, there are ways to accomplish that with herbs far more effective than charms." The woman busied herself with organizing some jars on her counter.

"The poor girl is not in my direct care, so I do not wish to interfere. But if she produces a son, it will ruin the lives of more than one." Three, to be exact: herself, her son, and her daughter, although if Marguerite could manage to marry well, perhaps she would not be so affected. For herself and Francis, it would mean the end of their dearest dream.

"So you do not wish to end the pregnancy, but to ensure that the babe is not male?" the wise woman asked.

"Yes, good woman. You have caught it exactly."

"I can give you such a thing, but with the understanding that I can make no promise that it will work."

"Understood. I will not hold you responsible, whatever the outcome."

"Very good, my lady. Allow me to prepare a sac. You should place it somewhere hidden away where you can go and pray daily for the result you desire."

"Will this work for more than one pregnancy?" Louise asked, intent on flicking a stray straw from her mantle.

"It will work for as long as you believe it works, my lady. Or not, if I may say so truthfully. But the stronger the conviction of the person believing it works, the more likely it will."

"Ah, then it sounds to be a strong charm."

"It's a set of charms, and I can't promise anything more than what I've already told you."

"I'll take them."

As the wise woman prepared the sac, Louise warmed herself before the fireplace in the small cottage, searching the fire's flames. If Father de Paule had said her unborn son would be a future king, then what was the harm in utilizing all possible channels to ensure it happened?

She had learned the benefit of careful planning from Anne de Beaujeu in the years she had grown up in her household. Her former guardian had been the master manipulator of the affairs of both France and Brittany in the eight years she had served as France's regent. Everyone had stood in awe of the woman known as Madame la Grande. Now Louise had a chance to be France's future Madame la Grande. She would use every means possible to step into that role one day as mother and closest advisor to France's king.

In a moment, the package was ready. Louise paid the woman, thanking her.

"It is I who thank you, Madame," the wise woman beamed. "It is rare to have such a great lady visit."

"I am surprised to hear that considering the concerns we have are those of all women, great ladies, too," Louise remarked.

"Indeed they are, Madame," the wise woman agreed as a girl of about eleven came up behind her. "Allow my serving girl to see you to your carriage."

"I know my way."

"She knows another that will guarantee no eyes upon you," the woman recommended.

"Very well, then." Louise set off with the serving girl, who led her down an enclosed passageway not visible from the street.

"There was another great lady expected the week before but she never arrived," the girl remarked as she led her through the passageway.

"Did she send her maid instead?" Louise asked.

"No, Madame. It was said some accident befell her on her way."

"Ah, then I hope she was not harmed," Louise remarked.

"I think not, Madame, as we would have heard by now."

"We?" Louise eyed the girl. How renowned was this lady, she wondered.

The serving girl looked flustered. "I meant we in the shop would have heard by now," she stammered.

"Then something else must have happened to change her mind," Louise said, thinking she never changed hers.

"Most likely, Madame."

The end of the passageway loomed ahead. Louise bade the girl good day as she wondered at her words. Concealing her face with her hood, she stepped out onto the street and into her carriage.

Once inside, she closed her hand around the small sac in the pocket of her gown, congratulating herself on her thoroughness. Even if the charms didn't work, they would be a focal point for her to whisper her request before daily.

If Jean asked what the charms were meant for, she would say it had something to do with regulating her flux. Men never wished to discuss such things, so he would inquire no further.

And if Marguerite asked, she would tell her they were to ensure their trinity remained intact. In a way, it was true. The point of their trinity was for Francis to be at its head as France's king one day with his all-powerful mother guiding him from behind.

Everything else was beside the point.

CHAPTER FIVE

November 1508

In Your Belly Lies a Future King

"As Petrarch has been called the first modern man,
so Anne might be called the first modern woman."
—Helen J. Sanborn, *Anne of Brittany*

Behind the arras in the receiving room at Blois, Anne picked up her ears. Two of her courtiers were deep in discussion just on the other side of the screen.

"He told her, 'In your belly lies a future king,'" the woman's voice said.

"No. Really?" a second voice asked. "Father de Paule said that to her?"

"That's what I heard."

"No wonder she's so protective of her son," a third voice chimed in.

Anne grimaced. It had to be Louise de Savoy they discussed. There was no more protective mother in all of France.

"Wouldn't you be if a holy man told you that when you were carrying a babe?" the first voice replied.

"I would think I was born under a lucky star."

Anne leaned back against the wall, the hair standing up on the back of her neck. She should be the one born under a lucky star, she who ruled Brittany, the only woman ever to have married two kings of France—not that unbearable woman in Amboise.

"And that's what she does think. Look at her, all high and mighty under the king's protection. She thinks she doesn't need anybody else."

"Is that why she never remarried?"

"I heard she carries on with her steward." The woman's laugh was muffled.

"You can hardly blame her for not wanting to marry again after the husband she had."

Anne held her breath as more whispering ensued, the voices so low she couldn't catch the words. As she strained to hear, she mulled over the woman's words: *In your belly lies a future king.* What powerful words those were, enough to hang one's dreams on. Why had the holy man not delivered such a prophecy to her, the one who rightfully should carry France's future king?

Moving closer to the screen, she sharpened her ears. In a moment, her attendant would return.

"Do you think she named her son after him?"

"I would if a holy man told me my son would be king."

"The queen hates her."

Anne froze. Hate was a strong word. But she couldn't think of another that came closer.

"Wouldn't you, if you couldn't manage to get an heir for the kingdom while the king's cousin's son grows up so fine a gentleman? It's the first duty of a queen, and she hasn't done it yet."

Anne's heart shriveled. Putting her hand to her throat, she fought to still her breathing.

"Even with two kings for husbands."

"That last one was a bit of a troll. But our king now is a fine figure. Think what a prince they would get together."

Anne touched her belly. So true. How fine a son of theirs would be. Far finer than that strutting bantam cock Francis, his feathers preened daily by his doting red hen of a mother. Yet what mother wouldn't dote on a son who had been proclaimed a future king while in her womb?

Anne searched her mind for anything of similar import that the Italian holy man might have said to her.

Francis de Paule's dark inscrutable eyes came to her, fixing on herself and her first husband as they asked about their son on their mad dash home in 1495. They had galloped back from Lyon at first word of Charles-Orland's illness, coming upon the holy man just outside Amboise's town gates. He had said nothing, only pointed with a spectral finger toward Amboise Castle where the boy's body lay, felled by measles at age three.

Anne's stomach roiled at the memory. She and Charles had spent over half of her son's short life away from him: Charles on campaign in Italy and she in Lyon just on the other side of the Alps to receive news from her husband the King.

Unlike Louise de Savoy, she had been the opposite of an overprotective mother. Was God withholding sons from her now for neglecting the only son she had had who had lived for any length of time?

The voices became fainter as the women moved away. Hearing the rustle of her attendant's skirts, Anne put on her court face. Later, she would ask Louis about what she had heard. Close to Louise's husband when he had been alive, he would know if any such prophecy had really happened.

Louis eased onto the low couch before the crackling fireplace in Anne's chambers. Once he sat he'd be hard-pressed to stand again. The years had taken their toll on his lean frame. There were moments he felt the litheness he had always enjoyed on the tennis court and dance floor. But, at other times, he felt the creak of his bones and needed to pause before unbending his limbs.

Fortunately, his wife kept regular hours and liked to fuss over him. Whenever they were home together he looked forward to their usual evening chat by the fire then early to bed.

Glancing over at Anne, he beckoned her to join him, prodding her Italian greyhound with his foot until the dog resettled to a more remote corner.

His wife's brow furrowed. "I heard something today."

"Come sit before you tell me." Her tone told him she was stewing over something. He would try to head her off before she started. Using his hands always worked best since his words rarely prevailed against hers when she had something on her mind.

Moving toward the hearth, Anne crossed her arms over her chest.

"What is it, *m'amie*?" She pulled away as he reached for her, but not before he snagged a handful of her gown.

Drawing her down onto the couch, he picked up the goblet on the low table next to him. A sip of mulled wine would fortify him for whatever lay ahead.

"Did Francis de Paule tell Louise she would bear a king when she was carrying Francis?" Anne shot off.

Louis groaned inside. He hated discussions about Louise de Savoy. They never went where they were supposed to go, and invariably left his *Brette* in a foul mood.

His wife's eyes bored into him. "Did he tell her she would bear a king or not?"

"How would I know, my lady?" Louis put down his goblet and picked up hers. Offering it to her, he was rebuffed.

"Think back, Husband. Did your cousin say anything to you when his wife was expecting Francis?"

"How would I remember? What would he have said that I would have given a second thought to?" Sweat broke out on Louis' temples. Vaguely, he remembered that Charles had said something about Louise back in 1494 when he had joked with him over how family life was going. It had been a remark that would not bear repeating in front of the ladies.

"Well, did he say anything about Father de Paule telling her something about the child she carried?"

"My lady, you don't honestly think men talk between themselves about such women's prattle," Louis tried to put her off.

"No. They have their own prattle with even less weight to it." Anne gave him a disdainful frown.

"Well, I don't remember anything he said about Father de Paule speaking to her other than that she told him she went to visit him."

"Ah, so you do remember something." Anne moved closer, trapping him in her gaze. Those violet-gray eyes delighted him when they were not searching out secrets he wished to remain that way. He didn't have many. But he had a few.

Sweat pooled under his arms. What he remembered was that Charles had joked that he was carrying on with a tasty dish, and Louise didn't care at all as she was with child and obsessed with visiting shrines and such to ensure the babe's health.

"He might have said that the priest had told her the child she carried would be special," Louis said, just to give her something to chew on. Charles had told him Louise had been animated coming back from visits with Father de Paule, and if he didn't know her better, he would think she was having a dalliance herself.

Anne stared at him. "Did he tell you that Father de Paule said the child would one day be a king?"

"I don't remember, *m'amie.* Why would I?" Hell's bells, if only she would take a sip or two of wine so they could relax. This was worse than his annulment proceedings from his last wife; no matter what answer he came up with, it was never the right one.

"How could you possibly forget if your cousin told you, or not, that his wife had told him she was bearing a future king?" His *Brette* looked ready to shake him as if he were a heavy-laden apple tree.

"*M'amie,* I was not king at the time, nor expecting to be, so why would I remember such a thing?"

"Because it is something out of the ordinary. Something extraordinary that you might have remembered from the mouth of your kinsman," Anne retorted.

"*M'amie*, women say many things when they're with child. Every woman thinks she's carrying a king or a hero or someone who will be special one day," he improvised. "With so many months to wait, a woman might spin some tales to pass the time." He was no expert on such matters. All he knew was that men went off to war, and women stayed home and replenished the population that men were responsible for killing off. It was an equitable arrangement.

"But what exactly did Charles tell you about what Father de Paule said to Louise when she visited him?"

Louis' face reddened. It was coming back to him that his cousin had jested that the more time his wife spent off on visits to Plessis, the more chances he had to enjoy the delights of his new mistress. There didn't seem to be any point in getting into all this, but he couldn't figure out how to get out of it either.

"He might have said that his wife seemed preoccupied." Charles had been preoccupied, too, happy to have Louise wrapped up in her unfolding pregnancy and out of his hair. Conversations with his cousin had tended to be on the lighter side. The Count d'Angoulême had enjoyed a singular lifestyle—one that had caused even Louis to raise an eyebrow.

It was a long-running scandal that Louise de Savoy's lady-in-waiting had been Charles's mistress, with two daughters by him before Louise joined his menagerie as his wife. Not only that, but the count had had a daughter by a second woman in his household. In the final year of his cousin's life, the man had been unfaithful to his wife, official mistress, and unofficial one with yet his latest favorite.

Just thinking about such a strenuous schedule exhausted Louis. It was hard enough managing one wife, he thought, avoiding Anne's eyes now scanning him like a torchlight.

It came to him that the effects of that complicated lifestyle might have caught up with his cousin at the end. Charles d'Angoulême had caught cold riding home from the funeral of Anne's son by Charles VIII and died on the first of January in 1496.

Trying not to smirk, Louis shook his head. His cousin had likely worn himself out from managing attachments to four women at the same time.

He glanced at his unrelenting consort, wracking his brain for what he might do to end the discussion.

Slipping an arm around her, he attempted a time-honored technique, honed over nine years of marriage. Massaging the back of her neck, he gazed into her eyes, waiting for the pupils to dilate.

"Stop it, Louis. I am not finished," Anne objected.

"Ah, but I am, my lady. And if you do not turn your concerns to more profitable enterprises, you will lessen your chances of making a future king yourself."

Anne scowled, but soon her eyes closed and her head fell back against his hand. He was not good at arguments, but he was adept at other pursuits. One that he had much practice with was calming his determined wife.

The red and gold papal seal with its distinctive gold cord adorned the sealed pouch Anne held. It had been sent from her archbishop and protégé in Nantes under plain wrapping to disguise its source. Cardinal Robert Guibé was Brittany's highest ecclesiastical authority and diplomatic envoy in Rome. Appointed to his position by Anne, she enjoyed a pipeline to the pope through him.

Julius II had written asking after her health, praising her for her care for the spiritual well-being of her Breton subjects and inquiring what she thought the main topic of discussion would at the King of France's suggested meeting at Cambrai the following month.

Immediately, Anne summoned her Italian private secretary to scribe a note back. Here was her opportunity to repair Louis' relationship with the pope and to ask his Holiness to petition God to favor her with a son.

> "Your Holiness, Be assured that the topic of discussion at Cambrai next month will be a formation of a league to push back Venice to its rightful borders. I am certain that my husband, the King of France, will welcome your inclusion in such an undertaking. I thank you, Holy Father, for inquiring after my health and ask you for your prayers for a son and heir to bless our family and to ensure orderly dynastic succession in both my realm and my husband's.
>
> Your Holiness' most obedient and humble servant,
> Anne, Duchess of Brittany

Writing to him as ruler of Brittany, she did not include her title of Queen of France. If the pope wished to hear from someone representing France, he could write directly to Louis himself. But given their chilly relations, she knew he wouldn't.

She pressed her seal into the soft wax and stamped it at the bottom of her response. Since Julius II's election in 1503, Louis and he had not been on good terms.

Louis had counted on the former Cardinal Giuliano della Rovere to vote for his senior minister Georges d'Amboise to ascend the papacy in the wake of Alexander VI's death.

But della Rovere had failed to support d'Amboise, and instead thrown his vote to Pius III. Old and weak, Pius III had died less than a month after ascending the papacy, even sooner than the cardinals who had elected him had anticipated. During that time, della Rovere had maneuvered to gain enough votes for the next election, which he won, to Cardinal d'Amboise's great disappointment.

Naming himself Julius II after Julius Caesar, the new pope had outfoxed both Louis and his senior minister. Anne guessed he would do so again if they found themselves on opposing sides. For the present moment, their mutual wrath against Venice's encroachment on mainland territories was the perfect project for them to come together on.

She shuddered, pushing away thoughts of the horrors that would be unleashed should they become enemies. Excommunication would be foremost amongst them.

Sealing the pouch, she inserted it in the larger pouch from Nantes and handed it to her secretary. It would return to Nantes where her archbishop would send it on to Rome.

As she sat back, she sighed with satisfaction. She had obeyed the Church's prohibition against relying on soothsayers and amulets to effect an outcome. Now she had asked its head to pray for her to produce a son. Was it not time for God to favor her?

The sound of a carriage rolling into the courtyard told Louise de Savoy she was not alone.

Hurriedly, she put away the charm she was sticking pins into, covering it facedown with the doeskin sac it had come in. She closed and locked the drawer of her desk, pocketing the key in the folds of her gown.

The great Beaujeu would scoff to know she was resorting to such childish measures to prevent her son from being replaced.

Let her scoff, Louise thought. One day she would wield power far beyond what the spider king's daughter had known. Just like Anne of Brittany, Anne de Beaujeu had been born to privilege and wealth, but not so Louise. And that would prove her trump card.

Her fingers drummed a dance on her desk as she smiled. Any tactic at all to prevent the queen from bearing a son that lived was within her consideration. She had no scruples about stooping low if it reaped the benefit she sought. Who truly knew what might work and what wouldn't? She had other measures working on her behalf at the royal court, intent on keeping the king as far from the queen as possible. One was arriving at that moment.

Rising, she smoothed her gown then straightened her headdress. It was always a pleasure to speak with her contact. Her suggestions to him to plant at court were so subtle that she wondered if he knew she was using him.

Whatever the man realized, she had made sure he was in her debt. Applying her former guardian's methods, she had woven him inescapably into her web by promising one of her husband's natural daughters to his wife's brother, who worked as the king's baker.

When that match took place, she would have yet another source at Blois Castle to report back to her. And when her son became king, the present king's baker would be married to the future king's half-sister, an unimaginable leap up in the world. The entire family would be indebted to her forever.

Crossing her arms she hugged herself. It was satisfying to do business with the commoner on the king's staff. She could sniff out the exact scent of his ambition because she possessed it too, only more so. She would vault to the highest level a woman could go: answering to no one and directing the king.

With a chortle she recalled the many chess games she had played with her husband. The year before he died, the chess queen's moves had been expanded to honor the great Spanish monarch, Queen Isabella, who had crisscrossed Spain in seeking out men and supplies to aid her husband Ferdinand, hemmed in by enemies at the battlefront.

Charles d'Angoulême and she had chuckled together over the queen becoming the most powerful piece on the board, able to move farther and in more directions than the king she protected. How well she intended to do the same when the moment arrived.

At the sound of her merriment, her steward appeared in the doorway.

"Madame, you are in fine spirits this morning," he remarked.

"Oh, Jean, you have no idea."

"I had thought perhaps I did," he remarked, a tinge of disappointment in his voice.

"Send my visitor in and tell the kitchen to bring refreshments," she ordered, deaf to his tone. The night before had been enjoyable, but it was nothing compared to the thrill she felt at moving toward her dream, one well-placed plant or pinprick at a time.

There was nothing better than having no lord above her. And when her son sat on the throne of France her happiness would be complete.

Chapter Six

February–March 1509

Journey to Nantes

"A legend in her own time with her
sparkling éclat of luxury with simplicity."
—Philippe Tourault, *Anne de Bretagne*

Inhaling deeply, Louis scented the tangy smell of the sea that surrounded his wife's homeland on three sides. Less than three days ride west from Fontevraud, Brittany was a different climate: more bracing and salty than the gentle landscape of the Touraine back in France's Loire Valley. It was good to be back. He always felt as if he could breathe more freely here, less encumbered by affairs of his own realm.

Brittany was his wife's duchy, and Nantes was the center of it. Perhaps not logistically, located as it was at the mouth of the Loire where it emptied into the vast Atlantic. Nor ecclesiastically, as Rennes was Brittany's clerical seat. But Nantes was the seat of the Dukes of Brittany, Anne's birthplace.

It was here that his *Brette* was born, in the castle whose courtyard they were about to enter.

The magnificent Chateau of the Dukes of Brittany had been built in 1207 by Guy of Thouars, consort to Constance, Duchess of Brittany, one of several female rulers of the duchy. Women in Anne's fertile realm were not barred from dynastic succession, as in France with its Salic Law.

Glancing around, Louis met his head huntsman's eye. If he were lucky, he planned to hunt the following day while Anne was in meetings with her ministers. Then she would attend the unveiling of the tomb of her parents that that expensive sculptor Colombe had created.

Anne had paid for the monument out of Brittany's coffers and her own sizeable income, so what did he care? He prayed she wouldn't pressure him to accompany her.

Riding over the stone bridge that crossed the moat before the portcullis of the main gate of the castle, Louis peered at his wife on her white palfrey ahead. Here Anne was sovereign, and he her consort.

Truth be told, he was delighted to switch roles for a few days. There were times he found it wearisome to be king: either beloved at home and hated abroad, or respected abroad and reviled at home. There was no middle ground, although he felt himself to be on an even keel since the December past when his chief minister had brokered an agreement at Cambrai with Margaret of Austria to ally against Venice. At least Europe's princes weren't ganging up on France.

He chuckled softly at the thought of having a few days' respite from it all.

"What comes over you, my lord?" Anne asked as his mount caught up to hers in the enormous courtyard of the castle. With flushed cheeks, she looked overjoyed to be back in her realm amongst her subjects.

Constance, Duchess of Brittany (1166-1201)
Courtesy of Wikimedia Commons

Louis leaned close to her ear. "*M'amie*, I remember your father in his night-clothes being chased over that bridge by demoiselles when we sported at punishing the last to wake up."

"Are you sure it wasn't you, my lord?" Anne batted her eyes at him. She was home. Finally, she could let down her guard. Except that she never did, other than with him.

Louis chortled. "It is good to be home is it not, *ma Brette?*"

"It is beyond words. But you may only remind me of my father's gay games when we are alone. Now 'tis business, my lord. Mine, not yours." She straightened in her saddle.

"Ah, *m'amie*, I am happy to serve you here as you serve me back in France."

"Do I, my lord? That's not what you say back in Blois." Anne flicked her riding crop against his leg.

A faint titter rose from the castle staff that had lined up to greet them. It was as if the merry days of Duke Francis' reign were back. Except it was his daughter in his place, making good cheer with her husband, the King of France.

Louis leaped from his mount and went 'round to Anne's palfrey, brushing aside the steward who stood ready to help the Duchess of Brittany dismount.

Louis reached up and grasped his wife around the waist, hoisting her off her horse. As he set her down with a subtle thump, the palace staff cheered.

"*Vive la bonne duchesse*," they called out.

"*Vive le roi!*" other voices cried.

"*Bienvenue, Duchesse*!" floated through the air.

Despite the February chill, it was a warm welcome.

Holding his arm out to her, he flamed as she gripped it. Memories of his first time in the enormous courtyard washed over him. He had been overwhelmed by the vast splendor of the Chateau of the Dukes of Brittany, far grander than his own ancestral home in Blois.

His thoughts bounded ahead as they strolled to the elegantly curved outer staircase. It was on those same wide steps that he had first laid eyes on Anne. He had been twenty-one; the proud elder daughter of his host had been seven. She had fixed him with serious eyes that shone violet in the sunlight, instantly commanding his attention.

Slowly, they climbed the Italian-style staircase that Francis II, Duke of Brittany, had installed. A connoisseur in his tastes, he had inhaled the fresh winds of art and design blowing westward from Italy before most of Europe's princes did.

In April 1484, Anne's father had been a gracious host whose capacity for entertainment and merrymaking had knit them together in shared sensibility and firm friendship. The duke's refined manner, combined with a great capacity for amusement and a passion for the hunt, had made an indelible impression on Louis.

They had spent days hunting in the forests outside Nantes, bagging deer, wild boar, and other game. Evenings they had feasted in an opulence that Louis had never before encountered. Despite his royal blood, he had grown up in reduced circumstances. Upon his father's death when he had been two, his mother had been left a widow, hard-pressed to provide for her son and his two sisters.

The dainty Anne had served as her father's host at table, her mother and younger sister both absent due to the lung illness that eventually killed them both. The young beauty's poise and maturity had struck Louis deeply.

"My home is yours, my lord, just as yours is mine," Anne said, cutting into his thoughts.

"My lady, your home felt like mine even before you were."

"How so, my lord?"

"Your father and lady mother were the most gracious hosts imaginable."

"And as for me?"

"You were an icicle, unmoved by every act of gallantry I offered," Louis teased. How well he remembered her fine hauteur, heralding at the tender age of seven the woman she would become.

Anne lifted her chin. "I am not one to give favors freely."

"Well I know, my lady. To be raised in such splendor made you the hardest of diamonds to scratch."

"Do you think you have scratched me, my lord?" Her chin tilted higher, imperious eyes staring him down. The same grave eyes had fixed on him for a full two days at first acquaintance before the tiny princess had finally offered a smile.

"'Tis a question only you can answer."

"I shall let you know later." She flicked him with the hem of her gown as she swished ahead.

Behind her, Louis grinned. He would gladly withstand her scratches and cuffs later that night; before it was over, he would have earned his day of hunting on the morrow.

Chapter Seven

February–March 1509

Anne Remembers her Past

Anne laughed aloud to feel the sea breeze ruffle her headdress. She was on her way to the Chapel of the Carmelites where her parents lay in eternal rest.

She loved Louis fiercely but she loved her parents with the same tender love that she held for her Breton people. Today was for her and them. Not for Louis or France.

Fortunately, her husband's passion for hunting was as predictable as his passion for her. He had wished to escape to the forests outside Nantes as much as she wished to be rid of him for the day. This was her realm, not his, and her monument to her parents. There was no reason for the King of France to be hanging about.

"Vive la bonne duchesse," a man's voice rang out. She waved in his direction, feeling as if she was ten again, riding behind her father on her way to the cathedral in Rennes. Francis II, Duke of Brittany, had named her his successor there in February 1487 before an assembly of Brittany's greatest noblemen and clergy. Some had been sincerely supportive, others restive with ancient rivalries against the Montfort claim to the ducal throne.

But the common people who filled the streets outside the cathedral had been unanimous in their support for her. The moment she had left the cathedral, she had felt as one with the good people of Brittany who had flocked to see her.

So it was again today.

"*Vive la duchesse-reine!*" a woman cried, warming Anne's heart to hear her call her by her dual title. She motioned to her attendant to shower her with coins.

At the entrance to the Carmelites Chapel, her chancellor came forward to meet her. Philippe de Montauban was an old friend, one who had served in her father's household before serving her. Along with her Breton cook, her elderly chancellor was one of those dearest to her from her childhood.

She had been overjoyed to see him again in meetings that morning. If only she could stay longer. But she had promised Louis that they would be back in France by the following week to learn if the pope had joined the Cambrai Conference's league against Venice. Once he did, she was sure Louis would begin plans to return to Italy. She would not try to stop him, only to bring him back as soon as possible.

Followed by her chancellor, she entered the chapel, her eyes adjusting before she could make out the outlines of the new installation to honor her parents.

"Your Grace, it is a wonder beyond all imagination," de Montauban exclaimed, his voice tinged with awe.

She sucked in her breath as she surveyed the magnificent monument. Fully assembled for the first time, its scope and detail were far beyond anything she had ever seen, either in Brittany or in France.

"Sire de Colombe has surpassed himself. He will be

remembered for all times for this masterpiece," she proclaimed, her heart full for her Breton-born sculptor, who stood in the shadows of the chapel unannounced.

As Michel Colombe blushed to hear his patron's praise, Anne traversed the four corners of the monument, pausing before each of the statues representing courage, temperance, prudence, and justice.

At the fourth and final statue, she turned to her chancellor. "Which of these four statues is me, Sire de Montauban?"

Philippe de Montauban smiled and raised a finger. "You must give me a moment, Madame."

Anne shot him a cheeky look. "You have known me all my life. Either you know which one it is, or you have never really known me." Her chancellor had been at her side in the darkest hours of her youth, fraught months when she had fought to hold onto ducal power following her father's death. Their bond gave them a jesting rapport that Anne enjoyed with no one else, save Louis.

The elderly minister's eyes twinkled. "Madame, you challenge me, as always."

"Take a moment, Monsieur, but don't take too long."

De Montauban strolled to the statue of courage and shook his head. "Too warlike. And I do not see my good duchess holding a dragon in her hand."

"Nor do I." She had tamed a few, she thought, the severe face of her first husband's sister, Anne de Beaujeu, flashing before her.

Moving to the statue of temperance, de Montauban frowned. "Your Grace, I know you too well not to know that you are marvelously temperate until you lose your temper. But then ..." His eyes rolled up, his mouth twitching with mirth.

"You are one of the few, Monsieur, who has had the opportunity to see my wrath unfurled." The man had supported her through countless power struggles with her unruly nobles. He had seen her temper flare more than once.

"And what a privilege it was, Your Grace. Never will I forget when you barked at the Marshal de Rieux and his men come to kidnap you 'til they slunk away like dogs with their tails between their legs."

"They needed reminding that the first to lay hands on their anointed and consecrated sovereign would have Heaven to answer to should they dare such sacrilege." Narrowing her eyes, she remembered how hard-pressed she had been to establish her authority as her father's successor in the wake of his death.

"Madame, no tongue's swordplay was faster than yours at that moment."

"Does my temper not stand me in good stead at times?" How good it felt to let down her guard with one who had known her since childhood.

"Only because your sharp mind delivers the right words to your tongue at the same instant."

"I am usually not so harsh, Monsieur."

"Your Grace, forgive me, but some of my greatest memories of you in your glory are of some especially harsh performances you gave."

Certainly, there were not many of those, Monsieur." But what displays of temper there had been had set others straight on who ruled Brittany, she recalled.

"Such moments will never be forgotten by those who witnessed you in full fury. Do you think any at the Estates-General in 1489 have forgotten the tongue-lashing you gave Alain d'Albret when he pressed his suit for your hand?"

"He deserved it! And there was no other way to make him back off other than to gain the support of the assembly." Exhilaration flooded her as she remembered the lecture at top voice she had given Brittany's most important political body that day. What fun it had been.

De Montauban's eyes shone. "Madame, you were only twelve years old and you were magnificent."

Behind him, Michel Colombe struggled to follow. His wife would wish him to recount this exchange between Brittany's duchess and her long-time chancellor. It was rich listening indeed, with secrets of his patron's early days in Brittany unfolding with every word.

"I simply asked if there was a single man present who would wed his daughter to a man four times her age, with two marriages and seven children behind him," Anne recalled, remembering her outrage on that day.

"You dispatched the great warrior so firmly that his suit crumbled to dust as you spoke." A grin widened on de Montauban's face.

"It needed to be done at the right moment. So I took it." The congratulations that poured in afterward had given her a taste for exercising political power ever since. Every man present had rallied to her support after seeing how effectively she had thumped the old toad back to his corner.

"When the moment comes, Your Grace, your political instincts are sharp."

"Sire de Montauban, you amuse me as no one does back in France."

"Because you must stand on ceremony there, Your Grace. But you are home here."

"So I am. Now, what of this statue? Is she me?" Anne

laughed like the carefree fourteen-year-old she had never had the chance to be.

"Madame, this one here wears the royal ermine but she looks more like a Queen of France than the good Duchess of Brittany," de Montauban observed.

"Is it me or not?" She gave him a mock glare.

"That one's justice," Colombe put in, although no one was listening.

"Let me examine the fourth and I will tell you," de Montauban said.

Michel Colombe held his breath. His sketch designer Jean Perréal had sworn the queen had chosen prudence to represent her, but she had not yet seen how well dressed Colombe had made the statue of justice. He prayed she would not be annoyed to see her own depiction dressed rather more like a Breton country woman.

Philippe de Montauban moved to the fourth and final statue, walking around it.

"'Tis strange indeed, with this old man's face on the back," he remarked.

"May I say that the old man symbolizes the wisdom of the past as the young woman looks to the future," Colombe interjected, beginning to sweat. Had he been foolish to listen to Perréal? The court painter who had sketched the designs had insisted that the queen had approved them, including the one she had chosen as herself. But his wife had told him the queen might prefer to be depicted as the better-dressed statue.

"So which am I, the one with the ermine trim or the one with two faces?" Anne pressed.

"Madame, there is no question which one depicts you." De Montauban walked back to the statue with the ermine trim and made as if to ogle it.

"Out with it!" Ready to burst, she waited to see if de Montauban would play the courtier or reveal his true thoughts.

De Montauban returned to where the queen stood and pointed to the statue with two faces: the old man, and the young woman in country dress. "This is my good duchess."

"And so it is," Anne agreed. She had always counted on him to tell her the truth. Her honest chancellor hadn't let her down.

Colombe felt his insides turn over. He would not have wished to return to his studio to come up with another statue for an installation of this magnitude. Already the queen had given him a list of new commissions that would likely take him to the end of his life.

"I would recognize that noble brow and self-possessed expression anywhere, Your Grace. Although the costume fails to capture your refinement," Brittany's chancellor observed.

"I am a simple country girl at heart, Sire de Montauban." Anne cocked her head, looking anything but.

As de Montauban choked back laughter, Michel Colombe bit his knuckles. Wait until his wife heard the Queen of France's description of herself. Not a single soul in France would believe that their regal queen had described herself as such.

"Madame, you are our duchess in clogs here in Brittany. But in France, it would be hard to mistake you for a simple country girl."

Anne put her hand to her chest. "My body will soon return to France, but you know where my heart belongs."

"So I do, *ma bonne duchesse*," de Montauban exclaimed, his eyes filling with tears as Michel Colombe put his own hand to his heart. "And may it ever remain so."

Tomb of Francis II, Duke of Brittany, and Marguerite de Foix
by Michel Colombe, with base bas-relief by Jerome Pachiarotti,
statues sketched by Jean Perréal, 1507
Nantes Cathedral, Nantes, France
Photo by Florestan, courtesy of Google images

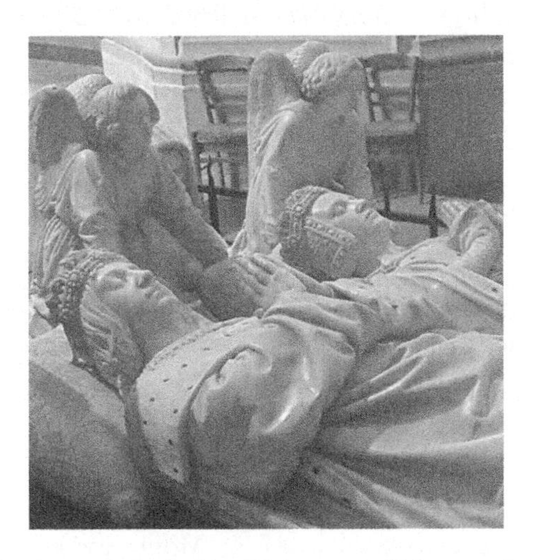

Tomb of Francis II, Duke of Brittany, and Margaret de Foix, parents of Anne of Brittany
By Michel Colomb, Nantes Cathedral, Nantes, France
Photo by R. Gaston

Statue of Courage
from tomb of Francis II, Duke of Brittany, and Marguerite de Foix
by Michel Colombe, with base bas-relief by Jerome Pachiarotti,
statues sketched by Jean Perréal, 1507
Nantes Cathedral, Nantes, France
Photo by Jibi44, courtesy of Google images

Statue of Temperance
from tomb of Francis II, Duke of Brittany, and Marguerite de Foix
by Michel Colombe, with base bas-relief by Jerome Pachiarotti, statues sketched by Jean Perréal, 1507
Nantes Cathedral, Nantes, France
Photo by Jibi44, courtesy of Google images

Statue of Justice
from tomb of Francis II, Duke of Brittany, and Marguerite de Foix
by Michel Colombe, with base bas-relief by Jerome Pachiarotti, statues sketched by Jean Perréal, 1507
Nantes Cathedral, Nantes, France
Photo by Jibi44, courtesy of Google images

Statue of Prudence
from tomb of Francis II, Duke of Brittany, and Marguerite de Foix
by Michel Colombe, with base bas-relief by Jerome Pachiarotti, statues sketched by Jean Perréal, 1507
Nantes Cathedral, Nantes, France
Photo by Paul Barlow, courtesy of Google images

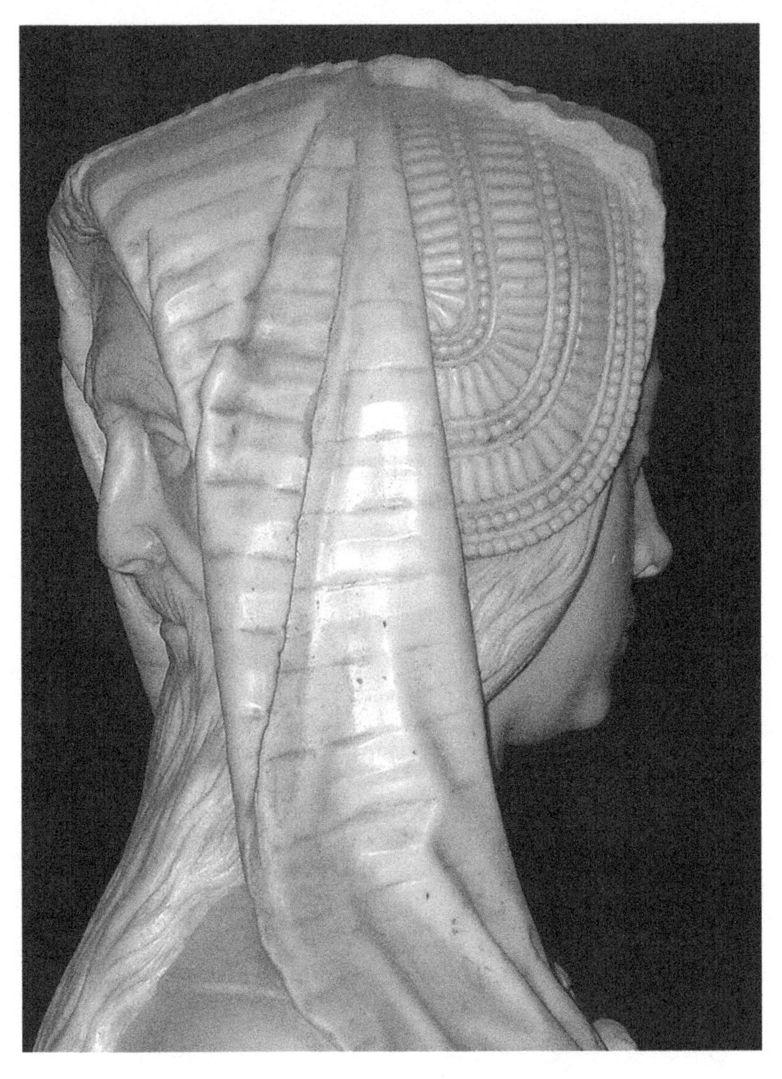

The Two Faces of the Statue of Prudence
from tomb of Francis II, Duke of Brittany, and Marguerite de Foix
by Michel Colombe from design sketched by Jean Perréal, 1507
Nantes Cathedral, Nantes, France
Photo by Jibi44, courtesy of Google images

Chapter Eight

May–October 1509

Louis' Victory at Agnadello

… in one day, the Venetians "lost what it had taken them eight hundred years' exertion to conquer."
—Niccolò Machiavelli, *The Prince*

"Good God, the pope signed our treaty!" Louis held out the message from Rome that had just arrived.

"Surprised, Husband?"

"Beyond surprised, *m'amie.* This is the first olive branch he's tossed me since becoming pope."

"I'd hardly call marching on Venice an olive branch, my lord." Anne smiled to herself. The pope had heeded her suggestion to join Louis' league, formed in Cambrai the December before.

"Finally, we can make our move," Louis exulted as Georges d'Amboise waddled into the room. The senior minister's hands were clasped over the scarlet cardinal's sash that reined in his ample midriff under his black cassock.

"What move, Your Grace?"

Louis' eyes sparked. "Georges, get your spurs on. We're going to Italy!"

D'Amboise groaned but took the message the king held out for him to read.

"Ah, so you convinced Julius to come in on our plan," the cardinal said.

"I didn't. You did, Georges!"

No, I did, Anne thought as she watched Louis dance around the room as excited as a boy. She could see that Italy was a sacred dream for him, one she mustn't touch, just as Louis knew he mustn't touch her sovereign authority over Brittany.

Let him play his grown-up war games, she told herself. She was busy with another boy now. The one forming in her belly since their journey to Nantes.

"Your Grace, the league will look to you to make the first move," d'Amboise advised.

"I'd call withdrawing my ambassador from the Venetian court a first move, wouldn't you?" Louis exclaimed. He had summoned his diplomat home at the end of January to let Venice know France did not approve of its territorial acquisitiveness.

"Well done, Your Grace. You have fired the warning salvo, but now we need to show them we mean business."

"By God, I do, Georges. Now that Julius is on our side, we'll deploy as soon as we can."

In April, Louis left for Italy at the head of the French army. Refreshed and energized, he was bursting to enlarge his territory in northern Italy and establish France's predominant position there. It was an opportune moment for Europe's princes to expand their holdings in Italy by pushing Venice back to its lagoon.

The Most Serene Republic had become increasingly unpopular through the years, for reasons of its inordinate wealth gained largely through trade with the Ottomans and the East.

The prosperous city-state had steadily expanded its territories on the mainland, encroaching into areas previously held by the Holy Roman Empire to the north and the papal states to the south. At Italy's southern tip, Venice had taken control of the two Adriatic ports of Brindisi and Otranto, next to Spanish-held territory.

But Venetian treatment of its subject cities as subordinates had resulted in alienating their populations. Spies returning to the French court from Venetian-held mainland territories had informed Louis that many of their inhabitants were fed up with Venetian rule and receptive to new overlords.

With Maximilian, Ferdinand, and the pope all wishing to regain territories lost to Venice, and Louis eager to enlarge Milan's territories to its east, the moment was ripe to curb Venetian power.

"Remind me of who gets what," Louis addressed his senior minister as he pulled up next to his litter on their journey over the Alps. Due to a flare-up of gout, the cardinal was traveling by sedan chair.

"I arranged Brescia, Bergamo, Crema, and Cremona for you," d'Amboise recounted.

"To be absorbed into Milan," Louis finished. How proud Valentina Visconti would be that he would expand the ancestral duchy she had passed down to him.

"Lady Margaret takes back Istria, the Friuli, Padua, Verona, and Vicenza for imperial territories," d'Amboise went on. Increasingly a power player amongst Europe's princes, Margaret of Austria had taken up the reins of responsibility her father Maximilian avoided and had negotiated at Cambrai on his behalf.

"What does the old fox get? Louis asked. Ferdinand of Spain had wrested Naples from him in 1503, the loss still stinging.

But Milan was his plum prize, more important to him than Naples, to which he held no family claim.

"Ferdinand regains Otranto for Naples," d'Amboise reminded him. "He needs the port to access the Ottomans."

"Let him have it," Louis said, thinking Spain could take the entire south of Italy so long as he held predominance in the north. "And the pope?"

"Ravenna and Rimini become part of the papal states again."

"That's it?"

D'Amboise smiled wryly. "That's it for now."

"But Julius will have something more up his sleeve," Louis snorted, his horse dancing in agreement.

"Your Grace, the papal sleeves are long and full. He has plenty of room to hide more schemes up them."

"Who do you think is the bigger trickster—Ferdinand or Julius?"

D'Amboise's laugh was hearty. "Your Grace, they are equally matched. But one fights to expand his holdings and the other fights to clear invaders from his lands."

"What's your meaning, then?"

"Which would you fight harder for, Your Grace? To take what is not already yours or to protect what is yours already?"

Louis gazed to the east. "I'd fight harder to protect what's mine," he answered. In his heart Milan was already his, rightfully passed down from his grandmother. The problem was that none of Europe's other princes saw it that way.

"And that's why the pope will prevail over Ferdinand," Georges predicted.

Louis weighed his minister's words. Julius II would fight. He had named himself after Julius Caesar for a reason. "And as for the rest of us?"

"Your Grace, let us hope time is on our side. Nature will take its course with Julius, as it does with us all."

"How old is he?"

D'Amboise cocked his head and thought. "He's seventeen years older than me."

"An old peasant," Louis said, thinking old peasants could make formidable enemies, honing their guile over years of experience, their bodies as hardened as gnarled olive trees.

"Sixty-five, my lord."

"Ancient," Louis observed, then thought of his own creaking knees and aching joints. Three years in prison, caged at best-forgotten moments, had aged him beyond his forty-eight years.

"We'll keep him close until . . ."

"Until what?"

The cardinal locked eyes with him. "Until nature takes its course."

"And France puts a true friend on the papal throne."

"Ah, yes, Your Grace, should fortune be kind to me." D'Amboise's sigh was deep.

"We will make sure of it, Georges," Louis encouraged.

"No one is sure of anything, Your Grace. But thank you." As d'Amboise shifted in his litter, Louis caught the wince of pain on his face. He prayed that he would be able to catapult his friend onto St. Peter's throne before God took him.

At the head of thirty thousand French troops, Louis left Milan in early May to march on Venice.

Ahead, luck awaited. At odds, the two generals of the opposing Venetian forces, cousins from the powerful Orsini family, were in competition with each other, both disdainful of the other's military skills.

Niccolò di Pitigliano was commander of the vanguard; his

cousin Bartolomeo d'Alviano led the rearguard. Both detachments, totaling about fifteen thousand men, were largely made up of Swiss mercenary troops.

Thirteen years his kinsman's senior, the cautious Pitigliano wished to hold off on engaging the French until the right moment presented itself. D'Alviano, who had successfully vanquished the French at Garigliano in 1503, was eager for battle. Both had been ordered by the Venetian city fathers not to attack directly but to track the French forces until they found an advantageous position from which to engage them.

Once Louis and his army crossed the Adda River to its east bank, the French were in Venetian territory. It was a formal invasion and d'Alviano itched to advance his army to meet him. Pitigliano held back, thinking it best not to engage yet. Instead, he moved his men farther south toward the River Po. His cousin grudgingly followed, both seeking out better positions from which to confront the French.

Five days later on May 14, the French army made its move. Near the village of Agnadello, an advance detachment under Louis' trusted commander Gian Giacomo Trivulzio attacked the Venetian rearguard. D'Alviano and his eight thousand men fought back, but were soon overwhelmed. D'Alviano sent an urgent message to his cousin for help.

Pitigliano sent one back ordering his cousin to refrain from pitched battle and resume heading south as he continued to do with his men.

It was too late. Louis' main army had caught up with Trivulzio's detachment and surrounded d'Alviano on three sides. D'Alviano's cavalry charged the center of the French forces, but they were outnumbered. Wounded, the brash Orsini commander was captured. Without his leadership, the Venetian cavalry fled the field, leaving the infantry to face massacre.

Meanwhile, the bulk of the Venetian forces was farther south. When news of the crushing defeat of Alviano's men reached them, terror struck at their hearts. Pitigliano's largely mercenary forces evaporated overnight, melting into the surrounding forests to make their way home.

Louis exulted in his victory. He had crushed the Venetian forces, as much due to the French army's cohesiveness as to the conflicting aims of the Italian commanders. Added to that, the Venetians had relied on a largely mercenary army in the field—never a wise policy.

Louis was well aware that once the tide of battle turned, paid soldiers—with no vested interest in the cause for which they fought—tended to disappear. He had made that mistake before with the Swiss. But, this time, he had used French troops under his own command, maintaining loyalty and discipline to defeat the enemy.

As the French celebrated their win, non-French signatories of the Treaty of Cambrai muttered that France was becoming too dominant in Italy. Louis now faced the same problem that had bedeviled the Venetians in previous years. Being too strong a power on the Italian peninsula invited enemies. Soon the King of France would learn just how many he had.

Anne was amongst the first to hear of France's triumph at Agnadello in a letter from Louis, scribed in his own hand.

She was delighted for him, but she wanted him back before the victory went to his head. It was time for the other signatories to the Treaty of Cambrai to step up and do their part to trim Venice down to size. She did not wish to see her husband in the position of enforcement marshal for the aims of the League of Cambrai.

Her political instincts told her that the more effective Louis was in such a thankless role, the more he would invite envy, especially from the pope. Since Julius II had sent word of his prayers for the child she carried to be a prince, she would do whatever she could to keep him and Louis on good terms.

The fire warming her insides since their journey to Nantes added to her joy at the king's victory. By fall she would have good reason to call him home.

As the first of June dawned, a songbird's gay chirps awoke Anne. Stretching, she smiled. There were no better months in the Touraine than May and June, followed by September and October. The babe would come at that time, just as Charles-Orland and Claude had. But the child had not quickened, so she would not yet share her secret.

Patting her belly, Anne exulted in its subtle roundness. As soon as she announced, she would be subjected to the court's assessing eyes, the guarded congratulations, the murmurs that would stop when she entered a room. Aware that all of France gossiped about her many failed pregnancies, she was in no rush to give them something more to whisper about.

"Ah, Your Grace, you are awake," Madame de la Seneschale's voice sang out. At Anne's bidding, she curtseyed and entered the bedchamber, morning drink in hand.

Anne took the hot barley drink and sipped. Lately, her stomach had settled but her appetite had not increased. She would force herself to eat more that day.

As her lady-in-waiting peered at her, Anne wondered if any at court were beginning to speculate on her condition. Let them. She would decide when to share her news. No one could take that moment from her.

One other can, a flutter-like voice whispered.

"Argh," Anne choked on her broth.

"Your Grace!" Madame de la Seneschale rushed to help her.

Anne held out her hand, palm up, to stop her. "I am fine," she said firmly. "Open the shutters so I may see the bird that woke me this morning."

As her lady-in-waiting went to the window Anne assessed what happened. Whether a flutter or a whisper, it had been as if a voice had spoken to her. Was it the babe quickening or had it been Father de Paule telling her something from beyond the grave? Had the voice said "one other can" or "one other king?" Her heart leaped at thought of the latter.

Rising from bed, she held out her arms for her lady to slip on her dressing gown. As she did, Anne noticed her glance at her belly. It would soon be time to tell, but the moment she shared her news that overbearing redhead in Amboise would rush to her chapel to pray for another princess for France.

Anne burned to think of it.

"Will you hold court in the garden today, Your Grace?" her lady-in-waiting asked.

"Not the garden. We will go to St. Sauveur to distribute alms," she said, referring to the main cathedral of Blois.

"Very good, Your Grace. Shall I get your gown?"

"No, call my maid to help me. And bring another cup of broth."

Anne watched as her lady-in-waiting left the room. The last thing she wanted was for her to help her dress, sliding her eyes over her belly then reporting to others on what she saw.

Anne's maid came in with her green gown.

"Not that one. The lilac one today," she told her. The purple panels of its over-gown would serve to conceal her secret.

As she waited, Anne moved to the window. Outside, she spotted the yellow oriole whose gay tune had woken her.

Thoughts stole over her of her caged linnet's song on the

day after Charles' death. Louis had come to comfort her and the moment the linnet had begun to sing Anne discerned that the new King of France's visit was not only to offer condolences. Feelings they had shared long ago began to flicker to life with the bird's joyous song.

"What do you tell me?" she asked the oriole. "Prince or princess?"

The bird cocked its head and studied her.

"Come now. Prince or princess do I carry?" she asked.

The bird remained silent, continuing to survey her.

It reminded her of another stare. She tried to remember from whom.

Suddenly, she shivered. Father de Paule had stared at her in the same way the day she had learned of her sweet Charles-Orland's death.

"Madame, is this the gown you wish for?" the maid cut into her thoughts.

Anne nodded, shaking off her phantoms. Why had she only received a stare from Francis de Paule when that harridan had received a prophecy that her son would be king? It should be a son of hers who would be a future king, not Louise de Savoy's son.

As her maid laced her into the gown inspiration struck. Instead of St. Sauveur, she would visit Father de Paule's priory of the Minims in Plessis-les-Tours. By boat, it was a short distance down the Loire past Amboise. There she could pray before the holy man's tomb, then give the prioress a donation to favorably dispose his soul toward her unborn child.

Looking back to the window, she saw the yellow oriole still contemplating her, motionless on its perch.

"Shoo," she called out, waving it away.

Fluttering its wings, the songbird flew off. As she watched, a ripple ran through her.

Shrugging it off, she turned and began her busy day.

That night, Anne recalled the day's excursion as she drifted off to sleep. The weather had been glorious, the waters of the Loire as calm and unruffled as she hoped the rest of her pregnancy would be. She had enjoyed the beatific smile that had spread across the Reverend Mother's face upon receiving her generous bequest. It had been larger than the one the Countess d'Angoulême had given two years earlier.

Wrapping her thoughts around her unborn child, Anne waited for a flutter, a kick, some sort of sign that he lived. When none came she fell into slumber, her final thoughts a prayer to Francis de Paule to help her deliver a prince. Would to God that she could do her duty for France and rest easy that her daughter one day would do her duty for Brittany.

Hours later, a cruel cramp wrenched her awake.

"Ahh!" she cried out into the dark, startling her attendant who had been asleep on a pallet at the foot of her bed.

"Your Grace!"

"Ah!" She doubled over, clutching her belly.

"Guardsman, rouse the doctor!" Anne's attendant called.

Not the doctor. Oh God, not again, Anne thought, unable to speak as a second cramp seized her.

The attendant ran for help, shouting to the other guard outside the door to light the torches.

Moaning, Anne clutched the bottom of her belly, pleading with God to save her babe. As she prayed, she felt a sticky wetness beneath her. It had happened before, it must not happen again. Perhaps it was just leakage, just an accident. *Cling to me, my love. Hold tight and do not let go,* she begged the unborn soul inside her.

Voices sounded and the room began to fill.

"Shut the bed curtains," Anne ordered. "Only my two ladies, no others." Curled up in a ball, she tried not to think about the spreading wetness beneath her. It was too dark to see, but the smell of blood was unmistakable. *Holy Father, do not take this babe from me*, she prayed, not knowing if she was praying to God above or to Francis de Paule. What did it matter? She needed help from them both.

"Madame, I am here," the breathless voice of Louise de Dampierre called out.

"I'm cramping," Anne gasped out.

"Your Grace, the doctor has been called."

"Send him to hell! It is my midwife I need."

"I will have them fetch her." Madame de Dampierre turned to an attendant and whispered orders.

Madame de la Seneschale appeared on the other side of Anne's bed. "Your Grace, are you bleeding still?"

"I think not." So others had smelled blood, too.

"Then let us help you sit up."

The ladies took an arm each and slid the queen further up on her bed, then propped pillows behind her head.

"Water," Anne whispered.

A goblet was brought. She drank deeply.

Madame de Dampierre shooed the pages from the room, bidding them to fetch more wood to stoke the fire then wait outside for further orders.

Within minutes, Anne's senior midwife appeared. Immediately, the woman placed linens under her lower torso then asked for several basins to be brought, one filled with water. Rolling up her sleeves, she rinsed her hands and got to work.

As she did, Anne fell back on her pillows, lips silently moving. Over her head, her two ladies-in-waiting exchanged glances. She had seen those looks before; never did she want to see them again. Wearily, she closed her eyes.

Finally, the midwife was done.

"Your Grace, shall I speak frankly?" The woman's eyes darted to the women on either side of the queen's bed.

"Yes. No. Get everyone out of here," Anne barked at Madame de la Seneschale. "I only want you two here." She gazed toward Madame de Dampierre, the woman's eyes glittering with tears.

As the room cleared, the midwife examined the contents of the basin she had just filled, a neutral expression on her face.

Shutting the door on the final attendant, Madame de la Seneschale returned bedside.

Anne fixed her eyes on the midwife. "Tell me."

"It is not what you wish to hear, Your Grace," the woman began.

She steeled herself. "Is it too late?"

"Yes, Your Grace," the midwife said, her eyes on the floor.

"Could you tell the sex?"

"No, Your Grace. It was early on, too soon to tell."

"I had no fall, no shock." Anne shook her head in disbelief, except that it had happened before, more than once, with no precipitating incident.

"Had you felt the babe quicken, Your Grace?"

"I hadn't. I wondered why not." A numb chill crept over her. The grim visitor she knew too well had come to steal another of her babes.

"Your Grace, if there was no quickening it is a blessing it went no further."

"Do not tell me what is a blessing," Anne's voice rose. "I have not been heavily blessed in this regard."

The midwife nodded, eyes averted. "Your Grace, with the

king away, you will have time to rest. Then you may try again," she encouraged.

Anne looked at her stonily. "Have you known any other to suffer so many losses?"

As the midwife answered the bells of prime began to ring for early morning prayers. "Your Grace, I have attended women who have lost every one and have no living child at all," she said.

"Thank God for my Claude." Anne clung to the vision of her sweet nine-year-old. Would she ever succeed in giving her a brother or sister?

"Yes, Your Grace," Madame de Dampierre spoke. "Thank God for the princess and for your—"

"Shut up," Anne snapped.

The women fell silent, their eyes resting anywhere but on her.

As the sound of the final bell ended, Anne shut her eyes.

She wished it were yesterday and she was back on the royal barge floating down the Loire on a perfect June day, a secret flame warming her insides.

She wished for Charles-Orland to be alive again and a young man, coming to her to boast of vanquishing Louise de Savoy's brat at sword practice.

And since neither of these wishes would ever come true, she drank the draught put to her lips.

Slipping into oblivion, she slept the sleep of the dead.

Chapter Nine

July–October 1509

Setbacks

"How sure are you of this news?"

"I was there myself when the midwife told her, Madame."

"Oh, how terrible for her," Louise exclaimed. *And how wonderful for my son and me.* She reached for the bag of coins she kept at hand.

"It was, indeed, Madame. The queen told her ladies to shut up when they tried to console her. I have never heard her speak so harshly."

"I would have, too, in her position," Louise tutted, assuming her most empathetic face. Fortunately, she would never be in that position. She had borne two healthy children and the next children she looked forward to in her family would be grandchildren whom she would fuss over then hand off to attendants when they fussed back.

"Did the midwife say what the sex was?" she asked, toying with the tassel on the coin bag.

"No, Madame. She said it was too soon to tell."

"I had not heard that the queen was expecting," Louise remarked. The haughty Breton had spent most of her adult life pregnant, yet with only one child to show for it. God grant that the princess Claude didn't inherit her mother's breeding problems.

"Nor had any of us. She had not yet announced, so perhaps we will not hear more of this."

"You said you were there. Who were you with?"

"No one, Madame. I was there to take the soiled linens. But instead of leaving, I slipped behind a curtain.

"Are you sure no one saw you?'

"No one, Madame. They were all at the queen's bedside. When the bells rang for prime, I left unnoticed."

"I will pray for her quick recovery and for a chance to try again," Louise lied. Perhaps she would send a gift to the wise woman she had visited to thank her for the efficacy of her charms.

"As shall I, Madame. Is there anything else you need for me to find out?"

"Nothing at the moment, good woman. But keep your ear to the ground and let me know if you hear the queen is pregnant again."

"Not likely with the king away in Italy," the woman quipped.

"Ah, yes, I'd forgotten," Louise lied again, ready to burst with glee. Such perfect timing for the queen to lose yet another child, unable to try again until Louis' return. After his win at Agnadello, she guessed he would linger longer, perhaps through the summer.

Handing the head of the laundry room at Blois the bag of coins, she dismissed her, waiting until she saw her cross the courtyard before unlocking her desk drawer.

She pulled the cloth off the charm, then held the tiny figure up to her face and kissed it. "Continue on your path," she whispered, thanking her lucky stars. The same stars lining up for her and Francis were the ones falling from the sky for the queen, one by one, as yet another of her babes' lives was snuffed out.

After reaping the reward of his victory at Agnadello, Louis was beginning to feel impatient with the Holy Roman Emperor. The regions his daughter Margaret had said were to be his at Cambrai he had not fully claimed. Why not?

Maximilian had asked for a meeting; Louis was eager to comply. But the emperor didn't arrive.

"Is he coming or not?" Louis railed on the final day of July. He was fed up with waiting to meet a man who so frequently used others to implement his policies. Remembering how Maximilian had deputized his ambassador to stand in for him when he had married Anne by proxy in 1491, Louis snorted.

"It is said, Sire, that he has not yet joined his army in the Friuli." General de la Trémoille lifted a brow.

"Does he want us to fight his battles for him?" Louis complained. "I sent him La Palice with five hundred lancemen, and he still loses Padua after us dropping it in his lap." The Venetians had retaken Padua on July 17, forcing the garrison of imperial troops stationed there to retreat to their fortress.

"It appears that he does, Sire."

"Tell Maximilian that we meet in person within the week or I return to France and take my army with me," Louis bellowed. The heat of the Italian summer was sapping him. He wanted to get back to his kingdom and Anne.

"A good plan, Sire. If we remain here we will end up doing his work for him and risk the wrath of the pope for our efforts," d'Amboise put in.

Louis threw up his hands. "Why would the pope be angered that we did the work of our allies?"

"Your Grace, the pope will find it too strong a dose of French seasoning in Italy," the cardinal observed.

"'Tis true, Your Grace. He wanted our help to curb the Venetians, not to take over the north of Italy," Trémoille agreed.

Frustration seamed Louis' face. "If Maximilian would claim his territories from the Venetians, we wouldn't look like we're trying to take over."

"Sire, I wonder if Maximilian is thinking to make a deal with the Venetians," Trémoille speculated.

"What sort of man double deals against an ally who just did his dirty work for him?" Louis thundered. He was disgusted by all these backroom deals. "What has happened to honor between princes? Am I living in the wrong age?" Kicking a filthy jerkin on the floor, he sent it scudding across the room.

"Every age is the wrong age, Sire, when it comes to honor between princes." D'Amboise's tone was dry.

"We know what sort of man he is, Sire. Did he not neglect to come to his wife's aid when her duchy was being sacked by us?" Trémoille pointed out.

"As he neglected to show up in person at Cambrai, but had his daughter negotiate our agreement," d'Amboise added.

Louis gritted his teeth. His wife hadn't known where she stood with Maximilian either back in 1491when he had failed to aid her in tossing the French out of Brittany. She had thrown him over when Charles VIII agreed to withdraw his army if she would consent to becoming his queen. In her shoes, Louis would have done the same thing.

One week later, Maximilian had not yet arrived, so Louis began his long journey back to France. He had had enough of Italy, enough of fighting, enough of allies who had done nothing to deserve French support.

But shortly after heading west from Milan, he was felled by a tertian fever and forced to halt in Biagrasso for some days in the extreme heat.

When a messenger brought word that Maximilian had

begun laying siege to Padua, Louis rolled his eyes. Based on his history, Louis doubted he would succeed. The man did everything halfway, including finalizing his marriage to Brittany's ruler nineteen years earlier. How happy he was to be the beneficiary of that union never coming to pass.

By the end of August, Louis had made it over the Alps. Reuniting with Anne in Grenoble on the other side, he was overjoyed to be back. Together, they headed home to Blois so he could pick up the reins of running his kingdom. There he would wait to hear what his allies' next move against Venice would be.

Early in October, news arrived. Maximilian's imperial army had abandoned its siege of Padua.

Louis flung down the dispatch as Anne watched in amusement. "Once again, your so-called first husband failed to complete his job," he scoffed.

"Aren't you glad he didn't, my lord?"

"In your case, yes; in the case of our alliance against Venice, no," Louis said.

"Think about it, my lord. He is consistent in his behavior. For how long do you think he'll remain your ally?

Louis felt the bile rise in his throat. Indeed, he had been thinking about it; he had gained nothing by having Maximilian as an ally.

"He will be your ally until the season changes. That is all there is to your game in Italy." Anne's smug look galled him.

"'Tis no game, my lady, to push the Venetians back from their encroachments on territory that does not belong to them," Louis lectured her.

"Just as the pope will consider it no game to push back foreigners who encroach on Italy," Anne countered.

"It is not his own kingdom, lady."

"It is Italy and he is Italian. He will fight to clear it of foreigners."

Louis studied her. "How can you know such a thing?"

"Because I know how hard I fought to clear my own realm of foreigners," she proclaimed, each word a swordstroke. "With marrying Charles, the price I had to pay."

"At least it prevented you from marrying that Austrian waffler."

"And led me to you." The look she gave him from under her lashes made Louis forget his sour mood.

Escorting his wife to their private quarters, he mulled over her words. They riled him, but Georges had said something similar. In his opinion, the pope should be grateful to France for helping him to push back Venice. But, instead, the man who had named himself after Julius Caesar appeared intent on pushing back France next.

Ungrateful double-crosser, Louis thought. Then a sheath of Anne's hair swept his face as the scent of violet musk filled his nostrils. Forgetting his problems beyond the Alps he reached for his wife and buried himself in the here and now.

Chapter Ten

December 1509

The Wedding of Marguerite d'Angoulême

Exasperated with the Holy Roman Emperor's flounderings, Louis turned his attention to matters at home. A lawsuit over Armagnac lands was before the courts. Charles, Duke d'Alençon and Count d'Armagnac, held a claim to Armagnac lands that Louis wished to see revert to the crown.

The Armagnacs had fought alongside Louis' grandfather then father against the Burgundians in the Armagnac-Burgundian Civil War of 1407-35. It had been a power tussle over who would control France during the reign of Charles VI, who had become insane. Louis was eager to consolidate Armagnac holdings with those of the monarchy to avoid a repeat of the disastrous political conflicts that had befallen France a century earlier.

It occurred to him that a way to settle the lawsuit would be by embracing the young Count d'Armagnac into the royal family. Taking a page from his wife's playbook of arranging marriage alliances to create a union where strife was brewing, Louis cast his eye on his dauphin's sister.

At age seventeen, Marguerite de Valois-Angoulême, daughter of Louise de Savoy and his late cousin Charles de

Valois-Angoulême, was overdue to be married. Her value as a young unmarried member of France's royal House of Valois could not be overestimated. The year before she had rejected the suit of the widowed English king, saying she wished to remain in France and marry a French nobleman.

Louis had just the candidate in mind.

What better way to effect a settlement than to have his cousin's daughter marry the heir to the Armagnac lands? Any children that would result would tie the region of Armagnac, near the Spanish border and formerly under English control, to the French crown. And Charles d'Alençon, Count d'Armagnac, could be nothing less than honored to move one step closer to the throne through a union with France's royal family.

Louis conveyed his decision to Louise de Savoy, who approved it then brought her daughter to him to receive the news from his lips directly.

With her mother at her side squeezing her arm, Marguerite d'Angoulême bowed her head and murmured her thanks.

Louis set the betrothal ceremony for October 9, to be followed by a December wedding. His satisfaction was great to think that by effecting such a union he had undermined any future legal battles over Armagnac lands reverting to the crown.

Even Anne was pleased as he had arranged exactly what she believed was the best method between noble houses to head off war or conflict. For once, she voiced no objection to an affair involving Louise de Savoy, since it was to the benefit of the French monarchy.

He set his *Brette* to work on what she did best: organizing and executing a sumptuous event. It would keep her mind off her latest miscarriage and focus her capable energies on providing France's most dazzling wedding of 1509 for his beloved cousin's daughter.

That fall was a joyous season for many at the French royal court. But not for Marguerite d'Angoulême.

"Can you guess what she told me when I asked what sort of cake she wanted for her wedding feast?" Cook's assistant Marie asked as they worked side by side in the kitchen.

"The usual, I suppose?" Cook asked as she kneaded dough for the mince pies they were making.

"She said she didn't care!" Marie exclaimed.

"Maybe she has more on her mind than cakes," Cook slung over her shoulder.

"She looked so glum," Marie mused. "Not like a bride-to-be at all."

Cook grunted. "Those high and mighty types don't always get a say in who they are to marry."

"I'd like a say if you're stuck with a husband for the rest of your life."

"Most of us would, Goose, but there's the rub."

"That our parents decide for us?"

"Worse, in her case. She turned down her mother's choice of the English king for her, but this one's the king's choice, so she has no say in it at all."

"Why did the king decide on a husband she doesn't want?'

"It's not what she wants, it's what the king wants that counts, and since she's high up in the order of things, who she marries is important to him."

"I'd like a choice if it were me."

"Your parents will want what's best for you. But they'll probably let you have some say."

"I hope they'll let me say no if I don't like him." Marie thought of her mother's struggles to put away money for her dowry. She had been saving up for years, but she couldn't imagine how she managed with only her wages as head of the laundry room.

"It's the royals, not common folk like us, who don't get any say at all."

"But the queen had a say when she married the king!"

Cook shook her head. "That's this king. But the queen had no choice when she was forced to marry the king before him."

"No! Really?"

Cook shot Marie a dark look. "You weren't yet born. But I served in her household when it happened. She married him to rid Brittany of the French. Believe me, she had no choice at all. It was either marry the gnome or watch the French army take over our country."

"Was she happy with him?" Marie tried to imagine the dainty queen married to a man who looked like a gnome.

"Not as happy as she is with this king." Cook lowered her voice. "He was ugly as sin and dallied with any woman who'd let him. But she put a good face on it."

"That would be hard to do." Marie fell silent as she contemplated the queen in a new light.

"Putting a good face on things is her job and she does it well."

"Do you tell me, then, that we have more say, in some ways, than those above us? Even the queen?"

"It's a funny thing, Goose, but the higher your rank, the less choice you have in anything."

"So I'm better off helping you in the kitchen than swanning about as a great lady?"

"You're better off right where you are, where neither the king nor queen care who you marry and don't try to marry you off to someone you don't like."

"I'm sorry for Mademoiselle Marguerite."

"Me, too, Goose. Her face was as long as an afternoon shadow when I saw her the other day. There's no joy in having your wedding day come up when your heart's not in it."

"I hope my heart will be in mine when the time comes."

"So do I. And when that day comes, may you move on to your own kitchen."

"I'd never want to stop helping you here!" Marie protested.

"Nonsense. I've taught you enough to run your own kitchen one day. If you miss me, you can come help out on feast days."

"It's strange how things look one way when they're another," Marie mused, her mind still on the queen. She always looked as if she got her way in all things. But she hadn't, really.

"Life has a way of evening people's positions out. So don't go envying those higher than you because they may just envy you."

"How jolly, Cook!" Marie exclaimed.

"I'm glad you think so, Goose. Just remember our chat so you don't go thinking others have it any better than you."

"I will, Cook! And I don't. Who could have it better than me making mince pies with you?"

"The queen would like your attitude, Goose. She's all for rank and order. If you know yours and stick to it you'll find her favor."

Marie shivered. Just thinking of the queen awed her. Now

that she knew something of the difficulties she had faced in her past, she was even more in awe. "I'm not looking for anyone's favor, only to be here helping you."

"That's why you'll find favor with her."

"She doesn't know I exist."

"Oh, yes, she does." Cook wagged a finger. "The queen attends closely to all she manages: her country, her court, her household, and her husband and the princess," she said as she counted off on the fingers of one hand.

Marie's eyes widened. "So she manages the king?"

"Of course, she does. You'll see, you'll have one of your own to manage one day, too."

"I'll have a king of my own to manage?" Marie erupted in giggles as Cook flicked a linen at her.

"You'll manage your husband. And you'll be glad he's not a king."

"That's for sure. Our king looks tired and worried most of the time. Except when he looks at the queen or Princess Claude. Then he lights up and looks as handsome as he must have once been." Marie's eyes shone as she imagined King Louis as a young man.

"Stick to your own kind and you'll do fine." Cook lifted a hand from her dough ball and painted a flour cross on her young assistant's nose.

Marguerite de Valois-Angoulême
by Jean Clouet, c. 1527
Courtesy of Wikimedia Commons, public domain

Charles de Valois, Duke d'Alençon and Count d'Armagnac
17th century portrait, artist unknown
Courtesy of Wikipedia Commons, public domain

On December 2, 1509, the wedding of Marguerite de Valois-Angoulême and Charles, Duke d'Alençon and Count d'Armagnac, took place. Louis XII, King of France, escorted the bride to the wedding chapel where Cardinal Guibé, Archbishop of Nantes, performed the marriage ceremony.

Louise could sense her daughter's unhappiness as she receded down the aisle on the arm of her new husband. Charles d'Alençon d'Armagnac was the least gifted of Francis's circle of childhood friends, but her daughter should not have thought she had some say in the matter.

The king needed the Armagnac lands tied to the crown. The only way to accomplish this was to unite the heir to the Armagnac holdings to the royal house of Valois to produce a subsequent heir with Valois blood running through his veins.

Marguerite was the means to achieve this end and if she couldn't understand why she needed to do her duty, Louise would remind her later that the most highly-ranked guests at her wedding, both male and female, had all had to do the same.

At the wedding feast, Louise sat at the head table along with France's two most powerful women. With her daughter next to her, the queen sat on Marguerite's other side. Beyond the queen sat Anne de Beaujeu, the Duchess of Bourbon. Louise chuckled to think all would hide their true feelings for each other with impeccable sangfroid. She expected Marguerite to do the same with her new husband later that night.

Venturing a smile at the woman who had raised her for half her childhood, Louise was met by the Duchess's usual indifferent gaze, focused somewhere over her head.

Stung, memories flooded Louise of the daily slights she had suffered as a child in her household, reminding her that she was a poor relation, indebted to the charity of France's most powerful woman. Anne de Beaujeu was renowned for many qualities, tenderness and maternal instincts not amongst them. The niggardly annual allowance France's former regent had given her as a year-end gift had been enough to buy one new gown a year, the same sum the laundry mistress received.

Scolding herself for seeking the Duchess's recognition, Louise vowed to ignore her for the rest of the evening. Louise de Savoy, thirty-three years old and a countess, mother of France's dauphin, would not be made to feel like an unloved cast-off.

Turning her attention to either end of the table, Louise recognized the ambassadors of Spain, Scotland, Burgundy, Florence, and Venice.

She watched as the queen steered the Venetian ambassador from the seat he was about to take between the Spanish and Scottish envoys, to one at the far end next to the lower-level Florentine diplomat. With an authoritative sweep of her hand, she motioned him to his place, reminding the Venetian envoy that his republic had been pushed back to its lagoon at the far eastern end of Italy.

An instant after the envoy was seated, Louise caught the king's grateful glance to the queen. Never would she understand the bond those two held. Anne of Brittany didn't want her husband in Italy at all, yet she had just delivered a diplomatic parry to support him there. And the king had his eye on Brittany for France, but unfailingly supported his wife as ruler of her realm and stayed out of her affairs administering it.

As the king's gaze passed over Anne de Beaujeu, Louise saw what looked like fear flicker in his eyes. Did Louis feel the same trepidation toward the great Beaujeu as she?

The woman had ruled France for eight years with the same cunning that her father had used to unite France. Louis XI's methods had been bound by no moral code. The spider king had woven his web to attach as many feudal lords as possible to the crown to break the power of the dukes and strengthen France's budding monarchy.

Anne de Beaujeu had sought to do the same, beginning with invading Brittany, then forcing its ruler, the fourteen-year-old Anne of Brittany, to marry her younger brother, Charles VIII, King of France.

The Duchess of Bourbon, with her usual icy hauteur, gave no sign she had noticed the king. Feeling less stung than she had the moment before, Louise recalled what she had heard of the king's dealings with the duchess long ago. All knew that in 1488, Louis had fought on Brittany's side to repel the French invaders under la Beaujeu's leadership.

She had heard worse, too. The French had defeated the Bretons and Louis had been taken prisoner. Anne de Beaujeu had sentenced him to prison for three years; some said she had ordered him caged at night.

The excessive punishment of a prince of the blood royal had scandalized France. Rumors floated that la Beaujeu had harbored an infatuation for the young Duke d'Orléans. Many whispered he had fled to Brittany because of her unwanted pursuit of his favors.

Louise marveled to think that the cold, carefully-controlled woman had sought to win his heart. As a young man, Louis d'Orléans had been as dashing and carefree a spirit as the forbidding Duchess of Bourbon was not.

Marguerite's sigh interrupted her thoughts.

"Save your sighs for another night and have some wine," Louise encouraged.

Marguerite gave her a sour look. "To fortify myself for the night ahead?"

"Every woman at this table had something to sigh about on her first wedding night. Take a sip, put on a good face, and do your duty later."

"My heart is not in it, *Maman*."

"Your heart has nothing to do with it. Do your duty until you produce an heir to satisfy the king. Then look to your heart." Louise's own heart was firmly and forever one with her children. She had never entertained the slightest desire to lose it to anyone else. It irked her that this particular child did not recognize the great honor of being given the year's most spectacular wedding by the king and his stiff-necked queen. For all her faults, the imperious Breton knew how to organize a splendid affair.

Sipping her wine, Louise savored its delicate elderflower bouquet. She watched with satisfaction as the first course was served, the gold plate of the serving platter set nearest her gleaming in the candlelight.

Glancing down the table she saw that individual gold plates had been set before her daughter, the queen, and the Duchess of Bourbon.

Waiting for hers, none came. Apparently she was to eat from the common platter as did those of lower rank.

Louise's face flamed as she took in the slight. Such distinctions in serving protocol would be the queen's doing. Coupled with similar slights from the lofty Beaujeu, she wished a curse on both women.

One day soon she would repay them in kind. At her son's coronation banquet she would seat them at far ends of the table, eating off a common platter. She would see to it that the dais where she sat with Francis was raised higher than theirs.

Disdaining to eat from the common platter, Louise surveyed the bridegroom's table. The insipid Charles d'Alençon was eyeing the serving girl, who had just placed a pitcher before him. It was just as well, since Marguerite felt no attraction to him.

Amongst those who sat at the groom's table, Louise noted Gouffier de Bonnivet shoot Marguerite an admiring glance. Laughing, handsome, and sure of himself, he raised his goblet to her.

A wicked thought wafted to Louise. If Marguerite was slow to do her duty, she could enlist Bonnivet to help her daughter produce an heir in a timely manner.

Stifling a snigger, Louise saw that Marguerite was scanning the banquet hall.

"Who are you looking for?" she asked.

"It is no matter," Marguerite said, her eyes veiled.

"Who, Daughter?"

"No matter, *Maman*. I will do my duty and serve the king."

"See that you do and stop mooning over something that cannot be when you have made a splendid marriage." Louise felt a twinge of alarm. She had so many secrets of her own that she had failed to note that her daughter might have some, too.

"Splendid, *Maman*?" Marguerite's voice dripped with irony.

"You will be one of the richest women in France."

"Do you think I care?"

"There will come a time when you will care, and then you will have the resources to do what you like, with discretion."

"Is that what you do, *Maman*?" Marguerite's almond-shaped eyes narrowed into slits, reminding Louise of her dead husband, Marguerite's father.

"I am far from the richest woman in France." *Although I intend to be one day*, Louise thought.

"But you practice discretion."

Louise felt the hairs rise on the back of her neck. "What is your meaning?"

"It would be indiscreet of me to say, would it not?" Marguerite checked her.

"I have no idea what you are talking about." Louise sipped her wine to hide her face, wondering which of her secrets Marguerite had stumbled upon.

"Like mother, like daughter, *Maman*." With a short laugh, Marguerite turned to answer a question from the queen.

Trying to ignore her daughter's jab, Louise glanced back to the bridegroom's table. Her incomparable Francis was there, laughing and gay, surrounded by his circle of friends: Bonnivet with an eye for the ladies and Robert de Fleuranges, whose high spirits had earned him the nickname of Young Adventurer. But where was Gaston de Foix?

Scanning the room, she didn't see the king's nephew anywhere. It was unthinkable that he was not there. Of high rank, Gaston had escorted Princess Claude down the aisle at her betrothal ceremony to Francis four years earlier. Always a favorite of both of her children, he had protected Marguerite when her brother and his friends had played too roughly. Marguerite had always referred to him as her knight. But where was her knight now?

A sly thought stole over Louise. Was it possible he was not celebrating for the same reason Marguerite was not?

Raking her thighs under the table, Louise scoffed at foolish hearts everywhere. Sentimental attachments were a waste of time.

For once, she looked to the Duchess of Bourbon as a role model. The woman had buttoned up her heart long ago and moved out from under its control over her. She didn't like the spider king's daughter, but how she admired her.

"Find my two pages," Anne bade an attendant. She motioned for the large two-handled silver urn on the sideboard behind her.

Francis de Bourdeille and Jean d'Estrées appeared, looking puffed up and pleased to begin their merry task. Grasping one handle each, they bowed to the queen as she put in a gold-threaded brocade purse. Next, they moved to the Duchess of Bourbon. "Largesse, largesse," they shrilled as the great lady placed a coin-filled crimson velvet sac in the urn.

The pages moved to Louise de Savoy, who waved them off.

Anne gave her a cool stare then turned to Marguerite, who looked mortified. Glancing to her other side, Anne locked eyes with the Duchess of Bourbon who had also taken in Louise's faux pas.

Once long ago at Anne's wedding breakfast to Charles VIII, she had let Anne de Beaujeu know that her duties as regent were over now that she had become Charles' queen. It had been a satisfying moment, painful for the Duchess, but she had swallowed it well, a royal down to her fingertips. So unlike Louise, who would never understand why she was not one of them and never would be.

Glancing again at the bride's mother, Anne saw her bite her lip, most likely ruing her social blunder. As always, Louise's gaffes were predictable. She had just declined to offer largesse to her own daughter in full view of the court. The flame-haired arriviste wore her faults on her sleeve; cheapness was one of them. How galling, Anne thought, that her grandchildren through Claude would have the woman's blood running through their veins.

Dismissing her, Anne looked for her husband. Stories had floated to her of the Duchess's personal interest in Louis when Anne had been a girl. The possibility seemed incredible. No two human beings could be less alike. Louis was effortlessly debonair but didn't stand on ceremony. The Duchess of Bourbon never descended from her dais, a female version of her father, that most effective monarch whom all had feared and none had liked. Anne's father had been one of them.

Duke Francis had warned her that the spider king would try to lure Brittany into his net. But by the time Anne came to power, Louis XI had died and it had been his daughter, Anne de Beaujeu, who had ordered French troops to invade Brittany.

The Duchess of Bourbon as France's regent at the time had been behind her younger brother the King's offer to withdraw French troops from Breton soil in exchange for Anne's hand in marriage. She did not doubt that the Duchess still wished to see her father's wishes carried out to fold Brittany into France.

Anne straightened in her chair, squaring her shoulders. It would never happen. With the Duchess a year older than Louis, Anne prayed the spider king's daughter would die before she did, to ensure her power to influence events was forever broken. Her husband Pierre was long dead and had exercised almost no authority, and their only child was a daughter, as meek and malleable as her mother was not.

Anne glanced at Claude, her similarly meek daughter. She loved her dearly, but she hoped the next child she bore would possess more of her spirit. Someone needed to take up Brittany's cause after she died. She feared that Claude would not be the one.

Moving off the dais the two pages wended their way through the great hall, shouting their lively refrain of "Largesse, a gift!" The wedding meal was transitioning to after-dinner entertainment with wine loosening both pockets and tongues.

After tossing a large sac into the silver urn, Louis shot a glance at his wife. Carefully, he avoided looking at Anne de Beaujeu beside her. After all these years, he still felt a chill in her presence. Most who had known her knew nothing of her heart. Louis sensed he was one of the few in the room who was aware that she had one.

Long ago it had been set on him, a burden that had sent him fleeing across France's borders to Brittany. He had returned as her prisoner, but she had failed to imprison his heart. That he had given to his *Brette*, but he was not of a mind to rub the formidable Beaujeu's face in it.

Too well he remembered the price he had paid to scorn the woman's affections. But for the greater good of France, he had vowed not to seek revenge on her for imprisoning him. He had seen the damage caused by France ripping itself apart in the Armagnac-Burgundian war with two branches of his own House of Valois bent on destroying each other. Now that he was king, he wished to see all factions of his kingdom united.

He guessed that the spider king's daughter would wish the same. Doubtless she had an eye on Brittany coming into France's fold, just as her father had. Truth be told, he did too, but not while his wife was alive.

As the strains of a lively galliard began, Louis' eyes traveled back to his wife. He longed to ask her to dance, but he wouldn't with the Duchess of Bourbon watching them both.

Later, he would dance with his sparkling queen before the fire in her bedchamber. Who knew, they might even beget an heir. And if they didn't, what did it matter? Francis d'Angoulême would be king after him, and his daughter Claude would be queen. All was well in the kingdom of France under his reign.

As for Italy?

Taking a sip of the fine Touraine wine Louis relaxed. Italy was a problem for another day.

Chapter Eleven

1510

A Dagger to the Heart

"He has stuck a dagger in my heart," Louis erupted.

"What is it, my lord? What has happened?" Anne cried as Georges d'Amboise came running from the other room, arriving out of breath and red in the face.

Louis looked as if he would explode. "The pope has made peace with Venice."

"Let me see, Your Grace," d'Amboise panted, peering over the king's shoulder.

"That peasant has cut a deal with the Venetians and cut the rest of us out of it," Louis sputtered, his face contorted.

"What are the terms?" Anne asked.

"The terms are unacceptable. Such perfidy!" Louis was beside himself. After all his hard work putting together the League of Cambrai, then sweeping back the Venetians at Agnadello, the pope had gone over to the enemy's side.

"The terms are here," Georges said, his eyes running down the list. "Ravenna and Rimini are to be returned to the papal states with Venice paying for the pope's expenses in capturing them. Venice may no longer appoint clergy and may not exert authority over papal subjects in her lands. In return, papal interdiction is lifted."

"That scoundrel went behind my back," Louis raged.

"He probably said the same thing about you when you appointed clerics to church benefices in Milan last fall without his approval," d'Amboise commented.

Louis felt as if his eyes would pop from their sockets. "Why should I seek his approval to appoint my own clergy in my own territory?"

"Because they are benefices of the Church and he is head of it," Anne pointed out.

"There was no reason for him not to approve them!" he snapped.

"The reason he didn't was that you didn't seek his approval first, Your Grace," d'Amboise spelled out.

"He hasn't communicated with me in months so why should I have reached out to him?" Louis shouted. "And now I know what he was up to."

"No doubt, you incited him when you objected to his cardinal appointments last month," Anne said.

"Of course, I objected! How am I supposed to get Georges elected pope without a single Frenchman amongst the twelve cardinals that trickster just appointed?" Louis noted the stricken look on his senior minister's face. It was evident the pope was trying to set up an Italian cardinal to succeed him when the time came. His oldest friend's dream of becoming pope was fast vanishing due to Julius II's machinations.

"Sire, the pope has probably been in talks with Venice for some time now," d'Amboise speculated, his eyes elsewhere. He looked as if he was struggling with the likelihood that he had lost his last chance to become pope.

"The Venetians probably begged him to lift papal interdict on them," Anne said.

"Fie on the interdict. What difference does interdiction

make when it comes from a warlord masquerading as a man of God?" Louis cried.

Anne and d'Amboise stared at him uneasily.

"What? What is wrong with you two?" He looked from one to the other, not seeing much support in either set of eyes. "Can you not see what a scoundrel he is?"

"He is the elected head of the Church, whatever else he may be." D'Amboise's tone was delicate. As a cardinal of the Church, his duty was to uphold its hierarchy.

"He does not belong on the seat of Rome but on the back of a war horse," Louis spit out.

"But because he is on the seat of Rome, we must submit authority to him in church matters," Anne reasoned.

"I will no longer submit authority to him in anything." Louis stormed from the room, heading for his private sanctuary.

As Anne began to follow, he stopped her. He didn't want to hear her lectures about Italian duplicity and why he shouldn't be surprised after sixteen years of dealing with them. All he wanted was a quiet moment before his grandmother's portrait without his wife's voice in his ears saying, "I told you so."

Anne turned to d'Amboise behind Louis' retreating form. "Why is he so surprised, Georges?"

"Your Grace, you know better than me what chivalry lies in the king's heart. He cannot bear the thought of his allies duping him."

"His chivalrous heart is valued by his subjects here but is trampled upon in Italy."

"That may be, Your Grace, but his heart is set on Milan as his birthright."

"No other prince of Europe will see it as such, beginning with the pope," Anne observed.

"I fear it is so, but the king is determined."

"Then help him to forget Venice and not goad the pope further by superseding his authority. He will get himself excommunicated if he does and cause France to be put under interdict, just as Venice was." Anne's heart beat faster. She could not afford that to happen for reasons only she alone knew.

"I will do my best to ease his anger, Your Grace. Let us give him some time, and I will continue building goodwill in other areas to take his mind off venting his rage at Rome."

"What other areas, Georges?"

"We are working on a treaty of friendship with the new English king."

"Ah, good, then direct him to find new allies, not to fan enmity with ones who have let him down, especially not the pope."

"They all dupe each other in the end, Your Grace. 'Tis the way of princes," d'Amboise said.

"My good man, how happy I am you are not one of them, but have served the king so faithfully," Anne told him.

D'Amboise bowed deeply. As he came up he met Anne's eyes. "I will serve him in every way I can until my last breath."

Anne's heart twinged as she contemplated the portly cardinal. Louis was in good hands with his dear and old friend, so similar to her in his shrewd view of the world. But she worried to think of the day when her husband's minister would no longer be there to guide him.

"I have good news," she told Louis weeks later as they sat before the crackling fire to stave off the March chill.

Louis' smile was faint. "After the tidings of these past two months, I am in need of some."

"It will take your mind off Italy," Anne said, noting new

worry lines at the sides of his mouth as she curled up next to him on the fur-covered divan.

"Nothing will take my mind off Italy, Wife. You must leave me to my affairs as I leave you to yours." Louis rubbed the top of his thighs as he gazed into the flames.

"'Tis an affair in common, Husband."

"Something at court?"

"Something between us." Taking his hand, Anne moved it to her belly.

Louis snapped to attention.

"Are you—?"

"I am, my lord."

"My lady, you are as fertile as a Breton field." Louis' broad smile set her heart dancing, reminding her of the breathtakingly handsome man he had been when she first met him.

"You have tilled it well, my lord." She gave him an impish grin, relieved to see her husband's worry lines disappear with her news.

"When may we expect the harvest?" he asked, looking down at her belly.

"At harvest time, my lord."

"Do you mean?"

"Our prince should arrive in the same month that Claude did."

"Ah, my lady, may God smile on us and bring this one to life."

"May he be the prince you seek."

May he be the prince you seek as well, *m'amie*."

"Do you remember our visit to Angers last fall?" Anne asked.

"Where we prayed at Saint René's shrine to bring us a son?"

"This is the son we prayed for," Anne declared, basking in the glow of the firelight.

Louis' smile was indulgent. "Unless there is a mix-up and another princess arrives."

Anne ignored him. She would name her prince after Saint René, she decided, thinking of the story of the 5th century saint who had brought a young boy back from the dead. She would need the saint's aid in shepherding this unborn soul to life.

"*M'amie,* I will stay with you until the weather warms, then I will tour Burgundy this spring," Louis announced.

"And after?"

I cannot say. But the cards have reshuffled in Italy and I must take a seat at the table."

"Don't take it too seriously, Louis. Remember what happened to Charles there."

Her husband's eyes hardened. "It happened because he did not take it seriously enough."

Anne studied him in the flickering firelight and decided to drop her objections. The news was too good to spoil the moment. Louis was on fire for Italy. She was on fire to bring their unborn child safely into the world. The pope had promised his prayers for her to deliver a prince, but if the pope and her husband were fighting, Julius II would withdraw his prayers. She would do what she could to keep them on good terms until this child was born.

"Why did the queen not accompany the king to Burgundy?" Louise asked her contact.

"Madame, it is said that the queen is again with child and has decided not to travel until the babe is born."

"Ah, what happy news for the queen," Louise remarked. "I had heard nothing of this. Has she announced yet?"

"No, Madame. But I have it on the best of sources."

"And who is that?"

"'Tis the head of the queen's laundry at Blois. It is thought that she is about two months along now, the babe due in the fall."

"And have you heard if the king intends to travel to Italy this summer?" Louise asked. The woman before her had no idea that the head of the queen's laundry was also in her pay. She wondered why she, herself, hadn't come to report such interesting news.

"I do not know for sure, but it is most likely that he does, Madame," the contact said, shifting from one foot to the other.

"Keep me informed, and let me know if anything happens to the queen," she said.

"Do you mean if she loses the babe?"

"Of course, that's what I mean," Louise snapped. "I would wish to know right away." It came to her that she might be one of the few to know that the queen had miscarried the year before. Perhaps her latest informant was unaware of the queen's last pregnancy.

"I will keep my ears open, Madame."

Louise dismissed her source with the usual sac of coins and went to the library, tapping her thighs as she walked. Why could it not have been her daughter falling pregnant instead of the queen?

Marguerite had been married for four months already, and Louise was impatient for happy tidings from Alençon. It would be a great pleasure to the king the day she produced an heir to attach the Duke d'Alençon's holdings to the crown.

Pulling out a book on medicinal herbs, Louise leafed through it until coming to the pages on pregnancy. Perhaps there was something in there she could have her kitchen staff prepare for Marguerite for her upcoming visit to Alençon.

Her daughter had described her new homeland as flat and uninspiring, as dull as her new husband's wit. With so little to do there, Louise wondered why she wasn't already with child.

As she leafed through the pages, she came to a section on herbs that brought on contractions, helpful in getting labor started, but also in ending a pregnancy. Of course, she would never prepare such a potion for the queen.

But there was no reason why she couldn't add such ingredients to her bag of charms to enhance their efficacy in preventing a male heir for Louis. It would be a discreet tool to add to her tool chest. No one would know what it was nor its intent. If anyone discovered the contents of her secret drawer, she would say she was hoping for grandchildren from her daughter. Who could blame her?

"Praise our king who keeps taxes low!" a voice rang out. Crowds lined both sides of the street to greet their king on his visit to Burgundy.

"I must be doing something right, Georges. What say you?" Louis called out to his minister. Behind him Georges d'Amboise plodded along on a chestnut palfrey as dumpy as he was.

"Sire, your subjects didn't name you Father of Your People for nothing." D'Amboise replied. The cardinal's face was florid, beads of sweat forming at the corners of his brow in the April warmth.

Louis' first progress through Burgundy since ascending the throne in 1498 was going well. He had set off to the northeast from Blois, wended his way down through the Champagne region, then south to Dijon, Burgundy's seat, in a joyous entry, with his senior minister at his side.

Georges did not inspire the crowds to riotous cheers the way the queen did with her dazzling hauteur and generous largesse. But his lifelong friend made for good conversation at a time when Louis had much on his mind.

He missed Anne, but they were taking no chances with this pregnancy, not after losing so many babes. Fortunately, their princess, although small for her age, enjoyed good health. Thinking of his sweet Claude, his heart warmed.

He prayed that this child would be male. It was easier to give free rein to his deepest desires without Anne around. When they were together, he took it upon himself to keep up her spirits, always reassuring her, whatever the outcome was of each of her pregnancies. He would never say so, but he longed for a son as desperately as she did.

Glancing over at Georges, he saw his minister was trying to hold up his end of pleasing the crowd. But no one cared whether a fat priest with a red face waved at them or not, although the coins scattered in his wake were eagerly swept up by children diving for them.

Watching two boys jostle each other, Louis imagined a strapping young son as athletic as he had been and as intelligent and attentive to duty as Anne.

His dauphin cut a fine figure, but there was something too cocksure and knowing about him. His mother had spoiled him. Besides, Louise didn't hold a pious bone in her body.

But it was more than that. Louis could already see Francis had inherited the profligate temperament of his father, who had been a great friend of his. It was all very well in a companion to pal around with, but such devotion to pleasure did not befit a king. He told himself Francis would grow out of it, but he had his doubts. Charles d'Angoulême had been thirty-six when he died, carrying on with four different women at the time. His dead cousin's son was only fifteen, yet Louis sensed the youth was cut from the same cloth.

Noting the pale pink buds on the trees lining the road, Louis asked God for a son who would possess the same devout spirit as his wife and the same chivalric values that made him a better king than he had been a young man. God knew such values weren't doing him much good in Italy, but here in France, they appeared to still be appreciated by his subjects.

"What say you, Georges, is it time to get off that horse?" Louis joked.

"Sire, it was time the moment I got on him," d'Amboise groaned, putting a hand to his right lower back as he shifted in his saddle.

"Straighten up, Cardinal. You're standing in for my wife and the crowd wants a show," Louis encouraged.

"Sire, there is no substitute for your wife in all of Europe, so I give up now."

"Then toss a few more coins and don't hold back. She says I'm cheap, so let's surprise the crowds."

"If I may say so, Sire, your common subjects love you for your cheapness."

"I tell the queen that they may mock me for my cheapness but they love me for not taxing them dry."

"Quite so, Sire. You are a good sport to take what your subjects say in stride."

"They can say what they want to me, just not to the queen. There I draw the line."

"Sire, you are as genteel as you are cheap," d'Amboise observed.

"What do you say—is it a good blend?" Louis enjoyed the candor of his oldest friend. It was a rare thing to have someone tell him the truth about himself—unheard of at court.

"It is a good blend as long as the queen's around, Your Grace."

"Well, she's not here today, so you'll have to stand in."

"I will do my best to demand luxury and refinement as soon as I get off this horse so that you will not miss her overmuch."

"You are in luck, Georges. The only place where one dines better than Dijon is Lyon, where we head next."

"How much farther?" his fat friend puffed.

"Not far, Georges."

"Hurrah for old King Louis!" a boy's voice piped up.

As Georges choked back a guffaw, Louis tried to hide his annoyance. He was coming up on forty-nine years, and he felt every one of them. He would never play another decent game of tennis and he would never joust again.

All he could manage now was to be a good king. It was on progresses like this, with the common people spouting truths never spoken at court, that he was reminded of how to be one. Keeping taxes low was at the top of the list. Showing largesse in the face of slights was another.

He tossed a coin to the cheeky boy to show him he didn't mind his salutation, although he did.

Within minutes, the procession reached the Hotel de Ville where the midday banquet would be held. Next to him, he heard Georges' grateful sigh as the horses came to a halt.

Louis' bones creaked as he began to dismount. As he did, several of his men reached up to help him.

"Hands off!" he roared, the sting of the boy's offhand address still ringing in his ears.

The young rascal had been right. He was old before his time, and he needed to accomplish his heart's desires before God called him home. He would claim his territories in Italy once and for all for France and teach his daughter Claude how to hunt and hawk before he was done. If he was lucky, he'd teach a son of his own one day, too.

By May, they had reached Lyon where Louis received the latest dispatches from Italy.

"I'm not going over there until Maximilian agrees I get Verona," Louis told Georges.

"He has not yet agreed, Sire."

"I'm not doing his work for him again for nothing."

"Then let us direct our generals from here and wait to see the result when our army meets up with the imperial forces."

"A good plan, Georges."

"Glad to hear it. I don't look forward to crossing the Alps so soon after our progress."

"What's wrong? Too much time spent on a horse?" Louis joked.

"Sire, I have chosen the priesthood largely to stay out of the saddle."

"Any other reasons?"

"I confess, I have no clue as to how to manage the fairer sex."

"The trick is to choose the right one, since they mostly end up managing you." Louis thought wistfully of Anne. To safeguard the growing life inside her he wished her to pass as quiet a summer as possible. By basing himself in Lyon before heading for Italy, he would avoid upsetting her by getting into arguments over Italy and the pope.

But he missed his *Brette,* even when they argued. There was no sport in just agreeing all the time. And if he was anything besides a king, he was a sportsman.

"From what I can see, Sire, you are managed splendidly by the queen," d'Amboise beamed. "But every man needs a moment to himself here or there," he added, taking out a linen cloth and mopping his forehead.

"I am thinking to take a few days in the Dauphiné to hunt," Louis admitted, in complete agreement. God's bones, what a blessed opportunity, with the queen back home, his general on his way to meet Maximilian's army to take Verona and Vicenza, and Georges looking as if he could use a rest.

His old friend's girth had grown in the wake of the fine dinners they had enjoyed on their progress, and he was walking with increasing stiffness. He would need a litter again to get him across the Alps.

"By all means, Sire, go. I will manage Italian affairs from here and send a messenger to you if something urgent comes up."

Louis' heart leaped. "You're a good man, Georges." The Dauphiné, nestled next to the Alps, was his favorite hunting ground in all of France. After more than a month of official functions, he wanted nothing more than to move his limbs, feel the thrill of the hunt, and escape from kingly duties for a few days.

"I am yours completely, Sire. The only one who is, besides your wife," d'Amboise quipped.

"Perhaps the only one, as my wife's heart belongs to Brittany."

D'Amboise's eyes twinkled. "You don't fault her for that, do you?"

"How could I fault her, when my own heart led me to Brittany to fight beside her father when I was young?"

"You would not have met her if it were not for those years," d'Amboise remarked.

"Thank God I met her in my youth." How reckless and carefree he had been in those days. Yet how he had enjoyed them. The price he had paid to fight against France invading Brittany had earned him three years in prison but also the undying devotion of his wife. For that, he could bear a few prematurely aching joints.

"Why so, Your Grace?"

"She sees the man I once was when she looks at me now." Louis conjured up the heart-shaped face of the young Breton princess, assessing him with serious eyes. When she finally decided she liked what she saw, her esteem had lasted a lifetime.

For a moment, he wished he was back in Blois, walking in the Queen's Garden with his *Brette.* Then the lure of the Dauphiné's wild terrain teeming with game washed over him and he forgot all about Blois.

"A fine quality in a wife, Your Grace."

"Fortunate for me since, otherwise, I would feel like an old man, just as the lad said."

"If you are old, Sire, then I am older," Georges cackled.

Louis threw back his head and roared with laughter. "Thank God someone close to me is."

Chapter Twelve

1510

Bleak News

Five days later, Louis had bagged a wild boar. Flush with renewed vigor and proud that his spear arm was still working, he felt like a young man again.

Hunting freed him from the constraints of endless decision-making, judging petty squabbles, and struggling to balance budgets that never balanced. What he needed to pay his troops and garrisons in Italy forever conflicted with keeping his subjects happy with low taxes. It was enough to stoop one's shoulders. But out on the flower-flecked meadows of the Dauphiné's alpine summits, Louis was in his element.

Ambling down the hill where he had bested the boar, he was startled to see a messenger approach on a fast horse.

Louis tensed. It was never a good sign when a messenger's horse was lathered. He hoped neither the pope nor Maximilian had delivered another outrage: the first, sure to be dastardly; the second, vacillating.

Jumping off his mount, the messenger knelt before him, sweeping his cap from his head. "Your Grace, tidings from Lyon."

"From the cardinal?" Louis asked.

The messenger raised his eyes, a certain pause to his delivery. "It concerns the Cardinal d'Amboise, Your Grace."

"What, then? Spit it out, man."

"Sire, the cardinal took ill a few days earlier."

"He is ill?" Louis cried.

The messenger hung his head. "I am sorry, Your Grace. He is ..."

"Good God, what is it?"

"He is dead, Sire. Of a gout attack."

"Georges is dead?" Louis stared at him stupidly.

"The Cardinal d'Amboise is dead, Sire. The doctors tried to save him, but the attack was too severe."

"Oh, God. No." Stunned, Louis turned away.

"Begging your pardon to bring such sad tidings, Your Grace."

"Get something to eat and drink then report back for my instructions."

"Yes, Sire."

Motioning his men to go ahead, he walked his horse down the hillside, so beauteous a moment ago, so invisible to him now. He had known this day would come. Georges had suffered from recurring gout for years, due to an excess of rich living. But nothing could have prepared Louis for this moment.

Dazed, he could hardly think. Normally, he would turn to Georges to arrange all affairs when a death close to him happened. Now, he must do it himself.

Pretending for a moment that he was Georges, he thought of what his friend might advise in this case. God knew he would wish his funeral to be as sumptuous as possible and to be buried near his beautiful Gaillon. His estate had been the finest mistress his generous and high-living minister had ever known.

Arriving at camp, his men grouped around him, crossing themselves as they bowed their heads.

"You will tell the bishop of Lyon that the cardinal is to lie in state in the cathedral for the next five days while transport is arranged to bring him to Rouen. We will organize a state funeral there," he directed the messenger.

"Yes, Your Grace. Shall I accompany you back?"

"You will go immediately. I will come later."

Dreading the myriad decisions that awaited him in Lyon, Louis lingered for two days more in the wild hills of the Dauphiné. As he hunted he grieved, unable to imagine a world without Georges in it. Nevermore would he say "Let Georges do it" when a problem came up. His right-hand man for his entire adult life was gone. It was an unbearable but inescapable fact.

Deep in the forest, away from his men, Louis did what he hadn't done since he was twenty-six years old, caged by orders of the fearsome Beaujeu, who had hated him with all the passion of a woman scorned.

He wept.

As Louis rode back to Lyon only one thought comforted him—he still had Anne.

Upon hearing news of the Cardinal d'Amboise's death, Louise penned a sympathy note to the king. Offering her utmost condolences, she expressed confidence in the abilities of his minister Florimond Robertet to help him in place of the cardinal.

She had known for years that the king was impressionable, just as her son was. Louis would be floundering, looking for a rudder to guide him with affairs both in France and Italy.

Now was the moment to plant the idea in his head that Robertet was the man most capable of serving him in d'Amboise's capacity. The king wouldn't regard him as an equal as he had the cardinal. But who could replace a trusted friend and advisor of over thirty years?

Trying to imagine how the king must feel, she came up short. There was no one she could think of with whom she held such a close bond. Jeanne de Polignac was her friend as well as her lady-in-waiting, despite being her dead husband's mistress before Louise had joined his household. But Louise had always held the reins in their friendship as her husband's legitimate wife and mother of his heir.

The king's loss of Georges d'Amboise was of a different order. Both nobly born, although d'Amboise had been in Louis' service, the cardinal had guided Louis as a peer throughout his life. In his absence, the queen would naturally step up as the king's most powerful influence.

But before that happened, Louise would get her own man in place to head off the queen. The Breton prig would consider it her most important duty at this time to safeguard her pregnancy, she guessed.

Opening her desk drawer, Louise tucked the cloth sac more tightly over the head of the small charm there, positioned face down. She would instruct her female contacts at court to mention to the queen how helpful Robertet had been in the past, so she would recommend him to the king to replace d'Amboise.

Once Robertet was installed at the king's side the queen could rest worry-free for the duration of her pregnancy. Or as worry-free as a woman could who had lost almost all of her children at birth, Louise thought, her spirits rising.

She would rest worry-free too, enjoying her daily devotions to the contents of her desk drawer. Shutting the drawer and locking it, she congratulated herself on doing whatever she could to ensure that her unholy trinity came to power.

Moving to the window she contemplated the blooming June landscape. How perfectly it dovetailed that Robertet had worked on behalf of both her and the queen to take down the king's overbearing marshal in 1504.

The Marshal de Gié had infuriated Louise by trying to take over guardianship of Francis from her. He had then enraged the queen by seizing her property when she had sought to have it shipped down the Loire to Brittany when the king had been thought to be dying.

The ambitious Robertet had supported both women, bringing the Marshal de Gié to trial and seeing him stripped of his powers. How fortuitous that this man was now in a position to become a senior advisor to the king, with the queen's full support.

Louise returned to her desk, writing out two more messages to be delivered to her contacts at court. She would see to it that the king was in the right hands, just as her precious Caesar would be one day. They would be her hands on his shoulders as she looked over them, ensuring that her son guided the kingdom of France to glory.

By mid-June Louis was back in Blois. He had organized a magnificent funeral for Georges d'Amboise in Rouen, arranging for the cardinal to be buried in the cathedral he had headed since 1493.

In Italy, Louis' general, Georges' nephew Charles d'Amboise de Chaumont, had teamed up with France's ally, the Duke of Ferrara, to win back Vicenza and Verona.

In retaliation, the pope, now allied with Venice, had excommunicated Chaumont, a heavy burden on top of the loss of his uncle.

Trying not to fret over Italian affairs, Anne took joy in her growing roundness and her husband's comment that the glow in her cheeks was as rosy as the rosebuds coming out in the gardens. She had safely sailed through the first four months of pregnancy. With Louis at her side and the pope's prayers for God to grant her a healthy prince, she felt a growing certainty that she would carry this babe to full term.

When Louis received a request from Maximilian to besiege Padua on his behalf, Anne exulted as he tossed it to the floor and shouted he was no longer going to do his work for him.

Instead, Louis instructed Chaumont to withdraw from outside Padua unless Maximilian showed up with his army. It was a withdrawal at a moment the French held the advantage that surprised many.

But not Anne. Louis was too angry with Maximilian to satisfy his request. It was a perfect opportunity to pay him back for fighting his battles for him the summer before. Still stunned by the loss of d'Amboise, for the moment Louis was no longer inspired to step so lively in Italy.

By July, the cards reshuffled once more. The pope informed France's ambassador to Rome that he regarded the King of France as his personal enemy and did not wish to hear anything further from him. He then ordered the French envoy to leave the city.

With diplomatic relations cut off, papal forces, fortified by Swiss mercenaries, began to harry French troops garrisoned in Genoa and Milan, both French-held territories.

Louis was now on the defensive with the pope against him. It was a complete reversal from his position of one year earlier.

Anne held her breath as well as her tongue. Although she knew her husband was sore put for advice, he wasn't going to listen to anything from her on the topic of Italy.

Instead, she pushed his fiscal minister closer to him, urging Florimond Robertet to step up and support the king in d'Amboise's place. Louis needed a close advisor and Anne was loathe to get into shouting matches with him over Italy while she tended her unborn babe.

In need of additional allies, Louis reached out to Florence for support against the new papal-Venetian alliance. His answer came with the arrival of a Florentine envoy that summer of 1510—one he and Anne already knew from visits to the French court in 1500 and 1504.

The moment Niccolò Machiavelli rose from paying his respects, Louis came straight to the point. "I need Florence's assurance of allegiance with the League of Cambrai," he told the seasoned envoy.

"Your Grace, since the pope is no longer a part of the league, such an assurance would put Florence at odds with the papal states," Machiavelli hedged.

"Do you not understand that the league is made up of France, Spain, and the Holy Roman Empire? It would be folly for Florence not to align with the interests of Europe's greatest powers," Louis said.

"Your Grace, Florence is situated next to Italy's greatest power, the pope himself. My republic can ill afford to incite his enmity or engage in conflict with the head of the Church," the Florentine countered.

Behind Louis, Anne silently thought that her own realm could not afford to incite the pope's enmity either. The authority His Holiness, Supreme Pontiff of the Church, held was far above that of other European princes. Incurring the anger of the highest spiritual representative of God on Earth would give Europe's princes pause, not wishing to bring down papal interdiction on their realms; nor, worse, the wrath of God.

"Sire de Machiavelli, I am sure you are not in the slightest interested in the Church itself, as the Cardinal d'Amboise filled me in on your humanist leanings when you were last here," Louis told him.

"Your Grace, my republic is interested in self-preservation. If we were to invoke the enmity of the papal states on its borders, it could mean our destruction." The envoy's mouth tightened into a thin line.

"The papal states are not in a position to destroy a republic such as yours," Louis said as Anne noted he did not specify his meaning. She had heard him brush off Florence as insignificant many times in the past. But now her husband needed every friend he could find on the Italian peninsula, great or small.

"Your Grace, they have gained the support not only of the Venetians but the Swiss as well. It is not just a question of the troops of the papal states but of the power of the pope to attract allies to his cause." The envoy lifted a brow with his veiled nod to the pope's greater reach than a mere monarch's.

"If Florence does not ally itself with the League of Cambrai, it will lose our support should it need help to defend itself against its enemies," Louis threatened.

"Florence will have to take its chances, Your Grace. I have been sent here by the Signoria to explain to you our position," Machiavelli responded, referring to Florence's governing body. "I beg you not to put us in a delicate position vis à vis the pope."

Anne exhaled silent thanks to God as well as to the subtle diplomat. Machiavelli could have taken the words straight from her mouth. Neither did she wish to see Brittany put in such a dangerous position. Unbeknownst to him, this godless Italian was arguing her own point on the importance of maintaining good relations with the pope.

Yet Louis would not listen. On July 30, 1510, he called for an assembly of the French clergy in two months' time. The ostensible reason was to discuss general affairs. But within a few weeks, it became clear its real intent was to discuss a plan of action in response to the pope's hostilities in Italy toward France.

Anne was horrified. Why was her husband firming up a position against the pope at such a delicate time for her? Julius II's promise of prayers for her to bear a healthy prince had given her great comfort during her pregnancy. Now, with her husband provoking him, she could no longer count on the pontiff's intercession with God for her unborn babe.

Angry with Louis, she tried not to show it while Machiavelli remained at court. She could guess he would be watching and reporting back to Florence on every gesture, every raised tone that passed between them.

Although she agreed with the man, she didn't want him around her husband. Her native shrewdness recognized the canny instincts of the Florentine. He would sniff out any weakness on the French king's part and report on it back home. It was time to send the diplomat on his way.

Instructing the kitchen staff not to serve the Florentine envoy, and the valet he had been assigned to neglect his duties, Anne did what she could to hasten Machiavelli's departure back to Florence. He had made his point, and there was no further reason for him to linger at the French court.

By the end of August, Machiavelli departed just as more bad news from Italy arrived. The papal fleet, combined with Venetian galleys, had attacked the French fleet in Genoa Harbor. In retaliation, the French navy captured four of their ships, sending the rest of them fleeing. This act of reciprocal aggression resulted in the pope's excommunication of the Duke of Ferrara, Louis' strongest ally in Italy who had helped to deliver France's victory at Agnadello.

With both General Chaumont and the Duke of Ferrara under interdict, Anne feared Louis would be Julius II's next target.

She shuddered to think of having her babe born without benefit of baptism, given the many times she had lost a child shortly after birth. Should the babe die, its soul would be in mortal peril, unable to return to God. The thought made her blood run cold.

Again she wrote to His Holiness, assuring him of Brittany's allegiance to the Church and thanking him for his continued prayers for her unborn prince. Signing and sealing the letter, she vowed to protect her Breton subjects from loss of the sacraments in their daily lives. In her view, the pope was the pope, good or bad. As Brittany's sovereign ruler, her duty was to uphold order, not to upend it.

At the end of September 1510, Julius II went to Bologna to lead the papal troops himself. The French monarchs soon received word that the sixty-six-year-old pontiff had fallen ill shortly after arriving.

Anne and Louis, together with the rest of Europe's princes, awaited news from Bologna on bated breath. Anne prayed for the pope's recovery; Louis did not.

But the sturdy old warrior pope recovered, surprising many who hoped for a change in leadership on Saint Peter's throne.

September gave way to October and Anne's hopes for a healthy birth loomed as large as her belly. She was bigger this time than with her other pregnancies. She took it as a good sign that her babe was due in the same birth month of the only two of her children who had lived. Charles-Orland had been born on October 12; Claude's eleventh birthday was October 13. How desperately Anne wished to give her a brother, finally putting that parvenue in Amboise back in her place.

As October's golden days progressed, Anne threw herself into prayers for no interdiction to be put on France, certainly not until after the birth of her child. If the babe were to live, she wanted him baptized. She shuddered to think he might not survive. But if the past repeated itself, she wished him to die in the arms of Holy Mother Church.

With the Florentine spy gone and Louis away in Lyon, Anne walked daily in the Queen's Garden at Blois, warming herself in the harvest sun. As she stroked her taut belly, she reveled in a peace she had not felt in years. A prince was on his way. A prince and an heir to the throne of France. This one, she felt sure, would live.

Chapter Thirteen

October 1510–January 1511

The Birth of A Royal

At nine in the morning on October 25, 1510, Anne of Brittany gave birth to a healthy child.

Upon hearing the queen had gone into labor, Louis had galloped back from Lyon, arriving at Blois at breakneck speed. Rushing to her lying-in chambers, he had stayed in the room with his brave *Brette* throughout the delivery, overriding all protocol and suffering with her every time she shrieked.

To his eyes, the child looked well-formed, pink enough, and with a loud bawl. He could see she was larger than Claude had been as a newborn.

"What name?" Louis asked.

His wife thought a moment. She looked as stunned as he felt to have delivered another princess. At least the babe lived.

"Let us name her Renée after Saint René."

"Ah, yes, the saint in Angers we prayed to," Louis said. *For a son*, he didn't add.

"She shall be my heir," Anne told him as he took the babe from her arms and brought it to the window to study its features.

Not wishing to argue for the moment, Louis handed his newest princess to the wet nurse then went to his wife. He willed himself not to think what she knew he was thinking. He would not. Or at least not admit it.

"Are you thinking what I am?" Anne reached out an arm to him.

"No. I'm not," Louis replied, trying to cut her off at the pass. He took her hand and ran his fingers along the back of it.

Anne narrowed her eyes. "How do you know you're not?"

"Because I am thinking what a fine princess you have delivered to me," Louis exclaimed in ringing tones. He was delighted to have another daughter. It was just that he needed a son.

"Husband, you are the world's worst dissembler. For that, I will always love you."

Louis sat on the side of his wife's bed and leaned over, lowering his voice. "And I, you, *ma Brette*."

"Even if I don't deliver the prince you long for?" Anne searched him with eyes that pierced his soul.

"Even so." He kept his voice steady. It wasn't hard because he meant it. Yet it was a disappointment.

"But I will do my best," Anne replied.

"You always do, *ma reine*. Which is why the people of France love you."

"The people of France will never love me, but they respect quality when they see it," Anne amended, smoothing back her sweat-drenched ringlets.

"Truth to that, but know you are highly esteemed." Reaching out, Louis grabbed a curl, twining it between his fingers. They could try again. At least this one lived.

Renée de Valois, Princess of France
By Corneille de Lyon, 16th century
Courtesy of The Monstrous Regiment of Women, Wikipedia Commons

Anne felt numb. Everything had gone right: the pregnancy, the birth—although painful—and, now, the evident good health of her newborn. But it was small consolation for not being able to produce the one most important requirement of her husband and his kingdom: a healthy male heir. The only two French subjects rejoicing at the birth of a princess that moment would be Louise de Savoy and her son.

She would counsel her attendants that if the Countess d'Angoulême tried to visit to offer congratulations they should tell her that late-season pestilence had broken out, such a shame she had already come in contact with several who were carrying it.

She smiled to think of Louise's horror; she, who was so vigilant to guard her precious Caesar's health. Once Marguerite found herself in the position of delivering her first child, she wondered if her mother would be able to pry herself from her son's side long enough to attend the birth.

"Ahh, the sun has come out. That's better, *ma chère*," Louis encouraged, caressing her cheek.

Comforted by his touch, she kept her thoughts to herself. Her husband already knew her feelings for Louise. She had just conceded his choice of godmother to him, relieved that he hadn't suggested Louise so that they hadn't needed to argue over it.

Anne agreed with Louis that their new princess required another princess of France to direct her in the ways of royal leadership. Louise knew leadership but was too much of a striver. Only one woman in France suited, and although she had once been Anne's rival for power, she no longer was.

Turning to Louis, she took his hand and slid it up the back of her neck under her hair. When she delivered their prince, she would see to it that her choice of godparents prevailed.

Louise de Savoy scanned the baptismal gathering at the private chapel at Blois. As custom dictated, the babe's mother was not present, still recovering from childbirth.

She smiled. It was hard enough to congratulate the Duchess of Bourbon on being named the princess's godmother instead of herself, but at least she didn't have to go through the motions of congratulating the queen on yet another failure to produce an heir.

Spotting the king she saw the commander of his army in Italy next to him. She had heard that General Gian Giacomo Trivulzio had sped over the Alps from Milan to assist at the ceremony.

As the Duchess of Bourbon passed the princess to her godfather, Louise hid her mirth at how awkwardly both godparents held the babe. Trivulzio was used to leading armies and la Beaujeu was used to leading France before she had been shouldered aside by the queen upon marrying Charles VIII. What had Louis been thinking to have asked either of the two to be the child's godparents?

"Congratulations, Your Grace, on your fine princess," Louise greeted the king with a deep curtsey.

"Thank you, Countess. I am delighted, as is my wife."

"I am sure you are, Sire. She is a blooming, healthy babe." Louise thought Renée already promised to be plain, but what matter did looks make when one was a princess born?

"She is indeed, Madame."

"I send my congratulations to the queen and pray for her speedy recovery," Louise offered, pleased at not having to lie. She was delighted that the babe was a girl.

As for the queen's recovery, she had already heard from her contact in the queen's chambers that Anne of Brittany was not bouncing back as quickly as usual.

"I will do so." Louis' brow rose in amusement as if to say he knew, as well as she, what his wife's reaction would be to receiving her best wishes. "And how is our Marguerite?" he asked in a lower tone.

"She is well and busy at Alençon." *She is bored to tears with her husband and uninspired by her new home in the middle of nowhere,* Louise neglected to add. Her daughter served at the king's pleasure in her new marriage. How she felt about it was beside the point.

"I am glad to hear it. I hope she will have good tidings for us soon." The King of France gave her a meaningful look.

"Your Grace, I will visit her shortly and perhaps by then there will be news to share," she encouraged, reaching for just the right degree of hopefulness without implying that Marguerite was with child. She had heard nothing to think that she was.

The Duchess of Bourbon passed by and Louise sensed the same shiver from Louis that rippled through her as the former regent's shadow fell over them.

"Has Madame congratulated you yet, Your Grace?" Louise asked, wondering if he felt as small and insignificant in la Beaujeu's presence as she did.

"She is waiting for me to congratulate her on accepting my offer to be Renée's godmother." A trace of irony laced Louis' tone.

"Your Grace, may I say that you rise above the past with a nobility that befits a true king," Louise breathed out, the first fully genuine statement she had made that day.

"And so, here I am." The king's tone was light, free of vengefulness's heavy weight. With a wry smile, and a pivot worthy of the superb tennis player he had once been, he turned to receive the next guest.

Louise moved back, a rare moment of awe cloaking her as she looked for her son in the crowd. The king had suffered at the hands of the woman he had just named godmother of France's newest princess. In his place she would never be able to rise above the wish to revenge herself on one who had treated her so cruelly.

But the king was cut from a different cloth. For the first time, Louise could see what it was the haughty Beaujeu had found so attractive in him: his nobility of spirit. She couldn't think of a single other man in France who possessed such gentility—heroism, truth be told—as to forgive a woman who had put him in prison for three years of his youth. Louis XII let bygones be bygones in a way that outdid any other ruler she could think of.

As she noticed Francis move toward the king, she imagined the queen arguing with Louis over returning to Italy. Perhaps

Anne of Brittany had a point. Such a noble soul would get rolled over there. And not just by the Italians.

He had overruled Anne on the choice of godparents, but he needed both of them. If no one else could understand his reasoning, it didn't matter. He was king and no one was going to argue with him except for his wife.

But his poor *Brette* was too disconsolate over the babe being a girl to have given it her all. Unusual for her, she had let him choose both godparents.

He needed Trivulzio's continued support in Italy, so he had tied him to his own family. A seasoned condottiero, the elderly Italian nobleman had served Charles VIII as head of his army in Naples, then Louis as Governor of Asti, then Milan in the late 1490s.

Leading the detachment that had won France's victory at Agnadello, Trivulzio had proven himself to Louis more than any other Italian commander he had used in previous campaigns. Louis hoped that the reward of a permanent tie with the French royal family might prevent him from switching sides in the future as the Italians were apt to do.

As for Anne de Beaujeu, the calculus was more complex. No one would understand except for Madame and himself, but he needed to sweep clean the wrongs of the past. She had caused him terrible suffering. But the suffering he had caused her by spurning her affections had also been grievous. No one but he and she knew of it. Yet it existed, all the same.

None thought France's former regent had a heart. But Louis knew she had one and he had stepped on it by accident in his gay thoughtless way when he had been young and cavalier. He had flirted with any woman he cared to, not wishing any woman to take him seriously.

But, to his horror, she had. As fast as he could he had fled France for Brittany, desperate to escape the pursuit of France's most powerful figure.

Fate had finally smiled on him at age thirty-six and given him the wife of his dreams. Not so for Anne de Beaujeu. She had put up with Pierre de Beaujeu as a husband until he had died a few years earlier, but Pierre had been as unfocused and pliant as Madame was disciplined and shrewd. She had not tasted her heart's desire and Louis knew the bitterness of that cup, not having tasted his own until he married his *Brette*.

At least he could offer la Beaujeu the honor that befitted a princess of France by naming her godmother to the kingdom's newest princess. He hadn't done it for her so much as he had done it for himself, to set his heart at ease. His grandmother would be pleased that he had shown the utmost gentility to a woman he had every reason to hate. And it would be far better for consolidating his kingdom to have an ally rather than an enemy in the powerful princess who had once sought his heart.

Anne was relieved that Louis had not been excommunicated and their daughter was baptized within the Church. The fact that she lived beyond birth brought her long-awaited hope. Should no prince of France be forthcoming, her second daughter would safeguard Brittany's independence from France as her successor. And perhaps an alliance could be made between Renée and a Habsburg prince to strengthen that safeguard.

Appointing her head chamberlain, Michelle de Saubonne, as her daughter's governess, Anne couldn't wait to get out of bed and back to the business of placating the pope while Louis provoked him.

But she found herself recovering less quickly after this delivery than with previous ones. She remained in bed through to the Advent season, unable to walk more than a few steps but fully able to issue directives to administer her realm and to receive news.

Meanwhile, Louis turned his energies to building support for an ecclesiastical council to depose the pope. In December, his position was strengthened when five cardinals from Rome fled to Milan. Anne's Italian secretary Fausto Andrelinus informed her that Louis had called upon these important defectors from Julius' Vatican Council to issue an invitation to the princes of Europe to send their senior clergy to attend an ecclesiastical council to be held in Pisa in September.

On the first day of January, Anne rose from childbirth bed to return to full-time duties. Aware of Louis' plans to convene an independent ecclesiastical council outside of the Church, she hid her dismay.

Her husband was misguided, but she loved him. She would do whatever she could to protect him, but as ruler of Brittany, she held a responsibility to save her own subjects from papal interdiction.

Within days she wrote to her archbishop in Nantes, forbidding him to attend Louis' proposed council. Well she knew the pope was likely to excommunicate all who took part. Then she had Fausto Andrelinus scribe her message to His Holiness in Rome, assuring him she had forbidden members of Brittany's clergy to attend any council convened outside the aegis of the Holy Mother Church.

It was now open war between Louis and Julius on both military and spiritual grounds. In January, the pope's army besieged Mirandola in the Emilia-Romagna, an outpost of the duchy of Ferrara. Once again, Julius II led his troops, unheard of for a pope, proclaiming himself appointed by God as Liberator of

Italy. Intent upon driving all foreign powers from Italy, beginning with the French, the warrior pope captured the town after a seventeen-day siege.

Soon after, rumors reached Louis' ears that Chaumont's troops had surrendered after he had left Mirandola to return to Milan to visit his mistress.

"God's bones, what was he thinking?" Louis raged.

Anne sniggered. "He was not, my lord."

Louis' nostrils flared. "I put him in charge and he abandons his post to run to his mistress!"

"It is not the first time it has happened," Anne recalled, remembering the disaster of her first husband Charles' campaign to win Naples in 1494. Marred by debauchery and misbehavior, it had ended in disgrace for French troops following the example of their philandering king and commander.

"It will be the last for him."

Saying nothing, Anne wished with all her heart that this latest defeat would convince Louis to leave Italy altogether. But lessons took time to learn. How well she knew from her years with Charles.

Chapter Fourteen

February 1511

Catherine of Aragon and Henry Tudor

Anne put down the letter, her lips pressed tightly together. "The English king's wife has just delivered her first child."

"I'm sure the new king must be happy," her lady-in-waiting said.

"A stillborn daughter." Anne turned her head to the tapestry on the wall.

A stag's face stared back, reproaching her. Queens everywhere who delivered only daughters were censured. It was a perilous job to be queen, one fraught with fear of failure and too frequent pregnancies that imperiled their health. Well did she know, still weak from Renée's birth. At age thirty-four, after thirteen pregnancies, she was not feeling her usual resilience after childbirth.

"Ah, Your Grace, that is sad indeed. But Queen Catherine is young and has many years ahead to try again," Madame de Dampierre said.

"How old is she?" Germaine had written from Spain with the news. Her husband Ferdinand had heard it directly from the English queen, his youngest daughter by Isabella.

"Your Grace, I am not sure, but a few years older than the king, I believe."

"Get Sire Lemaire here to fill us in."

Madame de Dampierre's face lit up. "Oh, Madame, what a sparkling idea. I will see if I can find him." The lady-in-waiting curtsied then bustled to the door.

"Have a pot of mulled wine brought and three goblets," Anne called after her. Lemaire was good fun and an incurable gossip. He would have something to tell them and not from the official English perspective, either.

Within moments, Jean Lemaire of Belgium appeared in the doorway. Four years older than the queen, he had served at Margaret of Austria's court in Flanders for many years. Some said that he had held his patron in such high regard that it had been best for him to find an appointment elsewhere. Anne had jumped to offer the cultured humanist his next position as her historiographer.

"Come," she greeted him. Lemaire was a boon to her as a conduit to Lady Margaret, Governor of the Netherlands and a valuable Habsburg connection.

Lemaire bowed gracefully. "I am at Your Grace's pleasure."

"What can you tell us of the young Queen and King of England?" Anne asked.

"Your Grace, I have heard news of the new queen and it is—"

"Sad, but not unusual," she finished. For once, it was another queen who had lost a newborn and not her. She would send a condolence note that day, but she would not allude to the depths of darkness she had felt at such losses over the years. No fellow queen would wish to walk the path she had trodden in childbearing.

"Quite right, Your Grace. She has many years to try again."

"How old is she?"

Lemaire paused a moment, counting. "She is six years older than her husband, the king."

"And he is ...?"

"Twenty this year, Your Grace."

"What do you know of the years she spent as widow of the young king's older brother?"

"Ah, Arthur..." Lemaire's voice drifted off.

"Did he not die of the sweat?" Anne asked.

"Indeed he did, Madame; only five months after his marriage to the Spanish princess," Lemaire related.

"I heard she had it, too," Madame de Dampierre put in.

"It has been said that the sweat takes more healthy young males than it does females," Lemaire observed.

"Mostly from the upper classes, they say." Madame de Dampierre tutted.

Anne shuddered. "May it not make its way here." Poor Isabella's daughter, sent to England to become a queen only to have her husband die after a few months of marriage.

Lemaire's face darkened. "It is dormant now, and let us hope it will remain so forever."

"What is forever in this vale of tears we walk, Sire Lemaire?" Anne asked, thinking of her ruddy Charles-Orland. He would have been eighteen if he had lived.

"Your Grace, you have just presented France with a bouncing princess, so I am surprised you speak of tears." Sire Lemaire's tone was gentle.

"My tears fall today for the English queen. I wonder that she was stuck in limbo so many years between marriages."

"It was six years, Your Grace, that the former English king and the King of Spain quarreled over her dowry."

"Let me guess. Was it her father who refused to complete the payments?" Anne curled her lips. Ferdinand was even more tightfisted than Louis. Much less handsome, too.

"Indeed, it was. But the old king was determined to get the

full amount, so he dangled marriage to his son up ahead as a way to make the king of Spain pay up."

"There was more to it, too," Madame de Dampierre added.

"Go on." Anne sipped her mulled wine, enjoying its warmth spreading in her belly. She looked forward to another type of warmth heating her there soon. Once she regained her strength, she would try again with Louis.

"It was said that the old king felt unsure of his legitimacy. He needed Spain's royal stamp upon his line," her lady-in-waiting filled in.

"Poor Henry Tudor," Anne said with a sigh.

"Your Grace, do tell. Did he not spend some years of his youth in Brittany as the guest of your father?" Madame de Dampierre asked.

"He was under my father's protection," Anne told them. "The York kings would have killed him had he set foot on English soil before he was fully supported."

Her lady-in-waiting's eyes shone. "Did you meet him, Madame?"

"I met him just before he returned to England and won the throne." She remembered Henry Tudor well. She had been a young girl, the Lancastrian exile a full twenty years older. Tall and lean like Louis, there the similarities ended.

Not debonair in the least, Henry Tudor had been tentative with a furtive hungry look that had puzzled her at the time. As a mother, Anne's instincts told her he had been separated from loving arms at too young an age.

Madame de Dampierre leaned forward. "And what was he like?"

"Timid and penniless. Unsure of himself." Her father had considered him as a match for her, but the idea had come to nothing when Henry had returned to England in 1483 and married Elizabeth of York. Their alliance had ended England's War of the Roses.

Marriage was life-giving, whereas war was the opposite, Anne thought. She had heard that it had been Henry Tudor's mother who had brokered the union, the indomitable Lady Margaret Beaufort—even more ambitious than that redhead in Amboise if such a thing were possible.

"That is it, Your Grace. He proved a good king, but he was uneasy on the throne," Lemaire agreed. "Marrying his heir to a Spanish princess legitimized his claim to the crown."

"And now Catherine needs a son to anchor her marriage to the new English king," Anne observed.

"Indeed, Your Grace. It would be most provident." Lemaire's tone was judicious.

"And how was her situation in those years between marriages to the two brothers?" she asked.

Lemaire's brows knit together. "I heard that before her marriage to the new king, the young princess was living in penury at the pleasure of the old king without means to support her household."

"Disgraceful," Anne said. "But Henry Tudor was always cheap. It was not his fault as he'd lived in hiding for so many years. But he should have supported his son's widow as her rank required until he decided what to do with her." What misery it must have been for Isabella of Spain's royal daughter to rot on the vine for six years of her first bloom, far from her family in a rainy, cold, foreign land.

"It was said at one time that he thought to marry her himself," Madame de Dampierre said.

"It would seem he thought to marry several great ladies," Lemaire added. "I heard a proposal was made to the Countess d'Angoulême—"

"It would have been a disaster," Anne cut him off. "Henry

Tudor was as contracted as the countess is grasping. I don't think he had it in him to take on a new wife after Elizabeth of York died."

"Your Grace, it was said that the light went out in his eyes the day his York wife died," Lemaire concurred.

"Sad for Henry Tudor that he achieved the throne he aimed for, yet could not sit on it with ease." Anne's thoughts fell on Louise de Savoy. She might acquire all she sought, but she would not sit easily once she had it.

"For fear of a pretender pushing him off," Madame de Dampierre put in.

"Let us return to Catherine," Anne directed them.

"She is finally the queen she was meant to be, as the young Henry's wife," Lemaire said.

Anne held out her goblet to be refilled. "What have you heard of him?" Henry VIII was a wild card thus far. Only in power since 1509, he was an emerging player on Europe's stage.

"Your Grace, it is said that the young king of England has inherited his York mother's confidence and his Beaufort grandmother's ambition," Lemaire described.

"I hope he will be good to his queen." Anne was no friend of England, but for the sake of Isabella, she prayed that the young Henry treated his bride as befitted the daughter of one of Europe's greatest monarchs.

"They say he is eager to prove himself."

"As I am sure Catherine is eager to prove herself by providing him with an heir." Anne weighed an entirely different thought that she would share later with Louis. *May the young English king not prove himself by entering into an alliance with his wife's father.*

Lemaire avoided her gaze. "Madame, I am sure it will come to pass."

"No one is sure of anything in such matters, but bring me my writing tools so I may send Catherine a note," she told him, guessing his thoughts. All of France waited for her to provide Louis with an heir. Let them wait. She had produced two princesses, and if French Salic Law forbade putting a woman on the throne to rule, it was France's loss.

"Right away, Your Grace."

As Anne awaited his return, she met her lady-in-waiting's questioning eyes. "What is it?"

"Your Grace, I am surprised you are reaching out to the English queen."

"She is the daughter of Isabella, whom I have always held in high regard. Unlike her husband." Ferdinand had never appealed to her. He lacked both gentility of spirit and the debonair courtliness that Louis possessed and that her father had had. How Isabella had put up with him she couldn't imagine.

Madame de Dampierre let out a titter. "Madame, she will be grateful for your show of support."

"I do not know her at all, but I know what it is to be queen and to fail at attempting an heir."

"Your Grace, she will be greatly consoled by a note from you."

"Perhaps not, but it may help." Anne waved her away as she contemplated other objectives in opening a line of communication to Catherine. It would be useful to have a conduit to the English court, should Henry VIII think to ally with one of Louis' enemies.

Wishing the Queen of England a speedy recovery, Anne sent her prayers for blooming health and a blooming prince to grace her family in the years ahead.

As she blotted and sealed the note, she prayed the same for herself.

"She said I was grasping?" Louise asked, careful to maintain an indifferent face.

"Begging your pardon, Madame, but that was the word," her contact replied.

"And that a match between Henry Tudor and me would have been a disaster?"

"Exactly so, Madame."

"I see. What did you say she said of Henry Tudor?"

"She called him 'contracted.'"

"As I am grasping ..." Louise gazed out the window, looking for something she couldn't find. Of course, she was grasping. How else was she to achieve what she reached for? But it galled her that she had not yet acquired the smooth veneer of self-possession that was the hallmark of the high born.

"Ah, yes, Madame. That was it."

"And she has written to the Queen of England."

"To offer her condolences, yes."

"Was there anything else she said she would offer?"

Her contact looked puzzled. "No, Madame. I don't think so. It was just to extend her sympathies to the English queen for the loss of her babe."

"How precious."

"Yes, Madame."

"You may go now." Louise stood and rummaged in her drawers. Finding the sac, she slid it across her desk. "For your efforts."

"Thank you, Madame. Is there something more you would like me to do?"

"The usual. Let me know if the queen is with child again and ..."

"Something else, Madame?"

"Keep track of her letters abroad, especially ones going elsewhere than Nantes."

"It will be difficult, Madame."

"Why?"

"There have been many, recently."

"Then keep track as well as you can and this sac will grow bigger as you report more." Louise pointed to the pouch still on the table.

"I will do my best." The woman reached for the sac then curtseyed.

Louise waved her out, eager to be alone.

As the woman crossed the courtyard, she went to the small looking glass on the wall.

"Am I grasping?" she asked her reflection.

The sharp-featured woman who stared back was not unattractive. But ambition had honed every angle of her face.

"Well then, is it a crime?"

The woman in the mirror smirked.

"It is what I must be to get where I need to go," Louise said.

The smirk widened, her reflection appearing to agree with her.

"Just don't give yourself away to others," she advised.

The image in the mirror straightened, tilting her chin and looking as if she needed nothing from anyone.

Louise studied herself, but it was no use. She couldn't hold the position, and she didn't look natural assuming it.

She needed lots of things and she would never stop needing them. She couldn't understand people who didn't: Louis, who didn't need revenge on the woman who had imprisoned him; Anne of Brittany, who didn't need the French to love her as long as her backwater Bretons did; and Anne de Beaujeu, who had once ruled France then stepped back and given it all up.

Turning from the mirror, she drummed her fingers on the

sides of her legs. She would never give up anything she had worked hard to achieve. Why should she? Why should anyone?

But what she wouldn't give for that ineffable quality her peers possessed that eluded her.

Frustrated, she tried to put her finger on what they had that she didn't. She was just as intelligent, shrewd, and well-educated as her powerful female peers. But Anne of Brittany and Anne de Beaujeu had both been born into wealth and privilege, with fathers who had adored them and molded them into rulers.

Louise stopped drumming and folded her arms over her torso, hugging herself. All she needed was a bit more of what they had to surpass them. With a little more wealth and a little more privilege, she would take her rightful place above both of those stone-faced snobs.

Rocking back and forth she pretended to be her own father embracing her, although she couldn't remember any time when he had. She would play his role for him, molding herself into the ruler of her son, France's future king. The father she would be to herself would shower her with treasures, acquiring the world for her if she asked for it. If that was grasping, then so be it.

Another peek into the mirror confirmed what she already knew. Naked neediness stared back at her, no matter how hard she tried to conceal it.

Yanking the mirror from the wall, she smashed it on the floor.

As her housemaid came running, she assumed her most dignified face, skirting the shattered pieces she had caused. She would grasp for the highest ring there was and hold it tight until death released her grip. What more was there to live for?

Louis XII of France
By circle of Richard Burchett (1815-1875)
Parliamentary Art Collection
Courtesy of ArtUk.org

Statue of Anne of Brittany
By Jean Baptiste Joseph Debay, 19th century
Luxembourg Gardens, Paris
Photo by R. Gaston

Statue of Valentina Visconti
By Victor Huguenin, 19th century
Luxembourg Gardens, Paris
Photo by Couscous Chocolat, courtesy of Wikimedia Commons

Statue of Marguerite d'Angoulême
By Joseph-Stanlislas Lescorné, 1848
Luxembourg Gardens, Paris
Photo by Remi Jouan, courtesy of Wikimedia Commons

Statue of Louise de Savoy
By Auguste Clésinger, 1851
Luxembourg Gardens, Paris
Photo by JLPC, courtesy of Wikimedia Commons

Claude of France
Portrait by Corneille de Lyon, 16th century
Courtesy of Wikimedia Commons

Portrait of Anne of France, a.k.a. Anne de Beaujeu, Duchess of Bourbon
From a triptych by Jean Hey, c. 1498
Courtesy of Wikimedia Commons

Terracotta statue of Anne of Brittany
By Alfred Caravaniez, 1884
Chateau of the Dukes of Brittany, Nantes France
Photo by Iolanda Andrade, courtesy of Wikimedia Commons

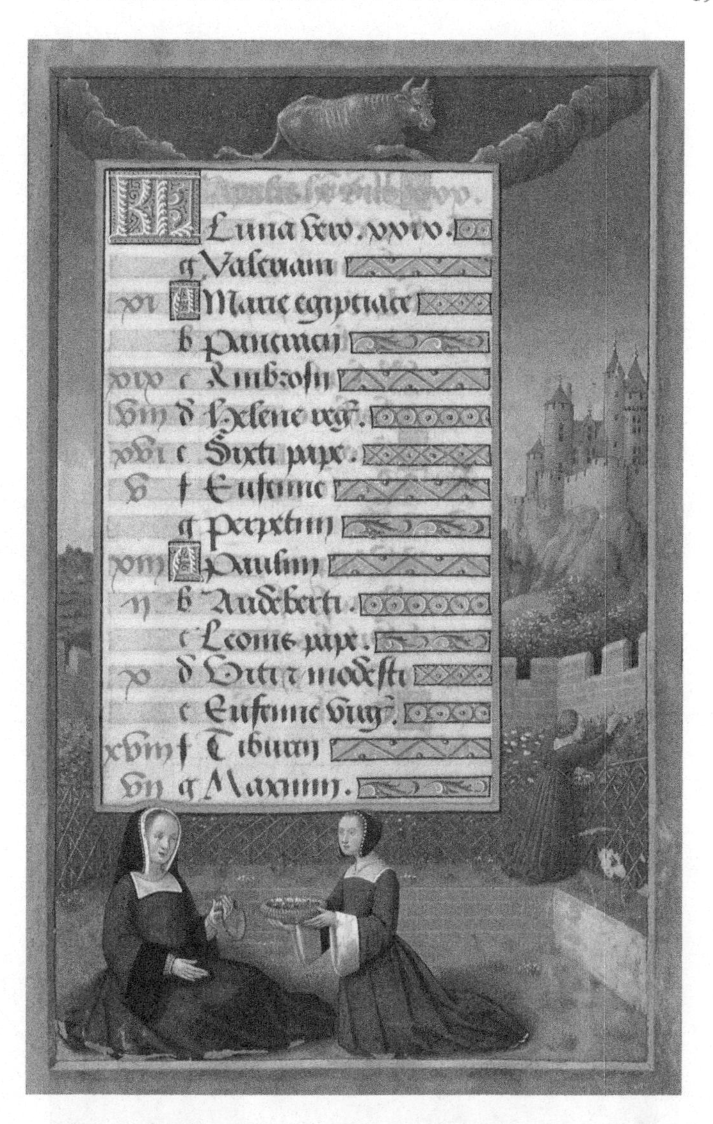

The month of April depicting Anne of Brittany and her ladies
from the *Great Hours of Anne of Brittany* by Jean Bourdichon
Reprint courtesy of © M. Moleiro, Editor (www.moleiro.com),
Great Hours of Anne of Brittany, f. 7r., Barcelona, Spain

Detail from the month of April depicting Anne of Brittany and her ladies
from the *Great Hours of Anne of Brittany* by Jean Bourdichon
Reprint courtesy of © M. Moleiro, Editor (www.moleiro.com),
Great Hours of Anne of Brittany, f. 7r., Barcelona, Spain

Detail from tomb of Anne of Brittany and Louis XII
Basilica of Saint-Denis, France
Photo by H. Bonné, Courtesy of Wikimedia Commons

Chapter Fifteen

Winter–Spring 1511

La Gravelle

Later that month of February 1511, word reached the French court that Charles d'Amboise, Seigneur de Chaumont and head of Louis' spring campaign in Italy, had taken ill in Coreggio and died.

The courier related that on his deathbed the Sire de Chaumont had prayed to be restored to the Church. A message to the pope had been sent, begging him to lift his excommunication.

"Did His Holiness lift the interdict?" Anne asked.

The messenger's face fell. "The pope did, Your Grace, but by the time the message arrived it was too late." He bowed his head.

"Do you mean Sire de Chaumont died believing his soul was in peril?" she pressed.

"I am sorry to say that he did, Your Grace. He was much distressed in his final hours. He was delirious, asking again and again if the pope had sent a pardon yet."

"Dear God, what torment to die without comfort of the Church's forgiveness." Anne's heart heaved to think that he had been pardoned but hadn't yet been told.

"He was in great anguish, Your Grace. It was a state no man would wish to find himself in to meet his Maker," the messenger added.

"That is enough. Go refresh yourself, and I will have my instructions by tomorrow for you to return to Italy with," Louis said.

The moment the messenger was gone, Anne faced her husband. "You do not seem too concerned. Are you not saddened by this news?"

"'Tis sad, but I am glad Georges is already gone so he doesn't have to grieve the loss of his nephew. And now I can have Trivulzio take over and do a better job."

"Fie on Trivulzio!" Anne cried. "I'm speaking of your general's soul. Do you not see how hard it is upon a man to suffer the pope's interdiction?"

Louis shrugged. "Julius is more warlord than pope and he will not be pope for much longer, so why should I care about his papal pronouncements?"

"Do you not care for the comfort of your subjects about to face their Maker, Husband? To die without solace of the Church is a terrible thing."

Louis' face reddened. "Which is why I intend to get rid of this pope and install one who attends to spiritual matters instead of making war."

"If you follow such a path, Husband, you will get yourself excommunicated."

Louis waved a hand as if flicking off a fly. "Madame, under this present pope, I do not care a fig if I do or not."

"I care! I care, Louis, and you should care too—for your own soul and the souls of your subjects!"

"Madame, this is a matter for the Church fathers to decide. Not you. You would do well to leave it alone and attend to your own affairs."

Louis' look made Anne's blood boil. If anyone cared about the concerns of Church fathers, she did. Knowing Louis, he had likely never given the Church fathers a thought until recently, now that he needed them to help unseat an enemy.

"This is certainly my affair and I will conduct my response to it as protector of the souls of my realm," she flung back, her face hot.

"No doubt you will. And you will excuse me now as I must get my general's new orders drawn up." Louis strode from the room, leaving Anne fuming.

He couldn't bear being at odds with his wife, but she needed to stay out of his affairs.

The problem was that managing affairs without Georges around was not the same. At Anne's urging, he had installed Florimond Robertet in his privy council chamber. But Robertet was not his old friend d'Amboise.

Georges had had vast experience in Italy and high connections as a cardinal of the Church. Robertet had never been to Italy; from a merchant family, he was not highly connected. He was good with fiscal affairs and that was something, just not the full scope of what Louis needed in an advisor.

With Chaumont dead, Louis was eager to get Trivulzio in place with orders. The seasoned Italian commander was his man but what orders to give him? Georges would know, with his experience and finesse. Robertet would not.

"Georges, where in God's name are you when I need you," Louis grumbled as he strode down the hallway to his privy council chambers. Up ahead, the narrower corridor to the castle's unused wing branched off.

As if shoved from behind by George's spirit, Louis diverted to the right and headed to his secret sanctuary. Usually, he didn't visit his grandmother's rooms when Anne was around. But his wife wouldn't be traveling until she was stronger and he needed advice now.

Help me, Valentina, he prayed as he made his way through the hidden door in the chapel. Within minutes, he was there.

The image of the daughter of Gian Galeazzo Visconti stared down at him, looking sadder than it had the last time he visited.

"I've lost Georges, Madame. And now, his nephew, too." To be honest, he wasn't too grieved by the loss of Charles d'Amboise. Ever since he and Anne had learned that the thirty-seven-year-old commander had lost Mirandola to the pope's forces because he had left his post to visit his mistress, Louis had wanted to replace him. It was a pity that his death provided the opportunity so soon after, but it worked to Louis' advantage.

His grandmother surveyed him, reminding him that he had forgotten something.

"Ah, yes. Our new princess! Thank you, dear lady, if you had anything to do with her healthy birth. I hope one day you will advise me on who to marry her to."

Chuckling to himself, he thought of his wife, then remembered their spat. Anne would have plenty of advice on who to marry Renée to, so he would need a trusted counsel in Valentina to help him stand firm with his own candidate.

It was not easy to hold his own when his *Brette* made up her mind. He had discovered as much when Anne had insisted on brokering a marriage alliance for Claude with Charles of Habsburg, the son of Maximilian's son Philip of Burgundy, and Ferdinand's daughter Joanna of Spain. He had gone along with his wife's plan until he had secretly arranged for Georges to convene an Estates-General of France to beg him to marry his daughter to his successor.

Louis studied the image of his grandmother, high on the wall, waiting for him to make her smile.

"Madame, the pope seeks to drive all foreign powers from Italy, the French most of all," Louis complained.

"But you are one-quarter Italian," Valentina Visconti reminded him.

"So I am, Madame. And it is my birthright to claim Milan." Truth be told, he didn't feel Italian at all. There was something about the impassioned sensibilities of the Italians that put him off. Everything seemed overwrought over there. The weather was too hot, the colors of the flowers too vividly-hued, even the blue of the sky too brilliant, unlike the delicate hues of his Loire Valley homeland.

He found the bold beauty of its women overwhelming, along with their shows of dramatic emotion. Such public displays defied ideals of courtly self-possession he had grown up with. As for Italian hand gestures, all the waving and flapping seemed excessive for his tastes.

To be faced with ruling an entire duchy filled with inhabitants who sought drama as naturally as flowers sought sunlight was an off-putting thought. To that end, his plan was to continue ruling Milan through a French governor to oversee administrative duties. Someone who understood the sort of people he was dealing with, although he couldn't think of any sane Frenchman who did.

His trusted Georges had gotten on well there, but when it had come to the 1503 papal election, he had fumbled winning enough votes from the other cardinals. Who, other than an Italian, could fully fathom the intricacies of the wheeling and dealing that went on to elect a pope, Louis wondered.

Cardinal Giuiliano della Rovere had plumbed the depths of backroom dealings, and in the guise of pretending to support Georges' candidacy, had stolen the papacy out from under him. Louis burned to think of the treachery of the man who had taken the name Julius II.

"Fight to hold your claim to my father's duchy, Louis. Do not let it slip from you," Valentina counseled.

"Madame, the man who sits on Peter's throne has done me wrong and will never support my claim there."

Valentina's eyes jumped out at him. "Then get rid of him."

Louis stepped back, shaken. He had been conjuring his grandmother's spirit. Was it possible he had summoned her?

"Madame, I seek to depose him," he answered, wondering if his grandmother had meant something more. If so, how innately Italian such a solution would be. The rumored tale of Cesare Borgia poisoning his older brother to claim primogeniture came to mind, chilling Louis to the bone.

Valentina Visconti released him, looking a bit more animated and less sad. It was time to return to the other side of the castle.

Kissing the feet of the image in the painting at face level, Louis turned and sped back to the castle's main wing. Approaching the end of the narrow corridor, he was about to turn into the main one when a sentry rushed past, not seeing him as he ran down the main hallway.

Curious, Louis followed.

"A doctor for the queen," the sentry shouted to someone up ahead.

Louis spun 'round and began to run toward Anne's quarters. All thoughts of their earlier spat forgotten, he raced toward his *Brette.*

"God help me!" Anne doubled over in her chair. She slipped to the floor as her ladies rushed to her.

"Your Grace!" Madame de la Seneschale gasped, reaching for her arm while Madame de Dampierre reached for the other.

"Madame, are you in pain?" Madame de Dampierre asked.

"Jesus God!" Anne shrieked, clutching her side as she curled into a ball.

"Get the court doctor," Madame de la Seneschale ordered the page standing near the door.

"I do not know where he is," the boy stammered, wide-eyed at sight of his queen writhing on the floor. Was a baby coming? If so, why had he been allowed into the birthing chambers? If this was women's pain, he wished to be far from it.

"Tell the kitchen. They'll find him!" Madame de la Seneschale barked.

"Yes, Madame." The youth scurried off, the queen's moans chasing him from the room.

"Your Grace, let us lift you so we can get you to your bed," Madame de Dampierre told her.

"Water," Anne gasped, clenching her side as she squeezed shut her eyes to hold back tears. She would not allow those around her to see her cry. It was unfitting for a queen; unheard of for her.

A goblet of water was brought, then Anne slowly stood, supported by both women.

"Your Grace, is there news we should know?" Madame de la Seneschale's tone was delicate.

"No. I don't know what it was, but it's gone," she breathed out, moving to the window.

"Sit down, Your Grace. Rest until the doctor arrives," Madame de Dampierre urged.

Anne paced back and forth, then sat. With a grimace, she stood again. Holding her hands to her lower back on either side, she resumed pacing.

"Is the pain back?"

She shook her head. "No, but it feels better to move."

"Your Grace, is it possible that you are in a condition you are unaware of?" Madame de la Seneschale asked again.

"I am not with child! It was like a stab, sharp as a blade," Anne snapped. A queen did not show fear unless it was in childbirth.

"Your Grace, let us get you to your chambers so the doctor may examine you when he arrives."

"God keep me from doctors and their stupidities!" Anne groaned as her ladies helped her toward her chambers.

"Your Grace, let him see you to hear what he says."

"He will say something useless, and I will get Cook to attend me. She'll know what ails me." On the way to her rooms, she thought of her fight with Louis. His plan to call a schismatic council was lunacy. If he was there now, she would tell him so—anything to get her mind off fear of the pain returning.

It was unlike her to fear anything other than childbirth. But that fear was mitigated by the certainty of resolution to come. This pain was higher up and sharper, an unknown enemy—the worst kind.

Within the hour, the doctor finished his exam and folded his arms into the loose sleeves of his coat. "Your Grace, I would surmise it is the stones."

"What stones?"

"Kidney stones, Your Grace. *La gravelle.*"

Anne looked at him sharply. They were quacks, most of them. "Was that not what the Cardinal d'Amboise suffered from?"

"Along with gout, Your Grace. The pain you describe is similar to what Sire d'Amboise suffered before, before—"

"Before he died," Anne finished. What a loss it had been for Louis to lose his right-hand man. She could see that he hadn't yet recovered by the stacks of unread documents piling up on his desk. "Did you treat him?"

"I did, Madame." The doctor cleared his throat, eyes avoiding hers. "The pain is severe when it comes, but it goes quickly until it comes again."

"No childbirth pain ever hurt so much." Anne trembled, in shock to think of it.

"Your Grace, take comfort in it being temporary, for soon the stone will pass."

"How soon?"

"Impossible to say, Your Grace. Perhaps a few days, perhaps a few weeks. I counsel you to drink more water than usual and make no plans to travel until it passes."

"Is this what the cardinal died from, Monsieur?" What a horrible way to die. Such agony that one could not even think long enough to commit one's soul to God, only to pray for oblivion to escape the pain.

"Your Grace, the cardinal died from a combination of maladies, of which this was one." The doctor's tone was vague.

"What were the others?" She wanted to slap the court physician. What good had any of them been to keep her Charles-Orland alive? Nor had any of them fixed whatever it was inside her that caused all her other sons to die at birth.

"Gout, Madame. Something you need not worry about at all."

"Was it gout that killed him or an attack of stones?"

"It was a gout attack to the stomach, Your Grace. One does not die of an attack of stones unless there are other circumstances."

"What other circumstances?"

"If there is fever present, there is mortal risk." The doctor's face was grave.

Anne put a hand to her forehead. "I have no fever."

"Thankfully not, Your Grace. I will instruct your attendants to watch carefully so we may know the moment the stone has passed. As soon as it is gone, you will not suffer further."

"But will other stones come in the future?" She couldn't bear to go through this again. God forbid that one should die in such a torturous way.

"Your Grace, it is possible that this may happen again in the future. But you are young and strong, and the moment the stone has passed your pain will be over."

"Do you think so, Monsieur?"

"I do, Your Grace, knowing your constitution and your resilience."

Disgusted, Anne recognized the usual flattering half-truths that courtiers fed their monarchs. Dismissing him she thought of Cook. Her good kitchen head would not lie to her. She would take one look and know what to do.

As her ladies sprang to their duties, Anne turned to the window, ruminating on the physician's final words. She had always had a strong constitution, despite her limp. But she knew her own resilience better than any court physician. It was not the same since giving birth to Renée.

"Ahh!" she cried, bending double over the table near her. Out of nowhere, the knifelike pain was back, stabbing her just below the ribcage on her right side.

"Your Grace!"

The pain was so piercing she would do anything to get away from it. Banging her head on the table, she moaned.

"Get the doctor again!" a voice called out.

"Not the doctor. Get Cook!" She needed her Breton cook. The woman knew everything there was to know about herbs.

She come up with something to stop the jagged shards of glass cutting into her insides.

In a moment, the pain subsided and she straightened up.

"Your Grace, let me help you to your bed," an attendant urged.

"Fie on my bed! I need to move to get this demon out!" Anne paced to the door, then to the window, then the hearth. It was as if a knife inside her was at work, not allowing her to rest the moment she stood still.

Before the hearth, she stretched out an arm to prop herself against the wall. Cook would help her. She had a cure for everything.

"Arghh!" Anne shrieked.

"Your Grace, she is coming. Hold on!" A woman slapped a cool lavender cloth onto her forehead, distracting her from the pain of a moment before. But the devil stalking her would be back.

"Your Majesty, I am here," Cook's voice sounded from the doorway. Her ample form filled the frame, exuding comfort and competence.

"God help me, Cook," Anne breathed out, relieved beyond measure to see her. "What can you do for stones?"

Cook grimaced in sympathy. "My lady, I will prepare a few potions. One to drink to ease your pain when it comes again and a few others to make the stone pass more quickly."

"Do it now or I will die from pain!" Anne moaned.

Cook came straight to her. "Begging your pardon, my lady queen."

"Do what you need to do!" she cried.

"Show me where the pain was."

"Here!" Anne pressed her fingers into the indent under her right ribcage. Whatever it was, it was no babe.

"May I?"

"Yes! Do something before it comes back."

Cook grasped her arm and led her to her bed like a small child, pushing her down onto it. She dug her fingers into the spot, massaging her body with up-to-down strokes as if easing the stone out.

Anne kept her eyes fixed on her broad honest face, taking comfort in its reassuring contours, ones she had known since childhood. Women healers always did something while male doctors just stood around hiding their useless hands in their sleeves. It was far more comforting to be tended by someone practical like Cook. If she saw her through this, she would reward her generously.

Chapter Sixteen

Winter–Spring 1511

A Ribald Song

Anne drank the pomegranate juice Cook gave her each morning upon awakening. Mid-mornings she sipped the basil tea Cook prepared for her. At midday dinner, she drank Cook's celery juice. But best of all were Cook's mid-afternoon visits when she brought dandelion tea and massaged her torso.

"Can you feel where the stone is?" Anne asked, relieved to surrender herself to her faithful Breton's hands as she rested after the midday meal. There were not many at her ladies' court with whom she let down her guard. Cook, from her birthplace of Nantes, was one of the few.

"Your Grace, I cannot feel the stone, but you can be sure it's there. And sooner or later, my fingers will move it down the path it must travel to pass out."

"You won't push anything else out while you're at it, will you?" Anne gave Cook a sly look.

Cook narrowed her eyes, the corner of her mouth twitching. "My duchess, if you tell me there's something more in there, I'll ease up."

"No, don't, Cook. I am just dreaming out loud."

"That is the way to see dreams come true, Your Grace.

First, you have them, then you give voice to them, and next thing you know they're on their way."

"What was the biggest dream you ever had?" Anne spoke with no one else like this. But with her trusted servant from her own realm, she could set aside her crown for a rare moment.

Cook laughed as her fingers worked their magic. "My duchess, I try not to dream too large so there's a bigger chance of what I aim for coming true."

"And what's the biggest thing you ever aimed for?"

"Your Grace, I won't say as it didn't come to pass."

Anne thought of her own biggest dream that hadn't come to pass. "Does it hurt too much to remember?"

Cook shrugged. "Not so much. It's just that I've put it aside now and moved onto dreaming other dreams."

"Why not go ahead and tell me? I'd like to know." Any other of her attendants she would order to answer her question. But not Cook.

"I could, but I don't want it to have any more power over me. The second I speak it aloud, it'll be out there hanging in the air, making me sad again." Cook didn't look bothered in the least. Instead, she kneaded efficiently, intent upon her mission.

"You don't spend much time being sad, do you, Cook?"

"You are right, indeed, Your Grace. There's too much to be busy about for me to waste time mulling over what didn't come to pass."

"I like your thinking." Even more, she liked her self-assurance. It rivaled her own.

Cook cackled. "Your Grace, no one has ever complimented me on my thinking before."

"But everyone admires you." There was nothing better than being in capable hands. She'd much rather be in Cook's hands than in a doctor's ones.

"I should say the same of you, Your Grace."

Anne sighed. "It's something, isn't it?" But was it enough to fill the hole left by dreams that hadn't come true?

"It's a great deal of something. You're the sort of great lady that other women dream of being like," Cook observed.

Anne laughed. Usually, she dismissed such words as courtiers' flattery. But coming from Cook's mouth, she could count on their true weight. "And why's that?" she asked.

The older Breton woman took a long moment, pressing and kneading along the side of her sovereign's torso from the top of her ribs to her hipbone.

"Because you keep a cool head even though you've been through a heap of troubles," she answered.

"Do I, Cook?"

"You do. Everyone remarks on it."

"Just after they've finished a good gossip over all my losses?"

"It's not the losses that linger with people. It's the way you get through them."

"How so?"

"Your Grace, most women know losses like the ones you've had, but not so many. And any woman who's had them looks to your example to get out of bed, on her feet, and back busy again with head held high and fresh dreams to come."

"Bless you, Cook. I'll remember that," Anne said, feeling infinitely comforted.

"And now will you finish your tea, my duchess, so we can get this stone out and you working on getting something else inside to worry about?"

Anne threw her head back and laughed, making her ladies-in-waiting appear in the doorway, smiles wreathing their faces. Cook had the same knack their queen did. Wherever either woman went, grace and order followed in their wake.

Louis was beside himself. Despite Cook's ministrations, his wife's condition worsened. By the end of March 1511, fever set in and Anne fell into delirium, unable to speak.

Fourteen and a half years her senior, it was usually he who was ill from time to time, due to the gout he had struggled with for years. To see his vital *Brette* so sick shocked Louis straight to his soul.

He conferred with the doctors, feeling the same frustration with their vague answers and lowered eyes that Anne complained about. Would to God she would find her voice to complain again as soon as possible. No one knew if she would live or die. But he couldn't bear to lose her. He needed her more than anyone realized, save Anne herself.

That morning he had received news that Trivulzio and the French army were outside Bologna's city walls, waiting for the papal states' northernmost city to surrender to the French army. The pope had already been there and left for Ravenna, further east, once he realized the Bolognese were more sympathetic to the French than they were to him. Such good news should have made Louis dance for joy, but, instead, he felt numb. Nothing mattered other than his wife's recovery.

Shooing everyone from the room, Louis sat next to Anne on her bed. Taking her hand, he leaned over her pale, sweat-beaded face.

"*M'amie*, come back. You know I can't manage without you. Don't you wish to argue with me some more? And what about Claude? You know you don't want her marrying Francis. There's only one way to prevent that, *m'amie*. You need to come back so we can make our own dauphin."

Restless, Anne stirred beneath his touch.

He didn't really think they would beget a new dauphin, but there would be no chance at all if she were to die.

Shock rippled through him at the thought. Running his hand through her hair in the way she loved he decided to return later. To shake grim thoughts, he would occupy himself with getting back orders to Trivulzio on besieging Bologna. But he didn't care about any of it anymore. He was bereft without her, even with her lectures on not goading the pope.

As he left, he instructed Anne's women to excuse the castle's head cook from all kitchen duties to attend the queen instead. He knew his *Brette*. She would only worsen if doctors stood around mumbling and annoying her.

She needed to want to come back; for that, a link to her past, to her loving childhood, would offer the strongest medicine. Cook was the perfect candidate to administer it.

The next day, Anne was no better, and Louis sat with her again. As she wandered in the deep, he wandered there with her, casting aside all thoughts of affairs at home and campaigns abroad.

"*Ma Brette,* do you remember the time we first met? How serious you were. I tried to entertain you and you wouldn't laugh for four full days."

Anne flung a hand out. But her eyes and mouth remained closed.

Chuckling, Louis continued, "Oh, you don't think so? It was at least three. I tried everything. You stared at me with big eyes and caught me in your lashes like a spider catches a bug." He had been hard put to coax a smile from the severe seven-year-old. How well he remembered her assessing eyes, the eyes of a full-grown woman.

His wife remained motionless, frustrating him. It was unlike her to be sick; she, who was so full of plans and projects. Perhaps if he could provoke her, she would come to life again.

Wracking his brain, he thought of japes he could depend on to catch a cuff from her. A chirp from Anne's linnet in his cage reminded him of just the thing.

Under his breath, he began to croon an old tune, one that he had shared some merry moments enjoying with his wife's father when Louis had visited his castle long ago.

> "*En baisant m'amie, j'ai cueilli la fleur.*
> (While kissing my sweetheart, I picked the flower.)
>
> *M'amie est tant belle, si bonne façon;*
> (My sweetheart is so beautiful, so good;)
>
> *En baisant m'amie, j'ai cueilli la fleur.*"
> (While kissing my sweetheart, I picked the flower.)

From behind, a faint titter rose to his ears. Apparently, some of Anne's attendants were familiar with the indelicate tune. It was strong seasoning, but his wife needed something well-spiced to rouse her.

Continuing, he tried the next few verses:

> "*Blanche comme neige, droite comme un jonc;*
> (White as the snow, straight as a rush;)
>
> *En baisant m'amie, j'ai cueilli la fleur.*"
> (While kissing my sweetheart, I picked the flower.)

As Louis sang softly, his thoughts wandered back to 1491 when he'd been sprung from prison to convince Brittany's young ruler to marry his cousin Charles, France's king before him.

Clapping eyes on Anne at age fourteen, Louis had been smitten. She had grown into the astonishing beauty she had promised to flower into when he had first met her. It hadn't been easy to make an argument for his cousin when he had desperately wanted her for himself.

> "*La bouche vermeille, fossette au menton;*
> (The ruddy mouth, dimple on the chin;)

Et en baisant m'amie, j'ai cueilli la fleur."
(And while kissing my sweetheart, I picked the flower.)

Once, long ago, Anne's father had thought to marry her to him, but too many obstacles had blocked the way. He had already been married and, besides, he had not been in direct line to become king. Then Duke Francis had died, and ten years later, so had Charles VIII, bringing Louis to France's throne.

Finally, he had been worthy of the Duke of Brittany's elder daughter. And so he had plucked the flower of his first love, his fiery *Brette,* with her splendid hauteur and ardent heart.

Leaning close to Anne's ear, he crooned the final verse, the one that invariably resulted in a slap or at least a cuff.

"La cuisse bien faite, le tétin bien rond.
(The thigh well made, the teat well round.)

Et en baisant m'amie, j'ai cueilli la fleur."
(And while kissing my sweetheart, I picked the flower.)

"Les gens de la ville ont dit qu'ils l'auront
(The people of the town said they will get it)

Mais je assure qu'ils en mentiron.
(But I assure you they will lie about it.)

En baisant m'amie, j'ai cueilli la fleur."
(While kissing my sweetheart, I picked the flower.)

No response. With a lingering kiss to his *Brette*'s still lips, he rose, promising to return soon. God forbid that those lips one day should be cold to his touch.

At the doorway to his wife's bedchamber, Anne's Breton cook curtseyed to him. "A word, Your Grace?"

Louis nodded.

"Your tune would rouse a soul from the dead, your Grace. I will feed her my potions, but if you feed her songs like that from her youth, you will give her the best medicine of all."

"So you heard my tune?"

Cook's face reddened, but her smile was broad. "It is one that brings me back to Nantes and gay times in my youth, Sire."

Then I shall sing it again until she wakes and scolds me to stop."

"Ah, Sire, you are the best keeper of the queen's heart if I may say so."

"And you are the best doctor she's got."

"The only one she'll tolerate, Your Grace."

"Go to her and coax her back."

"I'll do my best, Sire."

Louis passed as the woman curtseyed once more. He'd try their special song again the next time he came. Anything to rile her so she would return to him.

That evening, three court musicians appeared at the door to the queen's chambers.

Madame de Dampierre blocked their entry. "You are not allowed in here."

King's orders, my lady. Here." The first musician held out a sheet with the king's seal on it. Sure enough, the king had ordered music to be played in the queen's bedchamber every evening until she recovered from her fever.

Madame de Dampierre turned to Madame de la Seneschale. "Is this not unusual?"

The second lady-in-waiting shrugged. "Perhaps the king thinks this will snap her out of her fever."

"Let us see if it does any good." Madame de Dampierre stepped back to allow the musicians to enter.

Setting up in a corner of the bedchamber, the beat of the timbrel began, soon joined by lute and rebec. The room filled with the slow strains of *En Baisant M'Amie*, the earthy tune bringing a blush to the ladies-in-waiting's cheeks and a knowing smile to the faces of the sentries posted outside the queen's door.

"Do you not think this tune a bit brash for the queen's taste?" Madame de Dampierre asked Madame de la Seneschale.

"I think the king knows well what he is doing. I heard him crooning it to her the day before."

Madame de Dampierre frowned. "But Her Grace is not given to bawdy songs. Do you think this is some sort of secret between them?"

Madame de la Seneschale broke into a smile. "That is exactly what I think. The king is intent on provoking her so she will wake up and order the music stopped."

"Or wake up and order him to kiss her."

Madame de la Seneschale's eyes twinkled. "I don't think the king would need an order for such a task."

The dulcet strains that filled the queen's chambers that evening stirred the hearts of even the sternest of those present. Madame de la Seneschale's foot tapped and Madame de Dampierre wandered in private reveries of glory days of her own. Most in the room were familiar with the lyrics to the popular courting song.

Madame de Dampierre shuddered to think that the queen's maids of honor would catch wind of such a wayward tune. But tucked into the back of her mind, she guessed that many of the older demoiselles of the queen's court had already made an exhaustive study of the song's alluring lyrics.

On the fourth day of April, Anne awoke, her fever gone.

"Tell the king it was two days, not four," were her first words.

Her attendants looked at each other, fearful that the queen was still delirious. But the message was sent.

Within minutes the king arrived.

"So you were listening, were you?" Louis greeted her.

"How dare you sing that louche song!" Anne rebuked him. "And so sweetly, too, just as you did when I was seven. I had to stop you."

"*M'amie*, you were seven going on eighteen as I recall."

"Only because I was subjected to sorts like you," she riposted.

"And here you are. Queen of France stuck for all eternity with the king. Poor you."

"It is a cross I must bear," she teased, her heart swelling to see how relieved he looked. "But since you need me so badly, I will endure it."

"I will help you endure it more pleasantly once you are stronger." Louis took her hand and raised it to his lips.

"Call Cook and have her bring some elderflower wine and meat pasties so you may begin strengthening me this moment." She was famished. For food, drink, and her husband, who under no circumstances did she intend to go easy on.

"*M'amie*, it is good to have you back!" Louis exulted, looking overjoyed to see her restored to her usual spirited self.

"You may sing me that naughty song once more so that we may test my strength when I slap you," she ordered. How heavenly it was to banter with him again.

The queen's two Breton sentries at the door exchanged winks, eyes bright with amusement. The queen was back, sparring with the king as usual. None was supposed to overhear, but some did, then told others, until the entire castle rejoiced that the queen had recovered and was now lecturing the king on his bad behavior. What merriment it was to know that their monarchs shared a ribald joke between them.

With the fever broken and the stone passed, Anne remembered her vow to reward Cook.

Bidding an attendant to bring Cook's assistant to her, she asked her privately what Cook's concerns were.

"Your Grace, I think it's her daughter she worries about. When she mentions her she sighs and looks away," Marie told her.

"Is there something wrong with her then?"

"I don't know, Your Grace. All I know is that Cook sometimes says she would see her settled with a good man, but she has no dowry."

"Ah then, you have told me all I need to know. Go now and say nothing to anyone about our talk, do you understand?"

"I do, Your Grace. But may I tell my mother? She knows you bid me here and she will … she will …"

"She will stretch you on the rack until she gets out of you every word we spoke?" Anne gave her a merry look.

Marie giggled. "Your Grace, most certainly she will try. I will be hard-pressed to stay silent when she questions me."

"A good point, my dove. Here's what you must do." Anne leaned closer, enjoying the moment.

Marie's eyes sparkled. "Yes, Your Grace?"

"You must tell your mother that the queen has sworn you to secrecy on our talk, but when it comes to fruition you may tell her that you had a hand in it," Anne instructed in low tones.

"When what comes to fruition?" Marie asked, looking dazzled to be tête-à-tête with her queen.

"What I am planning, that shall remain secret."

"Your Grace, is it that you find a nice husband for Cook's daughter and pay her dowry?" the young woman asked.

Anne's laughter rippled through the room like a spring breeze. "Why would you think such a thing?"

"Because everyone knows you are the best matchmaker in all Europe and the most generous, too," Marie exclaimed.

"Tell your mother she must allow you to keep your talk with me to yourself. If she does, I will make a match for you, too," Anne promised.

The young woman's face lit up. "Oh, Your Grace, I would be most grateful!"

"But if she insists on prying our talk out of you, all is off. You will remain in the royal court's kitchen instead of heading up one of your own one day," Anne warned.

"Your Grace, such a rich secret between us!" Marie's voice rang with glee.

"Isn't it nice to have them?" Anne asked. "And, remember, the first rule for a woman to reap her own happiness is to keep her own counsel."

Marie looked worried. "That's not easy when it comes to my mother."

"You tell your mother that the queen herself has bid you to keep your secret, and if she pries it out of you, she will lose the reward that will make her most happy."

The young woman giggled. "She will know right away what I mean."

Anne laughed. "Let her. Just don't say anything about Cook."

"I promise, Your Grace. I promise!" Marie's eyes danced making Anne's heart dance in return.

Waving away the radiant girl, Anne's head filled with plans. With two new matches to make, she felt more herself than she had in months. What joy it was to solve another's problems and forget about one's own for a brief season.

EN BAISANT M'AMIE

Chant français du 15ème siècle

2. En baisant m'amie j'ai cueilli la fleur
La bouche vermeille, fossette au menton.
La cuisse bien faite, le tetin bien rond.
Et en baisant m'amie, j'ai cueilli la fleur.

3. En baisant m'amie j'ai cueilli la fleur
Les gens de la ville ont dit qu'ils l'auront
Mais je assure qu'ils en mentiront.
Et en baisant m'amie, j'ai cueilli la fleur.

En Baisant M'Amie
15th century French song
Courtesy of https://www.Partitions-domaine-public.fr
Public domain

Chapter Seventeen

Spring 1511

The Hunt with Claude

Within days of Anne's recovery, Louis received word that Maximilian had made a secret truce with Venice.

When he had heard of the pope's truce with Venice the year before he had been enraged. But with Maximilian's deceit, he only felt disgust. The Holy Roman Emperor was as useless, floundering, and impotent as Julius II was not.

Tossing the missive to the floor, Louis stomped on it. The League of Cambrai was fast unraveling, now consisting only of France and its staunch ally, the Duke of Ferrara.

Anne snickered when she heard. "Surprised, Husband?"

Louis gritted his teeth, aware that nothing would give her greater pleasure than the League disappearing altogether. He didn't care if it did because he had something else in its place to thwart the pope: his church council to be convened in Pisa in September.

For the moment, he would not mention it to Anne. He would not rile her after the gift God had given them of her recovery. His wife needed to rest, and he needed to get out into the early spring air to freshen his thoughts.

Leaning over the sill of the open window, he took in a deep breath. April's heady scents beckoned, deciding him instantly on how to avoid further discussion with his wife on Italy.

He would damn Maximilian to hell for the day and go out hunting with Claude.

Glancing over at his eleven-year-old Louis beamed to see her sit so straight on her mount. It was a fine thing to hunt with his daughter. His eldest princess was as malleable as his wife was not. Finally, a moment alone, with his quiet approving Claude at his side, happy to be with him, no matter whether he bagged any prey or not. What a good wife she would make. But would that young bantam cock Francis appreciate her?

Louis doubted his chosen successor would love Claude as tenderly as he did. All the more did he appreciate these moments alone with his daughter, hunting days that filled their souls with joy and their lungs with fresh air.

Falconry was their favorite form of hunt together. His princess was reserved and demure, a natural friend to creatures who sensed they had nothing to fear from her.

Horses quieted down when Claude drew near. Dogs ceased their barking. The smaller merlin falcons used by the ladies were unafraid to come to her, perching on her wrist on the large leather gauntlet she wore that extended up almost the length of her arm.

Neither was Claude afraid of the merlins, although they were fierce birds of prey. It was as if she had an unspoken understanding with dumb creatures. Louis could sense that animals and his daughter communicated in a different way than the noisy demanding types who surrounded them at court.

"Papa, did you see the way Pipette came to me when I called him, but not to you?" she teased, her high silvery voice piercing his heart.

"Minouche, any sensible falcon with sharp eyes would choose to come to you over me," Louis said.

Claude giggled. "But he is your favorite, Papa." She smoothed the merlin's long, pointed wings as it rested on her wrist, the two bells attached to each of its legs jingling as it shifted its weight.

"Apparently, I am not his." Louis hid a smile in his gauntlet.

"Do you think one day Francis will come to me when I call him, even if he is busy with something else?"

"*Ma chère*, if he is wise he will come to you. If not, he will continue what he is doing and miss the magic of your charms." Louis thought sadly that it was more than likely that his dauphin would miss most of Claude's charms. Her allure was as subtle as the pale lilacs and pinks of the budding spring that surrounded them. A cocksure swaggart like Francis would fail to fully appreciate her.

Claude cast him a sideways glance. "Do you think I have charm, Papa?"

Louis' heart swelled. "Minouche, you have the sort of charm that is reserved for the most special of God's creatures."

"Like you?"

"Not like me at all," he disagreed, remembering the bold vitality he had possessed in his younger days. He had dallied with the ladies who had flocked to him, then sidestepped them all, save one. Only Anne had obsessed him, equally as confident as he had been, his match in every way.

"So you don't think you're special, Papa?" Claude cocked

her head with an assessing look that reminded him of her mother.

Louis chuckled. "I do not, Minouche. And that is precisely why I appreciate you."

"What do you mean?" Claude asked. Grasping the purple and scarlet feathers affixed to the top of her merlin's leather hood, she gently pulled it off.

The hunting attendants nudged each other, enjoying this rare glimpse of their king in such fine spirits. Their sovereign was a man of simple tastes: a hard ride, a good day's hunt, a laugh or two with his daughter. When he indulged in his favorite pastime with the princess, it became clear why his subjects called him the father of his people. His enjoyment of pleasures came wrapped in a tender gentility, for which the common people of France adored him.

"I mean that you are one for those who do not seek fame and glory but peace and the comforts of home," Louis explained.

"*Maman* says you seek fame and glory in Italy," Claude said as Pipette cocked a hard eye at Louis.

He felt his face redden. "I seek our ancestral rights there, passed down by my grandmother, your great-grandmother."

"Who was she, Papa?"

"Her name was Valentina Visconti." Louis enjoyed the feel of the rounded syllables of her name on his lips.

Claude's eyes grew big. "What was she like?"

"She was noble, beautiful, and tragic," he described, thinking of his grandmother's portrait, her eyes staring at him each time he viewed it, waiting for him to carry out her wishes. Eyeing his daughter, he wondered if she could understand the insistent drumbeat that drove him to claim Milan. It was a legacy that might be passed down to her one day. But would she want it?

"Was she at all like *Maman*?" Claude asked.

Louis' horse snorted as he choked back laughter. "Not like *Maman, ma chère*. Your mother is not the tragic type."

"*Maman* is more the practical type. Like Francis' mother," Claude observed.

This time, it was Louis who snorted, causing his mount to shake his mane. His *Brette* would explode to hear herself compared with Francis' mother.

Yet Claude had a point. Neither was the tragic type, although both had suffered tragedies. Both women were firmly focused on the here and now, on getting things done, and removing from their paths people and obstacles that stood in their way.

"Minouche, don't repeat that in front of your mother," Louis advised.

"She hates her, doesn't she?" Claude's voice was matter-of-fact.

"Let us say that she does not appreciate her," Louis amended.

"Because they are too much alike." Claude smiled at Pipette.

"My daughter, whatever you do, do not point that out to either of them." Squelching his mirth, his heart swelled at his daughter's perceptiveness.

"But you agree, don't you?" Claude gave him a sideways glance, resembling the bird on her wrist for a moment.

"Minou, remember the secret pact we made in the past?"

Claude's face lit up. "Yes, Papa! How could I forget?"

"Let us make another one."

"What will it be?"

"Let us swear to each other that we will not tell anyone of

the secret between us that we both know how much alike your mother and Francis' mother are."

Claude's eyes twinkled. "It is amusing, isn't it?"

"Amusing secrets are the best ones," Louis told her. He had a few, but they would only remain amusing if they didn't reach his wife's ears.

"How will I know when you are reminding me of this one?"

"Shall I give you a secret signal?"

"Oh, yes, Papa! Like the one we made before when we touch our pinkies?"

Louis nodded. "Like that. But something else."

"What about this?" Claude rubbed her nose.

"A young lady does not rub her nose in front of others," he advised, remembering her mother's words to her of the day before.

"How about this?" Claude tugged her earlobe.

"When you are married, I might not see your earlobe under your headdress." A father's ache plucked at his heartstrings.

"Then what shall we do?"

"What about this?" Louis tented his hands and tapped his index and middle fingers together.

"'Tis like a dance," Claude exclaimed.

"Hunting with you is like a dance for me," Louis said, wishing with all his heart that every day could be like this one, and every evening spent by the fire with his fine *Brette.* Fie on kingship, he thought, until Valentina Visconti's stern eyes flashed before him, reminding him that it was only in his capacity as king that he could claim Milan for France.

"Let's use it," Claude agreed. "The dancing fingers shall mean we are keeping our secret of how much *Maman* and Francis' *maman* are alike."

"It's a very good idea to keep such a secret, Claude."

"Why, Papa?"

"Because either of those ladies would be greatly angered if they discovered you thought that." God's bones, what fun it would be to see.

"Many at court have noted it too." She shot him a merry look.

Louis laughed like the young and gay Duke d' Orléans he had once been.

"Let us not wander there, Claude. It is best not to go abroad in one's private judgments."

"Then we shall keep it between us, but you know it's true."

"What I know to be true is that I will always love you more than anything or anyone else, except for your mother," he declared.

"What about Italy, Papa?"

Louis choked. "What about it?" he tossed back, feeling sweat break out at his temples. No French woman ever asked about Italy without a hidden subtext, invariably negative.

"Do you love me more than Italy?"

Louis balked like a cornered stag. "Did your mother put you up to asking me that?"

"I cannot tell you, Papa." Claude looked as shrewd as her mother for a fleeting instant.

"Why not?"

"Because *Maman* and I have our own secrets." Like fairy dust, her girlish giggle settled over his heart.

"Then you must keep them, as you must keep your secrets with me." How his delicate princess beguiled him with her quiet charms. If only she would stay off the topic of Italy.

"I will do so, Papa, because *Maman* says the first rule of a queen is to guard her secrets."

"And so it is, Claude."

"What is the second rule, then?"

To produce an heir, Louis thought sadly. "I do not know, Claude. You must ask your mother, then let me know."

"She will probably say that it is to protect the king from doing foolish things."

Louis' blood rose. "Does this also have something to do with Italy?" he asked as Claude's falcon fixed him with a baleful stare.

"I will not say, Papa. *Maman* told me I mustn't." Claude sniffed as Pipette fluffed his feathers.

Louis' mount lifted his head and nickered. The horse shook his mane and stopped in his tracks. They had emerged from the forest and stood at the edge of a large meadow, a perfect spot for Pipette to demonstrate his skills.

"Let's hunt," Louis said. Anything to get off the topic of where his womenfolk thought he must stay or go. He loved them both, but nothing could wrest from him his dream of claiming Milan.

"Let's hunt, Pipette," Claude commanded her merlin. Smoothing back his feathers, she straightened her arm, riveting the bird's attention. Tensing, the princess thrust up her arm in a short sharp movement.

With a whir of its powerful wings, the raptor soared heavenward as if to say "Enough of all this talk."

As the bird sought its prey, Claude and her father spurred their horses and galloped across the meadow. With the wind in their faces and the hard fast stride of their mounts, all thoughts of forceful mothers and grandmothers were left behind. Only bliss remained.

Medieval Hunting Illustration
from *Book of the Hunt* by Gaston Phoebus
Courtesy of Google images, public domain

As she leaned over the windowsill, a merry laugh escaped Anne's lips. Catching sight of Claude in the courtyard below, she admired her elder daughter's fine posture as she rode out behind her father for a hawking jaunt. It was wonderful to be rid of them for the day. She couldn't wait to get to the nursery to spend time alone with Renée.

Enjoying the simple pleasures of being able to move about again, Anne stretched as her maid slipped her pale blue gown over her head. Her muscles were reawakening just as the earth was after a long winter's sleep.

Anne hurried to her daughter's quarters, her steps as light as her mood. She looked forward to seeing her babe's expression when she spotted her mother. They had played together every morning since Anne had risen from her sickbed. She wondered if Louise de Savoy had yet heard of her recovery. She would likely be praying that her illness had robbed her of the ability to conceive.

Anne smiled. How Louis' cheeky song had sustained her during her delirium. And how she intended to sustain him once he returned toward sunset. She couldn't wait to feel her next child quicken in her womb. What pleasure it would be to imagine her rival in Amboise's face turn as red as her hair as she raged to hear the queen was again pregnant.

Arriving at the nursery, she held out her arms to her youngest princess.

Renée's face lit up at sight of her mother. "Ba-ba," the babe burbled.

"*Ma petite,*" Anne cooed, taking her from her nurse's arms.

The sturdy babe reached for the glittering stones of Anne's necklace, tugging at the heavy gold collar they were set in.

"Do you like them, my love?"

Renée chuckled, her eyes lighting up.

"You have good taste, Mignon. Like your mother." Anne unclenched her daughter's fist from her necklace and kissed it's irresistibly fat dimpled surface until Renée squealed.

"Put a fur on the floor," she ordered an attendant.

In a moment, a thick mink pelt was spread, and Anne seated herself on it, steadying Renée with her hands as the babe stood, bouncing on her chubby legs.

Laughter filled the room as the six-month-old showed off an array of skills, rolling from side to side, scooting backward, and sitting up. Before Anne could stop her, Renée grabbed the gold-threaded silk cord that Anne wore around her waist and pulled with all her might.

"She is strong-minded, is she not, Your Grace?" Michelle de Saubonne asked.

"Like her mother," Anne declared, delighted to see such spirit in her second daughter. She would need it to hold Brittany off from France's grasp. God knew she must marry Renée to a strong prince to accomplish such an aim.

"Your Grace, let me wipe her mouth before she spittles all over you," an attendant cried, rushing over with a cloth.

Anne waved her away. "She already has, and I am happy for it." She laughed for joy as Renée drooled onto her chest, her milky scent as fragrant as the spring air wafting through the windows.

"She will spoil your dress, Your Grace," the attendant fretted.

"Let her!" Anne exulted, thinking how full of life this daughter was, bolder than Claude, and so like her Charles-Orland. She would keep her close and not travel anywhere without her. How she wished she had done so with her firstborn.

But God had given her another chance. She would embrace the lesson He had so painfully taught her just as she now embraced her burbling babe. Life had been cruel enough already. With spring's arrival, perhaps a season of joy would blot out all the seasons past that had dealt her harsh blows.

Her heart leaped as she hugged her youngest princess to her. This one would be like her. This one would save Brittany from France.

Chapter Eighteen

Summer 1511

Seduction Gone Awry

"Daughter, come quickly."

"What is it, *Maman*?" Marguerite asked.

"Gouffier says he's not well. Can you check what's wrong?"

Marguerite raised a brow at her mother. "Why don't you check yourself?"

"He said only you can help him," Louise urged. "Go see what he needs." If her daughter wasn't going to do her duty by the king, she would ensure that it got done, one way or another. Judging by the joyful hug Marguerite had given her childhood friend upon their arrival the day before, Gouffier de Bonnivet was the man for the job.

Louise watched as Marguerite disappeared down the hallway. Bonnivet was considered to be the most handsome gallant at court. He had held an infatuation for Marguerite for years and she had always been fond of him. If all went well Bonnivet would stir something more than fondness in her daughter's heart in the next hour.

Moving to the window to ensure that Marguerite's husband was not yet back, Louise willed her daughter to allow Bonnivet to do his job. Charles had left after the midday meal to confer with one of his estate stewards saying he would return to sup with his guests. The moment was ripe.

On the journey from Amboise Louise had briefed her son's and Marguerite's longstanding friend on what needed to happen. Bonnivet had laughed heartily, then put his hand over his heart. A Gascon from the south with its traditions of courtly love, his moral code was on the order of Louise's. His reputation as the court's most successful gallant meant he would be determined not to fail his assignment.

Settling down to enjoy a cool mint tisane, Louise was interrupted by the sound of a muffled scream coming from the direction of Bonnivet's room.

An attendant came running. Smoothly, Louise blocked the entryway to the hallway to the guest quarters. "Could you bring more tisane and another cup?" she asked.

"Yes, Madame. I will just see if the mistress needs help."

"I'll check while you get the tisane." She beamed. "Delicious."

"Thank you, Madame. I made it myself." Looking pleased, the attendant gave a short curtsey and took the empty pitcher Louise held out to her.

The moment she left, Louise tiptoed toward the guest quarters to head off any attendants who might interrupt. No more sounds emanated from Bonnivet's room, and she guessed her mission was being accomplished. Marguerite would thank her for it one day, should the outcome prove fruitful.

If she didn't thank her, no matter. The king would thank her for it. Besides, Bonnivet was a good deal more handsome than Charles d'Alençon with far more charm. If a male child ensued, she hoped he would have Bonnivet's personality but resemble his mother.

That night at supper nothing was said, but Louise sensed that Marguerite was upset.

"Out of sorts, my lady?" Charles d'Alençon grunted, barely glancing at his wife.

Eying the dull face of her host, Louise had to agree with Marguerite; her husband had the dynamism of a wooden block.

"Only some indisposition, my lord." Marguerite kept her head down until Charles turned to Bonnivet on his left, apparently uninterested in women's indispositions.

Louise caught the glare Marguerite shot her from across the table as the men conversed. She would get to the bottom of what had happened the next day.

"*Maman*, how dare you set him on me? Are you out of your mind?" Marguerite said the moment the last servant left the room. Charles and Bonnivet had gone out for a morning ride.

Louise de Savoy walked straight up to her daughter. Ripping the book by Erasmus from her hand, she threw it on the table.

"Do you not know that you have something more to accomplish here other than indulging yourself in new learning?" she asked.

"*Maman*, my virtue was attacked! Do you think my honor would allow such an assault?"

"Have done with your precious honor. You are the king's choice to produce an heir to secure Armagnac to the crown and you have yet to do your duty!" Louise snapped. Earlier that morning she had received word that the queen was again pregnant. At least that backcountry prig knew her duty, whether she managed to succeed at it or not. The thought that she might terrified her.

"You cannot force me to produce a child with a man other than my husband just because you wish it to happen!" Marguerite protested.

"You should be wishing it to happen yourself! What else do you have to do around here?"

"I have been improving my mind." Marguerite reached for her book.

"Daughter, you are the most well-educated woman in France. Use your mind to exercise some common sense. You must attend to what needs to be done so you will regain the king's favor."

"I didn't know I was out of favor."

"You will be, soon, if you let the years go by and don't bear fruit."

"My mind bears fruit daily, and I—"

"Forget that fine mind of yours and cultivate a fat belly instead," Louise cut her off. It was exasperating to have a high-minded daughter when one needed to accomplish down-to-earth goals.

"Allow me to manage my own affairs and attend to your own conscience, *Maman*. I will not be mauled by that knave again." Marguerite hugged her book to her chest.

"You have always been fond of him."

"I am less fond of him today as I am less fond of you." Marguerite's gaze was black.

"You will find yourself very lonely here if you don't bear a child," Louise warned.

"I am not lonely, *Maman.* I have my books, and I am close to Charles' mother."

"Pathetic," Louise spat out.

"Disgraceful," Marguerite spat back, slamming shut the door as she left the room with book in hand.

The moment she was gone, Louise sprang into action. Ringing for an attendant, she asked to be conducted to Marguerite's mother-in-law's quarters so she could pay her respects.

She would have a word with Charles' mother, the pious Duchess d'Alençon. Marguerite had alluded to their warm relationship, her only consolation as the second year of her fruitless marriage dragged on. Perhaps the good lady would have more common sense than Marguerite did and she could alert her to her daughter-in-law's need for a special potion or two to encourage conception.

"It is as God wills, and no man shall interfere in such matters," the duchess declared, one hand going to the cross that hung from her neck.

"But, Madame, it is a question of securing your son's succession." Louise balled her fist in the folds of her gown, trying to disguise her impatience. She had no time for pious types. The world offered too much opportunity for her to understand those who did not step up and help God steer their own course.

"As we see with the queen, it is a question that is out of our hands and in the hands of the good Lord alone," Marguerite's mother-in-law replied.

Louise gritted her teeth. Did any of these saintly women, her daughter included, see that the way to get things done was to help the good Lord if He appeared to be otherwise occupied?

Exhaling, she cursed impractical types everywhere. Would that they would cooperate when she was trying to get done what needed to happen. At least the queen managed to get pregnant with the regularity of a rabbit.

"Of course, Madame. I pray that He will soon grace His daughter and mine with a fruitful womb," Louise said, biting the inside of her cheek.

"I, too, will continue to pray for such an event to happen,"

Marguerite's mother-in-law agreed, her mouth set in a prim line.

Louise hated that look. It reminded her of the queen.

"Thank you, I'm sure that will help," she lied. Before she left she would have another word with Marguerite to shake her from her virtuous slumber.

Rising, she curtsied to the duchess, crossing her off her list of helpers for all times.

Another idea came to her as she went to find her daughter. The next time she visited she would bring Gaston de Foix. Marguerite worshipped the king's nephew. Perhaps she might find something else to do with him, too, given the chance.

Trying to imagine how it might come about, she wracked her brain. Gaston was as virtuous in act and as pure in spirit as her daughter was. For years she had noted how similar they were, both putting each other on a pedestal amongst their circle of friends. Both fanned the flame of courtly and knightly honor they admired in each other.

Louise sighed. Nothing would get done at all should she bring them together. She would take Bonnivet over Gaston any day. But not her high-minded daughter.

Gritting her teeth, she thought of the King and Queen. Marguerite and Gaston both reminded her of them, stuck on their high ideals, not recognizing they were getting in the way of where they needed to go. Privately, she doubted that Louis would last much longer in Italy. With his chivalric heart, he was too mired in the mud on his high horse to have a clue as to how to manage over there.

As for the queen, if Louise had been in her place, she would have made arrangements long ago for a healthy newborn male to be substituted for the latest one she lost, then present him to her husband as his heir. The rich Breton royal could have paid off any number of women to accomplish such a task. She wouldn't be the first queen to do so, either. But, of course, she wouldn't, being such a pious bore she would think God would strike her down to consider such a thing.

Sniggering to herself, Louise went to arrange for their departure. She and Bonnivet would share a joke or two on their way back to Amboise. And she looked forward to seeing Jean upon her return. He was a man as practical as herself: there when she needed him, out of her way when she didn't. How lucky she was to have him as a companion yet not as a husband, lording himself over her.

Fed up with virtuous types, Louise pocketed a handful of candied almonds from a silver bowl on the sidetable to eat on the journey back. They could all waste their time praying their way to Heaven while she reaped the bounty of her efforts right here on Earth.

Chapter Nineteen

Summer–Fall 1511

Tensions with the Pope

As 1511 progressed so did Louis' conflict with the pope. When her husband sent out a call in May for an ecclesiastical council to be convened in Pisa in September, Anne balked. Saying nothing on the day the invitations went out, she waited until they were alone that evening.

"Only the pope can call a council of the Church, Husband. What are you thinking?"

"To have Julius deposed." Louis sat back on the low couch in her chambers. Swinging one long leg over the other he looked as unconcerned as a newborn calf.

"You know he will excommunicate you if you do any such thing." She glared at the man she had lost her heart to since childhood. He was not getting her soul, too.

"That is as it is," Louis said. "It is time for the Church in France to have the power to appoint its own bishops, not for the pope to hand out favors to his bastard children and their families."

"Oh, Louis, what a good case you make," she volleyed back. "Except that everyone can see that this is all about France wishing to curb the pope's power in Italy so that it may enlarge its own."

Louis looked miffed. "And what is so wrong with that?"

"What is so wrong with it is that you will make a mortal enemy of every other power in Europe by doing so," Anne spelled out.

"The Holy Roman Emperor and I have already agreed to this council. He will send envoys to Pisa to join me in calling to depose the pope."

"Friends today, foes tomorrow. How many times must you relearn the same lesson?" Anne tossed down her unpinned headdress, fluffing her hair and enjoying the delicious sensation of freedom from its heavy weight. "If the pope is deposed and France gains more territory in Italy, you will enrage Maximilian, Ferdinand, and the Venetians. They will ally against you as they did two years ago, and who knows? Henry in England may join their game. I'm sure he'll be invited."

"Nonsense. They are all as sick of Julius as I am. We will make a sensible division of Italy and get a pope elected who stays out of politics."

"If you depose the pope, you open the door to being deposed yourself," Anne warned.

"The pope is corrupt and deserves to be thrown out of office."

"Any prince or cardinal who supplants his authority sets a precedent that could result in his own authority being overthrown one day. You must not think to do such a thing, Louis."

"My lady, you must do as your conscience bids as I must do as mine does."

"Wise words, Husband, and so I shall. You can be sure that I will pray for your soul, that it will not be put in mortal danger by breaking with the Church."

"*Ma Brette*, could you concern yourself with caring for my body and let me take care of my soul?"

"I will do no such thing. Your eye is on earthly aims in Italy, but mine is on your heavenly standing."

Louis reached out and took a lock of her wavy hair in his fingers. "Do you think you will need me so badly up there?"

"I will need you as surely as you will need me." She put her hands on Louis' shoulders, kneading them. "What would you do without me? And what will your people do without their Church?"

"My lady, one question at a time. Leave the latter for me to answer to. And as to the former ..."

Anne studied him from under her lashes, fighting with her will to continue arguing versus more immediate concerns. He looked ready to end the discussion. If he touched her hair again, she would be ready, too.

"I would be lost without you," he finished, his fingers running through her hair.

"Then give over." She squeezed his shoulders, shivering at the feel of his long fingers massaging her scalp. Perhaps she would take her own advice. For the moment.

"I am your king." He scowled at her.

"You are my Louis." She ignored his scowl. How well she knew and loved him. He must not lose his place in Heaven beside her.

"I am your Louis and you are my *Brette*." He made a fierce face.

"I am your wife and queen," she shot back with the hauteur she knew slayed him.

"You are my scourge," he complained.

"I am your conscience."

"I have my own."

"There are times when it needs wakening." Anne put her hand on his chest.

"It's fully awake now." He narrowed his eyes, his fingers finding the back of her neck.

"Then I have a job for you." She would work on his conscience another time.

"Really?"

"Really." Anne raked her nails down his back.

Louis groaned like steam escaping a pot whose lid has just come off.

Outside the queen's rooms, the guards exchanged amused looks. They had heard it all before. The King and Queen would not reappear until the following morning, refreshed and back in each other's good graces.

"Do you know what they were going at it about?" the first sentry asked.

"Something about the Church being here rather than there."

"Do you think the king really cares about where the Church is?"

The second sentry rolled his eyes. "He cares about enlarging his piece of Italy. And the only way to do that is to get the pope off the throne."

"Will the king get excommunicated?"

"Not just the king. All of us." The man looked grim.

"What do you mean?"

"It means we won't be able to take the sacraments. Or, if we do, it won't count for anything."

The first sentry mused for a moment. "It wouldn't bother me, but my wife wouldn't like it."

"That's about the shape of the argument they were having."

"What about Heaven?"

"What about it?"

"Any chance for us if the king gets us excommunicated?"

"Not much chance for you with or without the pope cutting us off," the second sentry jested.

His partner kicked his ankle. "Would he really do that?"

"If the king tries to depose him, he would."

"But wouldn't the king just appoint his own pope?"

"He would, but how would we know if that's the real one?"

"It would be the real one according to our king."

"But what about according to Our Lord?"

"I don't know. I'll ask my wife."

"And she'll know something that you don't?"

The first sentry snorted. "She'll be sure to have an opinion. She always does."

"Mine too." The sentries clapped hands over their mouths to squelch their guffaws.

Upon receipt of Louis' invitation consternation ensued amongst Europe's princes.

The invitation to the Conciliabulum of the Church, to be held in Pisa on the first of September 1511, was issued in the name of Louis XII of France, Maximilian I of the Holy Roman Empire, and nine cardinals of the Church, five of whom had left Rome for Milan in protest of Pope Julius's policies. The pope was duly invited, although all knew the council's intent was to depose him.

Within weeks, Julius II sent out word that anyone attending the Conciliabulum of Pisa would be excommunicated, and the city in which it was held put under papal interdict.

As a result, many invitees feared to attend.

Ferdinand II did not reply. Catholic Spain was not of a mind to break with the Church in Rome; not while Ferdinand needed Julius II's investiture as ruler of Naples.

Margaret of Austria sent word that no clergy from the Low Countries would attend as a Church council could only be convened by the pope. It was a point with which Anne wholeheartedly agreed.

As the first of September loomed, the city fathers of Pisa let it be known that they did not wish to host the meeting, fearing interdiction.

Anne feared for Louis' mortal soul. She feared for another soul, too. One that would be a French subject and would not receive benefit of baptism should France be under interdiction.

She was again pregnant. Hope glimmered within her at the thought that she had delivered three children who had lived beyond just days or weeks after birth. But with her weakened constitution, she would need every resource at her disposal, both temporal and spiritual, to bring another healthy child into the world.

Reaching out to her confessor, Anne unburdened her dilemma.

"Father, I am caught between my husband and my duty. What should I do?"

"You must do as your conscience bids you, my daughter," Father Mayheuc counseled.

"My conscience tells me not to put my subjects at risk of interdiction. But my husband will look grimly on me not supporting his council."

"My daughter, you must ask yourself where your true duty lies then uphold it."

"I uphold the authority of the Church. And the pope is at its head."

"Then follow your conscience and do what you need to do for the good of your subjects."

"I don't want them denied the sacraments, Father. Not to be baptized or married, or to receive Christian burial would be a terrible burden on them, all because the King of France pursues a personal fight with the present pope." For a moment she forgot she was married to Louis. She would sooner die than turn her back on the needs of her subjects.

"My daughter, this moment shall pass as all things pass, including all mortal souls."

"Do you speak of the passing of this present pope to solve this problem?"

"I speak of the passing of all things and all souls."

"I do not wish for the souls of my subjects to pass without benefit of the holy sacraments."

"Then do not be a part of denying them such comfort."

"Thank you, Father," she said, thinking of the practical gem he had dropped into her lap. It was the same point she had thought of herself. The pope would die one day soon, resolving Louis' conflict with him. But while God saw fit to keep him alive on Earth, she would submit to his authority.

Through her archbishop, she wrote to Julius II to assure him that no subject of Brittany would attend any ecclesiastical convocation outside the aegis of the Church. Knowing her support would put His Holiness in a benevolent frame of mind, she asked for his prayers for the safe delivery of an heir to the French throne.

The pope answered Anne's missive in October. He wrote that he prayed for a healthy male prince for her and asked her to use her influence on her husband to disband his schismatic council. The message was clear: God would hear the prayers of Christ's foremost representative on earth for the prince she sought if the King of France would drop his illegal council.

But Louis' course was set. On November first, the convocation began with only four cardinals and sixteen bishops in attendance. The Pisans, uneasy in the face of papal interdict, refused the attendees use of their main cathedral.

Within the first week, hostilities were exchanged between

French soldiers accompanying the French attendees and the townspeople of Pisa.

By November 12, Louis decided to change the council's location to Milan, under French rule. The move proved too strong a Gallic seasoning for most of Europe's princes.

It was the party to which no one came. As usual, the Holy Roman Emperor waffled. He sent envoys to the Conciliabulum, but Louis' spies informed him that the emperor was also in secret talks with the pope. Hedging his bets, Maximilian was not to be trusted.

Five days later, Louis received word that Spain and England had signed a treaty declaring their intent to defend the Church. They would not support any new pope chosen by the Conciliabulum but would send envoys to the new general council that Julius II had proposed to counter Louis and Maximilian's one.

To Louis' further dismay, the English-Spanish treaty also included the promise of the English to join Spain in an invasion of Gascony on France's southern border the following spring. The dispute was over areas that Ferdinand claimed belonged to Spain, and the House of Albret, which ruled Gascony, claimed for France.

Suddenly, Louis had enemies on two fronts: those in Italy who wished the French out of Milan, and the Spanish and English threatening to invade France on its border with Spain. If he was to regain Milan and expand French dominions south to Rome, he must move fast before Ferdinand and Henry VIII joined forces that would splinter his military resources in two.

Louis decided to play his newest trump card in Italy: his nephew, Gaston de Foix. Eager to take a chance on fresh blood leading his troops against the pope, he had appointed Gaston in August 1511 as governor of Milan and commander of the French army in Italy.

With the daring of Cesare Borgia but the character of a

valiant chevalier, Gaston was beginning to shape up as one of France's finest young knights. His nephew's nickname as a boy had been "the fortunate child." How fortunate Gaston de Foix would prove to be lay just months ahead, once Alpine snows melted and Louis could make his move.

By the start of Advent, Anne was heavy with child. When Louis blocked her archbishop from receiving his episcopal revenues, she confronted him.

"You have no right to seize Brittany's ecclesiastical revenues," she complained as she waved her archbishop's last letter to her, protesting the King of France's action.

"They are illegal since the pope's actions are illegal." The deep furrows lining each side of Louis' face from nose to mouth looked set in stone.

"But it was you who supported Robert de Guibé to become a cardinal of Rome. He has been a firm friend to us. Now, do you punish him?"

"He has been a firm friend to you, not to me." Louis' tone was nuanced.

"Why do you say that?" Anne challenged him.

Louis' eyes held a warning in them. "You know why."

"Because he is conscientious in carrying out his duties?" *And carrying my missives to Rome,* she thought, hoping Louis was unaware of this. It was within her rights as head of state to correspond with the head of the Church. But that wouldn't stop Louis from being furious to learn of it.

"Because he is not at my Conciliabulum, for one," Louis declared.

"Because I have forbidden him to attend," Anne stated flatly.

"And have you let Julius know?"

Anne eyed him, wondering what he knew. "It is none of your concern whether I have or haven't."

"Of course, it's my concern. Especially if you take the pope's side against me," Louis snapped.

Anne rapped the table with both hands. "It is not the pope's side I take. It is the Church's side, the Holy Mother Church that has existed since Our Lord asked Peter to head it."

"I am not trying to break with the Church but with Julius."

"They are one and the same."

"They are not the same, and I have sent word to Rome that all episcopal revenues are to be blocked until a determination is made on a new pope," Louis said.

"By whose authority do you decide to elect a new pope, Husband? Only the Church itself can elect its head, not some prince's idea of a council," Anne argued.

Louis looked ready to explode. "Am I just some prince to you, then?"

"Not to me, Louis. But in the Church's eyes, yes!" she hurled back.

"Madame, you vex me like no other," Louis spat out, then spun on his heels.

As he strode from the room, he knocked over a Venetian glass goblet from the wedding set she had given him twelve years earlier.

Anne stared at the jagged glass shards scattered across the floor, stifling the sob that rose in her throat. They had argued before, but never like this.

Chapter Twenty

January 1512

Hope for a Special Child

At odds with Louis and big with child, Anne threw herself into finding a match for Cook's daughter. A project that kept her mind off Louis' fight with the pope was just what she needed during her final weeks of pregnancy.

Bidding Cook to a private audience, Anne patted her stomach, feeling for the head of her unborn child as the big Breton woman arrived breathless from the kitchen.

"Your Grace, are you well? They bid me to come see you but wouldn't say why," she burst out as she rose from an awkward curtsey.

"I am well, and they did not say because I did not tell them," Anne greeted her, noting that Cook was no longer young. Her knees did not cooperate well with royal protocol, for which Anne forgave her.

"Ah, Your Grace, then I hope it's good news. I am too old to manage any more bad."

"Shall I tell you directly or would you like to guess?"

"I am too old for guessing, as well, my lady. I might guess wrong and offend you."

"Cook, you will never offend me because you are too dear to me," Anne said. "But if anyone were to do so, you would be the only one I would forgive."

Cook's eyes twinkled. "Oh, my lady, don't try me on that one. You might be hard put to hold to your word."

Anne shot her a merry look. "I have heard that your temper when things go wrong in the kitchen is as fierce as mine, so I will tiptoe around you."

"Your Grace, you have never tiptoed around anyone, not even as a young girl. The only tiptoeing I've seen you do is when you walk so nicely without your special shoe."

"So you know about my shoe." Anne shifted in her chair. Since the age of two, she had worn a built-up shoe to correct the difference in length between her legs, the left one slightly shorter than the right. Claude had inherited her limp, but fortunately not Renée.

"Your Grace, there is not much that those who serve in the kitchen don't know."

"Then do you know who it is I have a mind to marry your daughter to?"

Cook's eyes widened. "You know of my daughter, Your Grace?"

"I know of her, but I'd like to hear more."

Cook's throat contracted. "She is a special girl, my lady."

"How old is she, Cook?"

"My Bonne is twenty, Your Grace. As fine and pretty as I never was."

"Then she must take after her father."

"God rot his soul, I should hope not," the Breton woman burst out.

"Now that is a tale for another day, but tell me, why is she not yet married?" Anne asked.

"Your Grace, it is hard … it is hard for me to say," Cook spluttered, looking down at the floor.

"Nothing is hard for you to say, Cook, so it must be hard indeed." Anne wondered to see her sturdy countrywoman at a loss for words.

Cook nodded, mute.

"Is she touched, then?" Anne asked softly.

"She was born as bright as a silver coin, but she … she had an accident when she was young." Cook looked from the floor to the wall.

"What accident, Cook? You may tell me."

"I do not wish to speak ill of people, Your Grace. 'Tis a waste of time," Cook hedged.

"So what befell her was at the hands of another?"

"God rot him, Your Grace. God rot his bones in hell where he now lives."

"Do you speak of her father, then?"

Cook remained silent, her eyes averted. "I will speak no more, my lady, as there's nothing good to say."

"Let us say no more of him, but what of her?"

"Your Grace, she is a sweet and good girl. Her heart is golden, but her head is not always able to hold a thought."

"She will need a patient husband to appreciate her."

"A kind one, Your Grace." Cook's voice trembled.

Anne pondered a moment. "Does your daughter come to the castle at times?"

"No, my lady. She stays in my cottage on the edge of town and looks after my mother."

"Can she walk?" Anne kept her tone light, sensing Cook's distress.

"Oh yes, my lady." Cook nodded, finally meeting her eyes.

"Then bid her come to me tomorrow after the midday meal."

"She may lose her way, Your Grace. I'll be busy in the kitchen and won't be able to fetch her."

"I shall arrange to have the man I propose for her fetch her."

"Your Grace, who may that be?" Cook clasped her hands in front of her apron, her gaze anxious.

"I am thinking of a match between her and Sire Brunet."

Cook's eyes goggled. "You don't mean the stablemaster, do you?"

"I do."

"That would be a fine step up for my girl, Your Grace, but would he have her?"

"He will be sweetened after I let him know her dowry is to be one thousand livres with an annuity of six hundred settled on her for life."

"My lady, I cannot believe my ears!"

"Do you tell me you don't believe me? Now you have offended me," Anne jested.

"Your Grace, I am grateful beyond words if I have heard you rightly."

"A one thousand livre dowry, six hundred yearly to remain with her whatever happens to him. What do you think, Cook? Will Sire Brunet be interested to ask you for your daughter's hand?"

"That's an offer a man would be hard put to refuse."

"And what about your girl? Might she refuse it?"

Cook smiled broadly. "Not if she listens to her mother."

"I want her settled well so she can take care of you when you tire of bossing the kitchen staff around."

"I'll never tire of serving you, Your Grace. You know that."

"Your desire may not tire, but your body will one day." God knew she herself was feeling her body tire more easily at age thirty-four, but perhaps it was only due to being in the final months of pregnancy.

"Your Grace, I am speechless."

"'Tis unlike you, Cook. Your job is to speak your mind, and you do it well. Go take the rest of the day and ask Bonne if she is willing to marry."

"You can be sure she will be after I talk to her."

"Then let us see how Sire Brunet squires her tomorrow afternoon before I speak to him about her."

"Your Grace, I would rather have her stay with me all my days than see her in the hands of a man unkind to her," the Breton woman exclaimed.

"I agree, Cook. That is why we shall watch carefully to see where Sire Brunet's heart leads him when he finds she is touched by God."

"She was as perfect as a dewdrop until she was touched by the devil who sired her." Cook swallowed a sob, but Anne heard it.

"Let us not speak of the devil, but let us see how they take to each other. If Sire Brunet is impatient and scorns her, we shall find another," she said.

"Or none at all, Your Grace. Far better none at all than another who would do violence to her."

"We will find a match for her, Cook. You cannot live forever, and she needs someone to look after her when you are gone."

"Truth to that, Your Grace." Cook's sigh echoed with untold years of motherly cares.

"Leave it to me, Cook. Go and tell her to be ready tomorrow midday."

It had been a surprise to receive the queen's summons the day before to escort Cook's daughter to the castle. He had a long list of things to do and he worked for the king, not the queen. Yet he was happy to do it; Queen Anne was generous to all who served her.

Luc Brunet was head steward of the king's stables. At age thirty-five, he was a widower. Two years earlier, his wife had died in childbirth, his stillborn daughter laid to rest alongside her.

Thoughts of remarriage had crossed his mind, but the royal stables of Blois Castle were large and managing them consumed all of his energies. Plus, he was a commoner, and although the ladies of the court would cast an eye on him here and there, he knew the queen would not hear of it for one of her own to marry beneath her rank.

Hurrying along the path, he wondered why the queen had summoned Cook's daughter to the castle. Perhaps she was to be asked to serve there. It was the first he had heard that Cook had a daughter at all. No one ever spoke of her as having any family other than a distant kinsman who worked in the laundry room and an old mother stashed away somewhere.

Arriving at the door of the small timbered cottage on the edge of town, he knocked. In a moment the door opened, and as it did a rabbit darted out, followed by a young woman.

"Minou!" she called in a small, high voice.

The rabbit scampered into the woods as the maiden turned to him. Her hair was bright as wheat and her eyes hazel. All he could think of was gold as she curtseyed to him.

"Good day, Monsieur." Her voice was like a child's. But her body, when she rose, was not. Ripe as a late-September wheat field she stood staring at him, her eyes wide and guileless, unlike the eyes of any woman at court.

"Good day, Mademoiselle. I am Brunet, sent by the queen to escort you to the castle."

"I am Bonne. And my rabbit is Minou." She turned to look for the creature, and as she did he caught sight of the curve of her hip under her dark green kirtle.

"Come, Minou! Come back!" she called as she sat on a stump in the garden.

"Mademoiselle, the queen awaits you," Brunet said.

"He will come soon. You'll see," the young woman bade him calmly.

"As you wish, my lady." Brunet moved to the low stone wall that marked the borders of the cottage garden and sat. He wondered that the maiden did not concern herself that she was keeping the Queen of France waiting. Nonetheless, he would give Cook's daughter her moment.

They sat in companionable silence, the early November day not too chill. As they waited, the young woman began to hum as freely and naturally as if she were alone.

He was reminded of horse handlers he had worked with to break in the colts and foals of the royal stables. They all had their own unique tune or whistle that they would use to calm their jittery subjects. Every one of them had been quiet types, not given to conversation, with one foot in this world and the other in a hidden one.

The maiden stopped her tune and remained motionless.

Brunet felt himself relax. She wasn't watching him watch her as most women did. Her artlessness stirred him with conflicting desires: an instinct to protect her and an equally strong one to learn more about her.

The whir of a sudden movement jolted him. The rabbit had reappeared and hopped to Bonne's feet. As she picked it up and placed it in her lap, Brunet felt as if time fell away and all that was left was the tableau before him. In that moment he understood why unicorns only put their heads in the laps of maidens. Such innocence recognized its own.

"He is back, my lady, just as you said. And now we must be on our way," he ventured, sorry to disturb such a beguiling scene.

"Minou is not a he. She is a girl, and soon to be a mother."

"My mistake, Mademoiselle. Such a pretty rabbit I should have known was a girl," he said, thinking the woman before him seemed like a girl but looked old enough to be a young mother. The combination of both hit him hard as he thought of his dead wife and daughter.

"I will put her in the house and then we can go." She

disappeared into the cottage, then reappeared wearing a drab brown mantle.

As they made their way up the path, all he could think was that he should like to see the young woman in a green fur-trimmed one like the mantle his wife had once worn. It would match the maiden's gown and bring out the green of her hazel eyes.

Some might say they were vacant. But he had worked around animals and those who trained them for years. Her eyes were not vacant, they were just focused on something different from most other people's eyes. He wished he could know what it was.

"What did you notice, Francis?" Anne asked.

Francis de Bourdeille looked puzzled. "What do you mean, Your Grace?"

"What happened when Sire Brunet met Cook's daughter?" she spelled out. She had asked her page the day before to follow the stablemaster on the sly and watch him escort Cook's daughter to the castle.

"Nothing much happened, Your Grace. Except that …"

"Except what?"

"Except that Sire Brunet was very quiet."

"In a good way?" Anne dug in. "Or bad ?"

"What do you mean, Your Grace?"

"Was he quiet because he was bored or quiet in the way men are when a pretty maid walks by?"

Francis colored, looking as if he had gone quiet on such latter occasions too. "Ah, Your Grace, I know what you mean."

"I'm sure you do, Francis, as you are getting to be a very grown up young man these days."

The page's chest puffed out. "It was that, Your Grace. He didn't look bored at all, just struck dumb, you could say."

Anne chuckled to herself. "Did you notice anything about the demoiselle?"

"She had a tame rabbit that hopped away the minute he arrived."

Anne's heart danced to think of the charm of such a scene. "And?"

"She was quiet and didn't chatter like most demoiselles."

"Was Sire Brunet kind to her?"

Francis thought a moment. "I think so. He was patient while she waited for her rabbit to come back."

"Did he escort her nicely or did he hurry her?"

"Neither seemed in a hurry, Your Grace. They walked slowly and said little."

Anne smiled. "You may go now, and tell your friend Jean to do the same job for me tomorrow at the same time."

"What is the job, Your Grace? I wasn't sure what it was you wanted me to do."

"You have done it, Francis. Now go tell Jean to do the same tomorrow, and make sure Sire Brunet does not catch sight of him. He is then to report to me afterward."

The next day toward late afternoon, Anne's other head page presented himself to her.

"How did she seem to you, Jean?"

"Your Grace, she is touched, like Sire Brunet's stable boy who waters the horses."

"Is Sire Brunet kind to the stable boy?"

"Very kind, my lady. He has a good word for him whenever he's near and smacks anyone who treats him roughly."

"And was Sire Brunet kind to the maiden?"

"Your Grace, he seemed happy to see her and ..." He hesitated.

Anne caught him in her gaze. "And what?"

"And he brought her a gift."

Like a flame, her interest flared. "A gift, Jean? What was it?"

"My lady, it was a mantle with fur trim. Green, like her kirtle."

"And what did she do with it?"

"She took off her own and put it on straightaway. Then they came up the path."

"Did you notice anything else?"

"There was nothing to notice, Your Grace. They were both very quiet."

"A good sign." Anne crossed her hands over her belly, thinking of meeting Louis as a young man of twenty-one. For the first few days of his visit, she had been struck dumb every time she caught sight of him.

"What was it a sign of, Your Grace?"

She gave him a tender smile. "You will know one day."

"I think I know now, my lady."

Her mouth twitched in merriment. "Go on."

"Something was brewing and words would have spoiled it."

A laugh burbled out of her. "Remember that for the future, Jean."

"Remember to keep quiet if something is brewing?"

Anne's eyes danced. "Remember to bring a gift, too."

On January 4, 1512, Louis' Conciliabulum announced formal steps to depose Julius II based on various charges. Anne was horrified to learn that the charge of sodomy was amongst them.

"Husband, what are you thinking?" she stormed as she caught Louis heading out to the stables.

"I am thinking to go riding, wife. Is there something you

would say to me?" Louis' eyes widened in false innocence. Anne knew the look well.

"Louis, what can you be thinking to charge the pope with such horrendous crimes just before I am to give birth?'

"What does my business with the pope have to do with your lying-in, wife?" His tone hardened faster than it had in previous arguments.

"Louis, do you not realize that the pope will excommunicate you for making such charges against him?"

"Wife, do you not realize that it is men's business to tend to affairs of the Church, and the Church itself teaches that women should stay out of them?" he retorted.

"This is no affair of the Church, Louis, but of you and the pope over land!" Anne cried.

"The pope harasses me with temporal affairs that are not his domain; I will harass him back with spiritual ones."

"Which are not your domain, either! Oh, Louis, don't you see that the life of our child is at stake if you continue to provoke him?" If only she could tell him the pope had sent his prayers for her to bear a son if she succeeded in getting him to drop his schismatic council. But Louis would explode to hear of her communications with his enemy.

"Madame, I do not see such a thing at all, but I see you in a rage that is not good for the health of your child."

"Sodomy, Louis! Of all things. What were you thinking?"

"I am thinking to sweep this scourge from Rome, and I will do whatever I can to see him gone."

"Even at the risk of losing your unborn child?"

"My lady, the pope's crimes have nothing to do with our unborn child. But you must calm yourself to protect the babe's health."

"How can I calm myself when I see no understanding on your face?"

"Then I will remove my face from your sight and bid you a more pleasant day without me in it." Louis stormed off, his angry steps echoing through the cold stone corridor.

Behind him, Anne hugged her belly, distraught. The man she was bearing this child for, to give him an heir, was putting her in an impossible position. Either she supported him in his war with the pope or she protected the hope of salvation of the subjects of her realm and of her unborn child.

She loved Louis, but at that moment she hated him more.

CHAPTER TWENTY-ONE

January 1512

January Twenty-one

Back in Amboise, Louise de Savoy opened the desk drawer where she had hidden her charms. With a low laugh, she congratulated herself for having made sure her contact delivered the especially shocking news of the sodomy charge the king had leveled against the pope. She could imagine how upset the pious queen must have been to hear of such a charge when she should remain as calm as possible before the birth of her child.

May my Caesar's exaltation not be impeded, she prayed before the charms. *May she bear another princess or no life at all,* she continued. It was paramount that the queen not produce a male child that lived. She had worked too hard for all her plans to be shattered by the birth of a prince who would replace Francis as dauphin.

Carefully, she turned over the charm that represented the queen's unborn child. Covering it with the sac in which it had come, she pressed it over what she imagined as the child's head. The queen was prolific at delivering princes. But only one had lived for any length of time. Let that long-dead prince be Anne of Brittany's last one.

For the first time in her life, Anne found herself in the position of having two healthy living children and about to deliver a third. Her youngest was now over a year old. Renée of France had passed the first-year mark before which babes so easily succumbed. The royal toddler was hearty and thriving, having taken her first steps toward the start of Advent.

One week before Anne's thirty-fifth birthday, the babe dropped. Anne was intent on every precaution being taken for the birth of a healthy prince. Margaret of Austria had written from Flanders, wishing her a safe delivery and letting her know that her ambassador had reported in September that the babe she carried was certain to be a son.

"Certain! Pah! What certainty is there in childbirth other than the certainty of pain?" Anne exclaimed. Yet she took comfort in Margaret's letter.

The morning of January 21 was a sunny and cold one, with a bite to the air that kept most members of the royal court indoors. Anne had lost two princes on that date: one in 1503, the second in 1508. Pushing away her thoughts, she went to the nursery to visit Renée and confer with her governess on the princess' progress.

Standing in the doorway of Renée's bedchamber, she smiled as her sturdy toddler lurched toward her, ready to tumble at any moment.

"*Maman*!" Renée called out, collapsing onto her chubby behind.

Anne laughed, then lumbered into the room. Madame de Saubonne pulled up a chair and she sat with a resounding thud. The final weeks of pregnancy were exhausting. The only thing good about them were the frequent movements that told her the child she carried still lived.

Claude came into the room, the petite twelve-year-old as devoted to her little sister as she was to both her parents.

"Lady Mother, how fare you?" Claude asked, dropping a curtsey. A more delicate version of her mother, she was more like a fairy sprite than the sturdy girl that her little sister showed promise of becoming.

"Fed up and ready to unload this prince," Anne told her with a groan.

Claude giggled. "How do you know it's a prince, *Maman,* and not a princess?"

"Because I do, *ma chère*. It is a mother's instinct, and I have used mine many times already to guess correctly." *And to guess the outcome, too,* she thought as her stomach lurched. *But things will be different this time.*

"But, *Maman*, what if you are wrong and it is a girl who arrives?" Claude persisted.

She gave her daughter a joyful smile, feeling anything but joyful at such an outcome. "Then I shall have another princess for whom to make a match with one of the finest princes in Europe."

"To a king, *Maman*?"

"Why not an emperor?" Was it not time to unite one of her children with the House of Habsburg—either Charles of Habsburg or his younger brother Ferdinand? Not only would it provide Brittany with an ally to fend off France, but it would end the ceaseless struggle between Louis and Maximilian.

"*Maman,* shall Renée marry an emperor then, if I am to marry Francis?"

Behind her, Anne could hear Madame de Saubonne's chuckle.

Anne turned to her before answering her daughter. "What do you think, Madame? Can you instruct your charge in the duties and bearing of a future empress?"

"I will try, Your Grace. Already she is showing signs of wishing to take the lead." At that, the governess broke off and ran to Renée, who was about to collide with a table corner.

Anne laughed, then felt her stomach lurch again. Shifting her weight, she put out her hand to her younger daughter.

Renée held out both arms to be picked up. As Anne reached down, she felt the same strange sensation of the moment before. Gesturing to Madame de Saubonne, she pointed to Renée.

"Put her in my lap," she told her.

Madame de Saubonne lifted the toddler onto her mother's lap, where the fifteen-month-old cooed and gurgled, tugging at her necklace and grasping a lock of hair that had escaped Anne's headdress.

Claude came to her side and wiped her little sister's nose with a linen cloth. Already she showed signs of being a good mother.

Anne's heart beat faster as she tried to envision her two daughters with a new sibling to play with. She told herself she was capable of producing a healthy prince, the image of her sturdy Charles-Orland toddling to her on legs as chubby as Renée's.

She batted the vision away. If she had known then what she knew now, she would have kept him closer to her than Louise de Savoy did her precious Caesar.

A sudden twinge in her womb chased all further thoughts from her head.

"Take her," she ordered Madame de Saubonne.

Renée's governess lifted the girl from the queen's arms. "Are you well, Your Grace?"

Anne sat back, closing her eyes. "I am fine. But something is …"

"Your Grace, shall I call your ladies?" Madame de Saubonne's voice held a note of alarm.

Madame de Dampierre stepped forward. "Your Grace, shall we return to your quarters?"

Anne nodded, mute. God forbid that the babe was coming. She begged him to choose any other day than this one, the same cursed day of the year she had lost two princes before.

With Madame de Dampierre taking one arm and Madame de Saubonne the other, they lifted her from her chair and steered her toward the door.

"*Maman*!" Renée cried behind them, held tight by her older sister.

"*Maman* will come later, *Princesse.* Wait for a moment, and I will be back," Madame de Saubonne called to her.

Anne gave Claude a faint smile. "My sweet."

"*Maman*," Claude bleated, anguish shading her tone. She had been eight when her mother had delivered her last stillborn prince, old enough to feel her mother's heartbreak.

"You know what to pray," Anne bid her.

"I will pray it, *Maman*. With all my heart."

Anne turned and left the nursery. In the corridor, she shook off her two ladies. "I'm fine, it was nothing."

"I'm sure it was, Your Grace." Behind her, Madame de Dampierre exchanged glances with Michelle de Saubonne. Both of them had been with the queen through many of her pregnancies. Nothing was always something at this stage.

Back in her chambers, Anne felt restless. Refusing to lie down, she paced, moving around the room straightening and arranging. If only it wasn't the dead of winter she would throw on a cloak and take the sun on a walk in the gardens.

Madame de Dampierre conferred with Madame de la Seneschale. "She said she was fine, but something is …"

"She said something is what?"

"She didn't answer, just drifted off."

Madame de la Seneschale's brows knit together. "When does she ever drift off?"

"That's what I'm wondering."

Madame de de la Seneschale shook her head. "It's not like her."

"I think it's coming."

"Would that it not be today of all days," Madame de la Seneschale whispered.

Madame de Dampierre nodded, her face grim. "Shall I have the midwife called?"

"Let's just keep her occupied. No need to call the midwife unless her water breaks."

"Ahh," the queen's voice fluttered behind them.

Rushing to her, they both caught hold of an arm.

"What is it, Your Grace?" Madame de la Seneschale asked.

"Put some linens on my bed so I can lie down," the queen ordered.

"The bed is fully made, Your Grace. Come," Madame de Dampierre urged.

"Put old linens on top," the queen insisted.

"Your Grace?"

The queen pointed to the floor.

Looking down, the two ladies-in-waiting saw a pool of liquid at their sovereign's feet.

That afternoon the Queen of France's contractions began. By evening, she was in labor, her shrieks resounding through the castle—each one causing the king to nervously tap the sides of his thighs, begging God to grant them a son.

One who lived.

Louis tried to remain calm, but it was no use. He was father of his people, father of his princesses, and now he wanted a chance to be father of a son. A living breathing boy who smiled, cried, and made trouble for him when he wasn't making him proud. Not a dead son, like the three his wife had borne him or the one he had accidentally created long ago when he had fought for Brittany in 1488 in the Mad War against the French.

He had dallied with one of the camp followers, a *fille de joie*, who had borne him a son the following year. She had sent word that she had named the boy Michel, and years later, Louis had set him up as Archbishop of Bourges.

But two winters ago, a dispatch from Paris had arrived with the news that Michel Bucy had been felled by fever at age twenty-one. Louis had never known the boy and barely remembered his mother. He had ordered a candle lit and made a note to have a new archbishop appointed for Bourges.

When his wife's shrieks ceased, the silence that followed boded worse. Burying his head in his hands, he tried to pray. *God have mercy on my Brette. God have mercy on us both and deliver us a prince that lives. God forgive me for my anger against her these past months. God help and save my wife.*

Footsteps sounded in the hall outside, the murmur of men's voices.

Louis steeled himself. Depending on the outcome, he would either order the bells on every church in France to be rung or not. Not in the case of a newborn daughter. And not in the case of a newborn son who did not carry the breath of life.

A knock.

"Enter," Louis called out, willing himself to be strong. As strong as his wife had just been.

"Your Grace," the sentry bowed.

"What is it?"

"It is Father Mayheuc, Your Grace, to see you."

"Send him in." What the devil was his wife's confessor

coming to see him for? He broke out in a sweat as he waited for the Breton priest to make his bow as the sentry left the room.

"Your Grace, the queen is resting," the man of the cloth said, his tone flat.

"And?"

The priest bowed his head and clasped his hands. As he did, Louis felt his limbs go cold.

"She was delivered of a son, Sire, and—and …" The priest's hushed tone said all.

Louis shook his head, numb to what was to come.

"Your son is with God, Sire." The priest crossed himself.

"My son is with God?" Louis stared over the priest's head. He wouldn't look into his eyes because no answers lay there.

"The queen was delivered of a son, Sire, but no breath was in him."

"Good God, why could someone not do something?" Guilt flooded him as he thought of all the fights he'd had with Anne over the past few months. Had he brought this upon them with his war with the pope?

"Your Grace, the midwife tried, the doctor, too, but your child was called home on his journey to this world."

"Why the devil—why does God send us sons only to die before they are born?" A sob like a wave rose in Louis' chest. Lifting his eyes to the tapestry on the wall, he stared blankly at the unicorn being speared there. Had his son had any awareness of life at all? Why had he not wished to embrace his future as a king of France?

The sob escaped; he stifled the next one.

"Sire, there are mysteries we are not given to understand in this world. But all shall be made known to those who submit in obedience to the trials our Lord sends us."

Louis turned and stared at the Breton priest, feeling a bottomless well of disappointment open inside him. "How is my wife?"

"She was asleep when I left. They gave her a draught."

"And my son?" Louis' throat closed. *My son, for whom all the bells of France should be pealing at this moment.*

"He is still in the queen's chambers, Sire." The priest shook his head. "I am sorry, Your Grace. These are mysteries that no one can explain."

"Good God, may this be the last of them." Louis brushed past the priest, making his way to his queen and the sleeping prince who would never wake to meet his father's eyes. It was beyond any understanding at all.

"*Ma Brette*, you have given me two princesses, just as your mother gave your father. It is enough." Louis laced his fingers with Anne's as he sat at her bedside, trying to find a way to console her. He could barely conceal how disconsolate he was himself.

"Husband, have we brought this on ourselves?" Anne's voice was bleak.

"Shh, *m'amie*. Neither of us has brought anything on ourselves, other than caring for our subjects and treasuring our daughters."

"We both broke our marriage troths. Are we now being paid by God just as David and Bathsheba were served?"

"My sweet, these are questions for your confessor, not for me. I am your husband who would have broken any troth to make you my queen." *And did,* he thought. "If you and our princesses are my punishment, then I gladly accept."

"Fair words, Husband. But did we both do something that angered our Lord?"

"If we did, there is nothing we can do other than try to do our best now." Guilt pricked him at the thought of his saintly former wife. Jeanne of France's only crime had been to be as hideously ugly as she was utterly devoted to him, a combination that had revolted him. He had treated her appallingly until finally getting rid of her with his annulment.

Anne's sigh was deep. "I am tired," she whispered.

"*M'amie*, you are never tired," Louis encouraged. It wasn't entirely true. She had been worn out after Renée's birth, too.

"This time, I am."

"You are tired now, but after you recover you will be yourself again."

"I am not feeling myself these days," Anne's voice was faint.

"Remember your motto, *m'amie*, and follow it."

"What do you mean?"

Louis mustered a smile. "'*Non mudera.* I will not change.' Do you know how many times you angered me when I heard you say that?"

A wan smile flitted across her face. "Ah, Husband, it is always a pleasure to rile you a bit."

"Then rest now, and get up soon so you may rile me some more."

"If you keep provoking the pope you will give me cause."

"Then you will not wish to hear the latest from Rome." He would do whatever he could to get his lively *Brette* back, even endure her wrath.

"What have you done now?" she asked, her voice stronger.

"Not me. Julius. He has sent his army to Bologna with Ferdinand's forces."

"What do you care if he takes Bologna?"

"*M'amie*, he will not take it, not while I am King and Gaston heads my army."

"Louis, he will not stop until he sweeps your army from all of Italy. When will you realize that?"

"*Ma chère*, he has no right to do such a thing."

His wife's eyes narrowed. "Do you mean no more right than you do?"

"Madame, Bologna is ours. I will not let it fall to the pope's so-called 'Holy League.'"

"Bologna is yours until it is theirs, and then the Bolognese will tire of their new lords and throw them off when someone new comes calling."

"It is in French hands now and will remain French."

Anne's glance was cynical. "For how long?"

"For as long as we maintain our presence there."

"And what will happen when England and Spain press you in Gascony?"

"We will meet and defeat them."

"Husband, how are you going to pay for all these armies and garrisons, both in Italy and on your own border?"

Louis' gaze wavered. How precisely her words flew like arrows to his weakest spots. "I will find a way."

Silence fell between them like a thick fog. Both knew there was only one way to supply two armies on two different fronts. He would have to raise taxes. It was the one thing he was most loathe to do.

Anne lay back, spent. At least there was good news for her on the Italian front, if not for Louis. All she need do was nothing at all, and her husband's efforts in Italy were bound to come undone.

Both the French army and the Venetians hired Swiss mercenaries to fight alongside them. And the Swiss were devils to work with if they weren't paid on time. Her husband hated taxing his subjects to pay troops. But when he taxed his Italian subjects instead, they fomented rebellion against him. His success in Italy could only come at the expense of success at home in France.

Eyeing him from under her lashes, her heart hurt to think

of his dilemma. But she knew her husband. He was the father of his people. She could guess where his heart lay, just as hers lay with her beloved Brittany.

Anne closed her eyes. It wouldn't be the Italians at all who would chase the French from Italy. It would be the Swiss, enraged by Louis for not paying them reliably. The outcome was as inevitable as her luck in producing sons.

Two days later, Louise de Savoy shut her journal with a smart thump. She had just entered two supremely satisfying sentences: "The queen delivered a son but the breath of life was not in him. The exaltation of my Caesar shall not be impeded."

Opening her desk drawer, she smiled to see her charms lying undisturbed since the last time she had visited them. Lifting the sac off the back of the one lying face down, she held the small figure to her face then kissed it.

"Thank you for hearing my prayers," she whispered. She had no idea who she was thanking, but some power was working on her side, the same one that would vault her into the role of France's regent one day. She could only hope that Anne de Beaujeu would still be alive to see her step into her former position. How gratifying it would be to eclipse the haughty woman who had treated her like a poor relation.

Nevermore would she, Louise de Savoy, be anyone's poor relation. She would show the great Beaujeu how consummately she had absorbed all the skills she had exhibited in her manipulation of France and Brittany's affairs back in the 1480s.

Chuckling to herself, she thought of how France's regent had woven the net that had trapped Brittany's young ruler into marrying her brother, Charles VIII, so that France would one day absorb Brittany.

Louis was too besotted with his Breton prize to bring it about on his watch. But when Louise's son came to power, Brittany would come into France's fold. She would have the last laugh over Anne of Brittany on that day.

Chapter Twenty-two

February 1512

A Match for Marie

"… in our day we have seen Queen Anne of France,
a very great lady no less in ability than in station;
and if you will compare her in justice and clemency,
liberality and uprightness of life, with Kings Charles
and Louis, (to both of whom she was consort), you
will not find her to be the least bit inferior to them."
—Baldassare Castiglione
The Book of the Courtier (1528)

"*Maman*, did you hear that Cook's daughter and the king's stablemaster were married yesterday?"

"It sounds a good match for Cook's daughter, but what of it?" Marie's mother asked, folding linens as Marie pulled them from the line before the hearth.

"The queen said I may tell you a secret once it took place."

Marie's mother looked at her curiously. "What secret?"

Marie beamed. "I had a hand in it, *Maman*! I told the queen Cook wished to see her daughter settled with a good man, but she had no dowry."

"You did no such thing." Marie's mother flicked a linen towel at her daughter.

"I did, *Maman*. You can ask her yourself. And she said she would make a match for me, too, if I kept our secret until it came to pass."

Marie's mother stared at her, incredulous. "You told me the queen wished to speak to you about a kitchen matter!"

"She swore me to secrecy, so I could not say. But now that Cook's daughter is settled, she will look for someone for me next."

"Do you think you are so important that the queen has time to concern herself with you?" Marie's mother asked as she folded the queen's underlinens. No noblewoman she had ever worked for wore such dainty lace garments. She had heard they were sent from Brittany, where whole villages devoted themselves to lacework. The great lady in Amboise said the queen's realm was a backwater, but judging by the fineness of the garments beneath her hands and the queen who wore them, she'd guess not.

"No, *Maman,* I don't. Except that she has asked to see me tomorrow before the midday meal."

"My goose, you must have made an impression on her!" Marie's mother's heart beat faster. Who could imagine that her daughter and the queen had shared a secret together?

"Does she not usually follow through with her plans?" Marie asked.

"Whatever she says she will do, she sees to it that it's done." Marie's mother studied her daughter, her head in a swirl. She had been setting aside money for her dowry for years, ever since the dauphin's mother in Amboise had engaged her to keep her informed of the queen's doings.

"Such fun, *Maman*! I wonder if she will find someone as worthy as the stablemaster for me."

"Brunet is a good man, and I see the wisdom of the queen matching him with Cook's daughter."

"What do you mean, *Maman*?"

"She is a special one, from what I've heard, and needs a tender man to care for her. Not like you, who needs a sturdy husband to work with side by side and to argue with the rest of the time." She flicked another towel at her daughter.

"Queen Anne said if I kept our secret, I might head up my own kitchen one day instead of serving in someone else's." Marie's smile was bright.

"I like the sound of that," her mother retorted. She had worked in someone else's household all her life. It hadn't been her choice, but it had benefited her with extra income when the Countess d'Angoulême had sought her services. She could understand her interest in the queen, given if Queen Anne had a son the young Francis would no longer be dauphin. The countess was ambitious for her child, just as she was.

"Perhaps one day, *Maman*, I will wear such garments as the ones we are folding now!" Marie held up a lace chemise, admiring the intricacy of its design.

"Don't be getting above yourself, Goose. The queen is not one for upstarts. Remember what happened with the king's marshal when he rose above his station."

"What happened?"

"She had him tossed from his job and stripped of his title." It had been on the countess's visit to Blois to consult with the queen on bringing down the king's marshal that she had first met the dauphin's mother. All of France knew that the countess and the queen were rivals. But when the marshal had angered them both, they had united as one to dispatch him.

"*Maman*, I am happy with my station. I just hope the queen finds someone for me that I like."

"She will most likely find someone for you that you grow to like."

"I want to like him right away. And he must be handsome."

Marie's mother threw back her head and laughed. "Goose, you know nothing about what you need in a husband. Leave it to the queen and your father and me." She had heard that the queen provided generous dowries for her maids of honor. Might she do the same for Marie?

"*Maman*, make sure you only agree to a handsome one."

"The handsome ones spoil fast and are not the ones you want for a lifetime." Pressing her lips together she thought of the queen's delicate daughter to be married off to the dauphin. Already, he had an eye for the demoiselles at court. With his looks and swagger she worried for the shy princess. Likely, she would be used as a broodmare while her husband cavorted.

"Then one who is not too ugly."

"Take care of yourself, and we will take care of what is best for you."

"I do take care of myself. What do you mean, *Maman*?"

"Make sure that your kirtle is clean for tomorrow and change your underlinens."

"Yes, *Maman.*"

"Now take this stack to the queen's chambers, and come straight back so I can see to your bath."

"Not a bath! I will catch cold and freeze!"

"Oh no, you won't. I'll heat the water on the hearth now, and once you're done, I'll dry you 'til you glow like a bride."

"*Maman,* I am to meet with the queen, not prepare for my wedding night!"

"The better you look and smell, the finer the husband the queen might think of for you."

"Don't be getting above yourself, *Maman.* Remember?"
"Go on with you, Goose. And hurry back."

Straightening her headdress and smoothing the deep blue kirtle her mother had washed the day before, Marie entered the queen's antechamber and curtseyed with as much grace as she could. Gouffier de Bonnivet had told her she had more grace than any of the queen's maids of honor, but she had soon found out that his words held all the weight of a dandelion puff.

"Come closer, Marie. I would like you to know what plans I am thinking of for you." The queen beckoned with a reassuring smile.

Marie took a step closer, inhaling the scent of the queen's fragrance. It was a different one today—violet musk. Cook had told her Queen Anne only wore either of two scents: rose de Provence or violet musk. Both dazzled Marie, along with the one who wore them.

"Your Grace, I am honored that you wish to speak with me."

"You are lucky, too, because I have not made up my mind. So you may help me narrow the field."

Marie hesitated. "The field, Your Grace?"

"The field of candidates for your hand."

"Your Grace, I am only Cook's assistant. How wide a field could it be?" she exclaimed.

"With my blessing on your marriage, it has widened. Now tell me if there is someone you have already thought of—or one you have ruled out."

"Your Grace, I know of one I would not choose," Marie blurted out.

"Who is that, then?"

"He is of no account as he is titled and I am not."

"And were you clever enough to guess he only wished to dally with you?" the queen asked.

"Your Grace, my natural sense told me no future lay in that direction."

"Sire de Bonnivet has been sent on a mission to Milan. He will not bother you again."

Marie stiffened. So eyes had been upon her when Bonnivet had sniffed around. "My lady, I say nothing of him, only I thank you."

"You have friends who care about you, who noted his attentions to you."

"They were unreturned, Your Grace." At first, she had been flattered. Until she had seen that he ran after every other pretty demoiselle at court, too. Better to wait on the queen's pleasure and pray that her own desires aligned.

"There is Pierre Aubray, the son of Jean, the gardener here at the castle. Or there is Michel Tissard, who works in town with his father at the river," the queen proposed.

Marie felt her insides flutter. "Your Grace, I—I don't know what to say."

"Of course you do," the queen corrected. "You are a sensible girl, and you will choose wisely. Do you know either of them?"

Catching her breath, Marie nodded. "I know of them both from errands I run for Cook."

"And what do you think?"

"I scarcely know what to think as I've only glanced at either of them." Of medium height, Pierre was blondish and Michel was dark-haired. Both were passably good-looking.

"I have had their backgrounds checked. Neither is promised to another, and your parents would be satisfied with either."

"Your Grace, may I think it over?" Marie's heart flooded to think the queen was giving her a choice. It was said that she gave none to her maids of honor when she decided on matches for them. Remembering Cook's counsel, Marie felt lucky to be so lowly that her own marriage wasn't a matter of state concern.

"Take a few days, then let me know. I would see you settled soon, my dove. Both for your own good and your parents' peace of mind."

"Thank you, Your Grace. I will let you know as soon as I can."

"You will enjoy deciding, I am sure."

"Your Grace, to be given a choice is an honor, coming from you." Marie melted in the glow of the queen's aura. Like fairy dust, it settled over her, transforming her ordinary self into something finer.

"Why do you say so?" the queen asked, her eyes dancing.

"Because the demoiselles say that you choose for them and none may disagree," Marie confessed.

"As I have chosen two for you. But you may make the final choice."

"Why do you grant me such power, Your Grace?"

"Because you are prudent, Marie. You will choose wisely. Otherwise, I would decide for you."

"Which one would you pick, Your Grace?" Marie couldn't help but ask.

With a wave, the queen dismissed her.

Marie backed from the room with joy in her heart. Never would she forget that the queen had called her prudent. She would treasure such words forever. God knew they were more valuable to her than any piece of fluff Gouffier de Bonnivet had offered from his lying mouth.

Two days later, Marie rose from her curtsey to again face Queen Anne. Straightening her back, she thought of the future before her that the Queen of France had made possible.

"What have you decided, Marie?"

"I would be happy to consider Michel Tissard." She had run errands past both candidates over the last two days with another girl from the kitchen. Both young men had glanced at her when she had passed by. Then Pierre Aubray had glanced at her companion.

But Michel Tissard had looked only at her, making roses spring to her cheeks. She sensed he would be steady and true, keeping his eyes on her.

Remembering Bonnivet's wandering gaze, she wished him good riddance. He could tangle with all the Italian vixens he cared to, but should the pox disfigure his face, he would find his chances ended with women back in France.

The queen reached for a sealed pouch. "Then here is the letter to give to your parents to propose to them my arrangements."

"Arrangements, Your Grace?"

"Your dowry, my dove."

"Your Grace, thank you! But how did you have this letter prepared with the name of the man I had not yet chosen?"

"Little dove, I knew you would pick the man from town and not the castle."

"How so, Your Grace?"

"Because you would wish to be mistress of your own home one day. If you chose the gardener's son, you would remain in service here at the castle."

"I hadn't thought of that at all, Your Grace!" She would never be mistress of anything with Bonnivet, who would marry well one day and disappear from her life. Indeed, she was best off with a husband and home of her own, far from dangerous dalliances at court.

"Do you not remember I told you that you might head up your own kitchen one day instead of serving in someone else's?" the queen asked.

"Yes, Your Grace, but I am happy to serve in the royal kitchens!"

"You will be happier to serve your own family in your own kitchen."

"Do you think so, Your Grace?" Remembering Cook's words to her, she marveled to think how closely they resembled the queen's.

"I know so, and you may tell your mother I said so. Now go and deliver this to your parents." The queen handed her the pouch.

"Your Grace, I will never forget this kindness you have done me." With the queen's royal seal upon it, Marie's heart leaped to think of her mother and father's faces the moment they saw it.

"Come tell me again with your first child in your arms."

"I will do so, Your Grace. I will name her after you!"

"Enough!" With a tinkling laugh, the queen waved her away.

"Don't tell me she's pregnant again." Louise de Savoy flicked her eyes over her visitor as she placed a small sac of coins on her desk.

"No, Madame. The queen does well, but I am here to tell you that I cannot serve you anymore in this capacity."

"Has something happened?" Louise peered at the woman. She looked brighter than usual, more well-defined.

"I have what I need, Madame, and require no more."

"How curious." What was the woman thinking? And how was it possible that a laundrywoman could need no more coins for the secret store every housewife kept?

The woman's eyes shone. "I am content with what I have, Madame, and dare not risk the queen's wrath to serve you further."

"What wrath could the queen possibly have toward you for visiting me from time to time for a chat?" Imagine a laundrywoman telling her she was content with what she had. Perhaps she was touched in the head like the daughter of the cook at Blois. She had heard the queen had married her off to the stablemaster—ridiculous, but, then, so was the queen.

"It might displease her and I serve at her pleasure."

"If anything happened to you, you could come to serve me here." Recently she had arranged a fine match, herself, for her dead husband's natural daughter Souveraine. Earlier that month she had hosted her wedding at Amboise to Michel Gaillard, the king's baker and brother-in-law of Florimond Robertet. It would serve nicely to bind Robertet to her more tightly.

"Thank you, Madame. But I will not risk it. My family is settled in service to the queen, and I owe her my allegiance."

"You did not draw so fine a distinction over these past few years." Something had changed about the woman. Who, she wondered, was responsible for it?

"The queen has done me a great favor, Madame. I do not seek anything beyond it."

"And what favor is this?" Louise's curiosity was piqued. Both by whatever the queen had done and why the woman chose not to seek more. She couldn't imagine anyone not seeking more when there was more to be had.

"I may not say, Madame."

"Of course, you may. You are in my pay, remember." Louise nudged the small sac closer to her visitor.

"No longer, Madame. But I thank you for all you have given me."

Louise watched in disbelief as the laundrywoman from Blois Castle curtseyed and left.

The bag of coins she had offered remained untouched on the desk.

CHAPTER TWENTY-THREE

1512

Gaston de Foix - The Thunderbolt of Italy

"Italy is the grave of Frenchmen."
—Old French proverb from *Illustrious Dames of the Court of the Valois Kings* by Pierre de Brantôme

On April 19 after a pleasant day of hawking, Louis' spirits were high as he and Claude rode into the stableyard of Blois Castle.

Spotting a messenger waiting for him, Louis dismounted and threw his reins to his squire.

"What news?" he asked, his blood racing in anticipation of tidings from Italy.

"Your grace, a great victory in Ravenna." The messenger bowed his head. When he raised it, his eyes were hooded.

"Splendid. Gaston has outdone himself again," Louis exulted as Claude came to his side, her cheeks flushed pink from the fresh air of the spring afternoon. His twenty-two-year-old nephew and new army commander had already taken Bologna and Brescia in two stunning victories for the French earlier that year.

The messenger's Adam's apple bobbed. "Your Grace, Commander de Foix was felled in battle. As was Captain d'Alègre." The man hung his head.

Louis' throat closed. "My nephew was felled?"

"He died in glory, Sire, chasing the Spanish, who were running like dogs to escape our troops."

"Oh God." Reaching for Claude, he found her head with his hand. This was victory at too great a cost.

"Papa, is it our Gaston?"

Louis nodded, too stunned to speak.

"May the Lord glorify him in Heaven as he was glorious on earth, Sire." The messenger crossed himself, looking glum.

"Who took charge?" Louis choked out. It hardly mattered. Gaston was irreplaceable. No one could step into the void his death left.

"Sire de La Palice, Your Grace. He sent me to receive instructions for his next moves."

"Did we pursue the Spanish forces?" Louis asked numbly.

"We did not, Sire. It was a great victory, but our losses were heavy."

"How many men?"

"At least seven thousand, Your Grace. There were terrible artillery losses. Sire de La Palice overcame the pope's garrison in Ravenna and chased them out."

"Did they pursue them south?"

"No, Sire. Our troops were exhausted and ..."

"And what?"

"Sire, the loss of our commander hit them hard."

"As it does me." Louis smacked his chest.

"I am sorry, Your Majesty. The Commander de Foix fought to the glory of France. It was an honor to serve under him this past year."

"Go to the kitchen and I will summon you later to give details to my council." He couldn't bear to hear more for the moment. What good was one sole victory at the cost of his best and brightest commander? And seven thousand soldiers lost was a cruel blow to wives, mothers, and children who awaited them back home.

Sick at heart Louis squeezed Claude's hand, trying to blot out an image of his nephew's lifeless form, disfigured and hacked, lying in state in Ravenna—a city recently vacated by the pope. He wished he'd never heard of it and had never gone near it.

"Papa, I cannot believe Gaston is gone."

Louis shook his head. "Nor can I, Minou." It was a terrible loss, more devastating than the loss of his latest prince in January.

Gaston, his beloved older sister's boy, had been orphaned young. He had been raised in Anne and Charles' royal household at Amboise, then with him and Anne at Blois. His nephew had been like a son to him and now he had joined all the other sons Louis had, every one of them under the earth.

Louis punched the side of his leg with his leather hawking glove. Why had he sent him to certain death by appointing one so young as commander of his army? He should have known that Gaston's youthful sense of invincibility would lead him to make rash choices.

Moving in the direction of his wife's rooms, every muscle in his body ached—above all his heart.

"Husband, what ails you?" Anne cried. Her husband's face was ashen.

Louis sat with a dull thud on the side of her bed. "We have won Ravenna."

"I am glad, husband, but you are not. What more?" She put a hand on his back, feeling the knots beneath her touch.

"At terrible cost," Louis muttered, putting his head in his hands.

"D'Alègre?"

"Worse." Louis' shoulders shook, his face hidden.

"Not Gaston?" Let it not be Germaine's brother, the boy she had raised at court with Charles and then Louis. Anne had marriage plans for him, big plans to match his growing reputation.

Louis shook his head from side to side, saying nothing, telling all.

"Louis, our dear Gaston is—is he ..."

Not meeting her eyes Louis nodded, a strangled sob escaping him.

"May God have mercy on his soul!" Anne exclaimed, clasping her husband in her arms.

"Why did I send him to certain death?" Louis burst out, tearing at his hair.

"Husband, you did no such thing."

"I knew he would overstep himself in battle," Louis moaned.

"He was superb in battle and in leadership. You chose him because his speed and energy outstripped all others."

"It was his speed and energy that killed him!"

"How so, *mon cher*?"

"He had already beaten back the Spanish. They were

retreating, but he went after them." Louis punched his fist into the mattress.

"Ah," Anne exhaled. "And then what?" Gaston was not one to leave a job undone. She had watched Louis' nephew grow up at court. Both at play and at sport, Gaston never quit until the job was done or the game fully over. She could imagine him mopping up the end of a battle, careful to ensure that the enemy was in full retreat and not just regrouping.

"His horse stumbled and a bullet caught him," Louis choked out.

"Where were his men?"

"Trying to catch up with him."

"So the Spanish did first?"

"Yes, Madame, and what happened next is not for your ears."

"Husband, this reminds me of the end of Borgia."

Louis' face darkened. "Do not mention that cur in the same breath!"

Anne squeezed his shoulder. "He will not take a place beside our Gaston in paradise. But he came to a similar end because of his courage, racing ahead of his men to engage the enemy."

"It is what the bravest of young men do. And it is something that every fighting man of a certain age knows not to do."

"My lord, he died a hero's death."

"It is nothing to me that he died a hero!" Louis lamented. "It is a blow to my heart and to the heart of every soldier in my army that he is gone. No one can take his place. Certainly not La Palice."

"La Palice is now in charge?" She had heard Louis speak of Jacques de La Palice. A cautious, uninspired leader. A thick log to Gaston's thunderbolt.

Louis made a face. "Until I say otherwise."

"Do you see a better choice?" Would to God her husband would just pull out of Italy altogether. To what end was he there, gathering more enemies daily in a land where he didn't belong?

"I see nothing but a vale of tears with nowhere to shed them." Louis buried his face in his hands.

"Husband, you may shed them here. God knows this bed has been the site of enough of my own."

"*Ma Brette*, you have done battle in childbirth and lost your princes, one after the other. I have sent my own kin to lead my army, and lost our greatest hope in Italy."

"Louis, you are France's greatest hope in Italy, and none other."

"But I am losing my taste for the cost of being there."

Anne put out both arms to him, lying back with his graying head to her chest. She had waited for years to hear her husband say such words. But never would she have wanted him to lose his passion for Italy at so dear a cost.

"Husband, rest here. And when we have recovered, we will rise and face our subjects with fresh faces and good cheer," she encouraged.

"*M'amie*, I thought you were sick," Louis mumbled into her hair.

"I am better now." She wasn't really, but Louis' distress lit a fire under her. His most trusted minister was gone, and now his beloved nephew. Her husband needed her more than ever, and he had never made any bones about needing her every day of his life.

Gaston de Foix (1489-1512)
By Philippe de Champaigne, c. 1630-35
Courtesy of Wikimedia Commons, public domain

Funerary Monument of Gaston de Foix (1489-1512)
Sforza Castle, Milan
Photo by Richard Mortel, courtesy of Wikimedia Commons

Close up of Funerary Monument of Gaston de Foix (1489-1512)
Sforza Castle, Milan
Photo by Richard Mortel, courtesy of Wikimedia Commons

Over the next week, Anne comforted Louis, offering respite when he came to her chambers after long conferences with his advisors.

"Will you march on Rome now that you have secured Ravenna?" she asked, willing him to say no.

"I have not yet decided."

"If you do, Husband, are you prepared for the outcome?" Respite forgotten, Anne flew to her point.

"What outcome do you speak of, Madame?"

"You will be excommunicated, Louis. Your subjects will not be able to receive the Host. Think of it. Is your enmity with Julius worth the peril of your subjects' souls?

"Madame, this present pope has become the enemy of France. We will depose him and elect our own pope to head the Church."

"My lord, I worry that others in Europe will not follow France's lead."

"Why should they not follow our lead when we have proven ourselves the most powerful presence in Italy? Our victories at Agnadello and now in Ravenna—God rest my nephew, who brought it about—will make all of Europe fall into step behind us."

Anne eyed her husband. "Louis, France's power in Italy is no longer welcome by anyone there, Italian or foreign."

"They will all fight with each other, guaranteeing our dominance."

"As long as France remains dominant, they will unite as if blood brothers until death," Anne disagreed. "Better to come to terms with the pope and give your soldiers some relief since winning this latest victory at terrible loss of life."

"Madame, I must seize the advantage now that I have it." Louis moved to the door to leave for his council meeting.

"Think of the expense, my lord. How are you going to pay the Swiss to fight for you after you have settled accounts for what you already owe them?" Anne called after him. The salvation of French souls wasn't going to rattle Louis. But the milking of further taxes from his beloved subjects would.

"Enough, Wife!" he flung back.

"You do not mean that Gaston is gone!" Marguerite cried, her eyes wide with shock.

"Courage, my daughter. It was reported to the king that he fell on Easter Sunday, at the end of winning Ravenna," Louise de Savoy told her, shaken to think of that bright spirit dimmed forever.

"But where has he gone? Where is he now?" Marguerite looked as if she had seen a ghost.

"His body lies in state in Ravenna. I believe the king will have it taken to Milan where he will be buried in honor."

"What good is honor when he is dead!" Marguerite wailed, her hands over her ears as if to blot out the news.

"He won a great victory for France, but the losses were high. Many fine men died as well, the Captain d'Alègre amongst them," Louise related. What a waste war was. A waste of husbands, sons, and fathers who would never return. She would do whatever she could to keep her son from such a fate.

"I don't care! I don't care about any of them but Gaston!"

"He will be remembered forever for his victory for France," Louise encouraged. "Tales of his bravery will become legend." Even to her ears, the words rang empty.

"What good is all that if he is no longer here?" Marguerite ran to the window as if to look for him.

"My dear, life is for the living. It is time you focused on your own, which I do not see bearing fruit yet." A tinge of vinegar laced Louise's tone.

"I do not care to bear fruit when all that I love has been ripped from me!" Marguerite shrieked, rushing from the room.

Louise followed her with her eyes. It seemed that her suspicions about her daughter's attachment to Gaston had been correct. She had thought to bring him for a visit to Marguerite in Alençon after he returned from Italy. Now she would need to make other arrangements.

Louis smashed his fist down on the council chamber table. "They cannot possibly be thinking of marching on Milan! They have just returned home from supporting us in Brescia and Ravenna."

News had arrived that the Holy Roman Emperor had made a truce with Venice, enabling Swiss troops to pass through northern Italy to reach Milan. On top of that, the pope had made yet another agreement with the powerful Swiss cardinal Matthias Schinner. One word from Schinner was enough to bring home the Swiss mercenaries hired by Louis, reducing French forces considerably.

"Sire, as mercenaries, they support the side that pays them best," Robertet pointed out.

Louis swallowed hard as his conscience bit him. He was overdue on payments to his Swiss mercenaries in Italy. But he had been hard put to find funds to cover the army's huge expenses since Gaston had ravaged Brescia in February then captured Ravenna in April. Now he would reap the consequences.

"There are rumors too, Sire, that the pope has reached out to the English king with some sort of bull recognizing him as King of France if he wishes it," his finance minister, Thomas Bohier, put in.

"Preposterous! How dare he? And what does this have to do with overseeing the Church?"

"The pope is a warlike man, Sire. Only death will stop him from making alliances against you unless you come to terms with him," Bohier advised.

"And what business does the King of England have with France anyway?" Louis bellowed.

"With Sire de Foix gone, Your Grace, his claim to the seat of Navarre is being challenged by the Spanish King. England is his ally and will aid Spain against us."

Louis' eyes flicked from one minister to the other. "So we are being attacked at home and in Milan."

"The pope has fanned envy against France. It appears Spain, the Holy Roman Empire, and now England have taken the bait," Robertet observed.

"How am I to deploy troops on two fronts?" Louis' head spun at thought of such trouble.

"How are you to pay two armies, Sire?" Thomas Bohier asked, twisting a finger into the king's sore spot. "The coffers are exhausted from the Italian battles."

Louis glared at him, thinking that Georges would never have riled him like this by making so crass an observation. What good were courtiers if they didn't do their job of softening hard truths?

The following week, a messenger from London arrived. Henry VIII of England's ultimatum was explicit: make peace with the pope or prepare for an English invasion.

Louis quaked. The English army had decimated the French nobility less than one century earlier at the Battle of Agincourt. His own father, Charles d'Orléans, had been taken prisoner there and held in England for the next twenty-four years, destroying Louis' chance to get to know him. He could face anything but the English army on French soil.

Two days later, an official bull came from Rome, the papal seal upon it. The pope's own council was now opened, the Fifth Council of the Lateran, called to oppose Louis' Conciliabulum. Julius II announced that if the King of France did not disband his schismatic council and send French clergy to attend the Church's Lateran council, he would be officially excommunicated within two months.

Tossing the bull to the floor, Louis wished a pox on the pope.

"I know the game you play and you will not win it." Anne of Brittany's voice cut like a knife through the cake of Louise de Savoy's well-baked plans.

"What game do you speak of, Your Grace?" Louise asked, taking a step backward. She had been summoned to Blois two days earlier and had thought the queen wished to speak with her about her son's behavior at court—perhaps a dalliance with one of her high and mighty maids of honor.

But it was not that at all.

"You will not succeed in sowing enmity between the king and me," the Breton ruler said. Her sharp eyes pierced Louise, making her feel as small and guilty as a child caught in a lie.

"I would never seek to do such a thing, Your Grace." Louise felt the blood rush to her head. As a redhead, she colored easily. She must not allow her face to flush.

"You have engaged spies within my household to whisper in the king's ears of my communications with the pope. I order you to stop," the queen proclaimed.

"Your Grace, I would never think to do such a thing." Had the laundry-woman tipped her off? But she had used her for other tasks, not the nuggets of information placed to incite the king against his Breton queen. Perhaps Robertet?

"Of course, you would and I tell you now that you waste your time." Anne of Brittany's gaze raked her. "I am perfectly capable of telling the king myself of my concerns to keep the pope from excommunicating him."

Louise struggled to conceal her shock. The queen herself was telling her that she had already discussed with Louis the very issue that she had thought would turn husband and wife against each other. What hand had she left to play?

"Madame, I want only what is good for France and to serve at the king's pleasure," she stammered.

"You want only what is good for your son and yourself, and you serve at the king's pleasure only because he has named your son his successor," Anne of Brittany unequivocally spelled out.

What in the world was wrong with that? Louise thought, wondering how the queen had caught wind of her efforts to stir trouble between her and Louis.

"Your Grace, if you had a son yourself who was to be king one day, would you not do the same?" she asked. Instantly, she regretted her outburst.

"Your words seek to wound, but I know who I am and cruel words will not shake me," Anne answered, her face unchanging despite the barb.

Louise suddenly imagined the queen in an argument with the king. The woman was small, but the aura she exuded filled the room. Whatever rock Anne of Brittany stood on, it was a far different one from Louise's own. She had just delivered a sword slash, but the woman remained unmoved. For the first time, she saw that the queen's piety offered something more than just a topic of amusement for her and her circle to mock.

"I did not mean to be cruel, Your Grace. I only ask that as a mother, would you not seek to protect the interests of your child above any other?"

"The difference between us, Madame, is that your world is small and mine is large," the queen replied, ignoring her question.

"What meaning, Your Grace?" Once again she felt her face ready to flame. Anyone would say that her world was far larger than the queen's, whose interests lay with running her provincial backwater.

"Your duty is to your son and yourself. Mine is to my realm, my husband and his realm, and to my children."

"Is your duty truly to France, Your Grace? Some would say that it tends more toward your duchy," Louise ventured, hoping she was not treading the fine line of lèse-majestè.

"It is foremost toward my duchy as its ruler. But as queen of my husband's kingdom, I seek to improve all in France that is within my reach. And that includes the hopes for salvation of its people, which will die should the pope put them under interdict." The lucidity of the queen's words blocked Louise from countering further.

"You are very clear, Your Grace."

"It is important to be clear," the petite and precise queen said. "Both to my subjects and before God."

"I commend you for your attention to duty."

The queen's eyes shot daggers. "And I command you to cease meddling in my husband's and my affairs."

"I do not seek to meddle, only to—"

"I know very well what you seek," the queen cut her off, "and I order you to stop. Do not seek to sully that which is fine and clear, although hard and difficult at times."

"I do not know of what you speak, Your Grace." Was she referring to the married state? All she had experienced of it had been four years of murky immorality served her by her husband Charles d'Angoulême.

"You will never know of what I speak because you do not have the capacity to understand it," the queen concluded. "Now go." She waved a hand that brooked no further discussion.

Louise curtseyed and backed from the room. Outside in the corridor, the familiar infuriation stole over her. She would never possess the sangfroid of either Anne of Brittany or Anne de Beaujeu. Both women wore an invisible armor that she didn't know where to get and would never have the means to obtain. It galled her beyond measure.

Wracking her brain over how to acquire that elusive quality that her rivals possessed, she parsed the queen's words: *Do not seek to sully that which is fine and clear, although hard and difficult at times.* The absurd woman's convictions were based on her piety; it was something she would never understand.

But now she realized why the queen was so determined not to see Louis excommunicated. She truly believed that the path to salvation would be blocked not just for him but for all the subjects of his realm.

Louise snorted. It was nothing to her if her path to salvation was blocked. Her concerns were planted here on earth, and the only path she cared about was the one that led to getting her son onto France's throne.

Chapter Twenty-four

1512–1513

Italy Lost

Louis had lost Milan. The French army was straggling home to France in bits and pieces, chased from Italy by the Swiss and Venetians.

Under the uninspired leadership of La Palice, the French had retreated northward from Ravenna to Milan, demoralized and facing hostility along the way. As his men moved along the River Po toward the city, Swiss and Venetian troops joined forces to pursue them. News arrived from Milan that the Milanese were ready to revolt against their French overlords, angered by the burden of taxation that had been forced on them to pay for the French presence in Italy.

The Swiss had turned against Louis due to his chronic lateness in paying their mercenary troops. In his determination not to further tax his French subjects, Louis had instead overtaxed the Milanese to pay the Swiss. France was now without a friend in northern Italy.

Upon hearing that Milan would no longer welcome the French army, La Palice decided to bypass the city and continue farther west to Asti, traditionally more loyal to Louis as part of his family's hereditary lands.

But in mid-June, the Swiss and Venetians caught up to the French outside Asti. As French troops pushed their way onto a bridge across a small river to escape the enemy behind, the bridge collapsed, sending some to their death and stranding a large section of the army on the enemy's side of the river.

Those left behind surrendered. The ones who made it over skipped Asti altogether and fled over the Alps to France. It was an inglorious homecoming for the French army after thirteen years in northern Italy.

Secretly, Anne rejoiced that Louis was out of Italy. But her heart ached to see her husband so disconsolate at his loss. She was well acquainted with how terrible it was to lose one's dearest dream. After delivering her latest stillborn prince, her dreams of bearing a living son had fled just as the French army had fled Italy.

By July, the Swiss moved fully into Milan, occupying its city and installing Maximilian Sforza as its puppet governor. His uncle had been the strongman Ludovico Sforza, whom the French had captured and imprisoned in 1499. Everything Louis had worked for in Milan had come undone.

Sforza and the Swiss no longer wished to host Louis' Conciliabulum. The clergy attending moved first to Asti, then to Lyon in France, its number and appetite for ousting the pope dwindling with each relocation.

The worst was to come. At the end of July 1512, another papal bull arrived from Rome. Julius II had excommunicated Louis XII. France was now under papal interdiction.

Making good on his threat of two months' earlier, the pope declared Louis not only excommunicated but stripped of his crown. Julius II announced he would give his investiture to Henry VIII of England as France's new king.

The thought of the English King on the French throne enraged Louis as he prepared for hostilities on his southern border with Spain. At any moment an encroachment into Gascony by Ferdinand was expected. If the English joined forces with the Spanish, Louis would be hard pressed to protect his borders.

But, instead, an entirely unanticipated assault came, stunning both Louis and Anne.

On August 10, 1512, twenty-five English warships sailed into Berthaume Bay, just above Brest on Brittany's northwest coast. Under the command of Lord Edward Howard, they engaged the twenty-one ships of the French and Breton fleets that were anchored there. Among them was the crown jewel of the Breton naval fleet, the Marie de la Cordelière, commissioned by Anne and built in 1505.

The Breton and French navies were caught unaware. Some three hundred ladies and local officials were being entertained on the one-thousand-ton Cordelière by its captain, Hervé de Portzmoguer, and his crew.

At sight of the larger English fleet bearing down on them, nineteen of the French and Breton ships cut anchor and beat a retreat back to the port of Brest. The Cordelière and its second-largest sister galleon, the Petite Louise, raised sail and rushed the enemy.

Europe's first naval battle using cannons shot from lidded gun ports ensued. Soon the Petite Louise was severely damaged by the English flagship, the six-hundred-ton Regent, and forced to retreat, leaving the Cordelière to face the enemy alone.

With its cannons, the Cordelière destroyed the masts of two of the smaller English ships, but the Regent was its main target. Portzmoguer saw his opportunity when the Regent came alongside his ship downwind.

He ordered his sailors to grapple the English ship. Successful in their efforts, Breton sailors leaped onto the English ship, engaging in hand-to-hand, on-deck combat. Soon, an English gunner's shot caused a fire to break out on the deck of the Cordelière. Within minutes, it spread to the ship's gunpowder magazine.

The explosion that followed destroyed not only the Cordelière but the Regent tied to it. As Brittany's proud flagship went up in flames its captain climbed the mast of his beautiful galleon and flung himself into the sea, drowning under the weight of the full-body armor he wore.

With the two ships attached, the flames leaped to the Regent, blowing up their own gunpowder stores. The English ship exploded with only a handful of sailors escaping by jumping overboard. All but twenty of over one thousand sailors and civilians died, including the captain of the Regent.

Two days later, word of the catastrophe reached Anne and Louis. Anne was unconsolable. Retreating to her private chapel, she prayed for the souls of her subjects who had died in the conflagration. The Cordelière had been her pride and joy, built with her own funds. The centerpiece of her Breton fleet was gone along with her noble admiral Portzmoguer, hundreds of Breton sailors, and scores of Brest's most notable officials and their wives. It was an unthinkable tragedy, coming within weeks of the excommunication of Louis and all of France.

Just as her beautiful flagship had gone up in smoke, so did Anne's recent joy at saving her realm from papal interdiction. All she could think of was the unimaginable horror of the naval disaster.

Burning of the Cordelière and the Regent in the 1512 Battle of St.-Mathieu
By Pierre-Julien Gilbert, 1838
Courtesy of Wikimedia Commons, public domain

Within days, word came that a second English fleet had arrived by sea to join the Spanish in northwestern Spain. Their intent was to invade Gascony, but Ferdinand wished first to take Haute-Navarre, the small kingdom that controlled the border passage through the Pyrenees between France and Spain.

Louis' worst nightmares were coming true. Not only had he lost Italy, but the dreaded English were bearing down on him.

Swiftly, he reached out to Jean d'Albret, King of Haute-Navarre, to sign a treaty alliance. Louis promised to defend Haute-Navarre from Spain in return for d'Albret forbidding the enemy to cross his small but strategic kingdom to invade France. D'Albret agreed, incensing Ferdinand, who sent Spanish troops in early August to claim it for Spain.

Chased by the Spanish army, Jean d'Albret was forced to retreat northward over the Pyrenees. There, he joined La Palice's army, most of whom were veterans of the Italian campaign, tired of war and eager to reunite with their families.

Louis appointed his dauphin to head a division of La Palice's troops. At age seventeen, Francis d'Angoulême had no military experience, so Louis ordered Francis de Dunois, the Duke of Longueville and namesake son of one of the closest friends of his youth, to guide him.

Fortunately for Louis, the English refused to assist the Spanish. Their orders were to invade France, not the separate kingdom of Haute-Navarre. His spies reported that an even worse problem had dimmed their desire to aid their Spanish allies: there was no beer.

The soldiers disliked the rough Spanish wine and were unaccustomed to the excessive heat of the Spanish summer. The English officially complained that Ferdinand of Spain was not supplying the English troops properly during their stay on the Spanish coast.

"What else is new, Husband? An old fox does not change his tricks overnight, does he?" Anne chuckled.

"At least we can count on Ferdinand to remain true to his colors," Louis joked, gratified to learn he was not the only prince of Europe to be duped by the King of Spain.

The next dispatch was even more heartening. After doing nothing but complain for two months, the English army was leaving Spain to sail home. With the English gone, Louis gave orders to his army to proceed into Haute-Navarre.

The French troops separated into two divisions, one led by the eighteen-year-old dauphin, the other led by La Palice. In early fall 1512, they marched into Haute-Navarre to meet the Spanish army. True to form, La Palice proceeded cautiously, giving the Spanish time to retreat from the crest of the Pyrenees back to Pamplona, Spanish Navarre's main city.

The French pursued them and laid siege. But by early December, they still had not succeeded in taking the city. With supplies dwindling and winter setting in, the French army withdrew, retreating across the Pyrenees in bitter cold, a sorry remnant of what it had been only one year earlier in Italy.

In a final irony, Gaston de Foix as the successor to the House of Foix had held a hereditary claim to Haute-Navarre to rival the House of Albret. But with Gaston's death, his claim had passed to his only sibling and sister, Germaine de Foix, wife of the King of Spain since Queen Isabella's death in 1504. With Ferdinand's queen-consort holding a claim to Haute-Navarre, Spain conquered the small but strategically important kingdom that held the key routes over the Pyrenees. With Haute-Navarre's fall, yet another French ally was gone.

That summer, Anne's hopes to produce an heir flickered and sputtered like a flame about to go out. She had lost her latest prince and hadn't regained her full strength. Longing to visit Brittany to comfort her subjects who had lost loved ones in August's naval disaster, she couldn't go, her body still too weak.

Wrung out by the events of the year, she turned for solace to her Breton confessor.

"Father, I am losing my hope along with my strength," she confided.

"Your strength is in the Lord, my daughter. It is through our weaknesses that He is glorified," Father Mayheuc advised.

"I have done all that my conscience bids me do, yet my efforts have been in vain."

Father Mayheuc shook his head, his gaze compassionate. "They have not been in vain. You have obeyed the Church and saved your subjects from interdiction."

"But I was unable to shield my husband, who is attacked on all sides and is now outside the Church."

"You have done your duty to your realm by keeping it from the pope's wrath. Now do your duty by your husband."

"What do you mean, Father? Do I seek to convince him to return to the Church?" Her blood rose as she thought of her anger at Louis. But she didn't want to unload it on him when he desperately needed her support.

Father Mayheuc's smile was wry. "My daughter, you should love and forgive him as you are called to do in marriage and leave off seeking to convince him of anything. That is something only he can do for himself."

"But he is wrong to try to depose the pope!"

"That may be, my daughter, but it will not be you to convince him of that."

"Then what should I do to help him see the truth?" Anne's frustration mounted. She liked to solve problems and Louis was giving her one. Why shouldn't she use every means she had to fix it?

"You must see the deeper truth of the sacrament of your marriage promise. Support him as he has promised to support you."

"Father, it is my duty to guide him back to the Church. His soul is in peril if he doesn't return."

"It is not your duty to guide your husband anywhere," the priest counseled. "It is your duty to support him. Show him good cheer and be yielding as you pray for him privately."

"But he isn't learning from his error!"

Father Mayheuc laughed heartily. "Do you think that any man or woman learns from their error by having their spouse point it out to them?"

Anne pursed her lips. Her confessor seemed to know much about marriage.

"Then I shall pray for him and try to be his yielding wife." Feeling disingenuous, she couldn't imagine being a yielding wife, queen, duchess, or anything. As a child, she had failed to yield on most points, causing her parents to exchange knowing looks whenever she had been brought before them for defying her governess.

Yves Mayheuc's laugh rang out even louder. "Dear daughter, the Lord delights in you just as you are. Don't try to be anything you are not when your husband loves you just as you are. Be yourself and love him back, just as he is."

Anne showed him a sour face. "I do love him but he vexes me at times."

The priest chuckled. "You have just described the state of holy matrimony."

"Why does it have to be so hard at times?"

"Because everything precious in God's sight is hard at times. Just as our Lord's suffering on the cross was." The priest made the sign of the cross, giving her an encouraging smile. "Now go and continue to be a true and good wife to your husband while you pray for his soul."

Anne left the confessional feeling a hundred times lighter. Nothing was resolved but at least she knew her way forward. She would not hate her husband because he was in error toward the Church.

Departing the chapel she squelched a giggle. She couldn't hate Louis even if she wanted to. He was hers and she was his. God had knitted them together in a tapestry that no one, not even herself, would ever unravel.

In November 1512, Maximilian joined the pope's new Holy League, an alliance all Europe knew was really an anti-French league. Europe's rulers wished to reduce France's power, not only in Italy but in Europe as well. The new league's treaty neatly carved up France into separate spheres of influence amongst its signatories.

On the surface of it, Louis was sunk.

"Husband, you hold a trump card in your back pocket," Anne bolstered him.

"I do?"

"Your enemy Ferdinand is now almost as unpopular as you," she pointed out.

"How delightful to be in the same most-hated club," Louis quipped. Like himself, Ferdinand had lost most of his friends amongst Europe's princes, having angered the English over not supplying beer and quarreled with Maximilian over Venice.

"How opportune to be in the same boat at the same time," Anne observed.

"Should I reach out to him?" Louis asked. The Spanish king might prove receptive to finding a momentary friend in France.

"Husband, have you finally learned how to handle our neighbor below the border?" she asked.

Louis drummed his fingertips on the table as he sized up her point. "I might handle him before he mishandles me."

"Who would you send to open discussions?" she asked.

"Madame, if I could I would send you so that you could visit with Germaine, and tie that fox around your finger."

"When my strength returns, the next trip I make will be to my own realm. But you should send someone soon to forge an alliance."

"Although we know he will go back on whatever we agree to."

Anne's gaze was keen. "Without question. But that will be then and you need him now."

"To get this unholy League off my back." How good it was to have her counsel.

"Don't forget that his daughter is England's queen. She may induce her husband to back off France if her father's country is in treaty alliance with you."

"Such is the game clever princes play, my lady."

"My husband, you are more good than clever, and I would ever prefer you so."

"I am glad you value me in some ways, if not others." He wanted to be a good king, not a sly one. The problem was that to accomplish the first, he needed to act like the second.

Anne laughed. "It is no bad thing to be loved as the father of your people. Send someone to Ferdinand if you wish to pry him from the League."

"Who do you recommend?"

"Someone Germaine grew up with so that she will look favorably on the matter and soften him for you."

"Who would that be?" His niece had been one of Anne's most gifted maids of honor. Germaine de Foix was more capable than most to match wits with her much older husband.

Anne tapped a finger to her lips. "What about Fleuranges?"

"Our Young Adventurer?" Robert de Fleuranges was one of the more daring of his dauphin's circle of friends.

"Yes."

"Too young." Louis shook his head. At age twenty-one, Fleuranges was only a few years older than Francis d'Angoulême.

"He is polished beyond his years and charming to boot. She will be happy to see him."

"Ferdinand will walk circles around him."

"Ferdinand will walk circles around all of us. But, right now, he needs a friend and so do you." Anne stabbed at his chest with her index finger. "Why not tell him that bygones are bygones and you are ready to make peace with him?"

"*M'amie,* when do you ever let bygones be bygones?" Louis wanted to laugh but thought better of it.

"When they concern you and not me." Anne's chin tilted up.

"I am touched by your sudden flexibility."

"My lord, it is time you dropped this fight with the pope." Her violet-gray eyes bored into him.

"It seems I am to be dropped from the roster of Europe's princes if I do not."

"Neither of us wish to see your kingdom carved up by your neighbors, Husband."

"I will never allow it," he said with more confidence than he felt.

"You have exhausted your fighting forces. Your subjects still love you, but they no longer will if you raise taxes to supply your armies. Now is the time to make peace with Europe's princes."

"I do not see how," Louis confessed.

"See where their divisions lie, then widen them," Anne counseled.

Louis nodded. "I will send Fleuranges south."

"And reach out to the Venetians now that Maximilian has dropped them."

"A good thought, *m'amie.*"

"I am a good wife."

Louis narrowed his eyes. "When you are not going behind my back to appease the pope."

"I do not wish to see your soul endangered," Anne retorted.

"I would prefer if you allowed me to manage my own soul's trajectory."

"As long as it aligns with mine," she shot back.

"My soul could never stray far from yours," Louis said. His *Brette* was a rock. Immovable and, at times, in the way, but to be counted on.

"Then stop straying from the Church, and dispense with this schismatic idea before all of Europe abandons you."

"As long as you do not abandon me, I will manage." He

reached for his fierce consort. Without her, he would drown in the roiling waters of shifting alliances amongst princes. It was a game not to his taste. But he was a king, and he must play it to win.

Louise de Savoy was horrified to hear the king had commissioned Francis to lead an army division against Spain. What if something happened to her son? The loss of Gaston de Foix the year before had shocked her. But Gaston was expendable; her son was not.

"Jean, you must go to the king and urge him to put Francis in the rearguard," she told her steward.

"I have no clout with the king and you know the dauphin will seek a prominent position as befits the man you have raised him to be," Jean de St.-Gelais objected.

"I have raised him to stay alive, not to get himself killed in some foolish war! Louise cried. Francis thought he was invincible. So had Gaston. Not yet tried in the crucible of time, her eighteen-year-old son was at the top of his young man's game: footloose, filled with adventurous dreams, and eager to test his skills on the battlefield.

"Then advise him if he is to head a division he must stay alive to instruct his men," Jean said.

"You must advise him, not me!" Louise exclaimed. "He doesn't listen to anything I say when it comes to military affairs."

"I'm sure he will lead them bravely." Jean's soothing tone infuriated her.

"And there lies two problems, both of which you must warn him not to do!" Louise felt her hysteria growing.

"Which are?" Jean asked, looking ready to be somewhere else.

"He must not lead his men, but command them from a safe vantage point so he can keep an eye on the overall field." Frankly, she preferred him to stay home, but she knew the king wished to harden him.

"A wise strategy to keep him from the line of fire," Jean agreed.

"And what an eighteen-year-old youth thinks of as brave is what any seasoned soldier thinks of as foolhardy."

Jean laughed. "So it is and ever shall be. But he must learn what war is so he knows the sacrifice a king asks of his subjects when he sends them into battle."

"Sacrifice? I have sacrificed everything to raise my son to be king one day. Do not talk of sacrifice to me!" she screeched.

Avoiding her eyes, Jean edged toward the door as he put on his cap. "My lady, I must attend to the groundsmen. I will come again this evening to report on the day."

"Come in an hour," Louise directed, seeing it did no good to rile him. "I will have a letter for you to get to Blois."

"Very good, my lady." Jean dipped his head, looking relieved to make his exit.

The moment he was gone Louise went to her desk and penned a short note to Florimond Robertet. She would have him speak to the king and have Jean speak to Francis. Between the two of them, she would see to it that her son stayed far from the field of engagement.

Her precious Francis knew nothing at all about what war entailed. She would use all her well-woven connections to ensure that it remained that way.

Chapter Twenty-five

1513

The Pope is Dead

Relief arrived in late winter with two messages from Rome. On February 21 Julius II had died of a fever at age 69. Within weeks, a second missive followed: a new pope had been elected.

Anne exulted. There was now a chance that Louis' excommunication would be lifted, the hope of salvation restored to him and every one of his French subjects.

Louis was relieved beyond measure. The new pope was a less warlike and more cultured man. Taking the name Leo X, Giovanni de Medici was the second son of Lorenzo the Magnificent. As the Medicis were old allies of France, Louis' spirits soared to think that relations could be restored.

With Julius II out of the way, Louis signed a treaty alliance with the Venetians, who were looking for a friend amongst Europe's princes. On the outs with Maximilian, Venice had been tossed from the Holy League over a land dispute.

Soon after, Ferdinand of Spain responded favorably to Louis' peace offer, signing a truce of one year with France.

Four days later, Ferdinand signed another agreement against France with the Holy League, including the new pope and Margaret of Austria, Governor of the Netherlands. The

Spanish king's predictable perfidy gave Anne and Louis a merry moment.

A week later, Anne's joyful mood burst as she stood on the threshold to Louis' study. Overhearing him dictate orders for deploying the French army back over the Alps, she exploded.

"My lord, you're not thinking of going back, are you?" she exclaimed, Father Mayheuc's counsel flung to the wind.

Louis' eyes flashed. "Stay out of it, *m'amie*. It's my business, not yours."

Anne set her hands on her hips, blocking the doorway as if to block his path to Italy. "The new pope is your chance to start fresh. Do you really want to provoke him?"

Louis crossed his arms, staring her down. "I want what is mine by ancestral right."

"Folly, Husband! Look toward your salvation, not a piece of land outside your realm."

"Take care of your own realm, and I'll take care of mine, Madame."

Remembering her confessor's advice somewhat late, she shot her husband a black look and left the room. It was pointless to try to convince him to relinquish his dream. Let him keep his hopes for Milan as long as his soul was no longer in danger. She would work her back channels, writing to the new pope to congratulate him on his election and to say that her husband hoped for reinstatement within the Church.

The next day she went to find Louis' senior minister. Florimond Robertet owed his high position to her after she had urged the king to appoint him after d'Amboise's death. Now was time to call in the favor.

"Sire Robertet, I count on you to urge the king to remain in France whatever his plans are in Italy this spring," Anne told him.

"Your Grace, I will do what I can." Robertet looked strained. She rarely visited his office, but she had wanted to catch him alone before he met with Louis.

"He is too valuable here to risk his life there, wouldn't you agree?" Anne asked.

The senior minister's face blanched as she crossed the room between him and his desk.

"I agree, Your Grace, but it is up to the king whether he goes or not."

"We both know how important Milan is to him, do we not?" Anne asked, wondering what was most important to Robertet. It looked as if something was weighing on him.

"He believes it is a good moment to stake his claim again, Your Grace."

"And do you?"

Robertet coughed. "I serve at the king's pleasure, Your Grace. His pleasure is mine, so I—"

"Drop your courtier's tongue for a moment and remember who recommended you to the king for your present position," Anne reminded him in a pleasant tone.

"Alarm swam in Robertet's eyes. "Your Grace, I thank you every day of my life for my good fortune."

"As you should. But I count on you to keep the king's interests focused on France where he is well-loved."

"I try, Your Grace, but the king is committed to regaining Milan. With the new pope, he has more of a chance."

"Just make sure it is the army that goes, not the king himself," Anne specified.

"I can only try," he hedged.

"And I can only continue to support your favor in the king's eyes if you succeed," she spelled out.

"Ah, Your Grace—would that you would continue to do

so," Robertet exclaimed, his eyes darting to his desk then flitting away.

His tense tone surprised Anne. Was it her warning or was it something else?

Scanning the room, her eyes rested on the papers on his desk. At that moment, a sour scent hit her nose—the scent of fear. She had smelled it before on men, the first time at age twelve. Never would she forget the day she had stood up to her would-be kidnapper outside Nantes in his failed bid to wrest her ducal seat from her.

With three steps she was at the senior minister's desk, examining the papers on top.

"Your Grace, is there something I can find for you?" Robertet's voice was hoarse. Advancing toward the desk, he reached for the pile of papers closest to her.

Anne dropped her hand onto the pile, preventing him from sweeping it from her.

"I have already found it." She picked up the top paper as she took a seat. "Why not get some water to clear your throat?"

"Your Grace, shall we go refresh ourselves together?" Robertet asked, his voice tinged with panic.

"I am already refreshed. It is always amusing to learn what the Countess d'Angoulême is up to in her efforts to come between the king and me." Anne stared at the distinctive bold signature of her rival on the paper she held. She remembered it from 1506 when she had watched Louise sign Claude's betrothal contract with Francis.

Sweat broke out on Robertet's brow. "Madame, it is nothing of the sort. An altogether different matter, just a small request."

"I see." Anne read the short note above the signature.

> 'Urge the king to keep Francis out of Italy. He must not go should the king choose to go on campaign again. Your job depends on it.
>
> —Louise.'

"Your Grace, it is nothing. Just one of many requests I receive every day." Robertet shifted from one foot to the other.

"And yet your job depends on it." Anne surveyed the flustered man.

"I do not know what the Countess meant by that," the senior minister stammered.

So it was from Louise de Savoy. "Is it your job with the king or your job spying on the king for her?" Anne asked.

"Your Grace, you know I would never do such a thing."

"You wouldn't. But the Countess would use you to do it for her."

"I—I do not know what you mean. It is only a request from a mother who wishes to protect her son."

"A worthy instinct. What other requests does Louise make of you to whisper into the king's ear?"

"It is not so, Your Grace. Entirely not."

"Yet she signs herself 'Louise.' You are in close relation, are you not, Sire Robertet?"

"I know her from the years of the Marshal de Gié's trial, Your Grace. The same years in which I worked for you to bring the marshal to justice."

"So you are working for her now, is that it?"

"No, Your Grace. Of course not."

"Yet you are on a first-name basis."

"It is the way the Countess chooses to sign her name, I would think."

Anne flicked her eyes over him. "When was the last time you saw her?"

Robertet's face colored. "A while back."

"Here at Blois? Or at Amboise?"

"It was at Amboise, Your Grace."

"And what was your business at Amboise?"

"A wedding, Your Grace."

Anne smiled to put him at ease. "I enjoy weddings. Whose was it?"

"It was the wedding of the dauphin's natural sister."

"Do you mean Souveraine?" She had heard that Louise had married off the last of her husband's three daughters by his mistresses a few years earlier.

"Yes, Your Grace."

"Who did she marry?"

"She married the king's baker, Your Grace.

"And you are an especial friend of the king's baker?" She raised a brow.

"I—no, Your Grace. It is through my wife that I was invited."

"What is your wife's connection to the king's baker?" Anne pressed.

Robertet blinked. "She is his sister, Your Grace."

"Ah," Anne exhaled, allowing a moment of silence as Robertet absorbed the impact of what he had just divulged. She had heard of the baker's wedding to Souveraine the year before. It was interesting to learn that the baker was related by marriage to Robertet.

"And who arranged this match?" she asked, tapping the note from Louise under her hand.

"Who? I do not know, Your Grace."

"Of course, you do," she encouraged, her tone light. "Was

it not the Countess d'Angoulême who introduced them?" She didn't know, but she could guess.

"I believe it was, Your Grace." Sweat beaded at the senior minister's temples.

"Well done, Monsieur. You are now part of the dauphin's family."

"I—well, yes. I suppose I am."

"I see you are doing well for yourself, even without my help." Leaning back in the chair Anne rested both elbows on its arms as she assessed him.

"I count on your support, Your Grace. It is you who brought me to the king's attention in the first place."

"Then see to it that the king doesn't go to Italy," Anne demanded.

"Ah, Madame, I will do all that I can," Robertet replied.

"Even more than before I discovered you work for Louise?"

"No Madame! I would never—"

"If you wish to keep your position with the king, you must stop working for the Countess d'Angoulême," Anne cut him off. Rising and exiting the room, she passed the wrung-out courtier without a backward glance.

As she headed for her quarters, she thought of her rival's concerns. Louise was desperate to keep Francis out of Italy, safe at home, just as Anne was desperate to keep Louis out of Italy. Who could blame the woman?

For a brief moment, a twinge of sisterhood struck her. No mother in all of France fought harder to protect her son. The Countess was grasping, underhanded, and devoid of royal self-possession. But her passion for her son's interests was something to be counted on, as unshakeable as the sun in the sky. Would she have felt the same degree of protectiveness toward her own sons if any of them had lived?

Rounding the corner, she came upon Claude walking toward her, holding the hand of her tiny sister, their attendants behind.

Anne crouched and held out her arms to her daughters, her heart fierce with love.

Of course, she would.

Portrait of Francis I, King of France
by Jean Clouet, c. 1515
Musée Condé, Chantilly, France
Courtesy of Wikimedia Commons

Chapter Twenty-six

1513

Battle of the Spurs

In April 1513, twelve thousand French troops crossed the Alps and marched toward Milan under Louis' commander General Trémoille. Their aim? To overthrow the Swiss mercenaries and their puppet leader Maximilian Sforza now ruling Milan.

Louis stayed behind, directing actions from Lyon on the other side of the Alps. With rumors of the English king's plans to invade France from Calais, his advisors had begged him not to leave his kingdom.

Francis accompanied him, directed by Louis to sit in on council meetings. It was time his dauphin learned that kingship was more about endless meetings than about pageantry and heroism. Besides, Francis' mother had pleaded that he not allow him to go to Italy. After Gaston's untimely death, Louis could understand her concern.

Trémoille's army enjoyed quick success. As fed up with the Swiss occupying their duchy as they had been with the French the year before, many of the Milanese welcomed them back. Driving the Swiss from much of the duchy, except for Como in the north and Novara to the west, Trémoille followed Louis' orders to set siege to Novara until the Swiss mercenaries holding the town surrendered.

But before dawn on the same night the French arrived, Swiss forces slipped from town and marched on the French camp in a surprise attack. By the time the French awoke, thousands had been killed. All the cavalry could manage was to mount their horses and flee from the merciless Swiss pikemen.

French losses numbered over seven thousand, with Swiss losses at around fifteen hundred. Francis' close friend Fleuranges received multiple wounds and was carried from the field by his father. Louis shuddered to think what might have happened had he allowed his dauphin to go.

After learning of France's defeat at Novara, Genoa revolted next, rising up against its French overlords and restoring its former doge. Meanwhile, the Swiss swiftly retook Milan. What was left of the French army crept home, arriving in dribs and drabs just as they had the June before.

Nevermore was Louis XII to hold territories in Italy for France.

Too hard-pressed to grieve, Louis moved north to Paris by the end of June. Henry VIII of England had crossed the Channel the week before to join the English army in Calais. His plan was to invade France with help from Maximilian's troops. The young English king was determined to claim the title of King of France that Julius II had offered him the year before upon excommunicating Louis.

As Louis' troops trickled home from Italy throughout July, he redeployed some to Picardy to help push back the English and the remainder to Burgundy to stave off the Swiss on France's borders.

Back in Blois, Anne had Robertet draw up a document reinstating a French envoy to the papal seat in Rome and welcoming a papal envoy to France in the hopes of smoothing the path to reconciliation between Louis and the Church.

Henry VIII's first move came in August 1513. In the name of the Holy League, the English king's army besieged the French fortress town of Thérouanne. The onslaught was unthinkable for Louis when just one year earlier France had ruled northern Italy and no prince of Europe would have dared a military incursion on French soil.

Adding to his troubles an attack of gout delayed Louis from getting to the Picardy region to take command of the situation. His spies informed him that on August 13, Maximilian had been received by the English king under a tent of cloth of gold outside of Thérouanne.

Louis seethed that it was the twenty-two-year-old English king Maximilian had deigned to meet, not a peer such as himself, who had been the Holy Roman Emperor's ally far longer as a founding member of the League of Cambrai.

Stung by the insult and still unwell, Louis arrived at Amiens on August 14th, about nineteen leagues south of Thérouanne. There, he instructed his commander, La Palice, to bring provisions to the besieged town.

As French supply wagons lumbered past the village of Guinegate toward Thérouanne they met up with an unexpected surprise.

Henry VIII had sent ten thousand English troops down from Calais to block the road. Accompanying them was a detachment of imperial cavalrymen. Henry's troops were in fighting form, whereas the French, numbering about six thousand cavalrymen, had been tasked only with escorting the supply wagons.

Henry's army trained their mounted archers and artillery on the French cavalcade. With his men wholly unprepared for combat engagement and no orders from Louis in the event of an attack, La Palice ordered his cavalry troops to retreat.

But the English artillery and archers had already fired on the vanguard of the supply wagons. In a mad panic, French cavalrymen spurred their horses and turned tail.

Mounted English and imperial troops pursued them, capturing one hundred twenty French noblemen. The valiant Pierre Terrail de Bayard, France's most seasoned knight, numbered among them, along with Francis de Dunois, Duke of Longueville, who had helped keep the dauphin out of trouble in Navarre.

Francis d'Angoulême was not amongst them. Disporting at a nearby bathing spot with friends, he had missed the entire battle, much to his mother's relief.

Word of the rout spread like wildfire. Soon, all of Europe mocked the French, referring to the debacle as the Battle of the Spurs, since the French cavalry had used only their spurs to flee, instead of holding ground and fighting back.

"I would fly to Brittany if I could!" Louis burst out upon hearing the news. Those present who had known him the longest were not surprised. Brittany had always been a safe haven for him, a refuge where he could rest from the worries that beset him as a prince of the blood of France.

Without the supplies the French army had been on its way to deliver, Thérouanne fell within the week to the English and imperial armies. Margaret of Austria, Governor of the Netherlands, reasoned that her father Maximilian would not bother supplying or paying a garrison to hold it but would be ashamed to hand it over to the English. She ordered the town destroyed.

Henry and Maximilian turned next to Tournai, a French outpost that had existed within the Netherlands' territory for over three hundred years.

Surrounded by non-French territories, Tournai was as

ill-equipped to withstand a siege as Louis was ill-equipped to defend it. The flower of his officers had been taken prisoner. Additional troops could not be raised; already, they were engaged in Burgundy where the remainder of the French army was fending off the Swiss on its border.

Louis ordered Tournai's city fathers to hold out against the combined English and imperial forces. But without support or provisions, the town capitulated within six days. Most galling for Louis, Henry VIII insisted on receiving its surrender as King of France, the investiture offered him by Julius II the year before.

Louis now faced the Swiss pouring into France along Burgundy's border. His commander Trémoille did not have enough men to push back the twenty thousand Swiss pikemen, accompanied by one thousand cavalrymen sent by Maximilian.

Overwhelmed, the French army retreated to Burgundy's seat of Dijon, where the Swiss besieged them. On September 13, 1513, Dijon's city walls were breached. With no orders sent from Maximilian, the Swiss came to terms with Trémoille.

The concessions they demanded included a promise to give up all future claims to Milan and Asti. With no alternative, Trémoille accepted the terms in the king's name.

The Swiss pulled out and went home, grumbling over the Holy Roman Emperor's lack of follow-up after they had won French territory for him. Louis knew the story all too well.

The moment the Swiss left, Louis disavowed the treaty's terms, saying he had not agreed to them. Never would he give up all future claims on Milan and Asti. Those territories were his birthright. One day he intended to return to Italy to claim them for France.

Yet that day never came.

France's ally Scotland suffered similar devastation that

September, thwarting Louis' hopes that Henry VIII would be forced home to defend his own territory. Defeated by the English at Flodden Field under Catherine of Aragon's command, the Scottish king, James IV, had been killed. The turquoise ring Anne of Brittany had sent him, with encouragement to be her valiant knight, was found on his finger when his body was recovered.

Abandoned by those who had once been his allies, Louis vowed to rethink his strategy over the coming winter. With snow making the Alps impassable, he welcomed the respite after a long and difficult year.

Louise thanked her stars that her son had chosen to go swimming that fateful day at Guinegate. It was a shame that his friend who had protected him in Gascony had been captured, but all that mattered was that her son was safe.

"*Maman*, I should have been captured along with my friends," Francis complained. Tall, dark, and with the saturnine good looks of his father, he flicked the tassel on his burgundy doublet as he lounged against the door of her study.

Louise tutted. "My son, you were born under a lucky star. What happened at Guinegate confirms it. Do not think for a moment that you would have done the king of France any good by getting yourself captured."

"If I had been, I would have charmed the English and made friends with their king; he's only a few years older than me."

"War is no game, and capture by the English is something no Frenchman could ever wish upon himself." Louise tried to sound stern but it was no use. She drank in his debonair grace, every inch a future king.

"*Maman*, I have heard this new English king is sporting. I would beat him at tennis and he would release me, I'm sure."

"Francis, you know nothing of what truly happens in war. Do you not remember tales of King Louis' father? The English held him for twenty-four years after Agincourt. He was their prisoner for longer than you have been alive," she scolded, exasperated by his insouciance.

"He was a great poet, was he not?" Francis looked dreamy, as if mulling a poem on some future heroics he might achieve.

"He was unable to run his estates, marry and father heirs, and live the life he should have lived in his own country," she rejoined, thinking of further ways to ensure her son never saw military action again.

Francis shrugged in his usual disarming way. "He should have found someone to ransom him and come back sooner."

"It is not so easy!" she chided. "Ask the king if he is not saddened by his father's fate. He was so old when Louis was born that he died before he ever knew him."

She recalled the rumors circulated long ago about Louis' parentage. Charles d'Orléans had been sixty-seven years old when he had sired his first son, raising many a brow. Some said that in her eagerness to produce an heir for her much older husband, Louis' mother had turned to their steward for help.

Louise squelched a smile. Stewards could be handy at times, with or without husbands around. "You are incorrigible, Francis. Go now and promise me you will not seek any further military action."

"You smile, *Maman.* Is it because I am incorrigible or that you know I will not promise you any such thing?"

"Neither. Now leave me to my thoughts and return to your amusements."

"You as well, *Maman.*" With a wink, France's dauphin turned and strolled out the door.

Chapter Twenty-seven

Fall 1513

Renée's Dowry

Louis stood before Valentina Visconti's portrait, crushed to think he had let her down. It had been the worst year of his reign. Wondering how he might salvage something from it, he stared up at her image.

"Louis, do not give up on your birthright," she seemed to advise.

"There is nothing more I can do. I am tossed from Italy and pressed on all sides."

"For the moment, but not forever. Pass your rights on to your children so they may resume our family's claim one day. It is your birthright. Never forget it."

Louis thought for a moment. If he passed on his Italian rights to Claude, Francis would fight to reclaim his holdings. But he didn't want his successor getting himself killed over there. Thinking of Gaston, his heart hurt to think of his nephew's glorious future snuffed out in a moment of recklessness. Francis was even rasher and less experienced in battle. Besides, his mother had begged him to keep her son out of Italy.

"Give your rights to your second daughter," Valentina Visconti advised.

Louis stared at his grandmother's image. If he ceded rights to Renée instead of Claude, Francis would stay out of Italy and whoever Renée married could help her make her claim.

"She will need a powerful prince as a husband to help her claim them," Louis countered.

"Then marry her to a powerful one," his grandmother agreed.

"Who should it be?" Louis asked.

Valentina's eyes bored into his. "Tie your enemy to you so you may control him better."

Louis stared at his grandmother's portrait. His enemies were now Henry VIII of England, Maximilian of Austria, and Ferdinand of Spain. The Swiss didn't count because they were up for hire.

"Surely, not to the House of Habsburg," he said.

"You tie two of your most powerful enemies to you if you do," his grandmother pointed out.

Louis frowned. "I do not wish for France to be encroached on by Ferdinand or Maximilian."

"If you seek a marriage alliance with one of their mutual grandsons, they will be obliged as your allies to defend you against the English."

Louis' heart skipped a beat. Of all three of his present enemies, it was the English he feared most.

"'Tis a point. But what if Renée's husband tries to take her Italian holdings for the House of Habsburg instead of the House of Valois?"

"You will have a contract drawn up protecting her claim. Besides, her marriage will be years from now and much can change. In the meantime, you will have an alliance with two of your present enemies to protect you from the third one across the sea."

Louis shuddered. *England.* Images came to him of a field of longbowmen facing France's finest knights, his father—a youth of twenty—amongst them. Why not tie both Ferdinand and Maximilian to him now then shrug them off in ten years' time when Renée came of marriageable age?

"Madame, you advise me along the same lines as my wife would," Louis said, astonished to think of it.

"Your wife has her reasons for wanting an alliance with the House of Habsburg, and so do you. Different ones."

"Very different, Madame."

"Nothing need be set in stone. Remember that."

"My wife's mind is set in stone. But mine is not, so I will think on it."

As Valentina Visconti's eyes met his, they seemed to forgive him his failures. With the plan they had just hatched, all was not lost in Italy. Only put on hold for the present, waiting to be reclaimed at a future date.

"One last thing, Louis."

"What is it, Madame?"

"Make your peace with the pope."

"Hell's bells," Louis swore under his breath as he struggled to find the right words for his letter to the Medici prince Leo X.

"Just wrap it up with a sentence or two and send it off so I can get an answer," he ordered Robertet.

"Sire, I have no experience with penning a letter to the pope. I am sure your wife could do better than anything I can come up with."

"I'm sure she could too and already has. But this must be from the King of France, not the Duchess of Brittany."

Exasperated, Louis rued the loss of his former minister. Georges would have known exactly what tone to take as a cardinal of the Church. He would have written the whole message for him, just handing him the paper to sign. Where was his beloved stout friend when he needed him?

"You might say in light of the Conciliabulum being disbanded, you seek restoration to the Church on behalf of yourself and the subjects of your kingdom," Robertet suggested.

"Why not mention France?"

"Perhaps France has been mentioned overmuch in Italy in recent times," Robertet counseled delicately.

"Good point. Put all that in and remind His Holiness of our long time friendship, which I hope will continue throughout the duration of both of our reigns."

"Perhaps you should only mention his reign, as yours is no longer recognized in Rome since the last pope gave his investiture to—"

"Have done! Just mention his reign and let's get me back on the throne of my own kingdom in the eyes of my fellow princes."

"A good idea, Sire. Especially as your people adore you and have never sought any other as their king."

"Why should they? What prince would keep taxes as low as I do?"

"None, Sire. Which is why they love you."

"At least somebody does," Louis grunted.

"Certainly the queen does, Your Grace."

"She will love me even more once the pope lets me back into the Church."

"It is my belief that she could not love you more, but her relief would be great," Robertet offered.

"Finish scribing and hand me the signing quill." It was time to give the comforts of the sacraments back to his subjects. And God forbid that he should die outside the Church. It would be even worse than that sly diplomat Machiavelli being exiled from Florence.

He wondered if Anne had learned of the envoy's downfall at the hands of the Medicis. She would be happy to hear it, never having trusted the man.

He would let her know later as they sat before the fire in her chambers. Right after he told her he had written to the pope to ask for restoration to the Church. For once his sparkling *Brette* would have nothing to spar with him over. His blood raced to think of the evening ahead.

Louise captured her steward's bishop with her queen.

"Checkmate," she announced. Idly she wondered when Francis would arrive.

Jean de St.-Gelais stared at the board. "My lady, it doesn't seem possible."

"It doesn't seem possible, but it is." She sat back, satisfied.

"I am sure there is a way out of this."

"And I am sure there is not." She had won the game and soon she planned to win another one on a far larger board.

Francis was due to spend Christmas with her. Marguerite too, with her dull husband in tow. Hapless as well, Louise had heard he had broken his arm in a fall from his horse. She hoped it wouldn't interfere with their efforts to produce the heir the king needed to claim Armagnac lands for the crown.

"My lady, you have cornered my king," her steward acknowledged.

"Just what I told you." Louise contemplated Jean's king, hemmed in with no escape in any direction. She hoped Louis wasn't in a similar position.

"I look forward to a rematch, Madame." Seeing her mind was elsewhere, Jean rose and left the room.

As she swept the chess pieces from the board, she thought of the king. It had been a terrible year for Louis. The last time she had seen him, soon after Guinegate, he had looked harried and old. How much longer would he last with almost all of Europe bearing down on him and still under excommunication?

She caught herself. Of course, she didn't wish the king dead. She just wished her son to be on France's throne before she was too old to enjoy seizing the reins of command to direct him. Could she help it if she wanted to rule France as queen mother in the prime of her life? At age thirty-seven, she was ready.

Opening the drawer where her charms lay tucked away in their doeskin bag, she pulled them out. Patting the one shaped into a small wooden figure, she laid it face down with the bag covering it. *No more babes for you, high and mighty one*, she whispered.

About to place them back in the drawer, the clatter of hooves outside diverted her attention.

Louise's heart leaped. Had her one true love arrived?

As lightly as a hind she ran downstairs and out to the courtyard.

With easy grace, Louise's son jumped down from his horse, a broad smile on his darkly handsome face. Like a young god welcoming his devotees, he opened his arms to her.

"My darling!" she exclaimed, rushing into them.

Jean de St.-Gelais followed behind. Taking the reins of the dauphin's mount, he led it away.

Louise didn't notice. In her son's presence, she had no eyes for anyone or anything else. All that mattered was that her precious Caesar was with her, where he belonged. They would be together forever as soon as he was head of France, and she was head of him.

At age thirty-six, it had been almost two years since Anne had been with child. Never since her first pregnancy had she gone for so long without her womb ripening.

Pushing away thoughts that she would have no more children, she bent her efforts to getting Louis' excommunication lifted. In letters to the new pope, she congratulated him on his election and asked for clemency for her husband.

While waiting for Leo X's reply, she worked on a liturgical garment for him. As she wove she began to develop a plan for a Habsburg alliance for her younger daughter.

On November 16, 1513, Louis signed a document granting his hereditary rights to Milan, Asti, and Genoa to their second daughter, Renée of France. It was a grand coup, in light of the match Anne wished for her. Her sights were set on betrothing Renée to Charles of Habsburg, the thirteen-year-old Austrian archduke, grandson of both Maximilian and Ferdinand, raised by Maximilian's daughter Margaret in the Netherlands. No future prince of Europe would be more powerful, with his realms including the Holy Roman Empire, and Spain with its new dominions across the ocean, thanks to Queen Isabella's support of the navigator Columbus.

"Husband, let us present our proposal before another offer is decided upon," Anne urged. Both knew his gift to Renée was an admission he did not think they would have any more children.

"*M'amie*, the boy is likely promised elsewhere. I heard talk he will marry the English king's sister," Louis replied.

"Well, then, there's his younger brother Ferdinand."

Louis handed her the document he had just signed. "I will leave it to you since you are the matchmaker all Europe bends the knee before."

"Then let us send someone to Margaret's court in the Netherlands to broach the topic," she proposed.

"I will not stand in your way, *m'amie.* But do not place all your hopes on this alliance coming to pass."

Anne said nothing but silently rejoiced to have Louis pull together with her on such a plan. *May Brittany ally with the House of Habsburg to keep France at bay,* she thought.

As the royal court began the fasting days of Advent, Anne searched her heart to prepare for the holy season ahead. She and Louis still had not heard from the pope on their separate requests to lift Louis' excommunication.

"What more can I do, Father, to urge the pope to lift interdiction on my husband and his subjects?" she asked her confessor.

"You can pray to our Father in Heaven to move His Holiness's heart," Yves Mayheuc said.

"I will do so, Father. Is there anything else I can do?"

"You can search your heart and shine a light on dark corners so your prayers may be heard."

"How do I do that, Father?" She had spent her life mastering the art of dissembling. But the confessional was not a place to dissemble.

"Not by your own efforts. But by confession then surrender to the will of God."

"I confess that this year I have struggled to give up my dearest dream," Anne admitted.

"Tell me, my daughter, so I may help you hand it over to God."

"Father, it seems I am not to bear a son."

The Breton priest raised compassionate eyes. "In this holy season when the Virgin Mother bore our Savior, this must weigh on you."

Anne hung her head. "It does, Father. I had wanted to give my husband and his kingdom an heir."

"You have given them a good and virtuous queen," the priest observed.

About to accept her due, Anne's conscience stopped her. "Thank you, Father, but I have many unvirtuous thoughts."

"Tell me," Father Mayheuc encouraged.

"I am jealous of the dauphin's mother," she blurted out.

"And why is that?"

"It seems she will one day see her son on the throne of France when one of my own should be on it."

"And is she jealous of you?"

Anne snorted. "She is, Father."

"Why is that, my daughter?"

"I would guess it is because I have arrived and she is forever striving to arrive." She squirmed, aware that she was nowhere near her goal of cleansing her heart from sin.

The Breton priest's eyes twinkled. "Have you truly arrived, my daughter?"

"In all the ways I can control, I have. In ways I cannot control, I have not."

"And do you surrender those ways you cannot control to God?"

Anne's sigh filled the room. "I try, Father. But my mind always searches for what I might do to see my wishes met."

"Then you, too, are forever striving, my child."

His words settled on her like fine rain cleansing her soul. She didn't wish to think of herself as similar to Louise. But was she not also someone who strove with all her might to achieve her aims, just as her rival did?

"It is not in my control to have a son. But it is within my power to influence the pope to restore my husband to the Church," Anne said. "And I can't help thinking about what more I can do to convince him."

"Ah, my daughter. You are still intent upon convincing others."

"At least it's not my husband I'm trying to convince."

"Leave the convincing to others and seek to convince yourself that you have done all you can for your prayers to be heard by God," Father Mayheuc advised.

"Why would my prayers not be heard, Father?"

"Only you can answer that, my daughter."

As she knelt in her oratory that evening, Anne felt lightheaded. Hungry from fasting, she couldn't think clearly. Then it came to her that fast days were intended for God's people to approach Him in a state without too much thinking involved.

Too hungry to order her prayer, her mind drifted over her conversation with her confessor. The realization hurt that she would likely never bear another son. Yet there was peace in knowing it was out of her control and in God's hands.

Next, she contemplated Louis' excommunication. She had written many letters to the new pope that year. It was now for Leo X to decide the outcome. Giving up plans to sweeten him further, she let it go.

At thoughts of Louise, she stopped short. She had told Father Mayheuc she was jealous of her. But that wasn't all. She had put herself above the woman and mocked her for being an arriviste.

Of course, she was. Anyone could see it.

Her conscience slapped her. Were these not the dark corners Father Mayheuc had told her to shine a light on?

Shifting on her knees, she searched her heart.

Louise de Savoy was an arriviste only because she saw what could be and was ready to use all her resources to ensure that it came to pass. Would she not do the same if she were in her shoes?

She thought of the note scrawled to Robertet begging him to convince the king not to send Francis to Italy. Louise was as intent upon convincing Louis to do her will as she was. Her rival's desires and methods to achieve them were just like her own: insistent and unrelenting.

As if outside herself, Anne contemplated her rival. Was she not a woman more similar to herself than different? It wasn't Louise de Savoy who was ugly. It was her own heart.

In a swirl of self-reproach, Anne bowed her head and surrendered her dark thoughts to God. Even as they continued to fill her mind, she lay them out before Him. Powerless to stop them, she threw herself on His mercy.

Lord, cleanse me of my unkind thoughts toward Louise. My thoughts are as petty toward her as hers are toward me. She is an arriviste because she cares fiercely to get somewhere. I have striven just as fiercely, but because of the station I was born into I am not judged so harshly. There is no difference between what she wants and I do—we are both mothers who want what is best for our children. Release me from hating her. I can no more hate her than I can hate myself.

She lifted her head, humbled by such insight. Only the Holy Spirit could have authored it because she had never wished to think of herself as similar to her rival in any way.

Yet she was.

Rising, she went to meet her husband, the usual mocking thoughts about Louise de Savoy coming to her along the way.

But this time, her thoughts mocked her instead. The woman was a rock when it came to her son. And Anne's grandson through Claude and Francis would rule France as his father's successor. With both her and Louise's unrelenting determination in his bloodline, she expected he would make a strong king.

As she shook out her gown, she shook off her animosity toward her longstanding foe. Like a dandelion puff floating from her hand, her jealousy of Louise lost its power to torment her, blown away in the Advent season's winds of change.

One week later, the best possible news arrived from Rome: Leo X had lifted Louis' excommunication. France was no longer under papal interdict.

Louis was relieved but Anne was elated. She rejoiced to think that her husband would take his place in Heaven beside her, especially if she could keep him out of Italy.

That Advent season of 1513 brought great joy to both monarchs. With Louis' return to the Church, a possible match between their daughter and a Habsburg prince, and a lightened conscience toward Louise de Savoy, Anne felt more hopeful than she had in a long time.

But the winds of change still blew and none could guess how soon they would take an unexpected turn.

Chapter Twenty-eight

December 1513

A Flicker of Remorse

Marguerite arrived just minutes after Francis for her Christmas visit, her husband accompanying her with his arm in a sling.

Glancing at her daughter's mid-section, Louise saw it was as flat as ever. She would have another talk with her the following day. For the moment, it was enough to be in the company of the two people she loved most to celebrate a year that had brought her closer to her goal.

The king was worn out. Nothing more needed to happen other than the passage of time and the queen's usual bad luck with childbearing.

After the obligatory welcome greetings, Charles d'Alençon went to his room to see about his arm. The moment he left, conversation shifted to inside allusions and privileged references between Louise, Francis, and Marguerite that no one outside their trinity would ever be a part of.

"Our trinity back together!" Louise exclaimed as she settled in her study with her son and daughter.

Marguerite's almond-shaped eyes glittered. "Here we are, *Maman,* back under your roof and your spell."

Louise beamed. "Don't be foolish, 'tis I who am under your spell, Children."

"Of course, you are, *Maman*. You love being under my spell, don't you?" Francis teased. With a lithe movement, he tweaked her headdress.

Louise tossed back her head and laughed gaily. Could she help it? No one had ever delighted her more than the handsome young man she had brought into the world to one day become a king.

"Come, *Maman*. Take a walk with me before the sun dips. You know I can't sit still when there's fun to be had." Francis winked at her, making her heart flutter.

"It's cold outside. And we need to catch up," she protested.

"It's never cold when I'm here, *Maman*. You've said so yourself, many times." Francis turned and strolled from the study.

"Wait! I'll come!" Louise sang out. Following him from the room she would follow him anywhere. But once he was king, she would be sure to direct his steps.

"What are these for, *Maman*?"

"Where did you find those?" Louise's stomach roiled as she stared at her daughter's outstretched hand. The doeskin bag and its contents stared back at her. Unthinkable. Impossible.

"On your desk, *Maman*. What are you doing with these?"

Louise swallowed hard. Had she been so careless as to leave the bag of charms out?

With a shudder, she remembered Francis' arrival. All thoughts had flown from her head the moment she had heard the horses' hooves in the courtyard. She had run downstairs to fling herself into his arms, forgetting all about the sac on her desk.

Assuming a stern face, Louise pursed her lips. "If you must know, they are charms to bring about a pregnancy."

Marguerite's eyes narrowed. "How childish, *Maman*. Was it me you were thinking of?"

"Of course, it was you! Who else do you think I care enough about getting with child or not?"

"Well, there's the queen, of course. I rather thought these were on her behalf since I found this one lying face down with the sac over it." Marguerite shook the small wooden figure at her mother as if to taunt her.

"Don't be ridiculous. I got them on your behalf!" Louise reached for the charm, but Marguerite pulled away.

"And you see clearly they do not work," Marguerite replied. "You know relying on such things goes against the teachings of the Church."

"I am perfectly capable of deciding for myself what I choose to rely on to get done what needs to happen." Louise told herself not to get too worked up. Her clever daughter would know she had guessed right if she did.

Like a cat that has finished a bowl of cream, Marguerite gave a slow smile. "But you have not succeeded, have you?"

Oh, but I have. Entirely and utterly, Louise thought as she struggled to master herself. "It is my business, and I'll thank you to hand them over."

Marguerite glared at her. "It is my business too, since it is my child you are attempting to conjure."

"If you would just get it done, I would not need to resort to such methods. But since you defy your king, as well as me, you will give them back so I may continue."

"I do not care to have any child I create conjured through dark arts. Throw them out, *Maman.* They are worse than useless, used with intent to defy the teachings of the Church."

Bile rose in Louise's throat. "You're beginning to sound like the queen. Has spending time with your husband's mother made you more pious?"

Marguerite stared her down. "It has increased my respect for those who are."

"Little good it has done you."

"Yet here we are, *Maman*. I am at peace. And you?"

"I am perfectly at peace," Louise huffed, feeling like a thief caught in the act. "Just hand me my things."

"I know you, *Maman.* You cannot let go of anything once it's in your grasp."

"Of course, I can. Don't be silly." Damn her daughter to hell. There was nothing worse than being fully known by another. For that reason, she had never remarried. Only her children had such power over her, and they were old enough to use it against her. Especially this one.

"Don't worry, *Maman*. I know you can't do it, so I will throw these out for you."

Louise stepped closer. "I'll take them."

"No, you won't." Marguerite moved away, a mischievous smile on her face.

"Nonsense. Give them to me. They are mine to do with as I wish."

"I will give them to you if you destroy them before me," Marguerite bargained.

Louise sniffed, trying to emulate her son's effortless nonchalance. "I will throw them out, myself."

"Allow me, *Maman.*"

"No!" Louise threw herself at her daughter, reaching for her arm as she held it overhead.

But Marguerite was the taller of the two. Flinging the bag and its contents into the fireplace, she blocked her mother from fishing them out.

Avoiding her daughter's gaze, it was all Louise could do not to rush for the fire irons to retrieve the figures. But it would be what Marguerite expected her to do. Instead, Louise forced herself to remain still and pretend it didn't bother her to see her charms go up in smoke.

As she gazed into the flames, Louise assumed an impassive expression similar to ones she had seen on the faces of Anne de Beaujeu and Anne of Brittany. For a brief moment, she felt a flicker of remorse for the loss of sons she had wished upon the queen.

"You don't fool me," Marguerite broke into her thoughts. "I know you are dying to save your collection, but these are things you do not need."

Louise turned to meet her daughter's eyes. "What do you know of what I need?"

"I know that what you need you can't have because it is not something that can be acquired," Marguerite replied.

"What do you mean?" Louise stared at her, forgetting her role as mother for a moment.

Marguerite's eyes swept her. "It is something you either have within yourself or not."

Louise felt her blood rise. How dare her own daughter lecture her on what she lacked? "I will not ask if I do, then, because it is not for you to tell me."

"I don't need to, *Maman.* The queen does that job." Marguerite turned and left the room.

Seething, Louise stared into the fire until the last flame flickered and died. With it, so vanished her remorse. All that remained was rancor against those who possessed what she never would.

Chapter Twenty-nine

January 1514

The Ankou

On the second day of January 1514, Anne met with Fleuranges. He was just the man for the job she wished done.

"Sire de Fleuranges, I have another mission for you," she began as the handsome youth swept the floor with his hat in a gallant bow.

"Your Grace, I am at your service," he replied, his eyes rising to meet hers. At age twenty-two, he was one of the court favorites amongst Anne's demoiselles, a close second to Gouffier de Bonnivet. A second diplomatic mission would keep him away from her maids of honor until she decided upon a match for him.

"I wish you to take a message from me to Lady Margaret of the Netherlands," Anne said.

"I will do so gladly, Your Grace. May I ask what it is about?"

"It is to broach the subject of an alliance between the Princess Renée and Margaret's nephew Charles."

"Do you mean the young Habsburg archduke, Your Grace? The one whose grandfathers are the Holy Roman Emperor and the King of Spain?"

"The one."

"He is the most sought after prince in Europe, is he not, Your Grace?"

Anne felt her heart beat faster. There was no more suitable husband for her daughter. "He is."

"What if Lady Margaret tells me he is promised elsewhere?"

"If he is already taken then his younger brother Ferdinand."

"I shall deliver your message with utmost care, Your Grace."

"And I wish you to give Lady Margaret a gift from me and show her the greatest courtesies."

"I will pay court to Lady Margaret, Your Grace. Anything you give me to bring to her I will place in her hands with reverence."

"With all due pomp and ceremony, Sire de Fleuranges." Anne eyed him critically, to which the young man dipped his head. With his youthful brio and charm, he would do fine.

She sat back in her seat, contemplating what gift to send Margaret. Perhaps a portrait of Renée to assure her of the robust health of this younger Princess of France.

Her mind raced with plans. She could get her court painter Bourdichon to paint it. Or her other one, Jean Perréal. Better yet, have them both make a portrait and she would choose the better of the two.

"Shall I leave immediately, Your Grace, or when do you foresee this mission to be carried out?" Fleuranges looked ready to leap onto his horse and ride off the moment their audience was over.

"It will be soon, but not just—" A searing pain knifed through her. Clutching her abdomen, she moaned.

"Your Grace! Are you ill?" Fleuranges sprang to her side, catching her as she slipped from her seat.

"Mesdames, come quickly!" he cried, holding the back of the queen's head so that it did not touch the floor.

Unconscious, Anne, Duchess of Brittany and Queen of France, heard nothing.

The *gravelle* had returned. This time the pain was more severe. And fever accompanied it.

"*Maman*, you will rest, and when the stone has passed you will be better," Claude reassured her, holding her hand as Anne lay back on her bed.

"Thank you, Minou." She tried to focus on her daughter's delicate face, but the fever had addled her vision. The words of the doctor who had attended her two years earlier came to her: *If fever is present there is a mortal risk.*

Louis' face swam before her eyes. "*M'amie*, we will take good care of you. As soon as the stone comes out, you will be back to normal." His eyes were hooded. Whatever he was saying, she guessed he was thinking otherwise.

Anne shut her eyes, willing her mind to stay afloat. The pain was worse than childbirth. And childbirth had worn her out. Her spirit was strong, but her body was weak. She needed to tell Louis to get Fleuranges on the road to Margaret's court in Mechelen in the Low Countries. But she had not yet decided on what gift to send.

If she had Renée's portrait done, it would take time. Artistic creations, well done, could not be dashed off. For the first time in her life, she wondered if she had time to spare.

She needed to do so many things. She needed to rest, but she couldn't with this devilish torment inside, stabbing then subsiding, yet ever on its way back. Because of her previous attack, she knew how bad the pain would be when it returned. The thought struck terror into her, a terror she hadn't felt since 1495 when she received word that Charles-Orland was in extremis with measles.

"Bring Madame de Saubonne," she ordered.

Madame de Dampierre hurried away to find Renée's governess.

Within minutes, Michelle de Saubonne stood at Anne's bedside, her face composed but with eyes filled with concern.

"I entrust Renée's education and upbringing to you," Anne told her. "School her in the new learning, but give her a foundation in classical texts both ancient and modern."

"Your Grace, what examples do you give me of the more recent works she should read?"

"She must read *The Book of the City of Ladies* by Madame de Pizan and Monsieur Dufour's *Lives of Illustrious Women* that is dedicated to her mother."

"And of the new learning, Your Grace? Which of today's scholars do you wish her to study?"

"She should study the works of those who are not intent upon breaking with the Church as some new voices are. Have her read Erasmus. And get my Archbishop Guibé to guide her in the traditions of the Breton clergy. She must be familiar with them as my successor." Anne grimaced, her body doubling over.

"Your Grace, I will call your ladies," Madame de Saubonne exclaimed, backing from her presence.

Unable to stop shivering, Anne pulled the ermine-lined coverlet up to her chin. She couldn't get warm.

Madame de Dampierre came alongside her, tucking in the covers around her neck.

"Fetch Cook and have them send for the court doctor," her lady-in-waiting told an attendant. "Put another log on the fire and bring in more wood!" she barked to the two pages who stood in the doorway.

Francis de Bourdeille and Jean d'Estrées leaped to do her bidding. The queen had outfitted them with their jousting equipment. She was strict but generous. Everyone knew the king was less exacting but stingy. They'd choose the queen's service over the king's any day. If anything happened to the queen, they might not have the means to continue on their path to becoming chevaliers.

Anne closed her eyes, wishing she could sleep. But the cold was so fierce that she couldn't relax her body long enough to sink into slumber. Unable to rest between cutting bouts of pain, she couldn't recover herself the way she had done the last time she had suffered from stones.

Waiting for Cook to arrive, Anne sensed that this time was different from the last attack. Fever had set in sooner. It was wearing her out.

Lord, deliver me from this moment but not into the next world, she prayed. So much to do, yet unable to do it. How unlike her.

Two days later, Anne's prayer had shortened. *Lord, deliver me from this moment.* The pain, when it came, was unbearable. But when it ended there was no respite, just the ceaseless fever biting into her, imprisoning her in a state of endless shivering, her entire body shaking to warm itself. Nothing helped.

Finally, Cook brought a remedy that offered some escape. The poppy-flower tisane that she gave Anne to sip sent her into a strange sleep, unlike any she had ever experienced. Visions danced before her, some comforting, others not.

Her chancellor Philippe de Montauban came to her, holding up her special shoe that had fallen off in their escape from her enemies the year after her father had died. Philippe had rushed back to retrieve it on the dusty road they had galloped on, knowing she would need it to present herself with majestic bearing to her subjects. Smiling in her fitful sleep, she heard the crowds cheer as they acknowledged her as Brittany's new ruler.

"Is this a remedy you gave her the last time the *gravelle* came upon her?" Madame de la Seneschale's voice broke into her thoughts.

"Madame, it is not a remedy. And this is the first time I have given it to her," Cook's voice cut through Anne's fog like a flagship on the horizon.

"If it's not a remedy, then what is it? It seems the only way to get her to sleep."

"It is not a remedy but a poppy-flower tea to relieve pain."

"Why don't you make more of it to leave by her bedside? We can give it to her at night if she wakes in pain."

Cook's voice held a warning. "Madame, such a tea can make one float away and never return. It is not to be administered by unskilled hands."

"What is it, then, Cook?"

Whispered voices followed and Anne couldn't grasp what was being said. All she knew was that she was in a deep and unsettling sleep, one from which she would awaken into certain torment: if not from the stones, then from fever.

If only it could be spring. If only Claude were not to marry Francis d'Angoulême. If only Renée were ten years older and publicly proclaimed as her legal successor to Brittany's ducal throne. And if only Renée were already married to Charles, heir to both the Holy Roman Empire and Spain, with its vast new holdings in the lands across the ocean. If only she could get up and do something about all her plans.

But she needed to rest.

As she fell into uneasy sleep, the visions continued their dance. Muttering and murmuring she tossed. It was as if another being entirely was in possession of her body, a grim demon that clutched her in its maw and wouldn't let go.

Madame de Dampierre and Madame de la Seneschale clucked together as they moved from the queen's bed to warm themselves before the hearth. This was a state in which they had never before seen their sovereign. They prayed the stone would pass, the fever would break, and she would return to them.

Exchanging glances, both weighed the same thought. There was likely only one escape from this sort of pain. Should the queen take that route, their lives would inalterably change.

"Your Grace, there is blood in the queen's void," the court physician told the king.

Louis passed a hand over his eyes. "What does that mean?" Usually, it was he who was sick, except for the last time Anne had suffered an attack of the stones. He hadn't known what to do then, either.

"It is a sign of infection, Sire." The doctor's eyes were opaque, giving away nothing.

"Is that why she has a fever?"

"Yes, Your Grace."

"Can you do something to bring it down?"

"Sire, we are trying, but the queen is in a weaker state than she has been in the past."

"She is only thirty-six," Louis said, his voice rising. "There must be some way to bring down the fever so she can rest." No wonder his wife despised doctors. All they told anyone was the obvious.

"Sire, we will try, but you must know … you must know that—"

"I must know what?" Louis' tone was impatient. The doctor knew nothing more than he did. What more could he tell him?

"You must prepare for any eventuality, Your Grace."

Louis stared at the court physician. Finally, he had said something new. But it was something he was utterly unprepared to hear.

Waving his hand, he dismissed the doctor. He needed his wife. How could he go on without her? She had managed everything for him for years. Even things he didn't want her to manage.

He had lost his closest advisor and friend Georges. He had lost his beloved nephew Gaston. He had lost every one of his sons. But this was different. He could not bear to lose his *Brette.* She was his rudder like none other.

Louis clutched at the desk he sat before, as solid and immoveable as his wife. He had no idea what he would do without her around. Or he did, but he would do it wrong, and there would be no one he trusted to set him straight.

Crossing his arms on the desk, he buried his head in them. He had spent twenty-two years of unhappiness married to the wrong woman. Was he only to be given fifteen married to the right one?

As he rested, a perverse thought crossed his mind. If Anne were no longer around he could forge ahead with plans to retake Milan. Finally, no one would naysay him.

But at the thought of such an undertaking exhaustion filled him, paralyzing his will even to remove the nibbed quill that lay under his arm, pressing into him.

What was the point of it all? To what end? His daughters wouldn't want Milan to manage any more than their mother had. And without a son to pass it on to, why struggle to retake it? As soon as the Milanese found a more attractive suitor to rule them, they would shake off their French overlords just as they had done before.

Florimond Robertet slipped into the king's study, clearing his throat to announce his presence. He bowed as Louis lifted his head.

"Your Grace." Robertet took a step toward the king.

"It is not good." At least his new advisor had the decency

not to ask him for anything or prattle on about the latest bad news from abroad.

"Sire, I—I stand ready to fill in the gap until the queen recovers," Robertet stammered.

"Until the queen recovers?" Louis shook his head in misery. "God in Heaven, if only she would."

"Sire, we all remember how ill you were on more than one occasion. Yet here you are."

"I am here because she tended me. Now she is failing, and I don't know how to repay her in kind," Louis groaned.

"But, Sire, you know who does."

"Who?"

"The Breton woman in the kitchen."

"Ah, Cook."

"Yes. I heard she brought her back the last time the queen had stones."

"The last time the queen had stones fever didn't set in from the start."

"Your Grace, did the doctor say something more just now?"

Louis paused before uttering words he wished he had not heard. "He said to prepare for any eventuality."

Robertet hung his head then lifted his eyes. "Did not the doctor say that the last time she fell ill?"

"He did not. He also said there was blood in her void." Louis pushed away from his desk, staring blindly at the tapestry on the wall. It was a wedding gift from Anne: expensive, but worth it, just like her.

"I see." Robertet remained silent, his eyes on the tiled floor.

"I will check on her now." Louis rose and moved to the door, scanning the same tiles Robertet was gazing at. Black and white, Brittany's heraldic colors, they were arrayed in an artful pattern. Anne had commissioned them years earlier when she had first come to Blois as his queen. They achieved the effect of simplicity with elegance that was her hallmark.

Striding down the corridor toward his wife's chambers, Louis' thoughts raced. It wasn't just a question of losing her. He would lose part of himself, the best part if she were to go. His simplicity paired well with her elegance. His frugality curbed her extravagance. Who would temper him if she weren't around to do it?

Rounding a corner, he glanced at the fork that led off to his grandmother's rooms. *Dear lady, pray for my wife,* he begged.

Perhaps he'd still be the father of his people, but he would have no idea how to give them what Anne offered—pride in the glory that was France: morals, manners, refinement, taste. Without her, everything would be less well-ordered, less fine. He would turn into the crotchety old grandfather of his people.

Cook rose early the next morning. Her waking thought was to check on the queen. But she would first send Marie to see that the cloths were battened down over the herb beds. She missed her former kitchen assistant now that she had married and gone to live in town, but she had come back to help while Cook tended the queen.

"Go make sure the rocks at each corner of the herb bed cloths are still in place," she told Marie. "You can warm yourself by the fire when you're done."

Marie nodded and reached for her cloak. Heading out into the sharp cold of the misty January morning, she checked the herb beds, putting all in order. Then she looked about her. Down by the river she could see movement, perhaps a merchant on his way to market in the early morning chill.

Moving to a low point in the castle wall, she strained to see. Her Michel was down there, helping his father bring goods to the riverfront to load onto barges. How glad she was that the queen had brought them together.

But Marie couldn't make out her husband in the gray mist. Instead, a movement closer to her caught her eye. A tall, bent-over figure in a hooded cape was shuffling up the path.

Marie stared. What old man would be approaching the castle so early in the morning on such a frozen, gloomy day? Was it a holy man? A beggar?

A hawk circling overhead distracted her. When she looked again, the figure had vanished. Only tendrils of mist and fog curled in the air where she thought she had seen someone.

Hurrying back inside, she found Cook. "An old man is walking up the path to the castle."

"Alone?"

"All alone."

"A beggar perhaps. The guards will stop him," Cook assured her.

"It was strange. I saw him, then I looked again and he was gone."

Cook narrowed her eyes. "Did he turn the corner?"

"No. The path was straight where I saw him. First, he was there, and then he wasn't." She took the steaming mug of barley water Cook offered and sipped.

"What did he look like?" Cook pressed.

"I couldn't tell because he wore a cloak with a hood. He was tall and thin, and all bent over."

Cook looked at her strangely then reached for her mantle. "Show me where you saw him."

Going out into the chill morning mist, Marie led Cook to the chink in the wall where she had surveyed the river and pointed to the path below. "He was down there, just coming up the path."

"There's no one there now."

"And there was no one there the minute I looked again. Where do you think he could have gone?"

"You were seeing things, Goose." Cook's voice was muffled, unlike her usual commanding blare. She looked as if she had eaten a lemon.

"What does it matter, Cook? It was just some old man on his way somewhere." As far as she knew, the path led only to the castle. He would show up soon enough, and the sentries would learn his business.

"You were seeing the mist curl into figures, Goose. That's all." Cook's blanched expression didn't match her matter-of-fact tone.

"I guess so." Marie ran back into the kitchen to warm herself by the hearth. It wasn't the biting outside air that chilled her so much. It was the expression on Cook's face. She had never seen her look so shaken.

Cook hurried down the hall toward the queen's chambers, the mug of poppy-flower tisane warming her hands but doing nothing to stop the chill in her heart. The old man Marie had described to her resembled the Ankou of Breton lore.

It wasn't, of course.

Reaching the queen's chambers, she barely curtseyed in her haste to get to her patient. The queen lay still, her face a mask of exhaustion, the skin tight over her high cheekbones, her broad forehead sheened in sweat.

Cook sighed with relief. Sweat was a good sign. Her sovereign lived. She scolded herself for her overactive imagination. Yet as she did, her mind filled with childhood tales she had heard of the Ankou. Brittany's phantom harbinger of death came dressed as an old man: tall, skeletal, and bent over. It was a myth, that was all. Marie had simply seen an old man on his way somewhere.

Spooning a few drops of the tisane into the queen's mouth, Cook wiped her forehead with a lavender-scented cloth. Barking at the two useless pages who hung about wherever the queen was, she sent them for more logs. Then she returned down the hallway to the kitchen to give orders to her staff for the day.

As she walked, the thought of the old man came back. She shooed it away. An old man was an old man. Why or where he disappeared to was none of her concern. What was, was the queen's health. Her fever needed to break as soon as possible.

Or else.

Cook shivered. Would the fever continue until the old man reached the castle and climbed to the queen's bedchamber? Then it would end forever if the figure Marie had seen wasn't just an old man.

Smacking her forehead, the capable Breton woman told herself to stop.

Chapter Thirty

January 1514

Final Struggle

"Get the king and Robertet," Anne breathed out.

"Madame, you are in the mood for company today?" Madame de Dampierre asked, an uncertain smile on her face. Was the fever finally broken?

Anne shook her head. "Today I will make my testament." She closed her eyes, already annoyed at those who might not carry it out.

"Shall we send for the Countess d'Angoulême, too, Your Grace?"

"Not Louise," Anne rasped out. She couldn't stand the woman, but she could rely on her. She would entrust guardianship of Claude to her. With Louise as grandmother to Claude's children, Anne knew she would guard and protect her daughter-in-law as one of her own.

She gritted her teeth. She would bequeath her library to Louise, too. Anne knew the woman wouldn't let her vast collection of books and manuscripts slip through her hands. Once Louise acquired something she never let go. And however louche Anne found her to be, she was as adamant about noblewomen being well-educated as Anne was.

As fever gripped again, her judgments against Louise

dropped away like leaves falling from a tree. She didn't have to like her to know that putting her daughter and her books in her care meant they would be well looked after.

Within the hour, Louis was at Anne's bedside, his senior advisor steps behind.

"Bring in a desk so he can scribe all that I say," Anne ordered.

A desk was brought in and Robertet prepared his quill to capture the queen's bequests as stated to the king.

"Guardianship of my daughter Claude is to be given to the Countess d'Angoulême. She is to care for her like a child of her own."

Louis raised an eyebrow. His *Brette* couldn't stand the sight of Louise de Savoy. But he guessed his wife knew the domineering countess would watch over her daughter like a mother hawk, protecting the interests of the royal princess who would bear her grandchildren.

"The contents of my library are also to be given to the Countess d'Angoulême."

"My lady, I am impressed by your reversal of sentiment." Louis' voice held a tinge of irony.

"At least she will keep my library intact."

"Yes, my lady." He exchanged looks with Robertet.

"My duchy is to pass to our second daughter. The Princess Renée is to be ducal successor to the crown of Brittany."

"As it is stated in our marriage contract," Louis hedged, neither agreeing nor disagreeing. It wasn't the moment to argue.

"So you remember, my lord?" Anne's eyes bored into him, the fever appearing to clear for an instant.

"Of course, my lady. I remember well that you wouldn't

marry me without that clause." Louis' sap rose to think of Anne's spirited resistance to his suit. How pleasant a chase it had been to pursue his *Brette.* How she had challenged him and how gladly he had met her terms. He could think of no other woman in Europe more worthy of being a queen. Far more worthy than he was to be king beside her.

"And I wish to see Renée married to Charles of Habsburg or to his brother Ferdinand. Can you promise me you will attempt all to bring it about?"

"I will give it my all, *ma reine.* He couldn't promise what the outcome would be. After Lady Margaret being jilted by Charles for Anne in 1491, then Louis breaking off the marriage agreement for Claude and Charles in 1506, he doubted Maximilian's daughter would trust any marriage proposal coming from the French court.

"And I want you to keep Renée's dowry, as it is now, with Asti, Milan, and Genoa ceded to her by you. And Brittany ceded to her by me."

"As it stands, my lady." Surely she must know that as King of France he was not of a mind to give away French hereditary holdings in Italy to the House of Habsburg.

But time would have a way of making it all come right. Renée would need to marry an ally of France rather than a longstanding enemy. In the meantime, he would seek to tie his enemies to himself with a betrothal agreement just as Valentina Visconti had seemed to advise.

"I wish my heart to be buried next to my parents' tomb in Nantes," Anne dictated.

"*M'amie*, no!" Distraught, Louis slipped into his familiar address. "I wish you to be in the same place I, too, will one day rest." The thought of his wife's heart being anywhere but inside the living breathing woman before him was unbearable.

"I said my heart, Husband, not my body. You may have the comfort of my body next to you at St. Denis, cold comfort that it will be, but my heart belongs in Brittany at my parents' side."

"As you wish, *m'amie*." Louis' thoughts flashed back to Duke Francis' proud face as he introduced his exquisite elder daughter to him as a young man. What esteem the father and daughter had held each other in. Immediately, Louis had taken the young Breton princess seriously. He had done so ever since.

Robertet concealed a smile as he scribbled. His wife would enjoy hearing him recount this conversation that evening. As ever, he found the queen's attention to detail impressive.

Anne gave her husband's hand a weak squeeze. "I wish to see Claude." Whatever he did wrong after she was gone, she would settle the score when he joined her in paradise. How relieved she was that just the month before he had been welcomed back into the Church, so there was some chance of that happening.

Louis lifted Anne's hand to his mouth and kissed it. From a corner of the room, her linnet chirped once in its cage, reminding him they were not alone. He turned and motioned to Robertet to leave.

The counselor got up, bowed deeply, and backed from the room. As a commoner born, he greatly admired the queen, who upheld rank in all ways. She kept the old customs of Brittany, where gradations of nobility were as finely distinguished as the leaves of a mille-feuille pastry. Now that he had been admitted into the inner sanctum, he was a firm supporter of her high standards. If only she could forgive him his close relationship with Louise. God knew he would need to maintain it should the queen go. He guessed the king would soon follow, and then he would answer to Louise's son, whom everyone knew was controlled by his mother.

Seizing the moment of privacy, Louis leaned over and kissed Anne on the mouth.

"*M'amie,* you must not precede me home," he murmured.

"I would not if I could, but I am too weak to linger." Her loving look tore his heart in two.

"*M'amie*, I would be lost without you," Louis choked out, gathering her into his arms.

"You will, but I will be all around you."

He rocked her gently. "Would that it were so."

"Wherever you look in Blois, you will be surrounded by art that I commissioned."

Louis pulled away to smile at her through his tears. "*M'amie*, you have cost me a fortune."

"I have increased your prestige and added to the glory of your kingdom." Anne's linnet chirped in agreement.

"Amen, *m'amie*." All she said was true. And well worth it, every sou.

"Call my confessor," she commanded.

Louis' tears dropped onto Anne's hands as he bent over them. Kissing each one, he held his mouth against her skin, inhaling her scent of violet musk. Would that he could hold her forever.

Claude entered the room first, followed by Robertet and the Breton priest Yves Mayheuc. As Anne's two Italian greyhounds fled to a far corner, the princess rushed to her mother's bedside, grasping her hand in both of hers.

"*Maman,* you must not leave us," she squeaked, her voice trembling.

"Hush, Minou. I would not, but I am too weak to stay."

"No, *Maman*! Drink Cook's potions and the fever will

break. As soon as your stone passes you will be good as new." Claude's smile was unconvincing.

"Little dove, I will still be your mother in Heaven, watching over everything you do."

"I will do my best, *Maman*. I will do my duty by you and Papa."

Anne closed her eyes. Her heart filled with pride at words she had heard from her daughter's mouth before. When it came to duty, Claude was cut in her mold.

But she was well aware of where Claude's true heart lay. She would do her duty to her father and to France. Yet the children she bore would also possess the royal ducal blood of Brittany's House of Montfort. Her elder daughter would do her duty by them both. God grant that she would have more luck with bearing children than she ever had.

"You have always been my good girl. Now you must take care of Papa and Renée."

"Don't say that, *Maman*. You must get better and take care of them yourself. I can't boss Papa around the way you can. He is king, and only a queen can do that job," Claude protested.

"One day, you too, shall be queen."

"Not like you, *Maman*."

Anne smiled faintly. "You will be perfect, just as you are." *Not like me but with royal Breton blood in your veins, nevertheless.*

The queen's confessor bowed then approached the bed. It was time for the sacrament of extreme unction. The room fell still as Yves Mayheuc made the sign of the cross.

"Oh my God, I am heartily sorry for having offended Thee," the priest began.

Anne repeated the words, her voice a whisper.

"And I detest all my sins because I dread the loss of Heaven and the pains of Hell," he intoned.

The queen followed suit.

"But most of all because they offend Thee, my God, who are all good and deserving of all my love."

Louis felt a stab of jealousy, then caught himself. Of course, the Lord was deserving of all of his wife's love. Except that he needed some of it, too.

"I firmly resolve with the help of Thy grace, to confess my sins, to do penance, and to amend my life. Amen."

Louis watched as the priest pulled the vial of holy oil from his vestment and opened it. As he dabbed the sign of the cross on the queen's forehead and hands, he spoke.

"Through this holy anointing may the Lord in His love and mercy help you with the grace of the Holy Spirit. May the Lord who frees you from sin save you and raise you up."

Louis' heart caught. It was due to Anne that he had recovered all those times he had been close to death. He had been too worried about what she might do in his absence to die before her. Not that he had ever been able to control her. But the only way to ensure that his daughter marry his successor was to remain alive to see it happen.

Father Mayheuc began to recite the Pater Noster with those in the room joining him. The sounds of the Latin words rose and fell, comforting all present until the queen cried out as another attack seized her.

Louis wished he could rip the stone from her insides as Madame de Dampierre and Madame de la Seneschale bent over her. Anne moaned as they wiped her forehead and stroked her hair, her body convulsed in pain.

The priest completed the Our Father, then began the communion sacrament that followed. The attack subsided just long enough for Anne to swallow the morsel of bread given her and drink a sip of wine from the goblet he held to her mouth.

As the last rites ended, another attack began. In agony, she convulsed again.

"Get the queen something for her pain!" Louis barked at the two women who hovered over her.

"Yes, Your Grace."

"And take Claude with you." He didn't want his daughter to see her mother suffer so. He didn't want to see it either, truth be told, but he couldn't bear to leave her in such a state.

"Sire, you must rest," Robertet murmured.

"Leave me!" Louis snapped. He would rest when his *Brette* did. But he would rise again to face earthly affairs.

Gazing at Anne, he sensed she would face something different. He couldn't imagine her as feeble or as an invalid. She was born to make plans and order people around. He would be first in line to withstand her next order, if only she would give him one.

Noises at the door sounded and Cook appeared.

"Your Grace," she stated, curtseying. When she rose the face she presented was grim.

"Give her something for her pain."

"I heard she had another attack, Your Grace."

"Hurry. She can't take much more of this."

"Yes, Your Grace."

Louis moved away from the bed so that Cook could spoon the tisane into the queen. Drops of liquid dribbled from the side of her mouth, but enough reached her belly to do its strange work.

Within minutes Anne's moans ceased and she fell into sleep.

For the moment Louis could bear no more. He would come again soon but first he would take a stab at sorting through some of the papers piling up on his desk. Then he needed to give something to Fleuranges to bring to Lady Margaret in Mechelen. God's bones, he was no good at that sort of thing. What did he know about what gift to send the Governor of the Habsburg Netherlands? That was his wife's specialty, not his.

If only Anne could advise him next time he saw her. Glancing at his *Brette* he drank in the beauty of her heart-shaped face framed by its crown of dark wavy hair. Usually hidden under a headdress, it was a privileged sight reserved for only a few. He begged God to give him the chance to gaze upon those lush locks many times more.

The next day of Monday, January 9, 1514, Anne awoke to the dim outlines of her two Italian greyhounds on her bed. They weren't supposed to be there, but their fine bodies warmed her, so they had been allowed to stay.

The sound of her two best pages loading wood onto the hearth told her it was early morning. Francis de Bourdeille and Jean d'Estrées had finally learned how to manage their horses when carrying her litter. Since she had outfitted them with their jousting kits they would earn their knight's spurs one day. She prayed they would be valiant in battle and honorable toward the ladies.

The stones seized her, but she broke free from their grip. Caught by the vision of an image over her bed, she rose above the pain. The faint outlines of her Charles-Orland, a young man now, danced in swordplay with his younger brother, a youth with a dusting of hair on his upper lip. She soared toward them, eager to applaud the winner and grasp each of them in a loving embrace.

Her two princes' figures faded as the light grew brighter, guiding her to where she would reunite with her parents and sister, and the twelve princes and princesses she had borne who had left her too soon. Overjoyed, she flew to meet them.

Like a silk mantle slipping from her shoulders, her earthly cares fell away. Those she left behind would make mistakes in her absence, especially Louis.

But she knew her husband. She was on her way, and soon, he would follow. In paradise, she would teach him how to think big and spend big. They would fight and make up. It would be heavenly.

Chapter Thirty-one

January 1514

Louis

Louis awoke early the next morning. Anne would grumble if he didn't get Fleuranges off as soon as possible, but first, he needed to come up with a gift for Lady Margaret.

Throwing on his clothes, he headed toward the chapel for Mass then changed his mind. First, he would check in on Anne. If she was at all better, perhaps she might offer an idea for what to send the ruler of the Netherlands.

Heading down the cold stone corridor to his wife's chambers, he shivered. Knowing how his *Brette* disliked the cold, his heart ached for her to be so chilled by the brutally cold season on top of her fever.

As he rounded the final corner to her rooms, the back of Father Mayheuc appeared ahead, a ghostlike figure in the early morning gloom.

Louis froze. Anne had seen her confessor the day before. There was no reason for him to be there again so soon.

Icy tendrils crept over Louis as he took the final steps to her room. "Why is the fire not stoked? My wife must be freezing," he barked upon entering.

A sound like a sniffle came from the woman nearest him, her face crumpling as she curtsied. "She is no longer cold, Your Grace."

"If I'm cold, then she is," Louis told her. Then a shudder seized him as he took in the import of her words.

Behind him, a stifled sob. Whirling around, he flinched to see Madame de Dampierre on her knees before him.

"Your Grace, she is at rest," Anne's lady-in-waiting choked out, unable to meet his eyes.

Louis felt his senses go numb. The pain in the woman's voice told him what he couldn't bear to hear. He needed to warm his *Brette*, to rekindle the fire in her eyes, to feel her rage against him as they squabbled over Italy, the pope, Louise de Savoy.

Rushing to his wife's bed, he threw back the heavy velvet curtain.

Anne lay still, serene and at peace.

"The fever is gone," he cried, unable to think beyond how peaceful she looked.

"My son." Father Mayheuc came toward him, a crucifix in his hand.

Louis stared at him then back at Anne's face. Dear God, she was so peaceful she scarcely seemed to be breathing.

"'Tis wonderful to see her rest, is it not?" Louis babbled, not wanting to face what faced him now.

"She has gone home to her Heavenly rest, my son."

"She has … she is resting?"

"She rests in the Lord's arms, Your Grace."

"Dear God, no!"

"My son, be strong. She is at peace now and free from pain."

"She cannot—she cannot be …"

"She is, my son."

"Then I shall join her!" Louis flung himself on his wife's body as the priest backed away.

Muffled sobs filled the room as the dreadful day took shape.

Underneath him, Louis felt the strange coldness of Anne's body: inert, unresponsive, but finally at rest. Whispering to her, he kissed her face, more beautiful now than it had been since the stones had returned.

"*M'amie*, I will soon rest next to you," he choked out before his throat closed. Stifling his sobs, his chest heaved against her still one. No one would dare disturb him for however long he stayed with her. The anointed and consecrated body of a king could not be touched without permission. Except by his wife.

At the thought, a moan like a mighty wind escaped him. His beautiful *Brette* would never again reach up to touch him, to tease and provoke as she so loved to do.

"*M'amie*," he croaked, hiding his face in her hair. His great love was gone, his love of life gone with her.

The unusual cold of that January served its tragic purpose, preserving the queen's body for longer than was usual. For four full days, Louis wept and grieved, seeing no one and spending hours by Anne's side.

Refusing to wear the customary mourning white or purple of royalty, he dressed all in black as the lowliest of his subjects would wear and in keeping with Breton custom to please his beloved consort. God knew it reflected the blackness of his sorrow.

Unable to think beyond wishing to honor her in a splendor that befitted her, he ordered plans for the most magnificent funeral France had ever seen. He could get back to being cheap once his queen was laid to rest. But to esteem her in death with the resplendence with which she had lived would make her happy.

Hearing her voice in his head ordering candles and making arrangements, he vowed not to skimp. This was her final ceremony, not his. He would show all of France his regard for their queen.

An attendant appeared at the door to his study. "Your Grace, the men are here from Paris to ask about the vault."

"Send them in."

"Your Grace, my deepest condolences on the death of the Queen," the first man said.

"What do you need from me?"

"Sire, we wish to know what you would like done for the vault at Saint-Denis. The workmen will start on it as soon as we send the dimensions."

"Make it extra wide," Louis told them, his eyes straying to the window. If only he could rest beside Anne from that moment on.

"How wide, Your Grace?"

"Wide enough for me, for I will be joining her within a year."

The craftsman looked startled. "Ah, Sire, would that it not be so!"

"Would that it will be so, and see that it gets done." Louis shook his head. He had had enough of this world.

"Yes, Your Grace. May I measure your height?

"Whatever you need to do." Louis stood, his heart contracting to remember the exact point to which Anne's head came at the top of his arm.

The craftsman pulled out a thin measuring cord and held it up to the top of Louis' head as his partner held the other end to the floor.

In a moment, they were done. "Thank you, Your Grace, and may I say that all of France mourns with you."

"Go and light a candle for the greatest queen who ever lived," Louis dismissed them.

Outside in the corridor the first craftsman looked at the second. "Do you think he'll be gone in less than a year?"

"I think he'd like to be."

"He'll get remarried before a year passes. They all do," the first one observed.

"He looks as if he wants to join her now," the second one remarked.

"That's now, but wait and see. In a few months he'll be back in the game."

"It looks like he wants his game to be over, now that hers is."

"It doesn't matter what he wants," the first craftsman said. "He'll do what his subjects need him to do. And they're waiting for him to get an heir."

The second paused, rubbing his chin. "Do you think what we want has any sway with the king?"

"With most kings, no. But with this one, yes."

"God keep him, then. Long live King Louis."

"May King Louis live as long as he wants to," the first craftsman amended.

The second eyed him. "So you think he'll go within a year?"

The first craftsman nodded. "I'll wager an evening's drinks on it."

"He looks worn out so I'll only stand you a round."

"Done."

She couldn't believe her mother was dead. Now Francis' mother would look after her. Papa had already told her so.

Peering at him from the corner of her eye, Claude could see he looked as bad as she felt. Speechless, they sat side by side with their anchor and rock, mourning for the woman who had loved and shaped them. Each held a fold of the ermine-trimmed purple gown she wore as if holding on to it would bring her back.

Fighting back tears, Claude contemplated the months ahead. The Countess d'Angoulême would take charge of as much as the king allowed the moment she arrived. With her father undone, she guessed that would be a lot.

Claude steeled her shoulders. Her mother's voice rose in her head. "*Don't let her take you over. Stand firm, and see that you get your way when you need to.*"

How will I stand against her, Maman? She is a tiger, and I, a dove. She will run me over the second she arrives, Claude remonstrated.

"*No, Claude. You have two trump cards. Play them both.*"

Oh, Maman. You have ever been my trump card. And now you're gone. Claude crossed her arms at the side of her mother's body and buried her head in them.

"*Stop crying and listen to me. You wield power over Louise as mother of her future grandchildren.*"

She won't listen to anything I say, Claude argued.

"*Of course, she will. Don't even bother to raise your voice. Just tell her that you will speak to your father about whatever matter it is and she will back off in an instant.*"

Papa isn't always around. I will be a mouse standing up to a wolf. Recalling the Countess's sharp face, Claude shivered.

"*Remember the ermine whose pelt you now touch. Brittany's symbol stands up to its bigger enemies—wolves, hawks, foxes. Be like the ermine, my dove.*"

I will try, Maman, but I have no strong ally to support me. Only Madame trying to rule me.

"*Rely on Marguerite to be your ally.*"

But Marguerite is Madame's daughter! Surprised, Claude weighed the idea. She very much liked Marguerite, whose love of learning and sparkling wit she admired. She had always struck her as less fierce than her mother.

"Precisely. When does a daughter ever take her mother's side if she has a mind of her own?"

Maman, how can you say that? I always take your side, in all things, Claude protested.

"Except when you take your father's side."

Claude's conscience twinged, thinking of certain conversations she had shared with her father. *Forgive me, Maman.*

"There is nothing to forgive. I love your father and I love you for loving him. As for Louise, enlist Marguerite as your ally against her. She knows her weak spots and will guide you to them," her mother's voice counseled.

Oh, Maman, promise me you'll be there when I need you!

"I will be here, Claude. Just listen closely and do what you think I would counsel you to do."

But I am not you, and would not be able to do it your way, Claude argued.

"Of course not, my dove. You are like your father, so arrange things the way he would."

Do you mean indirectly? Claude asked.

"Yes, my clever one. In your own way, you will exert your power."

A glimmer of hope broke through Claude's grief. *Over Francis, too?*

"Especially over Francis. But the way you will do it is through his mother."

He doesn't listen to anything his mother tells him. He told me so himself! Claude thought, recalling his scornful tone when he had mentioned it.

Anne's merry laugh rang through the corridors of Claude's mind. "Whether he listens or not, he does her bidding."

How so, Maman?

"My joy, may God grace you with sons one day so you find out for yourself."

But not daughters, Maman?

"May God bless you with daughters, too. Just don't count on them to do your bidding."

But, Maman, I have always tried to do yours! Claude objected even as her heart told her otherwise. She sought to please her father more than she had ever tried to please her mother.

"Wait until you have daughters of your own. You cannot control them the way you will control your sons."

As Claude felt her father's arm steal around her she looked at him guiltily.

"You seemed lost in thought, Minou. Where were you?"

"I was talking to *Maman*, Papa. What about you? What were you doing?"

"I was talking to *Maman,* too."

"She hasn't really left us, has she?" Claude asked.

"She will never leave us, Minou. Because she is in our hearts reminding us to do something differently every time we do something she doesn't like."

Claude giggled, her sorrow lifting for a moment. "She told me something about boys."

Her father gave a low chuckle, the first one she had heard from him since her mother's death. "May I know?"

"No, Papa. It is a secret between *Maman* and me."

"Then guard it ever so because it is nice to have secrets with your *Maman*."

"Did you have secrets with her, too?" Claude asked.

Her father's smile dawned like the sun brimming the horizon. "Ever so many, Minou."

Louise de Savoy arrived within days to pay her condolences. As Louis remained sequestered with his wife's body, Florimond Robertet shared the contents of the queen's testament with her.

Skimming the document, she was pleased to see the queen had bequeathed Claude's care to her as well as the contents of her enormous library. Recalling the Marshal de Gié's trial, she smiled smugly to think the queen and she had come to terms when it counted.

As she read on, she sucked in her breath. The thought of Brittany passing to Renée instead of Claude was out of the question. The duchy must pass to Claude so that one day it became part of France. Francis would see to it as Claude's husband.

But if Renée were at Brittany's head and married to the Habsburg heir, France would be impeded from acquiring Brittany not only by Renée, but by the Holy Roman Empire and by Spain. Unthinkable.

Reading further, she saw that Louis had bequeathed his claims to Asti, Milan, and Genoa to Renée. That decided it for her. Should Renée marry Charles or Ferdinand of Habsburg, the Habsburgs and Spain would get their hands on the lands Louis had so determinedly fought to claim for France. Perhaps they were not in his possession at the moment. But she didn't doubt he would renew his efforts in Italy; so would Francis one day on France's behalf.

Louise met Florimond Robertet's eyes as she put down the testament. Slowly, she shook her head, and as she did, Robertet joined her.

"This will not be to the king's liking," she pronounced. Its contents, if fully carried out, would bring enormous difficulties to Louis and the kingdom of France.

Robertet glanced at the document then back at Louise. "The king will review it when this terrible moment has passed."

"You must ensure it is kept confidential until that moment

arrives," Louise said, her eyes boring into his. What was best for Louis was what was best for France. And what was best for her was what was best for Francis.

As for what was best for Robertet, she knew he would seek to follow her orders. He was far-sighted enough to guess the king would not be around forever and when Francis d'Angoulême ascended the throne, Louise would be the power behind it.

"A good idea, Madame," Robertet agreed.

Louise de Savoy watched as her agent slipped the testament into a plain pouch, then placed it in a pocket of his mourning robe.

You will see to it that this is kept from all eyes but the king's and ours," she ordered.

Robertet dipped his head. "You have my word."

Louise nodded with satisfaction. It would be such a pity should the queen's testament be misplaced. But if it were, at least the king and his senior minister had been witnesses to the points pertaining to her. As for the other points, who knew what they might remember and what they might forget?

On January 26, 1514, one day after what would have been Anne's thirty-seventh birthday, the funeral cortège from Blois to Paris began.

For ten days, an entourage of France's nobility followed the carriage containing Anne of Brittany's body. Through each town they passed, crowds lined the streets hung with violet and black mourning bunting to pay their respects to the queen whom all of France admired.

Louis was not present, as was customary. Nor were Claude or Renée, the former too grief-stricken, the latter too young. Although neither were there, Claude had spoken to her father to ensure the order of rank behind the carriage was carried out correctly.

She had not advised her future mother-in-law directly. Her father had done it for her after Claude had reminded him of how important it would be to the woman they loved most. Louis had instructed the head of the queen's Breton guard to restore the Countess to her rightful place should she decide to push ahead in the order of procession.

First in line behind the carriage France's dauphin Francis d'Angoulême walked, swathed in black mourning veil that trailed three horse-lengths behind.

Following him came Anne de Beaujeu, Duchess of Bourbon and former Regent of France, looking neither to right nor left.

Louise de Savoy, Countess d'Angoulême, trailed in Anne de Beaujeu's shadow, annoyed to hear the head of the queen's guards cite the king's orders as he escorted her back to her appointed position every time she stepped up alongside the Duchess of Bourbon.

For ten full days, the funeral procession wound its way from Blois through Orléans, turning northward through Etampes to Paris. In every town along the road vast throngs lamented the loss of France's much-admired queen with cries of homage to her virtue and piety, and prayers for her soul's rest.

After ten days, the cortège arrived in Paris where a service at Notre Dame de Paris was held. Hundreds attended representing all three of the age-old estates of nobility, clergy, and the common people. A magnificent funeral oration ensued, after which the procession began its final journey to Saint-Denis outside Paris.

There, Anne's Breton king-at-arms, Pierre Choque, took the rod of justice and the royal crown and placed it on his sovereign's casket. As Anne of Brittany's remains were lowered into the vault, officers of her household broke their staffs and threw them onto the coffin to signify the end of their service to their beloved sovereign lady.

Three times Pierre Choque's voice soared to the uppermost corners of the basilica, the final time his voice breaking.

"The Queen and most Christian Duchess, our sovereign lady and mistress, is dead, the Queen is dead, the Queen is dead."

Anne, Duchess of Brittany, and Queen of France, had come to the end of her journey at the Basilica of Saint-Denis, royal resting place of France's kings and queens.

Within a year the greatest love of Anne's life joined her there.

1514

Epilogue

Anne of Brittany's final testament was misplaced, never to be found.

Claude of France inherited the duchy of Brittany, as Anne's eldest child. She married Francis d'Angoulême on May 18, 1514, and produced seven children by him over the next ten years: four daughters and three sons, one of whom succeeded his father as Henry II, King of France.

As an adult, Renée of France contested the successorship of her duchy in court. She was not successful.

Neither did she marry Charles or Ferdinand of Habsburg, but Ercole d'Este, Duke of Ferrara. This minor nobleman, the eldest son of Alfonse d'Este and Lucrezia Borgia, was not of equal rank with Renée, a princess of the blood royal of France. A minor prince on Europe's stage, he was chosen for her by Louise de Savoy, power behind the throne of France since the day Louis XII died. Her aim was to weaken Renée's ability to fight for her rights to Brittany's ducal throne.

Renée of France became a supporter of the Protestant Reformation and enjoyed a strong friendship with John Calvin.

In the days after Anne's death, Louis swore he would never remarry.

But within months, the King of France had been convinced by advisors to remarry for the good of his kingdom and to attempt an heir.

In August 1514, Louis signed a contract to marry Mary Tudor, King Henry VIII of England's younger sister.

Mary Tudor arrived in October 1514, a nubile, attractive eighteen-year-old, with the man she was in love with in tow. Charles Brandon, Duke of Suffolk, was to become her next husband, another story entirely.

Louis was delighted, yet something was missing.

Anne.

As much as Mary Tudor charmed him, she wasn't his beloved *Brette* and she didn't behave like a wife.

Restless, energetic, and abundant in charm and beauty, Henry VIII's sister was the female equivalent of Louis' successor Francis d'Angoulême, whose eye she immediately caught.

If it wasn't for Louise de Savoy, watching them both like a hawk, Mary Tudor might have produced an heir for Louis that would have supplanted Francis d'Angoulême on France's throne. Except that it wouldn't have been Louis' child.

But Louise de Savoy wasn't about to let that happen. She had not struggled her entire life to see her son crowned king only to have some high-spirited beauty snatch it from him by bearing a child that would take his place.

After three months of marriage, Louis XII was worn out. Some say it was due to his young wife's lusty appetites. Others insist he was worn out to begin with, still grief-stricken over the loss of Anne; Mary Tudor simply made his final months more pleasant while serving Henry VIII's purposes on the Continent.

On January 1, 1515, Louis suffered a severe attack of gout. Toward ten in the evening, he gave up his soul to God. It is my guess that Louis' final thoughts were that he was flying home to Anne. In my considered opinion wherever Anne of Brittany was, Louis XII wished to be.

Together, their remains rest in a shared tomb at the Basilica of Saint-Denis, just outside Paris.

—Rozsa Gaston, Bronxville, New York

Tomb of Louis XII and Anne of Brittany
Basilica of Saint-Denis, Saint-Denis, France
Photo by Guilhem Vellut
Courtesy of Wikimedia Commons via Tudor Times

Bibliography

Abernethy, Susan, *The Freelance History Writer* blog.

Ameline-Le Bourlot, Annick, *Confessions d'Anne de Bretagne.* France: Gloriana Éditions, 2018.

Aubert, O.L., *Celtic Legends of Brittany*. Spézet: Coop Breizh, 1993.

Barker, Juliet, *Agincourt.* London: Little, Brown, 2005

Baumgartner, Frederic J., *Louis XII.* New York: St. Martin's Press, 1994.

Beauman, Sally, *Destiny*. London: Bantam, 1987.

Bolton, Muriel Roy, *The Golden Porcupine.* New York: Avon Books, 1977.

De Brantome, Pierre de Bourdeille, *Illustrious Dames of the Court of the Valois Kings.* New York: The Lamb Publishing Co., 1912.

De Brantome, Pierre de Bourdeille, *Lives of Fair and Gallant Ladies, Vol. I*. London and New York: The Alexandrian Society, Inc., 1922.

Brock, Emma L, *Little Duchess*. Eau Claire, Wisconsin: E.M. Hale and Company, 1948.

Brown, Cynthia J., *The Queen's Library: Image-Making at the Court of Anne of Brittany, 1477-1514*. Philadelphia: University of Pennsylvania Press, 2011.

Butler, Mildred Allen, *Twice Queen of France: Anne of Brittany*. New York: Funk & Wagnalls, 1967.

Carlino, Linda, *The Other Juana*. Durham, UK: Veritas Publishing, 2007.

Cassagnes-Brouquet, Sophie, *Un manuscrit d'Anne de Bretagne: Les Vies des femmes célèbres d'Antoine Dufour*. Nantes: Ouest-France, 2007.

Castiglione, Baldassare, *The Book of the Courtier*. New York: W.W. Norton & Company, 2002.

Chevalier, Tracy, *The Lady and the Unicorn*. New York: Plume, 2005.

Chotard, Pierre, *Anne de Bretagne: Une Histoire, Un Mythe*. Paris: Somogy éditions d'art, 2007.

Costello, Louisa S., *Memoirs of Anne, Duchess of Brittany*. London: W. & F.G. Cash, 1855.

Cushman, Karen, *Matilda Bone.* New York: Dell Yearling, 2000.

Davis, William Stearns, *Life on a Medieaval Barony*. New York: Harper & Brothers, 1923.

Downey, Kirstin, *Isabella: The Warrior Queen.* New York: Anchor Books, 2015.

Eco, Umberto, *The Name of the Rose*. New York: Harcourt, 1994.

Evans, Joan, *Life in Mediaeval France*. Oxford: Oxford University Press, 1925.

Fairburn, Eleanor, *Crowned Ermine.* London: Robert Hale, 1968.

Fairburn, Eleanor, *The Rose in Spring*. London: Robert Hale, 1971.

France, Marie de, *The Lais of Marie de France.* London: Penguin Books, 1986.

Froude, James Anthony, *Life and Letters of Erasmus, Lectures Delivered at Oxford 1893-94*. London, 1894.

Gobry, Ivan, *Charles VIII,* Paris: Pygmalion, 2012.

Greco, Gina L. & Rose, Christine M., translated by, *The Good Wife's Guide: Le Ménagier de Paris, A Medieval Household Book*. Ithaca and London: Cornell University Press, 2009.

Gregory, Philippa, *The Lady of the Rivers*. New York: Simon & Schuster, 2011.

Gristwood, Sarah, *Game of Queens*. New York: Basic Books, 2016.

Guizot, François Pierre Guillaume, *A Popular History of France from the Earliest Times, Vol. 2*. Charleston: CreateSpace, 2016.

Harrison, Kathryn, *Joan of Arc: A Life Transfigured*. New York: Anchor Books, 2014.

Harthan, John, *The Book of Hours*. New York: Park Lane, 1977.

Jogournel, Thierry, *Anne de Bretagne: Du Duché au Royaume.* Rennes: Éditions OUEST-FRANCE, 2014.

Lesage, Mireille, *Anne de Bretagne: L'Hermine et le Lys.* Paris: Éditions SW Télémaque, 2011.

De Lorris, Guillaume, and de Meun, Jean, *The Romance of the Rose.* Oxford: Oxford University press, 1994.

De Maulde La Clavière, René, ed., *Procédures politiques du règne de Louis XII*. Paris: 1885, pps. 915-16.

Mayer, Dorothy Moulton, *The Great Regent*. New York: Funk & Wagnalls, 1966.

Meyer, G.J., *The Borgias*. New York: Bantam Books, 2013.

Michael, of Kent, Princess, Her Royal Highness, *The Queen of Four Kingdoms*. New York: Beaufort Books, 2014.

Michael, of Kent, Princess, Her Royal Highness, *The Serpent and the Moon*. New York: Touchstone, 2004.

Minois, Georges, *Anne de Bretagne.* Paris: Fayard, 1999.

Morgan,Keira,https://keiramorgan.com/court/anne-of-brittanys-funeral/

Morison, Samuel Eliot, *Admiral of the Ocean Sea: A Life of Christopher Columbus.* New York: Little, Brown and Company, 1942.

Morvan, Frédéric, Anne de Bretagne. France: Éditions Jean-Paul Gisserot, 2019.

Partitions-domanine-public.fr. *En Baisant, m'Amie*, 15th century French song.

Pizan, Christine de, *Poems.* From *Christine de Pizan: Her Works* by Deanna Rodriguez, A Medieval Woman's Companion blog, 2013.

Putnam, Samuel, *Marguerite of Navarre.* New York: Grosset & Dunlap, 1935.

Reed, Joseph J., *Anne of Brittany: A Historical Sketch.* New York: Graham's American Monthly Magazine of Literature, Art, and Fashion, June 1858.

Richard, J., *Battle of the Garigliano.* HistoryofWar.org/articles/battles_garigliano.html

Rorimer, James J., *The Unicorn Tapestries Were Made for Anne of Brittany.* New York: The Metropolitan Museum of Art Bulletin, Summer 1942.

Ross, Jack, *Marie de France: Laüstic (c. 1180)*, from Ka Mate Ka Ora, issue 11, March 2012.

Ryley, M. Beresford, *Queens of the Renaissance.* London: Methuen & Co., 1907.

Sanborn, Helen Josephine, *Anne of Brittany, The Story of a Duchess and Twice-Crowned Queen.* Memphis: General Books, 2012.

Sanborn, Helen J. & Bates, Katharine Lee, Anne of Brittany: *The Story of a Duchess and Twice-crowned Queen.* Trieste: Victoria, Australia, 2017.

Shaw, Christine, and Mallett, Michael, *The Italian Wars: 1494-1559*. New York: Routledge, 2019.

Schoonover, Lawrence., The Spider King. New York: MacMillan, 1954.

Scott, Margaret, *Fashion in the Middle Ages*. The J. Paul Getty Museum: Los Angeles, 2011.

Seton, Anya, *Katherine.* Chicago: Chicago Review Press, 2004.

Siraisi, Nancy G., *Medieval and Early Renaissance Medicine: An*

Introduction to Knowledge and Practice. Chicago: University of Chicago Press, 1990.

Stewart, Cynthia J., *The Queen's Library: Image-Making at the Court of Anne of Brittany, 1477-1514.* Philadelphia: University of Pennsylvana Press: 2010.

Tanguy, Geneviève-Morgane, *Les Jardins Secrets d'Anne de Bretagne.* Paris: Éditions F. Lanore, 1991.

Tanguy, Geneviève-Morgane, *Sur les pas de Anne de Bretagne.* Rennes: Éditions OUEST-FRANCE, 2015.

Tourault, Philippe, *Anne de Bretagne.* Paris: Perrin, 2014.

Tremayne, Eleanor, *The First Governess of the Netherlands, Margaret of Austria.* London: Franklin Classics, 2018.

Tuchman, Barbara W., *A Distant Mirror.* New York: Alfred A. Knopf, 1978.

Tudor Times, *Anne of Brittany: Life Story.* London: www.tudor-times.co.uk, 2018.

Vieil-Castel, Alex, *Je Suis ... Anne de Bretagne.* Paris: Hoche Communication S.A.S., 2015.

Warr, Countess de la, Constance, *A Twice Crowned Queen.* London: Eveleigh Nash, 1906.

Weir, Alison, *Eleanor of Aquitaine.* New York: Ballantine Books, 1999.

Wellman, Kathleen, *Queens and Mistresses of Renaissance France.* New Haven: Yale University Press, 2014.

Willard, Charity Cannon, *Christine de Pizan: Her Life and Works.* New York, Persea Books, 1984.

Williams, Neville, *The Life and Times of Henry VII*: London: Book Club Associates, 1973.

About the Author

Rozsa Gaston writes historical fiction. She studied European history at Yale, and received her Master's degree in international affairs from Columbia University. She worked at *Institutional Investor*, then as a columnist for *The Westchester Guardian*. Gaston lives in Bronxville, New York, with her family and is currently working on *Dangereuse: The Untold Story of Eleanor of Aquitaine's Grandmother.*

If you enjoyed *Anne and Louis Forever Bound*, please post a review at http://lrd.to/anneandlouisforeverbound to help others find this book. One sentence is enough to let readers know what you thought. Drop Rozsa Gaston a line on Facebook to let her know you posted a review and receive as thanks an eBook edition of any other book of the Anne of Brittany Series.

Visit her at https://www.facebook.com/rozsagastonauthor
or the Anne of Brittany Series Facebook page
Instagram: rozsagastonauthor
Twitter: @RozsaGaston

An excerpt from Book Two of the Anne of Brittany Series
General fiction winner of the *Publishers Weekly 2018 BookLife Prize*

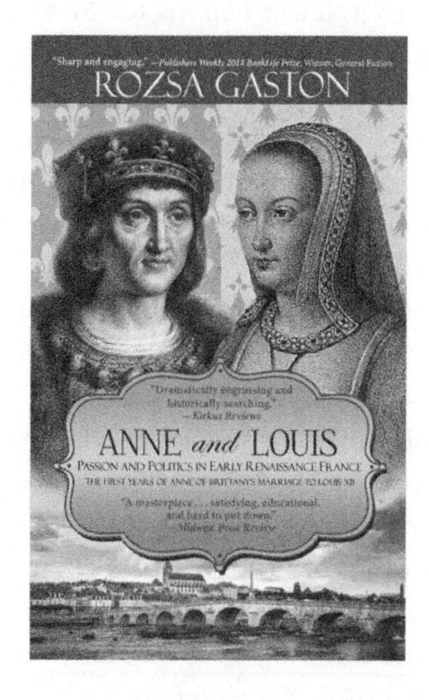

CHAPTER ONE

1498

Entice then Deny

She would return to Brittany. What better way to light a fire under Louis? He was mad to make her his wife. Too bad he already had one.

Anne flicked the insect from her forearm in the July heat of the garden. Ridiculous for him to speak to her of dreams and plans for a future together, when his future was tied to another.

He had an annulment to attempt. She had a country to run. She was itching to see her dear de Montauban again, the only one of her advisors she had truly trusted during those years of uncertainty before Charles had made her his queen. Would her beloved friend and ally of her father's be old and grizzled, worn out by the cares of being Brittany's chancellor once more, since she had reinstated him in the days following her husband's death?

Rising from the marble bench, she paced the wisteria-covered garden of the Hotel d'Etampes, residence of queen-consort widows during the required forty days of mourning after the death of a king of France.

An image from long ago washed over her, making her smile. De Montauban was vaulting off his horse, in search of her specially-made built-up shoe. It had come off as they had fled the outskirts of Nantes to return to Rennes. Their entire entourage stopped until he had retrieved it in the mud some ways behind them on the road. He had known how important it was for his people's sovereign, the eleven-year-old duchess Anne, to be able to stand tall and walk smoothly with an even gait when she greeted her subjects at the gates of Rennes. They would wonder why she was back so soon, and she would have a good story for her men to circulate among the populace.

Just outside Nantes she had narrowly avoided being taken hostage by the marshal de Rieux. He had offered his men to escort her into the city.

Escort her? Hah! The marshal her father had chosen to be her guardian after his death had stipulated that she was to enter the city of her ancestral home under cover of darkness through a minor gate, with only one attendant. Who was marshal de Rieux to tell her, sovereign ruler of Brittany, with whom and how she may enter her birthplace and Brittany's most important city?

Anne had sat tall on her horse, refusing to dismount when the marshal and his men rode out to escort her into Nantes. Dusk was creeping over them; she would act fast before they lost the light so the marshal's men could see her face as she told their commander exactly where to go.

"The duchess of Brittany, sovereign ruler of Brittany, will enter her city by its main gate in daylight with her full entourage, so that her subjects may greet her publicly." Anne's voice rang out sharp and clear, each word clipped so that every man in the marshal's party could hear.

"My lady-duchess, we have made arrangements for your comfort and are here to escort you into the city so that you may rest and greet your subjects on the morrow," Marshal de Rieux's voice oozed. He beckoned to his men to surround her horse.

"Halt!" Anne put up her hand and glared down her nose at the head guard. The man faltered, looking uncertain.

"Brittany's sovereign arranges her own comfort and safety with her own chosen men who will accompany her into her city in full view of her subjects. We will camp here tonight and proceed through the main gate tomorrow after breaking fast," she told the marshal and his men.

"But my lady-duchess, will you not be more comfortable within the city walls tonight?" The marshal's tone rang false. It was unlike him, a man used to barking out orders instead of coaxing recalcitrant counterparties. Anne sensed he was dissembling.

"Men of Brittany, you see your sovereign before you. Will you shame yourselves by dragging her against her will under cover of darkness into the city she and your ancestral rulers have made into Europe's most glorious port?" She might be exaggerating slightly, but she would guess that most of the marshal's men were native Nanteans whose chests would swell to hear their city described so glowingly.

Likewise, they would quake in their boots to lay a hand on a sovereign who had been consecrated by a priest, authorized by God Himself to rule over them. It would be sacrilege.

The marshal's men shifted uncomfortably on their horses and looked at each other.

"Who amongst you will be first to lay hands on your consecrated sovereign?" Anne's voice rang out like a bell.

She had had occasion to use it with authority just months earlier in Rennes, when she had challenged the entire assembly of the Estates-General to answer who among them would marry off their daughter to a man four times her age. That particular speech had resulted in shutting down talk once and for all of her accepting the wretched old Alain d'Albret's marriage suit.

How good it had felt to raise her voice in commanding tones that day. She would never forget the looks of shock, then approval on the faces of the men who made up Brittany's government. Not a single one had challenged her.

"My lady, my men only wish to ensure your safety as escorts for you into Nantes." The marshal's tone dripped honey. It was all she could do not to laugh.

"You see clearly, Monsieur, that I have my own men who will accompany me." Deliberately, she chose not to use his title. He may be his men's marshal, but she was their supreme commander.

"I am afraid they will not, Madame. They will remain here and we will accompany you."

"You are in no position to tell Brittany's anointed ruler what her personal guard will or will not do. I will either enter my own city on my own terms or I will not enter at all."

"*Madame duchesse*, we beg you to enter. Your people are eager to see you."

"On the terms I have stated or not at all." If he thought he would seduce her with words to puff her pride, he was singing to the wind. She was as eager to see her people as they were to see her, but in nothing less than a public entrance with all due pomp and ceremony. Otherwise her subjects would get the wrong idea, thinking de Rieux was in charge instead of her.

"But-but Madame—" the marshal stammered.

Anne turned her mount and commanded her men. "Turn your horses. We return to Rennes." All in her party did as they were told, preparing themselves in the event that the marshal's men overtook them. The jangle of steel being handled, knives patted in pockets, and spurs clanking informed the marshal's men they wouldn't be welcome should they follow.

None did.

ANNE *and* CHARLES

Book One of the Anne of Brittany Series
Available wherever books are sold or at
http://lrd.to/ANNEANDCHARLES

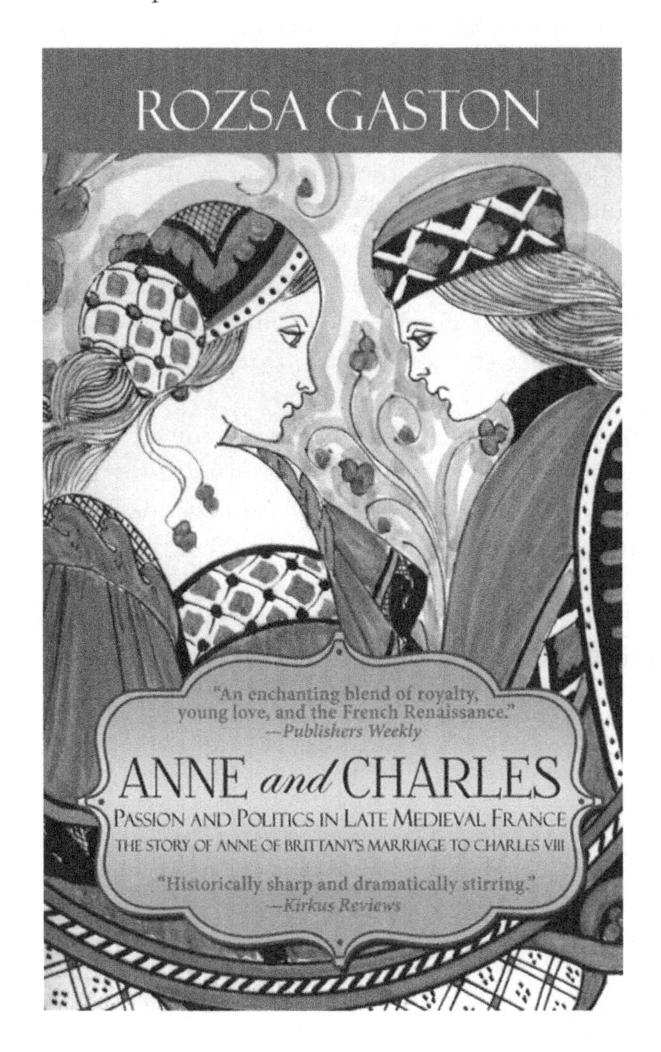

ROZSA GASTON
"An enchanting blend of royalty, young love, and the French Renaissance."
—Publishers Weekly
ANNE and CHARLES
PASSION AND POLITICS IN LATE MEDIEVAL FRANCE
THE STORY OF ANNE OF BRITTANY'S MARRIAGE TO CHARLES VIII
"Historically sharp and dramatically stirring."
—Kirkus Reviews

"An engrossing depiction of the meeting and marriage between Anne of Brittany and Charles VIII of France. This book excels in humanizing one of the most misunderstood of French kings."
—*RT Review Source*

It's 1488, and eleven-year-old Anne of Brittany is thrust into a desperate situation when she becomes ruler of her duchy. Besieged on all sides, she eventually agrees to marry Charles VIII, King of France, to save Brittany from plunder.

A passionate relationship ensues as they unexpectedly fall in love. Yet Charles cannot shake the bad habits he brings to their marriage, and Anne cannot pull him out of his darkest depths of struggle.

Together, they usher the Italian Renaissance into France, building a glorious court at their royal residence in Amboise. But year after year, they fail to accomplish their most important aim: to secure the future of their kingdom.

As they pursue their shared dream, will an unexpected twist of fate change the fortunes of Anne and Charles, two of fifteenth-century Europe's most star-crossed rulers?

Book One of the Anne of Brittany Series

"Masterfully conveys the passion, heartbreak, and determination of this royal couple."
—*InD'tale Magazine*

Fiction/Historical $14.95

ISBN 978-0-9847906-5-4
90000
9 780984 790654

Cover image by Adriano Rubino, courtesy of 123RF.com
Back cover photo of the Royal Chateau of Amboise, courtesy of Wikimedia Commons
Cover design by Cathy Helms/Avalon Graphics

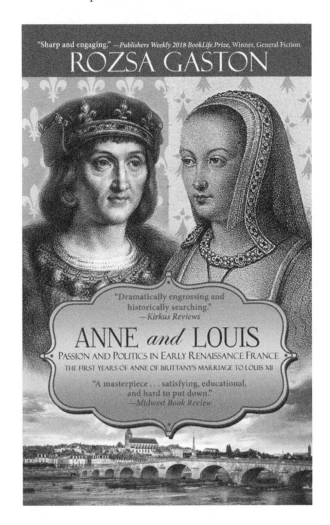

France admired her but Brittany loved her. Just as Louis did.

Anne, Duchess of Brittany, is the love of King Louis XII of France's life. Too bad he's already married. While his annulment proceedings create Europe's most sensational scandal of 1498, Anne returns to Brittany to take back control of her duchy that her late husband, Charles VIII, King of France, had wrested from her.

At age twenty-one, Anne is sovereign ruler of Brittany as well as Europe's most wealthy widow. But can she maintain Brittany's independence from France if she accepts Louis' offer to make her Queen of France once more?

With Italian arrivals to the French court from Cesare Borgia to Niccolò Machiavelli, Anne and Louis' story unfolds as the feudal era gives way to the dawn of the Renaissance. Their love for each other tested by conflicting duties to their separate countries, they struggle to navigate a collision course that will reshape the map of sixteenth-century Europe.

Book Two of the Anne of Brittany Series

Fiction/Historical $14.95

ISBN 978-0-9847906-8-5
90000
9 780984 790685

Cover image by Massimo Santi,
courtesy of shutterstock.com
Front and back cover illustrations
courtesy of Wikimedia Commons
Cover design by Cathy Helms/Avalon Graphics

ANNE *and* LOUIS: RULERS AND LOVERS

Book Three of the Anne of Brittany Series

Available wherever books are sold or at

http://lrd.to/ANNEANDLOUISRULERSANDLOVERS

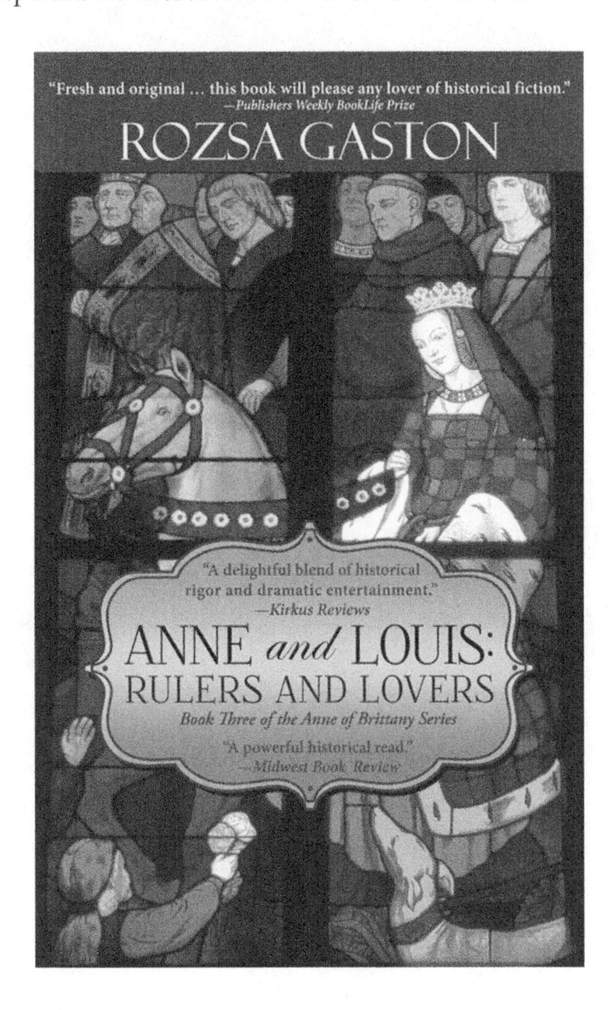

"As Petrarch has been called the first modern man, so Anne might be called the first modern woman."
—Helen J. Sanborn, *Anne of Brittany*

In 1501, Anne of Brittany devises the perfect match for her only child by Louis XII, King of France. Their daughter will become the most powerful woman in Europe if she marries the future Holy Roman Emperor. But Louis balks. Instead, he wishes her to marry his successor. How else to keep his own bloodline on the throne?

Anne is incensed. Why should her daughter not rule Brittany one day as her successor? Better to be a decision maker as ruler of Brittany, where women are not forbidden to rule, than only to sit next to France's future king as queen-consort, bereft of political power.

Anne wants Louis to stay out of Italy, but Louis is determined to gain a foothold there for France. Joining Ferdinand of Spain in a secret pact to partition southern Italy, Louis soon discovers, with devastating results, the age of chivalry is over.

As lovers, Anne and Louis are in accord. As rulers, their aims differ. Who will prevail?

Book Three of the Anne of Brittany Series

RENAISSANCE EDITIONS
WWW.RENAISSANCEEDITIONS.COM

Fiction/Historical $15.95

ISBN 978-1-7325899-4-0

Cover image from Church of St-Malo of Dinan, Brittany, France
Back cover illustrations courtesy of Wikimedia Commons and Pixabay
Cover design by Cathy Helms/Avalon Graphics

Acknowledgments

A special thank you to Helen J. Sanborn, author of *Anne of Brittany: The Story of a Duchess and Twice-Crowned Queen* (1917) who named many of the maids of honor and ladies in waiting who attended Anne of Brittany at the French royal court. Without her careful attention, these women of the early Renaissance would have been lost to the mists of anonymity.

Thanks also to Frederic J. Baumgartner, author of *Louis XII* (St. Martin's Press:1994), who wrote more extensively on Anne of Brittany's second husband than any other author I came across.

Thank you to my team: Susan Schulman of the Susan Schulman Agency, editor Cate Hogan, the meticulous Kim Huther of Wordsmith Proofreading, eagle-eyed manuscript reader Angela Loud Morris, Carol Thompson of Readers' Favorite, and Cathy Helms of Avalon Graphics.

I am also grateful to Larry Barrazotto, Michael Dandry, Claudia Suzan Carley, Keira Morgan, Maryvonne Cadiou, Philippe Argouarch of Agence Bretagne Press, Michèle Olive-LeClerc, Anna Words, Hilde van den Bergh, Donna Ford, Laurence Siegel, Annette Bressie Jackson, Diana Cecil, Ava and Bill Gaston, Sheila Jodlowski and so many others.

With you, and readers like you, Anne of Brittany's story will flame alive once more.

The Anne of Brittany Series

The gripping tale of a larger than life queen
http://lrd.to/anneofbrittanyseries

Made in United States
Orlando, FL
16 July 2023